Anarchist for Rent

Also by Douglas Fain

The Phantom's Song

2040 American Exodus

Anarchist for Rent

Douglas Fain

Bergen Peak Publishing, Evergreen, Colorado

This book is fiction, but the impetus for this work came from events all Americans witnessed on the evening news. All events and characters were created from the author's imagination. Any resemblance to actual people (living or dead) or actual events is strictly coincidental.

For information contact Bergen Peak Publishing
2964 Elk View Dr.
Evergreen, Colorado, 80439.

Cover and book design by Lorna Clubb

ISBN-13: 978-0692062623
Library of Congress Control Number: 2018933892
Bergan Peak Publishing, Evergreen, CO

First edition: March, 2018

i

This book is dedicated to the men and women who build America up as opposed to those who tear it down.

Acknowledgements

I would like to thank John Holstein for his assistance with technical military details. To my wife, Mary Jo, my friend, Tom Calandra, and Shirley Weaver thanks for your encouragement as I struggled through the process of telling yet another story. Thanks to Victoria Golden for her help with Russian names. Finally, I send a salute of appreciation to the artist, Lorna Clubb. Her art and her contributions are evident for all to see.

"This boy is Ignorance. This girl is Want. Beware them both, and all of their degree, but most of all beware this boy, for on his brow I see that written which is Doom..."

Charles Dickens

Major Characters

John McClellan – CIA agent, (AFL/CIO alias - Jason Kincaid)
David McClellan – John McClellan's son, (AFL/CIO alias - Carl Johnson)
Marcia Bartlett – fiancée of David McClellan.
Jessica Hanagan – waitress at The Cow Cafe
George Eldridge – elderly man in Morrison, CO. Lives with Jessica Hanagan
Walter Calandra – CIA agent and "money man" in Europe

Baltimore
Matthew – Police Chief
Dolph Metzen – Police officer
William Jensen – Police officer
Franklin / Richard – TV crew on local Baltimore

Citizens for a Free Tomorrow (CFT)
Frederico Gavalas – European billionaire funding much of CFT's operations
Dr. Lawrence Collingsworth – Wisconsin Professor, founder and leader of CFT
Hamad Al-Falani – high level operative in CFT and agent for terrorist group
Pierre – mid level operative in CFT
Lonnie Carver – paid assassin in CFT
Sylvia – CFT secretary who did research on Marcia Bartlett
Shorty and Ranger – two paid demonstrators in CFT
Anthony Rice – CNN photographer who filmed Marcia's death

Middle East
Prince Fakhir al-Shahri – Saudi Prince

Ammar / Hajid – Sons of Prince al-Shahri
Kahlid Bahir – friend of Ammar and connection to terrorists
Hamza – Head of personal security for Prince Fakhir al-Shahri

---

Russia

General Ivan Sergeevich Turgenov – Russian General involved in arms sale to terrorists
Major Rodion Mikhail Simkov (Rodya) – Adjutant to General Turgenov
Nina Andreevna Simkova – wife of Major Simkov
Vasiliy Petrovich Kirzanov – arms dealer in Moscow
Lidiya Kirzanova – wife of Vasiliy Kirzanov
Sergeant Petr Orlov – Noncommissioned officer in charge of bomb delivery squad
Nicolay – one of the troops on the bomb delivery squad
Ruslan – Russian intelligence officer and colleague of Walter Calandra
Colonel Pavel Matveevich Bazarov – Russian officer in charge of Russian forces in Chechnya

---

Seattle
Paul Hamilton – Seattle Detective

Hawaii
Boone – Bouncer at the Jetties Restaurant
Manny De Franco – owner of the Jetties Restaurant
Billy Wong – Maui Detective
Frankie Joe Carlotte – Mob assassin
Tony Valanetti – Mob boss and associate of Hamad Al-Falani

Chapter 1

Frankfurt, Germany, April 12, 2016

John McClellan looked down the length of the weapon in his hand, beyond the professionally made silencer, and into the startled eyes of his target. He was aware that the man before him had a gun in his right hand; he also knew that another man, slumped bleeding against the adjacent wall, was his contact, the man he had traveled so far to see. Perspiration ran slowly down his forehead and soaked into his eyebrows. John's heart was racing, but his hands were steady. Mostly he wanted more time; he wanted to negotiate. He had no desire to kill the man before him, but he knew he would. The weapon in the man's hand made that necessary. John knew the intruder would respond; he would move suddenly and fall backward as he fired at John. It was so predictable. But first the man had to acknowledge the threat John posed and then attempt to remove it. In that fraction of a second the intruder would be dead. John was certain of that as his finger was already squeezing the trigger. He had been in a similar situation before and had paused; it had almost cost him his life.

Just thirty-three minutes earlier John had climbed from a black Mercedes taxi that he had taken from the Frankfurt airport and handed the driver forty Euros as he stretched to relieve the discomfort of the long flight. He was forty-two years old, and his six foot two inch frame was ill fitted for commercial flight, even in an international business class seat. He refused the change but requested a receipt. "Rechnung bitte." It was

3

important to maintain his cover as a businessman. He was dressed in charcoal colored trousers and a dark blue sport coat over a black crew-necked shirt. He smiled to himself as he stepped away from the taxi and folded the receipt into his coat pocket. It was not his first trip to Frankfurt; he actually knew the city well. John travelled to Europe regularly as part of his normal business, which facilitated his clandestine activities for the past three years as a courier for the CIA. The agency had followed his frequent trips abroad, and after a thorough background check they had recruited him. It was two years after his wife's death, and John needed something to refocus his life, so he accepted. Now, three years later, he was a seasoned courier.

As instructed he walked south two blocks, passed number 20 Koenigstrasse, and then another half block, checking the numbers on the doors as if searching for a particular entrance. Per plan he stopped abruptly and turned around, checking the street and the people behind him. He carefully categorized each face, each walk, every aspect of those on the street. Slowly he walked back north along the same street, again checking the numbers as if lost. Carefully he peered down the narrow sidewalk from behind tinted glasses. It was deserted with the exception of an old woman sweeping laboriously and arranging flowers in a box that hung from one of the first floor windows across the street. He checked her quickly, noting that her movements and her apparent age did not correspond. She was rather spry for an older, overweight housewife. She never glanced in his direction as he returned to number 20 Koenigstrasse and turned to climb the stairs to the front door. It was a large white building with three rows of oversized, dark windows looking onto the narrow street. The roof of black slate gave the structure an ominous appearance of massive strength. As he climbed the worn marble stairs he glanced quickly around. No one was watching or following him, and the older woman across the street continued sweeping her sidewalk, never looking in his direction. John knew that sweeping one's sidewalk was common in Germany and continued into the building.

He was not anxious about the missed "drop" at the airport; it had happened before. Besides, he knew his contact by sight and could easily identify him for the delivery. He and Walter had worked together on three other occasions. Walter was a very intense and focused CIA field agent; he seldom smiled and took little notice of John. After all, John was not an agent, only a courier. John knew little about Walter, but it was not important—or encouraged—that he know anything about his contacts. He was simply to make his delivery as instructed and depart.

In the beginning all of this had been exciting; working for the CIA had given his life a new perspective he had needed after Sybil's death — purpose in an otherwise colorless existence. Now, after three years, it had become routine and, therefore, dull. Still, John did not allow himself to lose his edge. He was always alert while on "business" for *the Company*, as it was known to those working in the agency. He turned to the right and walked halfway down the dim hallway. Again he abruptly turned and retraced his steps, ensuring that he was not being followed. The cold, dusty, deserted hallway was reassuring. It had the smell of age, the stale smell of old wood and crumbling concrete. Dust had settled in these walls before John was even born; much of it still remained. He stopped at room 17 and knocked twice at the heavy wooden door, then stepped back a pace. Immediately the door opened, and Walter's stern gaze welcomed him. Once inside John touched his lips and held his right forefinger in the air. Walter replied quietly. "It's okay; it's been swept; just keep your voice down."

"You didn't show at the airport. Any problems?" The two men walked through a large sitting room with old and worn furniture, down a short hall, and turned left into a small alcove with several offices. They entered the farthest one. It was small and sparsely furnished and had the look of an office that saw little use; it was entirely too orderly. Only the new HP computer and two very large monitors gave it any indication of functionality. It did, however, have a window onto a small courtyard outside. That was the one thing that gave life to the otherwise desolate room. John noticed that the opening had double windows. Both were closed and secured.

"I had a slight problem. I think I was being followed."

"Followed? By whom?" John studied his contact carefully. Walter was an enigma. He was acknowledged to be the best at his trade — tracking money across the complex financial web that spanned the globe. It was rumored that on any day he could tell you exactly how much cash was in the pockets of the leaders of the five wealthiest countries of the world. Yet Walter didn't fit the general description of an accountant. He was shorter than John by several inches, but his body was compact and strong. John guessed that Walter was a man one would not want to cross. His physical fitness clearly matched his mental prowess. "The cold war is over; who would be watching you now?"

Walter nodded, a slight smile across his lips. "Don't be naive my friend, we still have many enemies out there." Just as suddenly he turned serious. "But I am worried that my cover may have been compromised. That's a concern."

John noticed how quickly the smile had vanished. "Should I include this in my report?"

"No, I've already alerted the proper people."

"Well, here's the package." John slung the computer bag from his shoulder and extracted the laptop.

"I have your replacement here, and, of course, it's identical, well, almost." As the agent spoke, a sound at the front door startled them both. It was not the sound of a polite knock but rather one of urgency, and it was continuous. After a moment there was a loud crashing sound; someone was obviously attempting to break into the office. "Quick, out this window." Walter opened the window, leaned out, and checked the courtyard. It was clear. "Good, they don't know about this additional suite of rooms. Now, go!" He was pushing John toward the window. "Wait! He handed the computer back to

John. "Take this one with you; we can't risk this information. Go to your hotel. I will contact you there."

"And you?"

"I'll follow. But first I need to see who's at the door." There was another loud crash behind them. "Now, go! Quickly!"

As John dropped to the courtyard, he heard the splintering of the doorframe. Above him, Walter leaned from the window. "There's an exit on your left; now go!"

"Come with me!"

"My job is here. Yours is to get that computer to safety. Now get the hell out of here." John quickly surveyed the small courtyard. It was paved with large stones and surrounded by the thick walls of the building with the exception of one exit forty yards on his left. Thankful for his own fitness, John McClellan sprinted as he headed toward the exit, dodging the accumulated trashcans that lined the narrow passageway. He paused briefly to catch his breath; his heart was pounding, and his lungs were burning from the exertion and the effects of the time change. Carefully he peeked around the corner to observe the window he had exited just moments earlier. It was closed, but two shadows crossed behind the finely embroidered curtains that covered the windows. One appeared to have a gun.

* * *

Walter faced the two men before him. Both had 9mm pistols with silencers attached. "What is this all about? What do you want?"

"To start with, I'll take that computer." The first man was tall and blond. He was of medium build, but he was young and strong. His trousers, like his sweater were black. Walter noted that his black shoes were specially made for moving silently; the man most certainly was a professional. He held the gun in his right hand and rubbed his right shoulder with his left

7

hand; obviously the door had been more substantial than he had anticipated. Walter handed the replacement laptop to the second intruder, a smaller man with dark complexion and a well-trimmed beard and moustache. He was wearing black slacks and a wine colored shirt. He was clearly Middle Eastern. "Abdul, watch the door. I'll take care of this." The entire time he spoke, the younger man held his pistol pointed at Walter's chest, his eyes glued on Walter's.

"You've gone to a lot of trouble to steal a computer." Experienced eyes studied the intruder carefully, memorizing his face, his clothing, his stature, the small tattoo on his left hand, everything that might be important later.

"The computer is meaningless. The information it contains, however, is something we both know to be very valuable."

"What could I possibly have that would interest you? I'm merely an engineer."

"Right, and I am merely a thief." The young man smiled. "We've been watching you for days, my friend. But enough of this; where is your visitor?"

"What visitor? I work here alone."

"I suggest you tell me now, Walter." He spit the name at the American as the smile faded from his rugged face.

"I don't know what you're talking about. And my name is Dieter."

In an instant the intruder lashed out with his pistol, striking Walter across the face. The blow cut his nose and his forehead above the left eye. Blood flowed freely from both wounds. The impact staggered him, and it took several seconds for Walter to stabilize himself against the wall. "I suggest you tell me now, Walter. I have little patience with your game."

"Why? You'll kill me anyway." Walter was wiping blood with his shirtsleeve to stop its flow toward his eyes. He was in great pain; the blow had stunned him, and for the first time in many years he was afraid. Perspiration beaded on his forehead and ran freely to mix with the blood streaking his left cheek.

"You're right, of course." The blond man paused to let this sink in. "But there are many ways to die. Some are preferable to others."

"Go to hell!"

The pistol lashed out again and smashed Walter's right cheek. He crumbled to the floor on his knees. Slowly he rose again before his tormenter. Very weakly, spitting blood as he spoke, he cursed the man before him. "Fuck you!"

An evil smile twisted the blond face. "Well Walter, I see you are going to make this difficult, but it need not be so. You have information I need. Give that to me, and I may even let you live." The taller man leaned toward the bleeding man and shouted. "Now give me the name of the man who entered this suite fifteen minutes ago."

"If he existed, he'd know you broke into my office."

"Perhaps."

"He might also have the information you want."

"Perhaps he would." There was a sound from the small hallway to the sitting room. "Abdul?"

"He might even have pictures of you." There was a forced smile on Walter's face.

"Pictures?" The man's eyes widened; the smile vanished.

"Of course. Do you think I was not aware that you were following me? You're not dealing with an amateur."

"Give me his name, now!" His voice was rising with anger. "Or I shall begin by putting a bullet through each of your knees."

Walter slowly wiped the blood across his face. He forced his mind to concentrate, in spite of the pain and the growing sense of fear. "I'll have to take you to him. You'll never find him without my help."

"Perhaps you think you are dealing with an amateur. Right or left? Which shall be first?" Slowly the man pointed the pistol at Walter's left leg, but before he could fire a sound from behind caused him to stop and turn. Standing in the door behind

9

him was the tall American for whom he was searching. John stood there, a pistol in his right hand, poised and ready. There was no time for the intruder to think, no time to react. He looked at the tall American in the doorway in total shock.

The soft spitting sound broke the silence as the 9mm pistol jerked upward from the recoil. As adrenaline surged through his body John grasped the weapon with both hands and returned to the firing stance, ready to fire again if needed. It was not. The man's head jerked back, the impact throwing him against the bookcase behind him. Slowly he slid to the floor in a pool of blood, the blond hair streaked with red.

"John?"

"You okay Walter?"

"John, there's two of them!"

"I know; that's where I got the gun." Walter climbed to his feet slowly, painfully. John stood motionless, staring at the body in the growing pool of blood.

"Is he dead?"

"Yes."

"Not this one, the other one."

"Oh, him. I don't know. I don't think so. That brick crumbled fairly easily. But he'll be out for a while." John's eyes had not left the dead man at his feet. Finally he looked at Walter. Visibly he collected himself. "Damn Walter, you look awful. Do you need a doctor?"

The agent wiped blood from his face with a handkerchief as he walked quickly from the room to check the second man. After a few moments he returned. "The door is in pretty bad shape. The damage is also obvious from the hallway." He was talking to himself. Finally he looked up at John. "We've got to tie up the one out there; we're going to need him. And keep your guard up. There may be more of them." Walter knelt and took the weapon from the hand of the dead man on the floor. He examined it carefully then nodded in appreciation of the weapon. "First class."

John studied the weapon in his own hand for a moment then stooped beside the body on the floor and began to unlace the dead man's shoestrings. After he had finished he tied them together as he turned toward the outer room. "This is a start, but we'll need more."

Walter's voice stopped him. "Thanks, John; it's a good thing you came back." John simply nodded. Walter rumbled through one of the drawers in the large desk in the back room and produced several flex ties. "I'm glad we got one alive."

"I had no choice on this one." John nodded toward the body on the floor.

"No matter; he was just a thug. I suspect the other will tell me all I need."

"Will he talk?"

"Oh yes, he'll talk." Walter discarded the blood soaked handkerchief; John handed him another from his own pocket. "We're not on US soil surrounded by bleeding hearts. He'll talk, dammit; I guarantee it. He'll sing like a nightingale before I'm finished with him." Anger was evident in his voice. Together they dragged the unconscious man into one of the empty offices. "I've got to get some reinforcements, and you've got to get out of here."

"You're right. I've got to plan a merger tomorrow, but I'll wait for the reinforcements." Suddenly John looked up, startled. "But first I've got to retrieve the computer from a trash can outside."

"The computer is in a trash can?"

John rushed from the room. "I'll be right back."

Ten minutes after John returned with the computer a team of workmen arrived and began repairing the doorframe. Inside their toolboxes were the familiar tools of their trade, plus an assortment of weapons. The leader of the team, dressed in workmen's overalls, walked into the first office with Walter. He laid a large paint spotted tarp he was carrying on the floor and unwrapped a Browning shotgun. He checked it carefully, and laid it on a nearby table. John sat nearby watching the still

11

unconscious intruder. The team leader looked at Walter and nodded toward John. "Who's he?"

"He's okay; he's a courier."

"He shouldn't be here."

"He just saved my life. If it weren't for him I'd be the one back there lying in a pool of blood."

"Oh." The man, short and stocky, studied John carefully. "In that case, thanks; now get the hell out of here." John nodded. "Hold on." The man dialed his phone then placed it to his ear. "Franz, we have a courier here who needs a ride to his hotel. Would you please take care of that? Walter will escort him out." He placed his hand on John's shoulder and guided him toward the door. "Don't worry. We've got things covered outside. These two appear to have been working alone."

John and Walter walked quickly down the hall in silence. Outside, a panel truck with black stenciled letters on the side pulled up. It was white, with a ladder strapped to metal framing atop the vehicle. It could have been any carpenter's vehicle. John climbed inside then turned back to Walter. "Here, I don't think I'll be needing this." He pulled the pistol from his belt and handed it to the bleeding agent.
"Thanks John."

"You'd better see a doctor; you're still bleeding pretty badly."

"Just as soon as I take care of our friend inside, I'll do that." He pushed the pistol inside his belt. "Thanks again, and be careful till we sort this out."

"I will; take care."

"If you need anything, just give me a call, and check in before you leave for the states. We'll need a short debrief."

"Will do."

The truck pulled away and headed for John's hotel near the middle of the city.

Two weeks later John received a visitor from Langley with notification that his status had been upgraded to Agent. Formal training would start in a week.

12

Chapter 2

Baltimore, Maryland, August 12, 2016

William Jensen rambled through his locker searching for his badge. He had been a cop in this suburb near Baltimore only three months and still struggled with all of the paraphernalia that a police officer must carry on his belt. Standing nearby, Dolph Metzen watched with amusement. Dolph had been training the "newbie" and had grown fond of the young man. He knew Will would develop into a fine officer. "You ready, Will?"

"Yeah, just need to find my badge. It might be useful." There was humor in his voice.

"Be sure to get your vest. These goofballs who are rioting are unpredictable."

"They certainly don't care much for the police, that's for damn sure."

"If you were a drug dealer or a petty criminal, would you like us much?"

"Good point, but a lot of them are just young kids. What do they have against the police?"

"What is it they say about how long it takes for the human mind to mature?" Dolph laughed at this own joke. "Hey, it's just another excuse not to study and do homework. Besides, there's lots of marijuana and drugs flowing freely at the demonstrations. Someone is making a fortune out there." He watched carefully as Will checked his pistol and holstered it. "Be sure to secure the strap on your weapon. There are some really stupid kids out there, and I wouldn't put it past one of them to try to steal a shiny new Glock if the chance presented itself."

"Good point. I don't want this gun out of its holster at all tonight. But I sure hope we can catch some of the looters and send them away for a few years."

"Never happen. The politicians wouldn't allow it. They might get a slap on the hand, but not much else. Remember, idiots get to vote too." Dolph frowned. "Hell, I wouldn't be a bit surprised to see several of our elected officials leading the riots. Those are their people, their base out there, a bunch of losers who need someone else to blame for their own failed lives."

"Well, don't forget, we are here to protect everybody— even those crazies in the riots." There was derision in the young man's voice. "Remember the kid who doused himself with gasoline trying to build a Molotov cocktail and damned near burned to death last week? If the guys from the fourth precinct hadn't been there he would have died on the spot."

"As my physical therapist keeps reminding me, remember the bell curve. At least half of the population has an IQ below average." Dolph smiled broadly. "And the last I heard there are at least a dozen lawyers lined up to sue the guys who saved that kid's sorry ass."

"Your PT's right, and average is not very high as I remember." Both men walked out to their patrol car smiling.

*　*　*

Five miles away three young men sat on the steps of an old brownstone laughing and sharing crack cocaine. The evening was cool, but not cold enough to require a coat. They were all dressed in dirty jeans and T-shirts displaying various obscene messages. One had a large picture of Che Guevara on his chest, the Cuban who had become a folk hero to many liberals. The fact that Che had been a murderer was inconsequential since he was a communist who hated capitalism and America in general. That was good enough for his ardent followers. A fourth young man approached the group and was obviously upset with his comrades. Unlike the others, he was dressed in slacks and a dress shirt open at the collar. His hair was trimmed; he could easily pass for a graduate student or perhaps even an up-and-coming young executive. "What the hell you guys doin? You know we got work to do tonight. If you get picked up by the police, you'll be in big trouble. They'll hang your ass out to dry if you're stoned. What are you thinkin?"

"Come on, Shorty. What you so upset bout? We just havin' some fun 'for we bust a few cops' chops."

"You dumb shit. You'll get your sorry ass thrown in jail. Then we'll see how funny this is."

"Ain't no cop going to take me in t'night. I'll slit his damn throat." The tall young man pulled a switch blade knife out of his pocket and waved it in the air.

"Put that thing back in your pants and leave it there. We got us a chance to make some real bread tonight. I don't want to waste this opportunity. We're talking about some real money, so stash those drugs and get ready to move. The guys payin' us want results, so let's get this riot organized. Anybody got any questions about tonight? Remember, we keep the school kids out in front when the police arrive. We'll have spotters out there keepin' us informed. We'll know where the cops are, and the Control Center will tell us where the cameras are. Keep the college kids movin' toward the police and try to start a fight if you can. If the police stand back, charge them, and in the scuffle, knock a couple of the kids' heads together. We need a few of those respectable students with busted heads. Just make sure the press can get pictures of them bleedin,' and remember to scream it was the cops. I want this on the nine o'clock news in bright colors tonight." Shorty looked at his crew in disgust. None of them were paying him any attention at all. He knew that in a few months most of them would be back on the street broke or selling drugs. Not him. He had learned the business back in Oslo during the World Trade Organization demonstrations. Since then he had made a lot of money, and he had also made a reputation for himself. If he kept up the successes he had shown in the past, he had a bright future with the men who funded groups like *Citizens for a Free Tomorrow*. He reckoned that CFT might last a year or so, maybe three if they were lucky. But there would be more CFTs down the line, and he intended to be the man they relied on. It was a spigot that flowed with money, money he intended to tap into for many years. "Dammit, stash those drugs and get ready. We're leaving in ten minutes." He walked across the street where a group of the students were forming. Several were smoking marijuana, and all seemed excited.

"When do we get started?"

Shorty looked at the pretty young woman's blue hair and studied her carefully. She was young, beautiful, and obviously stoned. There was enough metal hanging from her nose, ears, eyebrows and who knows where else to set off the magnetometer in any airport in the US. "Soon." He climbed onto the back of a pickup truck and shouted to get everyone's attention. "Listen up, everybody. We'll be movin' out in a few minutes. Remember to stay together and follow your leader." He pointed to one of his lieutenants, a young man wearing a red cap. "He's your lead — the red cap, and he knows the route and will direct you where to go. Pay attention to him. When the police arrive we all start shouting and raising hell. Don't worry, they won't hurt you. They're in so much trouble already they'll just form a line and keep backing up as we approach. And watch for the press. When you see cameras, turn up the volume. Let them know we are here to be heard. Remember we ain't goin' to put up with police brutality no more. We had enough!" The young people cheered, and Shorty smiled. *They're ready*, he thought. *But ready for what?*

* * *

Shorty opened the vacuum bottle and took a long sip of the coffee inside. It had cooled significantly, but he didn't mind. He wasn't looking for taste; he wanted the caffeine. It would be a long night, and he had to stay sharp. His cell phone buzzed, and he quickly checked the message:

> "Keep the crowd moving down Westbury street. The cops are two blocks ahead. Five TV camera crews are between you and the police. Notify your team to start the approach plan. Keep the cameras rolling. I've notified them that you will be there in about five minutes. Make it quicker if you can. We need this on the evening news."

Shorty tapped out a reply on his phone and waved to one of his guys. He left the college kids and circled his personal team of paid pros. "Get this thing movin'! Cameras are a block away! I want to see fires; I want to hear yellin' and chantin'; I want to see broken windows, and don't forget your oil bombs; I want smoke! Remember, it's just like they told us in the class. Demonstrations are all about organization and leadership. A few of us can lead hundreds of sheep and achieve remarkable results as long as the press supports us. Be smart; let the sheep do the work, and if arrests are made, give them the kids. They all have parents who will bail them out, and if not, they can easily be replaced. Now get movin'!"

* * *

The patrol car was approaching the demonstration when three TV news trucks blocked the road and made it impossible to move forward. Dolph slammed his fist on the steering wheel and cursed quietly. "Damn, do you see any way around this mess?"

Will stepped out of the patrol car and began looking around the intersection for a way to proceed. He was approaching one of the TV vans when a brick flew through the air and struck him on the side of his head. He fell into the street, blood streaming down his neck. Dolph rushed around the car and pulled him into the cruiser, checking the injury. He locked

17

the passenger door then turned to the three punks who stood fifteen feet away laughing. One had a brick in his hand. Dolph drew his weapon and pointed it at the three. "Drop that brick and put your hands up."

"Why for? We don't take no orders from you!"

"I said drop the brick and put your hands up."

"Fuck you! What you goin' do, shoot somebody?" The tallest of the three pulled a knife from his pocket. The switchblade swung from the knife with a snap and reflected the light from the top of the car. "Hey, you want some of this? We ain't fraid of no cops." The three started walking slowly toward the officer. They were clearly unsteady from the drugs, and one stumbled and fell. Then the man with the knife started to run directly at Dolph. The cop shouted "stop!" twice as he backed toward the cruiser. The young man only laughed and continued his attack, but he took only a few more steps when his right leg crumbled beneath him. He fell into the street with a scream of pain, blood flowing from his right knee. Dolph raised the gun toward the other two men, and they backed off quickly. That was when he saw the camera crew hovering a few feet away, filming the entire episode.

* * *

The local news crew from the national TV affiliate arrived at the downtown news room with broad grins on their faces. "We got it! We got a cop shooting one of the demonstrators."

The evening chief stood and approached the two young men quickly. "Did the demonstrator have a weapon?"

"Just a knife."

"We can work with that. I need to see that film ASAP." The older man thought for a moment and added. "Edit as you need to, but I don't want to see that knife in the film. Understand?"

"Got it chief."

"Somebody get on this; call our contacts in city hall. I want everything the cops have on this incident, and I want it fast. We're on the air in less than half an hour." Smiling, the chief dialed his cell phone. "We got a cop shooting a demonstrator. This is great; I'll call you back in five minutes."

Twenty minutes later the evening news anchor decried yet another example of police brutality. The clip showed the three young men facing the cop with the gun. The next scene was the young man falling into the street after the sound of a gunshot. No mention was made of the wound sustained by the young cop in the hospital. An hour later two police cruisers were burned in the streets and several shots were fired at officers. The next morning all national news outlets except one led with the story. The injured demonstrator's mother was interviewed as was one of several lawyers who had taken up the cause against police brutality. The woman assured everyone that her son was a "good boy," and the lawyer demanded justice and compensation by the city. Will Jensen remained in a coma, and Dolph Metzen was placed on paid leave pending an investigation of the events surrounding the shooting. The mayor joined the chorus of those demanding an investigation and assured the public that proper action would be taken against the officer involved if warranted. The Police Chief called for calm and order until all details were clearly understood. Dolph had been experienced enough to get the knife from the punk he had shot. Before morning four individuals came forward to deny that the demonstrator had a knife. They all swore they had seen the cop pull the knife from his own pocket.

*   *   *

Shorty stood in the hospital room beside the bed of his friend. The antiseptic smells and the bright lights made him uncomfortable. He said little until the nurse gathered up her things and left the room. "You know, Ranger, for a total screw-up, you did manage to make the demonstration a successful operation. We be on every television station across this nation today." The thin man on the bed was paying Shorty little attention, but Shorty continued, talking to himself. "Actually you weren't really even in the demonstration, but you got us the credit anyway."

"Fuck you!" The words were barely audible.

"Hey man, I was givin' you a compliment."

Ranger was suffering terrible pain from his knee and the drug withdrawal was not helping at all. "You think this was worth it?"

"What you talking 'bout, Ranger? You was the wiseass with the knife. You was the one looking for trouble, and I guess you done found it." Shorty would have continued but his cell phone interrupted the conversation. He walked into the hall to answer. "What do you mean they want to go home? You tell them I want folks in that cop's yard 24 hours a day until I say otherwise." He listened for several minutes and then interrupted the caller. "Look, I got three TV stations comin' out there this afternoon, and I want signs, singing, chantin', everything. You understand that? If I have to come out there and run the show, why do I need you? Huh? I got yo' money in my right pocket right now. Maybe I should give it to someone who can get this done, or do you think you can step up to the job?" He listened for just a few seconds. "Good, I knowed you could do this. Now get out there and take charge. I've already ordered the signs; they'll be there by noon." Shorty looked back into the hospital room and paused for a moment. Did he really want to go back and spend more time with Ranger? Ranger was of little use to him now. He would be out of action for a long time, and Shorty had a riot to plan. Besides, Ranger was an idiot, but a useful one in the streets—until today. A crippled idiot was of little use in leading a demonstration. But Shorty also realized he couldn't abandon Ranger entirely, not yet. He would have to coach him through the endless interviews Ranger would face next week and try to keep him on script. If he could just keep the moron from talking too much they had a good chance of creating weeks of favorable news coverage. Shorty turned and quickly walked down the hall. He dialed his cell phone while waiting for the elevator. "Shandra, you ain't give no money to the troops this week have you? Good, don't. I'll take care of that later today. Just put the cash in my bottom drawer like I tol' you. Thanks."

* * *

The Mayor and his chief-of-staff watched as the three leaders of the minority community walked out of his office. The Mayor spoke first. "I don't have a good feeling about this."

"Neither do I. There are a lot of inherent risks in what we're doing, but we have few alternatives as long as they're playing the race card."

"They're always playing the race card, dammit. They can find a way to do that for almost any problem you can imagine, real or otherwise." The mayor was looking out his window at a deteriorating brick building across the street.

"And why not? We've made sure it always works for them. In essence, we have created the monster that may well destroy us all." The younger man rose and refilled his cup with coffee remaining from the meeting. He also took a donut as well. "But the inner city is our base, a base we can count on when elections roll around."

"So we keep them happy. We need them." The mayor placed his coffee cup on his desk and tossed his napkin into the trash can by the door.

"Right, and they think they need us, even though we haven't really provided much in the way of jobs or education that they need. The chief-of-staff looked carefully at the half of the donut remaining, made a decision, and tossed it into the waste can by the door. "Have you seen the backlash we're getting from the business community about the cop? We're tossing him under the bus, and some folks don't like it."

"You can put Matthew in that crowd. He's a good Police Chief, and he supports his men. I understand that. I also think he understands the political necessity of making it look as if we are supporting the demonstrators, but it's hard for him to swallow. I had to lean on him pretty hard."

"It's the old cop code, the long blue line. Surely you understand that. That's real too."

"I know Dolph Metzen. He's a good man. I hate what we're doing to him."

"But it's him or your job. It always comes down to a choice. You're the mayor, and it's your job to make those choices. No one said it would be fun. It's just a necessity that has to be taken care of. You need the minority vote; that's all there is to it. We own them, and, in a sense, they own us."

"This is one decision I would like to avoid."

"I know, but you can't. So just do what you have to do. We can lean on the judge to take it easy on Dolph. I'll suggest that Judge Gore gets the case; he'll do whatever we need. I'll stop by this afternoon and brief him." The chief of staff stopped for a moment in thought. "That video of the shooting will do him in for sure. I'll make sure they destroy the original. That could lead to serious problems."

"Good idea." The mayor walked back to his desk. "Now that has been taken care of, let's have some lunch. I'm starved."

The chief of police was just exiting the restaurant when the Mayor and his chief-of-staff walked in. He smiled and tipped his hat as they passed. Chief Jackson was a life-long cop. He had spent his entire adult life working in police organizations, first as a beat cop, then finally as a detective in Oklahoma City. He was elated when the opportunity finally came to be chief of his own team in Baltimore. He loved police work, but he did not trust the politicians who gave him orders, and for good reason. The most recent order to back-off in his defense of one of his best cops did not sit well with him at all. There were always cops on the beat who he worried about. Some were still new on the job, a few others were hot-heads, but the one cop he had never

22

questioned was Dolph Metzen. Dolph was solid. The chief slid into his black sedan and stared at the passing traffic. There was another issue he faced regarding support for Dolph. There were the other cops on the street as well. They would all know what he did. He was their leader; he was also their friend. Damn the punks on the street. They were all a bunch of idiots. What was it they wanted? Respect? Opportunities to improve their lives? You can't force people to respect you. Respect is earned. Maybe they were just too stupid to understand that. Maybe they were also too lazy. Or perhaps, just perhaps, they had bought into the myth about what they "deserved." Didn't they get it that in order to deserve something you must first do something to earn it? He grimaced and pulled into traffic. He had work to do. He had to find a way to keep his department together and save Dolph as well. Finally there was the community. Already some of them were calling him an "Uncle Tom." Being a black Police Chief in a major city was no easy job. If he could just pull this off, he would truly "deserve" the respect of his men, and maybe he could even earn respect from the more thoughtful folks in the community as well. As for the others, damn them. He had given up on most of them a long time ago.

Chapter 3

Baltimore, Maryland, August 18, 2016

The mayor read the paper he had been handed and looked up at the Police Chief in genuine surprise. "You are resigning?"

"Yes I am."

"Why? You've done a good job here. You're a respected man in this city."

"That's exactly why I'm resigning. I'd like to keep that respect. I worked very hard to earn it."

The mayor's chief-of-staff sat on a couch across from the mayor's desk and watched the spectacle before him. "The price of that respect is very high. Are you sure you want to do this?"

"I've been thinking about this for some time now; it's the right thing for me to do. I cannot be a part of this charade. We all know the kid was doped up and had a knife. This whole affair is not about justice; it is about politics—and we all know it." The chief looked both men in their eyes. "I'm sorry, I just can't be a part of this."

The mayor's mind jumped to the obvious. "You're not going to the press are you? That would be a disaster."

"So now my telling the truth is the disaster? What about Dolph Metzen's career? His life?"

"Will you at least stay on long enough for us to find a replacement?"

"I'll give you two more weeks." The chief nodded and then left the room, his head high.

After they were alone, the chief-of-staff rose and looked at his boss. "Well, I didn't expect that. Can you believe that a man would give up his job, his career, that easily? He must be a fool. What does he see in all this?"

The mayor stood and looked out his window for several moments before answering. "Obviously something we don't." The mayor's voice trailed off as he stared ahead.

"The chief is black. This could get real dicey. Maybe we can spin this as him being fired for poor leadership in controlling his cops. After all, he is the chief-of-police who was in charge."

"That won't be necessary. He's supporting the cop; that will be enough. Don't say anything except that he is leaving. If he stayed the community would probably turn against him anyway. I suspect he probably knows that; it may have even led to his decision."

* * *

The dark blue Prius pulled to a stop in front of a small house in a row of similar homes, with one exception; this one was meticulously kept. The yard was freshly mowed, and there were flowers neatly arranged around the small walk that extended from the freshly painted picket fence to the brightly colored door. The young man in the passenger seat leaned over and kissed the man behind the wheel. "Knock 'em dead tonight, Richard. I'll be watching."

Richard glanced into the mirror and arranged his hair. He was a handsome young man and had all the characteristics that made him a natural selection for television. His chin was square and his dark hair was thick and well groomed. The one slight imperfection in his skin was carefully concealed under makeup to complete the image. "I'll see you after the ten o'clock news. It's taken awhile, but they finally gave me a chance in the anchor seat. The boss seems to like my reporting. Now, if I can just get him to pay attention, I may get the position full time."

25

"Oh, you're much better than that dinosaur they've had for the past hundred years. For heaven's sake, can't they see beyond the end of their noses?"

"I've got to run or I'll be late. Lots to report today. Keep my wine chilling; see you." Richard leaned over and gave Franklin a quick kiss on his cheek as Franklin slid out of the car. In a second Richard was off to review the evening news.

Franklin watched the Prius as it rounded the corner then turned toward the house; he stopped to pick up a few stray leaves that were spoiling the freshly cleaned walk then searched through his small case for his keys. It was dark inside the small home, but that did not bother him at all. He knew every inch of the small dwelling and could walk it easily blindfolded. He was just reaching for the light switch in the kitchen when a voice startled him and caused him to freeze. "Good evening Franklin. I've been waiting for you, and leave the light off please."

The young man turned slowly and looked carefully at the shadow standing five feet away. He could see the slightest glint of light reflecting from the barrel of the gun pointed at him. He tried to speak, but his voice broke involuntarily. Finally he got the words out of his mouth. "What do you want? Who are you?"

"First of all, you can relax. I did not come here to hurt you. I just came to collect something for our mayor." When Franklin stood silent, the man continued. "I understand you were the cameraman who filmed the cop shooting the demonstrator last week. Is that correct?"

"Yes."

"I am here to get the complete, unedited copy of that tape. I assume you have it, right?"

"Why do you want that?"

"Oh, I don't want it, myself. I'm just the person who was sent to collect it. The mayor wants it."

"Why does the mayor want that tape? What does it mean to him?"

"Well the mayor seems to feel that if that tape ever got out in its entirety, it could be very embarrassing for him since he naturally came out in favor of the demonstrators; in this city they are a big part of the Democrat base, his base. Politically it would be very embarrassing if the full story got out. So, I need you to give me that tape, and I need it now; the mayor is waiting, and he is not a very patient man."

"I'm not sure I have it here." Franklin's words were not convincing.

"Franklin, let's not make this difficult. I saw you bringing all of your cameras and your case of tapes into the house earlier today. I know the original tape is here, because the tape used at the station is a copy. I need the original."

"I'll have to call the station and get permission to release that. They have very strict rules, you know."

The voice in the dark became very cold and threatening as the shadow moved toward the frightened cameraman. There was just enough light in the room to see the outline of the gun. It was large and threatening. "Franklin, let me be clear. You are going to give me that tape, and I want it now. I really don't want to hurt you, but I will if necessary. You and I both know the station doesn't even know you have the original. In fact, it might be a problem for you if they found out you did." Then the voice became loud and demanding. "Get that tape, and get it now." The gun was leveled at the younger man's head as a round was chambered.

"I'll get it right now. It's right here."

Get your camera too. I want to see what is on that tape, and it better be what I expect."

"Here, here." Franklin struggled with his equipment for a few minutes. He had handled these cameras for five years; they were old friends who knew his touch well. He pressed a button and the small screen on the side of the Sony camera flooded with light. The picture was surprisingly clear. Franklin was obviously good at his job.

In the dim light the intruder watched the tape play, carefully concealing his own face in the dim room. Finally satisfied, he took the tape from the camera and put it into his pocket. "Very good, Franklin. I'll tell the mayor you were helpful."

"How did you know I had the original?"

"Oh, I know a bit about TV news, and I also talked to one of your colleagues this afternoon. After a short conversation he suggested you probably still had the original. I was also confident you probably realized that this might be valuable someday. Leverage, shall we say." The man stood silent for a moment then raised the gun again. Franklin began shaking. "One last question. Is this the only complete tape remaining? Are there any others? And don't lie to me Franklin. I know where you live."

"No, no, that's the only one. I promise."

"Let's be sure." The man took the case of film and put the strap over his shoulder. He then lowered the gun and turned to leave but stopped abruptly. As he did he reached inside his pocket and secretly flipped a small switch. "Who all knew about the tapes being doctored, Franklin? The mayor needs to know in case he ever has to cover his ass. I need all the names. All of them."

Franklin began to mumble but spoke up when the man moved toward him again. "Well, the editor at the paper knew, two guys in the edit group, me, and, of course the mayor. The boss told everyone to keep our mouths shut about this, but we already knew that."

"Names Franklin. I want their names." Slowly the frightened man listed each man individually. He also listed a man who was unknown to the intruder. "Who is "Shorty?" What does he do?"

"He's one of the leaders of the demonstrations. He's a relatively lower level manager for that group."

"Is he from here? Locally?"

"No, he's one of the paid guys that organizes the demonstrations."

"One of the goons they brought in from outside?"

"Something like that."

"Who paid them? Gavalas?"

"Most likely one of his guys and maybe Crowley as well."

"Who's Crowley?"

"He's the guy who runs the school for demonstrators. You know, he's the one married to that representative in Congress. It was in the news."

"Yeah, I've heard of her. So her husband trains these guys on how to organize a demonstration."

"That's right."

"Who pays for all that?"

"You know, various liberal groups. Probably Move-On and groups like that."

"What about campaign committees?"

"Oh yeah, them too."

The man put his hand into his pocket and another small click was heard. "The mayor will not admit to knowing me or why I am here, but I assume you are smart enough to figure that out, so don't expect him to acknowledge my visit." The man turned and walked to the front door. "Don't turn on any lights for twenty minutes. Don't call anyone, and don't mention this to anyone, especially Richard. Let's just keep Richard out of this, shall we. The mayor would be very displeased if the press started making a fuss about this tape, so this never happened. You destroyed the tape after the copy was made—that is your story. Got it?"

"Yes, yes."

The man dressed in black turned to leave but stopped abruptly. He turned and looked into Franklin's eyes as he spoke. "You know, a lot of good people have fought very hard for your rights and those of other gay men like you. You should be the last to participate in a lie to ruin another man's life. I seem to remember officer Metzen standing up to a group of skin-heads

last year for you guys. How could you forget that, Franklin?"
With a nod he was gone. Franklin leaned against the sink for a
very long time in thought. The fear was gone; it was replaced by
a deep sense of shame. When he finally reached for the switch
he saw many of his things strewn across the floor. It was obvious
the man had searched the house carefully. He surveyed the
mess for a moment then started cleaning up the room. He didn't
want it in disarray when Richard returned.

* * *

Dolph Metzen sat at his kitchen table reviewing his life;
he could feel the knot in his stomach tightening. It was the first
time he had known this type of fear. So many years of service
to his community; so many criminals apprehended; twice he had
been wounded in the process. An entire life of doing his job and
protecting his community, and now it was down to this. There
was even talk about prosecution coming from the mayor's
office. But that didn't surprise him. The mayor was a cheap
politician who would do anything to further his political career.
He knew the people in the inner city, and he was playing their
song. Only the Police Chief had come out on his side; Dolph had
heard that the chief had even turned in his resignation. That
might help a bit, but it was difficult to measure. It's hard to fight
city hall. The old cop pulled a beer from the refrigerator and
sipped it slowly. What to do? The union was pissed and had
come to his defense, but they had offered only a pittance toward
his legal fees. How would he possibly afford a real defense?
Lawyers, like politicians, were a greedy bunch, and they had him
where they wanted him—desperate. His kids were already
being harassed, and his wife wouldn't even go out of the house
because of the punks parading on his front lawn with signs. He
had produced the demonstrator's knife as evidence, but that
was in question since several demonstrators had lied about who
originally had the knife. Basically he was at the end of his rope
when he heard a sound at his back door. He placed the beer on

the table and walked through the kitchen carefully. It was more than likely one of the demonstrators taunting him further. He kept reminding himself that he could not lose his temper. No matter what they did or said, he could not react. Dolph looked out the window but saw nothing. He slowly opened the door and glanced outside, his temper rising by the moment. Then he saw the small envelope lodged between the screen door and the door frame. He angrily grabbed it and started to tear it up. Then on second thought he decided to see what the bastards had written. He tore it open and walked back into the kitchen for better light. He looked at the paper and a small smile broke across his face. The message was short and would have meant nothing to anyone else except him and four other men who would have known immediately what the correspondence meant.

Got your six. Intel confirmed. Stand Proud! Semper fi!

Dolph didn't know how or why, but he suddenly knew everything was going to be okay. There are some men who can be trusted with anything, including our very lives. When one of them said it was going to be okay, he knew it would be true. He finished his beer and walked quickly to his bedroom and his wife. He was smiling when he entered the room.

The very next evening the local nightly newscast suddenly blanked out. For a moment the entire city watched a dark screen, then a tape began playing, the total tape showing a young punk charging a cop with a knife drawn. The cop told him to stop twice before shooting. Then two voices were heard discussing how the mayor and the news staff conspired to convict an innocent policeman. No one knew who hacked into the TV station's system, or where the tape was found, but it was obvious that whoever did it was a pro.

The next morning officer Metzen reported for work in freshly pressed blues. Four of his fellow officers had dispersed the crowd that had camped on his front yard, and two of the demonstrators were arrested for trespassing. Investigations were opened on the mayor and two of the executives at the TV station.   Within two days the demonstrators were nowhere to be seen.   They left burned buildings, broken windows, a crowded emergency room, and a tab in the hundreds of thousands of dollars for hard working taxpayers to bear. The anarchists considered it all a big success.

* * *

In a very ornate office in the nation's capital, a young lawyer stood behind his desk and listened to the voice from across the globe.   He said nothing but focused intently, answering "Yes Sir" repeatedly. Ten minutes later he placed the phone back into his pocket and walked into the reception area of his exquisitely appointed office.

A pretty brunette watched him pace and finally spoke as she rose. "Coffee or Scotch?"

"Scotch, and make it a double."

"I assume that was Gavalas." She looked back at his face as she searched the cabinets for a clean glass.

"One of his lieutenants, and he was not happy."

"The demonstration issue?"

"Yes, seems the demonstrators we recruited this time were the dumbest bunch yet."

"If they were bright, they wouldn't be doing Gavalas's dirty work for him."

"Well, they are getting some pretty good money for their efforts."

She turned and handed him the drink. "Tax free, of course."

"Cash on the barrel head."

"How much do you guys pay them? Is it really that much? Like, for instance, what did it take to get someone to go to the Republican convention and start one of those fights?"

"Actually not that much; these thugs are essentially cheap and willing workers. We're not dealing with the brightest elements of our society, you know. Gavalas funds a good part of the operation, along with the ACLU, Democrats, and some union groups, but no one really knows how the details work at the bottom of the pyramid. I'm guessing every layer skims a bit as the money makes its way to the actual demonstrators."

"Well, I suppose it does help keep the local economy going." There was almost laughter in her voice. "And the pot shops!"

"Adam Smith would have been proud." He was smiling as he watched her walk back to her desk. "Well, they do pay *us* well. I'm billing them a lot of hours each week, and they never question it."

"It's too bad you didn't get to speak to Gavalas, himself."

"He's far too smart for that. He handles everything through his staff. And now he has that clown, Crowley, running a school for these knuckleheads. There is even talk Crowley is going to be placed in charge of operations for the group. I'm sure old Collingsworth will be pissed to hear that. He has such illusions of grandeur that he has actually begun to believe that he, himself, is in charge of everything." He looked at this watch briefly. "Damn, it's almost noon. Let's go. I'm taking us to a great restaurant for lunch. We need to celebrate these anarchists. They're making us rich." He held his glass high in the air. "God bless the idiots, one and all. May they never wise up."

"It's been a good month. Our revenue must be up five hundred percent. Do you think this will ever be over?"

"Over? My dear, this is just beginning. The Democrats lost the election. We'll have at least four more years of riots, mayhem, and unrest. Anything to make the Republicans look bad. We're going to be able to retire in style."

"And when the Democrats win?"

"Who knows, maybe we can find some Republicans pissed enough to launch some payback. Neither side is worried about the country; they both just want to win and hold power."

"And everybody else just gets up each morning and naively goes to work without a thought."

"Well, somebody has to go to work to pay for this show."

She paused a moment and looked into his face with concern. "Then how does this finally end?"

"With a nation in debt up to its ears and a population so divided that civil war might again be possible." Neither were smiling as they locked the office to leave.

Chapter 4

Madison, Wisconsin, April 14, 2017

David McClellan sprinted across the poorly lit campus toward the bright lights of the dorm cafeteria. It was dark, but he could see the crowd of students inside as he rounded the sidewalk that curved toward the science building. David was twenty-one and was a member of the track team at the university, but he did not feel the breath flowing in and out of his lungs or the constant rhythm of his legs as they propelled him onward. He was aware of only one thing, her. Marcia would be there in the crowd. His Marcia, his fiancée, the woman he loved and adored. He was still over a hundred yards away, but he could see her in his mind. He could feel her, smell her. It was so unreal for him. He was dizzy with love for her, and best of all, she loved him too. How had he been so lucky to find her? She was smart; she was beautiful; her mother was a famous actress; how had he been so lucky?

A man at the front of the crowd rose to speak as David entered the back door of the cafeteria and began searching for the blond head he knew so well. The man smiled and raised his hands to quiet the excited students as David took his seat beside Marcia. Instinctively she reached and placed her hand in his.

A young man with long curly brown hair walked to the small podium and raised his hands to the crowd. His dark hair and eyes contrasted dramatically with the pallid color of his skin. He gave the overall impression of one who had not eaten well for much of his life, or perhaps a young person who imbibed in the drugs that were so prevalent. "Hello, everybody; I'm Pierre and I'm here for *Citizens for a Free Tomorrow*. I think most of you know about our organization. We stand for fairness and decency in a world run by a small number of privileged people who have enslaved many. We've all seen the reports of the outrageous salaries and perks of corporate CEOs while the world struggles to feed the poor, provide healthcare to the downtrodden, and build homes to get the less fortunate off the streets and out from under bridges. Our new president paid himself hundreds of millions while laying off tens of thousands of the very people who produced the products that made him rich. He's merely a puppet of the ultra-wealthy. His policies are clearly those of a fascist. He doesn't represent our values, and he is not our president. He stole the election, and everyone knows it. We aren't going to stand for this any longer. Join us and help us reclaim our country. We'll show the world who he really is! It's time to stand up to this imposter. Join us; join the fight for what we all know is right for this country. If we don't stand up, who will?" He paused as the crowd cheered. The applause was intoxicating, and the young man continued with wild gestures. He searched the eyes of those in the crowd as the frenzy rose to a fevered pitch. "What gives this man the right to decide who will and who will not live in America? When did he become God? We live in a world of unfair distribution, and we at CFT intend to stand up for those unfairly manipulated by the system, those who are little more than slaves. We will not live under a fascist pig. CFT stands for fairness and decency." Pierre stopped speaking and looked out over the crowd for several long minutes. The effect was dramatic. Finally he spoke again, his voice rising from a whisper to a thundering command. "I hope that you will join us. Help us win this battle for the heart and soul of this nation."

Marcia leaned toward the young man who sat watching her. "David, let's join. He's right. I've read their literature; it's just so right. Have you followed the latest reports on the news? How did that man ever get elected?"

"Sure, if you want to." He pulled her close, feeling the touch of her hand as it rested lightly on his thigh.

Pierre raised his arms and calmed the crowd as he began again. "What we are looking for is commitment. We need more than just your approval. We need your hands, your voices, your commitment." He looked out over the crowd and smiled at the excited throng. Tonight he would make his quota for sure. It all sounded so good, clichés spooned to naïve students, and he was the master manipulator.

From somewhere in the crowd a young man shouted back. "What can we do? How do we help? We believe in that."

Pierre looked at the young face, in actuality a CFT "plant" in the crowd. "I want you to understand the seriousness of this commitment. I hope you are as sincere as I am. This is not a thing to be taken lightly. Are you ready to stand up to this joke of a president, to the police if necessary?"

"Hell, yes." The young man shouted back. Then he turned to those around him. "Are we committed? Or are we just cogs in the system?" The answer shook the room.

Pierre stood smiling, waving his arms to quiet the crowd. "Please, please, let me share a short video with you that we got from a major news outlet. In this video you will see a dozen examples of the greed of this pompous man. You will witness a racist and sexist man running for the highest office in this nation. Is this the man you want leading our country?" He paused again, this time even longer. He looked intently at the crowd as if he were looking into the hearts and souls of everyone present. Finally he spoke as the room stood silent before him. His voice was low, almost a prayer. "If you can watch this video and walk away unmoved, turn and leave us. You are not one of us. We are soldiers for truth. For this is the evil we fight; this is the greed and bigotry that dominates the world we live in. This is the man who must be stopped, stopped by committed men and women like us — people who are willing to use their lives to make a difference." As his words echoed through the room and the emotions of everyone present, the large screen illuminated and the lights dimmed. The first scene was that of a small naked child crying. It was interspersed with clips taken from the President's campaign speeches, forming a montage of half completed sentences from a contorted face speaking from a podium while scenes of naked children, frightened adults, and ICE agents ran in the background. The scene changed to an opulent New York penthouse and a smiling group of wealthy people sipping wine while the candidate spoke in sentences repeated over and over again. Then suddenly the scene changed to one of dilapidated tenements in a poor neighborhood where neglected children stood with tattered clothes and vacant eyes staring into the camera. And all the while the president stood like a manikin speaking the same clichés over and over again. Seventeen minutes later when the program ended the entire room was stunned. The final words of the video were from the leader of *Citizens for a Free Tomorrow*, Professor Lawrence Collingsworth. He blamed the shocking scenes to a system run by a man full of contempt, a man greedy for power. He further invited, no, commanded, commitment from everyone to defeat that monster and all he stood for.

The silence was broken by the young CFT plant who had spoken earlier. "What can I do? How do I join?"

Pierre smiled at his colleague and held a stack of paper above his head. "You can do two things right now. You can join the organization, and you can participate in our next demonstration."

The young man pushed his way forward shouting to the others in the room. "You can count on me!"

Another young man from the other side of the room stepped forward and joined his fellow CFT operative. "Me, too. I'm in." Soon the room was converted into a long line of students, all waiting their turn to join *Citizens for a Free Tomorrow*.

As the line of enthusiastic young people moved forward, Pierre raised another piece of paper above his head. "How many of you would like to go to Chicago to join the demonstration next week? CFT has tickets to get some of you there and back. All you need is spending money and enough to cover food. We've reserved hotel rooms and a hostel. If you are interested, sign up on this sheet. He placed it on the table and smiled as the line moved from one roster to the other. Yes, indeed, it had been a very good night. His quota was in the bag.

When the meeting finally ended and small groups of students began to filter into the night, Marcia and David walked out into the brisk evening air. She was excited about the meeting; he was enthralled with her. "You see, David, that's what I was talking about. There is so much injustice in the world. We need to stand for the things we believe in. I really liked Pierre's emphasis on commitment. Most people just exist; they don't really stand for anything. I don't want to live like that. I believe our lives should have meaning and purpose." He watched her enthusiasm, smiling. He loved it when she got excited about something. Marcia was a bit far out sometimes, but she was never boring. She was full of life, and he was in love. Life was always a rainbow of colors when she was around. The only time he had ever seen her demure was in bed. Then she was like a little girl, uncertain, unsure. That had surprised him; it had also pleased him. He had guided her through the night, feeling more of a man than he had ever felt in his life. It was his moment, their moment, a night he would never forget. As they walked he suddenly noticed the dark spots on the sidewalk under the street lamps. He looked up at the falling rain as it streaked under the dim lights high above his head, small white lines etched against the black sky. As he peered into the darkness, a large drop splashed on his cheek. He began to laugh. He had not even noticed the rain; soon they would both be drenched. No matter, they had a warm room and lots of towels. He looked into her face and saw that she was laughing too. "Race you home." She broke into a run and turned toward the apartment. Once again the body sprang into action, oblivious to the cold, the wet, or the exertion. He saw only one thing, Marcia laughing and running through the darkness. His legs, like his heart, were light as feathers as he chased her through the night. The organizer's words were already forgotten. He was aware of only one thing—the beautiful young woman running before him.

* * *

Hamad Al-Falani, one of the leaders of the Citizens for a Free Tomorrow, sat in the crowded meeting and nodded congratulations to the young CFT recruiter. Pierre had just reported the success of the prior evening, much to the approval of the CFT team. The meeting was not crowded due to the number of people but rather due to the small room into which the CFT staff had stuffed themselves. In all there were less than a dozen present. At the head of the long, scarred table stood the leader of Citizens for a Free Tomorrow, Dr. Lawrence Collingsworth. Collingsworth reminded Hamad of a large, soft, stuffed teddy bear, but without the smiling face. He looked up as the professor from Wisconsin droned on. He was in rare form, as he should be. Collingsworth had just received a very large check that enabled him to fund his relentless diatribe against the new administration. Hamad looked intently around the room. No one else in the room knew that the "donation" was actually fifteen million dollars, and only he and Collingsworth knew that the entire amount had eventually come from two sources—a billionaire in Europe, Frederico Gavalas, and a Saudi who had not been identified. He watched the faces of the excited volunteers. They were being used as surely as he. There was one difference, however. He was being paid very well by the same Saudi interests. Even the esteemed professor didn't know that. Hamad's head began to pound as Collingsworth ranted on with no end in sight. Did students really have to listen to such drivel in order to get a degree? How was it possible that they paid for such abuse? Perhaps, he thought, ignorance would be a better choice. He detested Collingsworth. He detested his haughty arrogance, his obvious assumption of his own superiority. He also hated the fact that Collingsworth was his boss. It infuriated him to be treated with such condescension.

Around the table the others sat attentively, looking at Collingsworth, nodding affirmation to his various pontifications. Hamad was a small man, but his dark eyes shone with the same brilliance as his penetrating mind. His sharp, angular face matched his cutting mind. He was not listening to the babbling leader of CFT. No, he was thinking about his own plans, his own future. He had lived most of his life in south Florida; he was even a professor like Collingsworth. Still, Hamad was treated like hired help. Perhaps it was his Arabic ancestry; perhaps not. Hamad was still considering his plight when he glanced up from his iPad and noticed that everyone was looking at him. His head jerked toward Collingsworth who was also looking in his direction. "Let me repeat the question, Hamad. Were the press advised of the last two demonstrations? And if they were, why did so few of them show? All we got was a few paragraphs on page 99 of the want ads." There was derision in the professor's voice.

Hamad's mind sprang into action. He quickly calmed himself and answered as professionally as he could. "The press were all invited, and I personally called to remind the mental midgets who should have shown up. Every major network promised to be there, but they were too busy covering a dog show instead."

"A dog show?" There was surprise in Collingsworth's voice, mixed with anger.

"The Poodles came in third." Hamad knew that Collingsworth loved Poodles.

"Must not have been a high class dog show."

"It got more lines in the news than we did."

41

Collingsworth rubbed his forehead with his left hand as he stared off into the distance. He appeared to be thinking carefully. "We've got to find a way to get the press back on board. We damn sure can't go out and buy advertisements for our demonstrations."

A young man near the center of the table spoke up. "What about a few shekels in the hands of the reporters? That might work."

Collingsworth stared at him for a moment then continued without addressing his comment. "Come on people, I need some suggestions. You're not being paid to be spectators. Someone come up with an idea." He stared back at the young man. "Ideas that will work would be helpful." The young man slid further into his chair and said nothing in return. He had no idea that his suggestion had already been tried with little success and great risk. "Have we met with the right people to inform them of our goals? The media should be sympathetic to our cause. A year ago they were avid supporters, but now they seem too busy to get involved."

Hamad spoke up again. "I've met with the right people, and we've made substantial donations to all the politically correct causes as well as to key individuals in those organizations." He glanced quickly in the direction of the young man who had spoken earlier. There was a tone of frustration in his voice. "And they are sympathetic to our cause, or at least most are. I think these demonstrations are just getting to be old news. ABC, CBS, NBC, CNN, they all were onboard for months. But after a while I guess it just got to be old news. The problem is that we simply aren't 'exciting' enough for them now."

"Exciting?" Collingsworth's voice was considerably higher than before. "Exciting?"

"That's what they say."

"Well, dammit, let's generate some excitement." He scanned the group as his eyes glared at them. Finally he stopped and stared at Hamad. "That's your job, Hamad. Figure out how to make this exciting." Collingsworth shook his head and turned for the door. "I want to see results in Chicago; that gives you a week to come up with something...exciting."

Hamad shook his head slowly. He knew that he had been given the impossible task. But he also knew he could not allow Collingsworth to fail. His secret contract with the Saudis said as much. He was trapped.

As he walked down the narrow hallway toward his office, Hamad motioned for Pierre to join him. He closed the door as the two entered and turned to the younger man. "Good report today. Collingsworth liked your numbers." Hamad sat behind his desk and motioned to the chair in the corner of the small office. "Now we have a different challenge. We've got to find a way to get the press excited about this next demonstration. Any ideas?"

"Money to the right folks?"

"Been there; done that."

"More money?"

"That might work, but it has to be discreet." Hamad made some notes on a pad on his desk.

"Of course."

"Think about it and let's get together after lunch. Let's get innovative; you know, think out of the box."

* * *

It was just after one o'clock when Pierre walked into Hamad's office. He was discouraged; he had not been able to think of any good ideas, and he knew his boss was anxious to get the extra TV time Collingsworth desired. "Sorry boss, I'm totally out of ideas." He noticed that Hamad was smiling as he relaxed in his chair and stared at the ceiling in the office. After an awkward moment of silence he spoke. "Why are you grinning?"

"Because I have a plan." Hamad sat up straight and looked over at his subordinate. "But I'm going to need your help."

"Will it work?"

"Yes, it will work." Hamad's smile grew wider. "I'm sure of it."

"Well I hope it's something better than more looting and more burning cars. We've done enough of that, and it isn't working."

"No, it's better than that—much better, something really unique."

Chapter 5

Chicago, Illinois, April 22, 2017

The sky was dark and foreboding as the demonstrators surged through the late afternoon mist towards three rows of police, all armed with long riot sticks and large Mylar shields. They were dressed in black uniforms and wore military style helmets and dark glasses. They appeared inhuman, a wall of dark robots standing firm against the screaming crowd of young demonstrators. Overhead, helicopters hovered below the threatening clouds, tracking the chaotic crowd and filming their progress. High atop several adjacent buildings CFT staff tracked the demonstrations as well. They used cell phones and portable radios to report the movement of the police and the media to CFT headquarters in a large suite of rooms in a nearby hotel. Inside the makeshift control room Hamad watched the large map with interest. They marked the movements of those on the streets below like generals in a battle. Red arrows tracked the demonstrators, blue slashes the police. A cell phone rang; he grabbed it immediately; it was one of his lieutenants down on the street. "The police are moving about thirty of their force East on Balboa toward South Michigan Avenue. They're about five blocks from Michigan Avenue now." A young man with long hair reached and drew two large blue dashes on the map.

"Good, they're not a problem yet." Hamad was handed a cell phone by a young woman at his side. He motioned to the map as he relayed the message. "A water cannon truck has been spotted parked south of Grant Park." He responded into the phone. "Keep an eye on that. Let me know if it moves west toward our people." Hamad shouted across the room to an attractive young woman manning the phones. "Julie, what's the location of the press?"

"TV crews are proceeding north along South Michigan toward the Hilton. They should be there in five minutes."

"Good! Call Shorty and tell him it's time to get his guys into action. I want several cars burning south of Grant Park—near Balboa and more fires near the Hilton—before the press gets there. And have them break some windows too. And tell them to hurry and to be sure to put enough oil on those fires to make lots of smoke." Hamad picked up his phone and dialed the Hilton hotel. After a few rings the operator answered. "Room 437 please. Dr. Collingsworth."

"Hamad, how is it going? I can see the crowd moving in this direction. They are about a block and a half away now."

"All our TV buddies are in place. I personally talked to each of them before our briefing today. They'll be ready."

"Well I hope you gave them a good pep talk. We need them to get the word out for us. Without the press we are nothing. They are our mouthpiece."

"Don't worry, everything is under control. We'll get all the coverage we need tonight."

"Promises, promises!"

"Just watch the evening news!" Hamad hung up smiling.

* * *

Collingsworth turned to the well-dressed man sitting in his hotel room sipping a fine port. "The team is confident, and we have about five hundred people marching on this hotel. We're making progress."

"That's good, because Gavalas is not happy. He wants more results. You fools lost the last election and allowed the conservatives to take over the country. You not only lost the presidency, you also lost both houses of your Parliament."

"Congress. It's not a parliament here."

"Parliament, Congress, it's the same group of idiots either way."

"That wasn't my fault. Hell, half of my own friends refused to vote for that woman. She was a joke, and everyone knew it. Her arrogance pissed off enough people to cost her the election. How could the Democrats have made such a mistake? What were they thinking?"

The man eyed Collingsworth with a smile. "They weren't! They were simply playing politics, and now we have to clean up their mess. But this is just a small delay in the overall plan Gavalas and his friends have for one world government, a government they will establish and control."

"Is that what they want, really?"

"Of course. They know the people aren't capable of governing themselves. Smarter people like the *Commission* will take care of them and make decisions for them. Just look at the recent election. Could more sophisticated people have chosen better candidates for the most important leadership role in the world? Of course they could."

"You make a good point there. But of course there is also great danger as well. Hitler, Stalin, Mao, Castro – they all felt they knew better than the people. And we both know their experiments did not do so well."

"The men in the Commission are far smarter than that. The only things they share in common with a Hitler or Stalin is their total willingness to do whatever is necessary to win control."

Collingsworth didn't like the direction the conversation was taking and smartly decided to change the topic. "How ticked is Gavalas?"

"Let's just say he's not happy." Antonio Moreau smiled broadly. "Why do you think I'm here?"

"Did he get in touch with the Democrat leadership? They should have their heads handed to them. What a bunch of idiots."

"Oh yes, they were talked to. Three of them were contacted personally, and he let them know he was displeased with their performance. They know that a major source of funds is in jeopardy so they agreed to get their act together. They are all supposed to have a meeting soon. I hope to be able to be there. It will be interesting to hear the innovative excuses they devise." He sipped his port and rose to look out the window. "They obviously don't know Gavalas well. He's not an excuses kind of man. Their foolishness has left us with only one recourse, block the president at every turn, and make sure he fails."

"How do you propose to block a president?"

"Congress. The Democrat leadership will block anything he tries to do."

"What will that do to the country?"

"That is the price the fools pay for electing a conservative—or populist, as the case may be." Moreau smiled as he sipped his drink. "And for the country, we don't give a damn if it founders; that would even make our job easier. What matters is that we gain control. Once we do that we can set it straight."

"Well, we are doing all we can to make that happen."

"No you're not. You're failing. Your citizens groups are making very little impact on the political landscape. Thus far you're no better than the Democrat party. Both are failing. You need to, how is it you Americans say, *step it up* a bit."

Collingsworth loathed the impertinent man smugly drinking his port while passing judgement on all those who were actually working to change things. Nevertheless, he maintained his smile. He knew he had to humor Moreau; he was key to the money that Collingsworth needed to keep his operation afloat and in the news. A new donor from the Middle-East had recently contributed a sizable sum and seemed to be viable, but that source was not yet tested and was therefore risky. That left Gavalas as the primary funding for CFT. "Don't worry, my team assures me they have a new plan to put us on headlines across the country." Collingsworth was hoping that was true.

"That would certainly be helpful. You need a big success about now."

* * *

Three blocks away the demonstrators surged forward toward the police lines that were forming on South Michigan Ave, just south of East Balboa. David and Marcia were a block away, walking quickly to catch the crowds. Earlier in the day they had been asked to stop by CFT headquarters and had been delayed there for almost half an hour. Marcia had insisted that they be in the crowd when they reached the police lines. She, unlike David, found the looming confrontation exciting.

As the two approached the screaming demonstrators, they were suddenly engulfed in the shifting chaos. David felt the excitement of the crowd; he also had a disturbing feeling that the demonstration was becoming uncontrollable. He was several inches taller than Marcia and could see the long lines of police running into the street ahead of them and the surging mass of taunting students. He knew the police had orders to avoid physical violence; he also knew that would be impossible. At least some of the demonstrators wanted violence, and they were prepared to do whatever it took to incite it. At least he and Marcia were in the back of the crowd, not so near the danger. He looked up to his right at the tall buildings and wondered how they would look on a peaceful summer day. To his left, Grant Park looked inviting and serene. How beautiful the city would be without this chaos. Suddenly he saw a figure above them on a rooftop, then another, and another. He wondered if they were from CFT or if they were police. It could be either, or both.

When the mass of young bodies hit the first lines of police, the sound rang from the buildings and echoed down the streets. Suddenly there was an explosion on their left as an overturned car was torched. The sound of breaking glass surrounded them on the right side of the street as shops were destroyed and looted. A movement above them caught David's attention; he watched as a Molotov cocktail arched through the afternoon sky and disappeared through one of the broken windows. In an instant flames exploded and raced through the building. Almost immediately a siren sounded as police and firemen struggled to reach the burning building. Ahead of them students were staggering back along the sidewalks. Several were holding their heads and bleeding profusely. David felt Marcia's grip tighten on his arm as she continued to pull him forward toward the screaming crowd. He held back as he assessed the danger and searched for a safer location. But they were caught up in the movement of the crowd, dragged forward into the screaming mass of humanity. In the midst of the chaos a voice called out behind them. Someone distinctively called Marcia's name. David felt her grasp suddenly tighten then release; as he turned, she fell into his arms, blood flowing across her face. He gasped in disbelief; she had been shot. It took a moment for his mind to comprehend what had happened. The scream that rose from David's throat echoed down the burning street and across the shouting mob, but it was lost in a sea of pandemonium. He held her to his breast and stared in shock. The woman he loved had just been murdered.

Chapter 6

Denver, Colorado, April 24, 2017

It was an innocuous message; it simply stated that there were seven unheard messages on his cell phone. John McClellan looked at it wearily as he walked through the crowded concourse toward the main airport terminal. It had been a long flight from England, and it had been a difficult week before that. He had completed consulting work on yet another merger, and it had been successful. He had guided two very nervous CEOs through the marriage of their two companies. It should be a successful union, he mused. Both were on the verge of bankruptcy; together they had a chance at survival. He had convinced the senior man to step down and retire, leaving a younger and more innovative man in charge. Yes, it had been highly successful, and he had also made a lot of money. John thought briefly about the "other" work he had done there, then pushed it from his mind. His life had many secrets, some he even tried to keep from himself. He thought about that for a moment. He had kept much of his earlier professional life from Sybil. The thought of her created an instant sadness in his heart. How he still missed her, even after seven years. His business trips were welcome diversions that made life easier, but when he returned home he again had to face the overpowering emptiness. Sleeping alone in the same bed they had shared reminded him of her warmth and the joy they had shared in their marriage. The thought of her brought on the depression he knew would follow. It was hard to live without her; she had been the center of his existence, the source of his laughter and joy. Now she was gone. He shook his head slightly and forced the thoughts from his mind. It was headed toward things he was not prepared to handle.

John's phone buzzed loudly; he glanced down; there was a message from his son, David. That surprised him; David seldom called his dad. Their relationship had been rather rocky the last few years, and communication between the two was rare. Invariably the call would be a request for more money. He joined the crowd surging toward the baggage area and put the phone back into his coat pocket. He was in no mood for a confrontation with his son; he would handle it later. Surely David could stretch his funds for one more day. He would graduate from the university next year. Maybe it was time to take him on a trip to Europe, get to know him better. John frowned, thinking of the son he barely knew. David had been cast from the same mold as his father, and the two of them had clashed repeatedly. Only his wife's calm had tempered the frequent conflicts between father and son. Sybil's death had been a horrible blow to them both. What might have pulled them closer together had somehow created just the opposite effect. Their attempts to communicate usually deteriorated into shouting matches with both of them leaving angry and frustrated. When David finally left for college, John was relieved. The constant confrontations were exhausting, but it was his guilt that pained him most. He recognized that David was struggling with his mother's death and the difficult process of growing into manhood. John also knew that he was the adult, the one to act calmly, the one to diffuse the explosive mixture of father and son. But he, too, was struggling; he, too, was lost in grief. Somehow his own anger was fueled by his son's; they fed on each other and created an impasse it seemed neither could or would reconcile.

He shifted his computer bag to the other shoulder and decided to wait until after he had collected his bags before listening to the variety of messages a busy businessman would invariably get when out of town for two weeks. That would give him time to grab a cup of coffee at the Starbucks on the main level of the airport and shake some of the weariness that slowed his thoughts. By the time he could down his latte, the bags would almost be arriving. He had a plan; that was enough for now.

The first message on the phone was David's. So were three others. "Dad, it's David. Call me as soon as you can. It's important." John stared at the phone as he tried to focus his tired mind. David's voice was near panic. Something was terribly wrong. Perhaps he had been involved in an accident. Could he be in jail? Had he become involved in drugs? John's weary mind quickly ran through a father's checklist of things that might have elicited such a tone of despair. He stood silently staring at the phone, forcing his mind to focus. He had to be prepared. Every time he dealt with David it had the potential of becoming a disaster. He wanted to understand his son; he wanted even more for his son to understand him. But both seemed to have a high propensity to say the wrong thing and always at the wrong time. He thought about the voice. What was it that he recognized? Fear? Pain? Anger? Perhaps a bit of all three he thought. What could have precipitated such a call? It had to be significant. David would not actively seek a conversation with him unless it was absolutely necessary. Just a month earlier John had landed in Dulles Airport from a trip to Europe and had changed his itinerary to fly up to Madison for a brief visit. He had been surprised to learn that David was no longer living in the dorm but rather had rented an apartment that he was sharing with a young woman. John had decided not to make a major issue of that in order to avoid another confrontation with his son. The three of them had met for dinner at a nice restaurant where it was understood that John would pick up the tab. When David ordered an expensive bottle of wine for dinner, John had said nothing, surprised that his son would order wine but also surprised that it was an excellent choice. Was there a class in wine appreciation at the university? The waiter never asked for an ID; he obviously knew David as a regular and expected a good tip. It quickly became evident that David was putting on a very good show for the young lady. Marcia was beautiful in a young, breathless sort of way. Her hair was naturally blond and streaked by the sun. She was thin and graceful; in many ways she reminded John of Sybil. As he watched the two his mind wandered back many years when he and Sybil had been young, when he, too, had tried to act mature for the woman of his dreams. He smiled, knowing exactly what David was feeling; had he not been there himself? Suddenly he felt old. Forty-two was certainly not old, but as he watched the youth before him, he realized how many experiences they might have together that he had already experienced. Would he ever feel that way again? Is true love a once in a lifetime gift? When Sybil died, something inside him died with her. He feared those feelings might never dance in his heart again.   Were his emotions really dead, or, like the legendary Phoenix, were they simply waiting to arise again from ashes to bring him the joy of love, the feelings of desire?

The evening had gone surprisingly well until desert was served. Then Marcia had announced that the two of them were going to Chicago to participate in the demonstration against the new administration. John knew Marcia's mother was from the "Hollywood crowd," but still he was a bit shocked and curious. He paused for a moment then asked why she thought they should get involved. Slowly, but as surely as the rising of the sun, he felt himself moving into his "father" role. In less than three minutes the sides were drawn, and he was arguing with both of them. It had not gone well, and he left, as always, angry and disappointed. His last words were "I will not pay for you to join a group of crackpots to demonstrate against the new president, or anything else for that matter. Anyone who agrees to try to run this country needs all the help he or she can get, not a bunch of anarchists bent on destroying the nation and all it stands for." They had not spoken since.

John walked quickly to the Starbucks kiosk and bought a latte breve and then turned toward the baggage area as he sipped the hot liquid. As he did, he studied the preset numbers in his iPhone and dialed his son. He mentally braced himself; he didn't know whether to expect a verbal attack or perhaps simply a request for money. Mostly he didn't expect that he would reach his son. They had a system that worked for both of them. John called and left a message; David would return his message with one of his own. That way they could communicate without speaking directly to each other. John was surprised when his son answered. "Hello."

"David, it's Dad."

"Dad, I need some money." The voice more than the words conveyed a sense of dread in John. He waited a moment before answering; he was weighing his options.

"How much do you need?" The question gave him time to think.

"About seven hundred dollars." David's words were short and clipped, but still his voice was filled with an emotion that puzzled his father.

"What's it for, David?"

"I just need it. Okay?" The voice was now angry.

John remained calm as his mind raced to categorize his son's voice. Was it a mixture of fear and pain or anger and pain? It was difficult to determine. He tried to imagine his son's face. "I'd like to know what's going on; you sound as if you're in trouble."

"I'm not in trouble; I just need the money. If you won't send it, forget it." David was nearly shouting, but he did not hang up. He clearly needed the money badly.

John waited a brief moment, struggling with his words. "David, what's wrong?"

"Nothing; I just need to fly to Seattle."

"Seattle?" John raced through the various snippets of information filed neatly in his ordered mind and struck pay dirt. A major demonstration had just been announced for Seattle. It had been widely publicized, and the city was already bracing for violence. John breathed deeply and spoke without considering his words. "Did Marcia put you up to this?"

There was a long silence, then a small, defeated voice spoke. "Dad, she's dead. They shot her."

"What? Who? What are you saying, son?" Now there was complete shock in John's voice.

"Marcia. Somebody killed her." John barely recognized the voice that shook his reality as he stood in the busy airport. It was a David he did not know. It was the voice of a defeated young man. The bravado of the night at the restaurant was gone. He was five again, and someone had hurt him. John listened to the words, but they barely registered in his mind. It might have been the fatigue; it may well have been that his mind refused to hear the words from the instrument in his hand. "What happened, son?"

"We went to Chicago. We should have stayed here." The voice trailed off as if the speaker had dropped the phone and walked away.

"David, where are you?"

"I'm at the apartment."

"I'm on my way, son. I'll be there as fast as I can."

"You don't have to come. I don't need your help. I just need the money."

"I'll be on the next flight. I'm already at the airport." He put the phone into his coat pocket without waiting for an answer. Adrenaline surged into his body. Perhaps it was the caffeine; perhaps it was the shocking news; probably it was both. John looked over his shoulder to the escalator that led to the ticket counters above. He checked his watch—two o'clock. If he were lucky he could get out on the next flight to Chicago, and perhaps he might still make the last flight to Madison. He needed some luck, but he was determined to get there tonight.

It was almost eight fifteen when John pulled the rental car to the curb at a drab apartment house. It was a two-story brick building, built in the late fifties when functionality was far more important than aesthetics. John wondered how much this was costing him; there was certainly no way David could afford it—especially in Madison. The windshield wipers drummed their monotonous cadence as John sat in the car peering through the rain to the second floor window on the corner of the building. What should he say? What should he do? He desperately wanted it to be right; he wanted to help his son. But he had no idea at all what David needed or even what he had to offer his son, so he simply opened the door and dashed through the cold rain toward the dim light at the entrance. As he did, he said a short prayer for Sybil's intercession. He knew he would need it.

It was a moment that John would remember for the remainder of his days. When the door opened they stood face to face, father and son, and each noted how the other had suddenly aged. John was facing a young man to whom life had dealt a cruel blow. The eyes that met his own stopped him in the doorway. In them he saw the despair of death mixed with something he could not identify. Whatever it was, it sent a chill up his back. David was dressed in worn jeans and a dark gray Wisconsin athletic shirt, but it was the eyes that John saw first. They were blank, and his face, like his eyes, was red and swollen. John had imagined the scene, but his father's mind had not envisioned the pain that faced him. Then he realized that his son had borne the shock alone. His mother was dead; there was only he, his father, with whom to share the loss, and it was a loss David had not chosen to share until absolutely necessary. What had he endured? Awkwardly John reached and embraced his son, half expecting him to dissolve into tears, half expecting him to withdraw. As he pulled David to him, John felt a strength in his son he had not expected. He stepped back and looked into his eyes again. At that moment he recognized the emotion he had questioned earlier. It was one he had not expected. It was rage.

"Have you eaten?"

"I don't know. I'm not hungry."

"Grab your jacket. Let's get something to eat."

57

"I said I'm not hungry."

"I know, but I am." John lied as he turned for the door. "Get your jacket; it's raining outside." It was an order, not a request.

John found a small diner with a mixture of cars and trucks parked outside. Once inside he ordered for both while David sat silently across the table, holding his head in his hands. After the two had eaten most of their meals, John finally broke the silence. "Do you want to tell me about it?" He studied his son's eyes; they were clear; they were determined. It was the rage that fought back the tears. John knew that rage was the demon that sustained David and the one force that could destroy him. All it needed was a focus; then like a malignant cancer, it would grow unchecked. It frightened him; he knew there was much he did not understand; he also knew what the young man was going through. Had he not walked that same path just seven years earlier when he lost Sybil? He could still remember the hollow feeling of grief, then the panic. His life, once a rainbow of bright, vivid colors, changed to a colorless gray in one short breath when he heard the doctor's diagnosis of Sybil's illness. A year of hell later his world was practically black. Slowly he had climbed from the pit of despair, but seven years after her death he was still lost in a spectrum of dark gray. It was painful to know that his son would now be lost in that same colorless existence.

"It's been in all the news. Didn't you hear about it?"

"I've been in a small village outside Berlin. I haven't seen a TV or read a paper for two weeks. But I did check the reports on my cell phone before leaving Denver." He had also made a quick call to friends in the CIA as well. They had done some quick research on the death, but John didn't want to discuss that with his son.

"I had no idea anything could hurt this much." It was a small, quiet voice, and it came from a place of great pain. Suddenly David looked up at his father, a look of recognition on his young face. "But you understand this, don't you Dad."

John could see the struggle on the swollen face, the glistening tears that hung precariously in his eyes. "Yes son, I do."

The two men sat silently regarding each other as they sipped coffee. It was John who finally broke the silence. "How long did you know Marcia?"

"About two years."

As he watched the young eyes it occurred to him that he still had not gotten over his own pain from Sybil's loss. Would David also be alone seven years from now? Would his pain still be as real as that which John still knew?

Finally the young man spoke, his eyes locked somewhere in the middle of the cluttered table. His voice remained small and far away. "I should have protected her better." It was a simple statement, but John understood what had given it birth. David's eyes never left the table as he spoke. His voice, however, regained its strength. "We never should have gone to that damned demonstration. If we had just stayed here." Then, in a weaker voice. "I thought I could take care of her." There was a long silence between the two men, then David spoke again, rapidly, staccato. "The whole demonstration was crap, and I knew it. I also knew the types of weirdoes who would attend. I really didn't want to go, but she insisted. She wanted to stand for something she felt was important." His voice dropped again. He spoke slowly once more. "I thought I could take care of her."

John waited for David to finish then spoke deliberately; he knew how important his words might be a year from now, maybe three. "How could you have protected her from the police?" He watched the young man carefully. "Who would have expected them to fire on a bunch of kids? How could they have done that?" There was anger in his voice.

"The police didn't shoot Marcia." It was said bluntly.

"What?"

"The police didn't shoot her. The press was lying or stupid, or both."

"They didn't?" John's voice was incredulous.

"No."

"You're sure? The newspapers said…"

"I was standing next to her, Dad." The eyes were locked on the table again, but the voice was raw with emotion.

John rubbed his forehead with his fingertips and stared off into the distance for several moments. He was breathing slowly, trying to understand what his son was saying. Finally he turned and looked directly into David's eyes. His voice was calm and professional, detached even. "David, tell me exactly what happened, everything you can remember."

"What difference does it make?" David's voice remained defiant, angry.

"Because I want to know." There was frustration in John's voice.

David leaned forward and again held his head in both his hands, his elbows on the table. There was a long silence before he regained control and began to speak. "It was late afternoon. We had been briefed about the police. All of us were walking toward the Hilton hotel where the new administration officials were to meet. We had to stop by the CFT offices and were delayed and arrived after the confrontation with the police had begun. There were police everywhere. They all had helmets and those large plastic shields." David's eyes grew larger as he relived the terrible moments of that day. "We were late. When I saw the first wave of demonstrators hit the line of police I knew we should leave, but Marcia wasn't afraid." There was moisture forming in his eyes. There was clear panic on his face as his mind revived memories it wanted to forget.

"Go ahead." John was leaning toward his son, concentrating on every painful word.

"We were suddenly in a crowd at the back of the demonstration. There were cars on fire and people throwing rocks at windows. Then someone called her name behind us, and she turned to answer." David's lip quivered like a small child. A single tear slipped down his left cheek.

"Someone called her name?"

"As I turned to see what was happening, she fell into my arms. There was blood all over her face; she was dead."

"Wait, you say you were in the *back* of the demonstration? Someone called her name? Someone called her name?"

"Yes." David's face was merely inches from the tabletop. His hands were gripped into tight fists.

"Behind you?"

"Yes."

"Then the police didn't do it." John paused a moment in thought. "And the report said there were powder burns on her face." John's voice grew louder; he sat upright, stiff, both hands flat on the table before him. "You're right, the police didn't do it. But who? Why?" He talked more rapidly now. "Did you report any of this to the police?"

"No. I was so shocked, and the CFT people told me they would take care of it." David looked quizzically at this dad. "What report?"

John looked directly into his son's eyes and ignored his question. "David, did you hear the gunshot?"

"No. I had no idea what was happening until I saw the blood." He struggled visibly with himself as the image spread once again across his mind. His hands were shaking, and tears flowed freely down his cheeks.

"Are you sure? You heard nothing? The shooter had to be within six feet."

"I didn't hear the shot."

"Did you see who did it, or anyone with a gun?"

"No."

John sat silently, analyzing the new information. Finally he spoke, very quietly, to himself. "You were in the back of the demonstration. She turned and was shot from behind. There were powder burns on her face, and you never heard the shot. Then it had to be a silencer—otherwise you'd have heard it." He looked back into David's eyes. "Or you may have blocked it from your mind."

"I haven't blocked anything from my mind." The young man's eyes were almost pleading when he continued. He was almost shouting, then in a much smaller voice, "But I wish I could."

"You didn't hear anything or see anything." John's voice was once again calm.

"Only the voice calling her name."

"Then that's all we have, isn't it." Suddenly John's eyes narrowed. "Wait, you said you stopped by CFT headquarters. Why?"

"She got a text asking her to stop by for directions. We didn't know what that was about so we did as they asked."

"Did anyone else get that same instruction?"

"No, just Marcia, as far as I know."

"When you arrived at the headquarters area, what directions did they give you, son?"

"None. No one seemed to know anything about the message. So we just left."

"Did anyone leave with you or did you notice anyone following you. Perhaps a group walking along in the same direction?"

"No. We just hurried off to join the crowd. Marcia was so excited."

John slid out of the booth and stood by the table thinking and processing the information he had received. Finally he spoke. "We have two things we know for sure: the shooter was a professional, and you heard his voice. Those are the facts we have to work with. We also have a suspicion that whoever did this might have made the call regarding the directions at CFT. If that is true, this was planned in advance, and Marcia was a designated target."

"Why would anyone target Marcia? She's just a student. She wouldn't hurt anyone."

"I don't know son. That's what we have to find out." For a long while they looked at each other in silence. Finally John leaned closer to his son and spoke very slowly. "David, do you think you could recognize that voice if you ever heard it again?"

"I'll never forget that voice. Never in a lifetime." David's head jerked up. His eyes met his father's; for a long time they stared at each other, saying nothing. "I've got to find that voice."

"No, David. *We* have to find him." When David said nothing, John continued. "So that's why you wanted the seven hundred dollars." It was a simple statement.

"Yes."

"How?"

"There's only one place I know to look, Dad—at the next CFT demonstration." The pain left David's face. His eyes were suddenly cold and hard, fed by the unquenchable rage burning inside. "That will be in Seattle in two weeks."

"It's a long shot, son. If the shooter were a part of that group, he will probably be gone by now."

"Maybe so, but I'll be there. I've got to try."

"Then I'm going with you."

"That's okay Dad. I can do this myself."

"I know son, but you're going to need this." He held up his credit card. "And besides, I may have a few ideas that might help."

The young man lowered his head slowly, again examining the dirty tabletop. "Let's face it, Dad, neither of us knows shit about how to find this guy. I'm just a student, and you're just a businessman." There was despair in his voice.

"Perhaps. Perhaps not." John threw some bills on the table. "Come on, son, let's go back to the apartment and get some sleep." He paused for only a second. "Then we'll make a plan."

* * *

John rolled to his back and sat up in the darkness on the uncomfortable couch in his son's living room. It was not the cheap cushions that kept him awake but the Italian food that he had lingered over too long, or perhaps it was the wine. He had consumed only a small amount of each, but the combination, or the stress of the day, was just too much for his tired body. He regretted that he had no antacids with him, and his son was far too young to need such medicines. John thought about David and the pain he was facing at such an early age. It angered him that David had experienced such loss so soon; that was a burden for much later in life. He had already lost his mother; perhaps he had never really had a dad. John had traveled almost continuously when David was young. Was there time to recover all they had lost? The self-recriminations were lining up in his consciousness, ready to parade across his weary mind when they were interrupted by a sound at the door. It surprised him, because he immediately knew what it was. It was not a key but a very fine set of tools that were probing the lock. He was immediately alert, but before he could move, the intruder expertly turned the tool and opened the door; he had obviously done this before. John quietly rolled to the floor beside the couch and peered through the legs of the small end table that stood between the couch and the hallway. The man entering the door was slightly less than six feet tall and moved with the dexterity of a young man. As he silently closed the door, John saw the long dark shadow of a knife in his right hand. The intruder stood inside the door briefly and waited for his eyes to adjust to the darkness, then walked slowly and quietly toward the back bedroom where David was sleeping. As he approached the couch, John covered his own eyes and switched on the lamp sitting on the end table above him. After a second he switched it off again. The man cursed loudly and grabbed for his eyes; the unexpected light had temporarily blinded him. Before he could recover, John grabbed the end table and swung it with all his

64

might at the man's face. The impact stunned the intruder and knocked him backward against the wall. John immediately struck again, this time the man's right hand, and the knife went flying across the floor. The shocked man cursed loudly and vainly attempted to avoid the punch that landed squarely in the middle of his face, breaking his nose and sending him into the wall. John grabbed the stunned man and was just preparing to hit him again when the door crashed open. He had not anticipated that there might be an accomplice outside. The second man stood against the light from the hallway struggling to find the light switch inside the apartment. A glint of polished steel flashed from his right hand; he had a gun. John grabbed the figure sliding slowly down the wall, screamed loudly, and shoved the half-conscious man in his grasp through the darkness toward the door and the second intruder. He heard the shot as he dived back behind the couch. The second man, much larger than the first, stared in shock as his companion gasped loudly and fell at his feet in the light from the opened door. The shooter knelt beside his partner and cursed loudly. "Shit! Bill, is that you? What the fuck is going on?" There was panic in his voice. The sight of the blood on the first intruder's face stopped him cold until he saw the red hole in the man's right shoulder.

The gunshot had hardly echoed down the hall when several lights flashed beneath the uneven doors in the old building and several young men stuck their heads into the hall. "Hey man, what's going on down there? Knock off the fucking noise. Some of us have to work tomorrow."

The man stood for a moment and looked at his injured partner. "Shit!" The panic was setting in. His initial response was to flee, and that is what he chose. With strength enhanced by fear and adrenaline, he lifted the wounded man, and the two struggled awkwardly from the room.

John crawled rapidly across the room and retrieved the knife. He was heading for the door when the large overhead light blinded him. After a moment he saw David standing behind him, confusion on his face. "What's going on in here?"

"Turn off the lights. Quick!" David did as he was told.

"What the hell is going on?" As the lights went out David instinctively lowered his voice.

"We've had visitors." John was peering into the darkness outside from the bottom of the dark window. He cursed as a car sped from the parking lot. "Damn, no tag. Must be them." He walked into the kitchen and opened the door to the refrigerator. It shed light into the small room and drew David there as well.

"Who were they? Was someone trying to rob us?"

"Not armed with this." John held up the large knife; it was clearly military issue. "My guess is they were after someone, not something." The two men looked at each other for several moments before John continued. "Get packed. We're getting out of here."

"Do you think they were after me?" There was both fear and anger in the young man's voice.

"David, I don't know what they were up to. We'll sort that out later. For now, just pack what you need. We're getting out of here, tonight." He thought a moment and added. "Take all you might want; we may not be back for a while."

"Do you think it's okay to turn the lights on now?"

John stood in the middle of the living room and fumbled through his small blue bag. After a moment he withdrew a 9mm Beretta and cocked it. "Yeah, you can turn the lights on now."

"What's that?" David's voice was one of shock and surprise.

"It's a weapon."

"What's that for?"

"This is for men who sneak into people's bedrooms with knives. Now get packed. We're going to Colorado." It was a voice David had never heard from his father before; he did as he was told. As the young man packed his things, John walked onto the small porch and dialed his cell phone. It was a number he knew well. "Walter, this is John. I need some more information..."

Chapter 7

Seattle, Washington, May 12, 2017

The 757 taxied to the gate and lurched to a stop. The familiar tone sounded over the intercom, and the excited passengers rose and waited impatiently for the ground crews to pull the Jetway into place. John and David climbed from their economy class seats and moved slowly forward with the other passengers. John nodded to David. The younger man was still in shock. After Marcia's funeral there had been little time or interest from David to establish a plan, but John had quickly completed that task. Each had fake Id's, assumed names, and traceable backgrounds. David thought this unnecessary, but John insisted. They argued intermittently, especially when John insisted they disguise themselves. They changed the color of their hair and wore facial hair and eyeglasses. They were dressed in cheap slacks and worn sport coats. Neither wore a tie. John turned to the younger man, "You watch for the bags. I'll get the rental car."

The drive to the middle class hotel in the center of the city gave them time alone to review their plan one more time. A call had been made to CFT from a "union office" near Chicago. Two mid-level shop stewards were being sent out to evaluate CFT's work. They would support the demonstration and report back to AFL/CIO leaders regarding future support efforts. Names, Id's, etc., were faxed out. They were easily recognizable; Mr. Jason Kinkaid was of medium build, fifty-one, and had gray hair, while Mr. Carl Johnson was twenty-four with blond hair. They would present proper union Id's upon reporting in. And, of course, the union would appreciate all due support they would receive.

"The hard part are the names and the glasses. You've got to remember both."

"Is all this crap really necessary? This dyed hair is for the birds." David looked into the car mirror again. "Damn, Dad, how did you come up with all this? You've been watching too much TV. This is ridiculous."

John turned to his son in frustration. "Think, dammit. They know your name; they know your face; they saw you with Marcia. Do you think the shooter will just introduce himself to you when he recognizes you? You'll recognize a voice; he'll recognize a face. Who has the advantage there?" John glanced into the rear view mirror and assessed his own dyed hair. "At least it doesn't make you look ninety."

David looked away, clearly unconvinced. "Where do we start?"

"Let's check into the hotel, then report to CFT headquarters. Our "union" secretary has made all the arrangements."

"How did you do all of this?"

"I had some help from a friend." John continued before David could question him further. "CFT will be expecting us."

"Then?"

"Then we simply circulate. Let's hope our man is still around."

"Do you think he will be?"

John carefully maneuvered the rental car through Seattle's traffic; finally he answered. "Frankly, no. My guess is he was hired to do a job and then left immediately. If he is still around, he's either on his own, or those who hired him are stupid."

"But who would have hired him?"

"I don't know." John was silent for a moment. When he spoke, it was the voice of a professional, not a concerned father. "If we just knew why, we'd have a much better idea of who might have done it." John was perplexed; he had already done a preliminary investigation and could find nothing that might have led to this incident. Whatever the reason Marcia was killed must be connected in some way to CFT he surmised. Nothing else made sense. There were no flags in her background—none!

"You know, Dad, I keep wondering if this was simply a mistake. Maybe he thought Marcia was someone else."

"Perhaps, but you said the shooter called her name."

"Oh yes, that's right."

"David, we probably won't find her killer, but we'll try."

"I understand."

"Don't be too disappointed if we come up empty handed. This is really a long shot."

"I know." He waited a moment then added, "Thanks, Dad."

It was not much, but it was something; David had at least made a small overture. John nodded in return and drove on quietly for a few minutes then turned to the young man beside him. "After we check in, we'll try the briefing rooms, the bars, restaurants, anywhere the demonstrators congregate."

"Do you think it was someone with the demonstration?"

"I don't know, but whoever it was, he was in the crowd of demonstrators with you in Chicago, so the odds are that he was one of them. We know it wasn't the police." John looked directly into David's eyes. "In spite of what CFT reported." John had secured a copy of the police report and had studied it carefully. The police denied any connection to Marcia's death, but the press was reporting what they wanted people to believe.

"Right." There was a sudden realization in the young man's eyes, a vague question that had not yet been verbalized.

"We only have three days, so we need to cover as much ground as possible. Remember David, I didn't hear the voice. I'll help you circulate, but it's you who will have to identify this man if we get lucky."

"These guys are all over Seattle; I'm not at all sure we can cover that much ground in three days."

"I know; we just do the best we can."

"What if we don't find him?"

"We try once more; then we quit."

"We quit?" There was surprise and disappointment in the young man's voice.

"David, I really don't think the shooter will still be hanging around with these nuts. It's just too dangerous for him."

"I hope he's still here, and I hope we catch the son-of-a-bitch."

John looked over at the intense dark eyes. "So do I, David. So do I." John weighed the determination of his son; he weighed his own resolve as well. He understood the anger; he also knew that anger could betray a man. An angry man was a dangerous man—to himself especially. He was concerned that David might also become a victim in a scenario he had yet to understand. The chances of finding the shooter were practically nil, but he would help his son temper his grief, and he would protect him while David fought his demons. And if they got lucky? Well, that was an eventuality that would probably not happen. If it did, he'd handle that when the time arose.

* * *

The two union reps marched into the makeshift CFT control room. It was a large suite of rooms in one of the nicer hotels in the center of Seattle. John surveyed the suite of rooms quickly, but carefully. There were three young women answering phones, typing various items into networked computers, and greeting the various visitors and press personnel who crowded into the foyer. In the rear were two other rooms. Inside each were groups of CFT "captains" huddled over large maps of the city. Strategy was being developed to embarrass the new president and to try to sabotage any successes he might have. John would have liked to study this group further—they were obviously well financed considering the venue they had chosen—but that was not his mission. He had one task, to escort David through the maze of weirdoes and intellectual idiots as fast as possible. He simply needed to find one man, just one. "Hello, Brenda." John spoke to one of the young receptionists. She was surprised that he knew her name, even though it was prominently displayed over her left breast with a large CFT nametag. "We're from the AFL/CIO; I believe our paperwork was sent earlier."

"Yes, we got it two days ago." She looked at the stacks of paper spread across the desk. A half-eaten sandwich stood atop the stack nearest her. "It's here somewhere." She threw up her hands in exasperation.

"No problem, I'm Jason and this is Carl." John noticed how Brenda smiled at the younger man. She obviously liked blonds he surmised. "Mind if we look around?"

"No, not at all."

"Hey, do we need nametags or anything like that?"

"Not really, but if you want one, just let me know and I'll print one up for you."

"Not a problem, we have our union Id's. They should do."

John walked through the rooms and began making mental notes on the staff and the various volunteers there. He stopped by one of the briefing rooms and listened to a small group of young men being instructed regarding their next assignment. Two of them were large black men; two were white. An older man was talking to the attentive team. "Now remember Ben, you and JR wait until the president gets into his speech about five minutes. Then you stand up and start shouting and waving your arms. Just start shouting racist! Racist! as loudly as you can. That's when you try to start a fight if possible, and remember to wave your arms so the press can find your location easier. We've given them the approximate location, but it's impossible to know how the crowd will be forming, so wave your arms high above your heads so they can focus on you quickly."

"What if no one wants to fight?"

"Then Mark and Joe here will take a swing at you guys. When someone tries to break it up, take a swing at them or someone else nearby. Just try to get as many people involved as you can."

One of the young white men grinned at the largest black. "I'll have on a sweat shirt with the Confederate flag on front, so you won't have any problem finding me. And remember Ben, make it look good, but don't hit me in the face. I just got my teeth straightened."

"Then you better duck fast." Ben patted his friend's shoulder. "I'm guessing we'll have some red-necks in the crowd. We'll get a real fight pretty quickly."

The "coach" looked up at John and watched him listening in the doorway. "You need something?"

"No, just admiring your planning." John held up his union name tag.

The man smiled at John as he handed each of the young men an envelope with money inside. "Our news contacts will be looking for you in the crowd, so give them a show. If you make the evening news, there will be another envelope—only thicker."

The team opened their envelopes and checked the money inside. They were smiling as they passed John and disappeared into the crowded hallway.

The "coach" followed the young men but stopped long enough to touch John's badge as he passed. "You guys were doing this a long time ago. We've learned a lot from you, but we have something you didn't—we've got TV."

"It's a powerful tool when you have the media on your side."

"You're right about that." He paused at the door. "By-the-way, you got any guys who might like a part of this action? We could use a few who know how to throw a punch."

John answered quickly. "You bet. I'll make a few calls." He took the man's card as he left.

The coach stopped suddenly and signaled a young man walking quickly down the crowded hall. "Lewis, hold up a minute." He stepped through the throng of young demonstrators and pulled the man aside. "Any luck with the NFL guys?"

"Yeah, the quarterback thought it was a great idea, and we didn't even have to pay him."

"Pay him? Are you kidding, he makes more than all of us combined."

"Yeah, but as soon as I mentioned the press and the notoriety, he was on board."

"That was enough?" The older man was genuinely surprised.

"Yeah, he's a pretty mediocre player. I'm guessing he thought the publicity might help keep him from getting cut."

"What about the other three?"

"One was a vet. I thought he was going to slug me. He wasn't happy about this at all. Something about flags on coffins and real men. Not sure what that was all about." He paused for a moment and searched the hallway as if looking for someone. "The other two were easy. It didn't take much to recruit them. I told them that once they started the demonstration it would grow into a movement. They weren't the sharpest knives in the drawer, but kneeling down really isn't all that hard."

"Good work. Did you give your card to the veteran?"

"No."

"Good. Don't approach him again. Just keep working with the others. I figure we can pull this off with only four or five guys to start. It will grow quickly when the press gets involved and makes them heroes. Then they will all want on board." He scribbled on a pad and handed the sheet to the younger man. "This is a reporter for one of the main news organizations. I've already alerted him that you would be in touch. Give him a call and sit down and work out a plan. We need this in the mainstream press. I'd like to see that Thursday morning. Any questions?" He handed an envelope as he patted the younger man on the shoulder. "I told you this would be easy. Just keep the conversation all about them."

"Yes you did. And you were right."

* * *

The rest of the day was spent moving through the offices and meeting CFT volunteers and staff. That night they visited four bars and three restaurants. At a little before two am they returned to the hotel exhausted.

Breakfast the next morning began the hunt anew. The two visited three restaurants and two brunches near the hotel before ten o'clock. Lunch followed the same pattern. That afternoon the pair attended three briefings and visited two of the sites where the demonstrators would assemble. Five bars finished the evening before they returned, tired and frustrated, for five hours of sleep before beginning day three.

John stood amid the crowd of older "delegates" watching as a young man in jeans and a Berkley sweatshirt spoke to a large group of young people over a bullhorn. He was giving them instructions. Many, it was hoped, would be arrested. If they weren't, several professionals were on hand to torch a few cars and break some windows—anything to feed the insatiable press who generally showed up to cover the demonstrations. They were identifiable by their large cameras. They could go anywhere and do anything; the cameras were world class passes to everything, anywhere in the world. Several small teams were working with the press corps to pre-film "shorts" that could be interspersed with actual footage of the real demonstrations. The CFT personnel clearly courted the press. TV coverage was one of the primary reasons for the demonstrations in the first place, and coverage had waned considerably in recent months. It was as Dr. Collingsworth had proclaimed: "Nothing activates demonstrators like TV cameras, and nothing activates TV cameras like demonstrators." As John watched, fascinated at the planning and organization behind the event, David left a group of young college students and walked slowly toward him. He was clearly depressed. John left the group of observers and met David, pulling him aside. "There's a coffee house up the street. Do you think it would be unseemly for a shop steward to order a latte?"

David smiled weakly. "Yeah, sounds good."

John ordered the coffee while David went into the men's room. Several minutes later the two sat at a small table in the corner looking out into the gray day. It was beginning to rain. Dark clouds rushed overhead, racing across the city, dampening the body and the spirit alike. It was 4:30, but it might as well have been 8:00. Only the hot coffee kept the dampness at bay. "Damn, just what we didn't need—rain."

David smiled briefly, trying to encourage his partner. "Well, it won't help the demonstrators either. I hear they melt in water."

"Let's hope." John watched as two policemen entered the premise and began to scout the clientele. As they approached, John noticed they were not actually police at all but a local security service, obviously hired by the local businesses to keep some semblance of order during the demonstrations. John sipped his coffee slowly then turned sharply to look at the two burley uniformed men. Suddenly he thrust his coffee to the small table by his seat. "Of course!" He dialed his phone rapidly, looking at a number he had scribbled earlier. "Hello, Brenda? Jane? Look, we've got a problem at the coffee house on Kilgore Street." He listened briefly. "That's right, about one block east of site number four. Got that?" He listened briefly then added, "Get our security folks down here fast—all of them—now!" He hung up the phone and picked up his coffee. "Quick, grab that table by the door."

David looked at John in confusion. "What's that all about?"

"If the shooter happened to work with CFT on a regular basis, what job do you think he'd probably have?" John was looking at the two uniformed men leaning against the counter.

75

"Security?"

"It's just a hunch, but it makes sense to me, and I'm quickly running out of ideas." John stood up. "While we wait, want a piece of cheesecake to go with that coffee?"

"Why not."

Eighteen minutes later four CFT men walked into the room. John recognized two from earlier in the day. The other two were tall young men. One was large, the other relatively thin. Both looked fit. As they surveyed the crowded room John rose and greeted the group. "Hello gentlemen. How about a coffee?"

One of the two recognized John and approached. "We got a call from someone that we were needed here."

"Really? No problem here, but there was some kind of altercation outside earlier."

"What happened?"

"Who knows, looked like two drunks to me; a lot of shouting and some shoving."

"Our guys?"

"How should I know?" John turned to David. "Carl, these are CFT troops. You remember Derek from this morning."

David rose and stepped forward. "You guys also with CFT?"

"Yeah," the larger man grunted. The thin man simply nodded in the affirmative. "Jason and I are AFL/CIO. We're here to help if we can. Say, you guys sure you don't want a coffee?"

The thin man turned to leave. "No, I'd rather have a beer."

John saw the sudden jerk of David's head; he watched his jaw clench and then the sudden redness that spread upward from his neck. John stepped immediately between the two. "I don't think we've met. I'm Jason Kinkaid."

"Lonnie." The man nodded to John.

John studied the man carefully as he spoke to the group. "Who called anyway?"

"Who knows? It might have been a diversion. We've got to get back to CFT. See you guys later."

"Sure you don't have time for a coffee?"

"Maybe later." The group turned and left.

John watched them until they were gone, then turned to David. "You're sure?"

"I'm sure!" David's face remained crimson. "It was all I could do not to strangle the bastard!"

"All in good time, David. All in good time."

"What now?"

"Have you ever done a stakeout before?"

"No. Why would I know that?"

"Well, you learn how tonight. And this is for real." John watched as David fought to compose himself. His fists were still clenched, and John could see the small tremor in David's lower lip. He reached and placed his right hand on the younger man's shoulder. "It's okay David. We've found him, but we need information; we still need the reason." David slowly turned from the door to face John. His eyes were looking beyond his father, perhaps through him. John watched as the young man conquered the rage that was coursing through his body. He blinked twice then turned his eyes to John's.

"I'm okay."

"Good, finish your coffee. You need to be very alert tonight." The young man downed the remainder with one gulp. John sipped his own before continuing his thought. "David, you did well. If you had reacted, it would have been a mistake." He watched the dark eyes glare into the dim light. "Right?"

"I suppose."

"One seldom acts rationally when coming from a place of anger. This has to be well thought out." He waited until the young man's eyes met his. "Understand?"

"Yes, but it was difficult to just stand there."

"I understand, but first we have to be absolutely sure. Okay!"

"I'm absolutely sure. He's the one."

"Good." John downed the last of his coffee. "Now, let's go get that bastard."

"Dad?"

"Yes son."

"How do you know all this stuff? You're damn good at this."

"Like you said, David, I watch a lot of TV. Far too much I guess." John nodded to the door. "Come on, we've got work to do."

The two men stepped out into the rain and walked the two blocks to their rental car. Neither spoke as they drove to the hotel; each was lost in his own thoughts, his own memories. For one the memories were of a small, smiling child; for the other, the memories were of a budding young woman testing life, tasting love.

The rain intensified as a low front moved south of the city and became stationary over Mossyrock. Thick clouds settled over Seattle and hung like curtains from the dripping treetops and the glistening buildings. As the cold and the dampness increased, the wet students lost their enthusiasm for the demonstrations, and since their leaders had already retreated to the warmth of bars and restaurants, the youthful crowd drifted away in groups and pairs. Soon only the most ardent were left to condemn an idea none of them truly understood. For them it was so much easier to think with emotions than their intellect, emotions that were so easily manipulated by the trained CFT staff and, in some cases, frequent use of illegal drugs.

As the last groups disappeared into the overcast night, two men stood silently in the dark shadows of a storefront and watched one of the last organizers to leave. The light played off the wet streets, reflecting the lone streetlights that lined the thoroughfare. Lonnie collected the remaining documents and stuffed them in a nearby trash receptacle as he left the last demonstrators and turned to walk south, his raincoat collar pulled up around his neck. David followed closely behind in a crowd of young people, never more than twenty yards from the dark-headed man. John trailed both, about ten yards behind David. As he walked, he prayed Lonnie wouldn't get into a taxi. What would David do if he did, pull him out and start a fight in the street? Besides, how could he be sure this was the right man? How well could David actually recognize and identify a voice? He had to know for sure; there was no room for an error in the course of action he had chosen. Slowly he began to formulate a plan. Only Lonnie could confirm that he was, indeed, the right man. That would be the hard part. If he were, what would they do then? He checked the recorder in his pocket. Would that be enough? The rules in international espionage were really quite simple. The American judicial system was another matter altogether. John thought for a moment and made a conscious decision. He took the recorder from his pocket and turned it off. If he could just get a confession out of Lonnie, that would be enough for him. He didn't need an army of lawyers to debate the finer points of rehabilitation of criminals. This one had stepped over a very dangerous line when he murdered Marcia. David would never have to sit through the killer's trial, and a fake rehabilitation was not an option that the public would have to pay for. But first he needed information; who ordered this murder?

Lonnie turned east and continued to walk briskly in the rain. He stopped once and made a quick call on his cell phone then continued turning south at the next intersection. David passed him in a crowd of people but ducked behind the next corner to watch until he passed again. The cold and the rain were assets in his pursuit of Marcia's killer. David was wearing a Berkley hoodie pulled close around his face and John pulled his fedora down across his forehead. In the dark, they were difficult to identify. John stopped in front of a store window and waited until the CFT security man turned east. David stepped behind him from the corner as the dwindling crowd continued to break up into pairs and singles. Two blocks later Lonnie turned left and climbed the steps into a small hotel.

The Windsor was a typical inner city hotel. It had been built in the late fifties or early sixties and was well maintained. The hotel had one hundred thirty-four rooms. It also maintained a restaurant of some reputation in the neighborhood and fed locals along with the mid-level businesspeople who appreciated its convenient location. It was built of tan brick, accentuated by dark green canopies that stood above the large windows on the street level. Over all it gave a pleasant appearance and a welcome home for travelers who frequented the establishment.

David, then John, followed the man into the hotel. Lonnie stepped into the elevator, shaking rain from his coat. David watched carefully as the elevator light indicated a stop at the eleventh floor. John walked to the reception desk and talked to the desk clerk. As he left he handed the man some bills. David returned to the lobby, staring at the wall, wondering what events the evening held in store for him. His mind was clouded by confusion and anger; thus far the anger was predominant. Five minutes later he was still considering his situation when the elevator opened and Lonnie waked into the lobby. The man appeared slightly older than David had thought, perhaps his late-30s. He wore a beige sweater and blue jeans that were damp at the ankles. He scanned the room carefully as he turned into the small lobby bar.

John returned and stood beside his son as he whispered. "His name is Lonnie Carver."

"Well, Lonnie Carver just walked into the bar, and his room is on the eleventh floor."

John's head swung around quickly. "The bar? Great."

"What do we do now?"

John rubbed his forehead and eyes as he spoke. "Go in there and strike up a conversation. Tell him you knew him from an earlier demonstration. Chicago." Both men's eyes met momentarily before the older man continued. "Be sure to keep your glasses on. That and your facial hair will probably be enough to ensure he doesn't recognize you. Buy him a drink. When I walk in, invite me over. We'll continue the AFL/CIO ploy.

80

Then I'll offer to buy the next round of drinks. After we've had a few and he's getting drunk, we'll go up to his room. He'll probably be getting sick and need some help."

"How do you know he'll get drunk?"

"Trust me; he will." There was a slight smile on John's face.

"Then what?"

"Then we find out how good your voice recognition really is." John's face was serious as he stared at the younger man. "David," he grabbed the young man's arm and looked squarely into his eyes. "Can you do this without losing it? It's going to be hard to keep your cool if he's really the one who killed Marcia. Can you do that?"

"He's the one, trust me." David looked into the eyes of his father and stood silently for a moment, cold, hard, like a stone. "And yes, I can handle it."

"You're sure, son? This is important. He has information we need, and we have to be sure."

"I'm sure." Grim determination framed David's face. "I want this guy; I want the others too."

"And that is why we have to play this carefully. Just be patient until we get all the information we need." John put his hand on his son's shoulder and turned him toward the bar.
"Okay, go! I'll join you in about five minutes; that should give you time to make an acquaintance." David started off slowly, uncertainty on his face. "Just remember why we're here. This guy is just the shooter; we want the brains and the reasons behind this as well."

David looked back momentarily. "Yeah." He straightened his shoulders and walked very deliberately into the bar.

When John entered the crowded room five minutes later he felt the tightness in his guts and the anger welling up in his heart. Part of him desperately wanted resolution, to know that this was the man who had caused such pain, but also he hoped it would be a mistake. Either way, they had to know.

Someone had done the unthinkable. It was a sin neither he nor his son could ever forgive. That was not something a McClellan could do. John wanted revenge; he wanted to strike out at the man who had murdered the woman his son loved. His son had been wronged; evil had touched his family. But there was another specter that haunted his mind. Why? Why would anyone want to harm Marcia? What was the purpose? John understood violence with purpose. He lived with that, but why Marcia? She was just a kid; what was the purpose in killing her? He would protect his son from himself; he would also seek to understand this tragedy. Then he would have to figure out how to deal with her killer. He owed that much to David, and even to Marcia. Quietly he calmed his body and breathed deeply. He forced a smile and walked casually into the crowded room. The bar on the right was circa early 1900s. Behind the chest high bar were two bartenders and mirrors that stretched along the entire wall. Booze of every type stood displayed before the mirrors and reflected into the windows on the opposite wall. The familiar smell of beer penetrated the dark bar. On the left side of the room the large windows looked out onto the rain-drenched streets. Before the windows were small tables crowded with chairs. Tiny candles blinked through their glass containers and shed warmth into the room which, like the bar, was crowded with young people from the demonstration. It was dark; it was also very loud. One had to shout simply to be heard. Above everything else was loud, raucous music that added to the din inside.

John had walked half way through the room when he heard David's call. "Jason! Jason Kinkaid! Hi. Come join us; want a beer?"

John peered through the smoky haze to find the two men sitting together. "Carl. Where did you disappear to this afternoon? I lost you after the coffee shop. Were you at the demonstration?"

"You bet."

"Great." John allowed himself to be guided toward the small table.

"Jason, this is Lonnie. Lonnie, Jason."

"Hi Lonnie. Say, didn't we meet at the coffee shop this afternoon?"

The man looked up and smiled. John judged him to be in his mid-thirties or perhaps a bit older. He was good looking with straight black hair. "Yeah."

John extended his hand. "Well, this is my first demonstration. Guess I'm a beginner."

David motioned for the waiter as he pulled John's chair into place. "Can I buy you a beer?"

"Sure, as long as I get the next round. And since we're on a union expense account this trip, we'll let them pay for the beer." The men drank, joked, and talked as the crowd grew around them. Finally, John looked around furtively for a waiter. "Damn, I'll get them myself. What'll you have?"

"A Sam Adams for me."

"Make mine a Killians."

"Done." In a few minutes John returned with the beers. In the darkness of the room, no one noticed that one of the drinks had slightly more of a "head" than normal. Ten minutes later Lonnie was leaning slightly to one side. David looked questioningly at John who simply sat sipping his beer, smiling. "Hey, Lonnie, maybe we'd better get you upstairs; you don't look so good."

"Yeah, I feel like shit. Damn, I only had three beers."

"Come on, man." David helped hoist Lonnie, and they started out of the room. Lonnie looked as if he were going to be sick there in the bar. "What's your room number? I'll help you."

"1114."

John heard the number and nodded to David. He continued to drink his beer and watched David help Lonnie out of the bar. Seven minutes later he walked out and entered the elevator alone and pressed the button for the eleventh floor. After checking the hallway carefully, he walked to 1114 and knocked twice. David opened the door and John stepped inside. Lonnie was slouched on a couch in the sitting room of the suite. David stood nearby watching the inebriated security man. Lonnie did not appear to have improved much. "Hi Jason, Lonnie and I were just talking about Chicago." David looked quickly into John's eyes.

"Yeah, that was a big one. That got us on the map!" John watched for a reaction in Lonnie.

"Yeah, Lonnie and I were both there, man."

Lonnie nodded. "Yeah."

John sat down and began pouring vodka into glasses from a bottle he produced from his pocket. He handed one to each of the other men.

John glanced at Lonnie and then back at David. "Let's see, Chicago was when that girl got killed and the press blamed the police wasn't it?" Lonnie nodded slightly. After a moment John continued. "That's right, the shooter even had the good sense to use a 9mm."

"Just like the police." Lonnie had finished the vodka and John was pouring another.

John looked directly at the intoxicated man. "You know, Collingsworth told me the original plan was to use a .38, but whoever ran the show had the good sense to tell the shooter to switch to a 9mm. He must have had a good man in charge."

"Collingsworth's full of shit!" Lonnie spilled most of the second shot down his shirt. "Pierre wouldn't know one end of a gun from another."

John picked up the name and continued. "That's funny, Pierre told Collingsworth it was his idea."

"Pierre is an ass. He always acts like he's in charge of everything. But I know different. I've heard him on the phone. He sounds like a kid pissing in his pants when the brass calls."

"The brass?"

"Yeah, whoever they are. Collingsworth I guess."

"Collingsworth said he paid Pierre fifty thousand for that hit." John spoke to Lonnie, but his eyes were locked on David. Lonnie's eyes were closed, his head back against the couch.

"Then Pierre must have held a lot out for himself. Rotten bastard." Lonnie leaned forward and poured himself another vodka, spilling as much as he poured.

"Yeah, he has a rep for stiffing his folks. But, I suppose ten percent is fair."

"Ten percent, hell. That scumbag took fifty."

"So they only paid you twenty-five thousand to whack that girl?"

"And Pierre kept the rest, that son-of-a-bitch. Wait till I see him again..." The remainder of the sentence was lost as David lunged across the couch and struck Lonnie as hard as he could. The intoxicated man was taken completely by surprise as the younger man beat him mercilessly. Tears rushed down David's cheeks as he lashed out blindly. From deep within his throat a moan of pain escaped as he wiped his eyes to focus on Lonnie's shocked face. The killer instinctively rolled to the floor, assumed a fetal position, and covered his head. John stood aside and watched as David kicked and beat the prostrate figure. Finally, exhausted, the young man stepped back, trembling with anger.

"You bastard! You killed her!" Again he kicked the downed man in the back, then stepped away, his energy spent, but not his anger.

The injured man moaned loudly and glanced quickly at his attacker. David had lost his fake glasses in the melee, and Lonnie suddenly saw him clearly in the dim light. "It's you!"

John firmly placed his hand on David's shoulder, speaking in a soft but commanding tone. "That's enough." David looked up. "For now, that's enough." John, too, was having a difficult time controlling his emotions. He reached down and pulled Lonnie to his knees. The injured man kept his eyes locked on David.

"It's you. You're him." As his voice grew louder John struck him again. The impact of the blow flipped Lonnie over onto his back. He lay there motionless, dazed.

Before he could recover, John rolled him over and tied his hands behind him with pieces of silk hose that he pulled from his own pockets. With David's help he lifted Lonnie into a chair and gagged him with another piece of silk. Then he tied Lonnie's ankles to the legs of the chair and tied his arms in the back. John turned to David and nodded toward the bedroom. "Look for a computer or cell phone — and check around back there. See if there are any weapons."

"Right." David was rubbing his right hand and moving slowly. After he turned into the bedroom John pulled the small tape recorder from his pocket. He keyed it briefly and listened to their voices. After it played a few sentences, he replaced it and turned to the bound and gagged man.

"You're going to fry, Lonnie. Murdering young girls for hire is not tolerated here. Even liberals don't stand for that."

John was still standing over the frightened murderer when David walked back into the room. The young man held up a 9mm pistol in one hand and a silencer in the other; his face filled with sorrow and anger. "Look what I found." Frantically, David began to screw the silencer onto the muzzle of the pistol, all the while staring at the bound man in the chair. John looked at him momentarily then quickly reached and took the weapon and the silencer from his son. He studied them both briefly, then put them in his pockets.

"Look what else I found." He held a laptop in his left hand and handed John a stack of photos with his right. The first was a picture of David and Marcia, obviously from Chicago. The second was the same as the first, with the exception that a circle had been drawn around David's face. The third was a blowup of David's face. John's face turned suddenly white.

"So that's what he meant. He recognized you."

"What does that mean?"

"It means they're worried about what you might say. It

means if you had come here without a disguise you'd probably be dead now." John reviewed the pictures again then placed them in his pocket. "This also explains those two thugs in your apartment." He stood silent for a moment rubbing his forehead with his fingers. He mumbled to himself. "This changes everything. Those bastards!" John paced across the room twice then turned, resolved, to his son. "David, check again. Make sure there aren't any more of these photos around. Check everything, but leave the room in order." He wrote quickly on a page he tore from a hotel notepad and handed it to David. "See if Pierre and Collingsworth are on his email list. If he is, send them this note, then put the note in your pocket. Be sure not to leave it here." He glanced at Lonnie then looked back at David. "And copy his email list and his own email address onto this flash drive." David's eyes never left the killer until he walked back toward the bedroom. John turned to Lonnie and bent close to the killer's face. Very quietly he whispered, "You know, you really blew it this time." He rose, still looking into the eyes of the man who had murdered Marcia, the man who also planned to murder his son.

The bound man was sobering quickly as the adrenaline flowed through his body. He watched apprehensively as John pulled another chair before his and loosened the gag. "Now Lonnie, we're going to have a little talk, and you're going to answer some questions. If you don't, I'll get the information the hard way. It's up to you." John held a knife before Lonnie's face. "Now, first of all, tell me about Pierre." His voice was cold and deliberate.

"Who are you?" Lonnie's eyes were wide with a mixture of fear and anger.

"Let's just say I'm your worst nightmare right now. Now tell me about Pierre or I'll carve you like a Thanksgiving turkey. I'm a professional just like you, Lonnie. I will get what I want. It is just a question of how much pain you have to experience first. You and I both know that torture really does work, don't we?

You hold no allegiance to those idiots in CFT; you were just on contract. So make it easy on yourself and start talking." John moved the knife before the frightened man's face and placed it gently against his neck.

"Pierre recruited me in March, just before the Chicago demonstrations. He said he'd pay me to do some security work."

"When did he tell you to kill the girl?"

"That morning, before the demonstration."

"Had you killed anyone before that?"

Lonnie looked down momentarily, trying to understand what was happening to him. He was in great pain and sweating with fear. When John pulled his arm up against his back, he groaned and spoke quickly. "Yes."

"Did Pierre know that?"

"Of course. Why do you think he hired me?"

"Did Pierre make the decision to kill the girl, or was it someone else?"

"I don't know." John put more pressure on the arm. Lonnie cried out loudly. "Dammit, I already told you, I don't know. They don't tell me things like that."

"What about his friends or associates?"

"Pierre is the only one I know."

John released some of the pressure. "Where do I find Pierre? And what is his last name?"

"It's Marcharant or something like that. I think he lives in Pittsburgh; I haven't seen him here in Seattle." Lonnie lied, looking up at John. "What are you? A cop?" Lonnie was sobering quickly. "I want my lawyer."

"No lying lawyer is going to make a lot of money trying to save your sorry ass, Lonnie. Not this time" John pulled his wallet from his back pocket and flipped it open to a small picture. He held it and one of the pictures David had found before Lonnie's face. Lonnie's reaction was one of sudden understanding and instant fear. "You were right. It is him. He's my son, and that was his fiancée you murdered."

"I was just following orders." There was defiance in Pierre's voice.

"Do you really think that matters to me?" John pulled the gag back into place; he had heard all he needed, all he wanted to hear. He rose, his face set with anger and resolve. He walked quickly across the room as David returned, picked up the vodka glasses and stuffed two of them into David's jacket. John was mumbling as he moved around the room. "You picked the wrong kids, Lonnie. They're my family, you made a huge mistake." John straightened the room, wiped the doorknobs, then picked up the vodka bottle and walked back to Lonnie who was desperately trying to speak through the gag. John stood there looking around the room for a moment then turned to his son. "David, wait for me on the street corner one block west." John said it coldly, deliberately.

"What are you going to do? You're not going to let him go are you? I'm not through with that sack of shit." David's eyes flashed from his father to the killer. "Give me back that gun, Dad. Let me have it." His voice was calm, cold, and determined.

John walked to the door, looked out quickly, then shoved David into the hall. "Turn right out the front door. That's west. If I'm not there in twenty minutes, go on to our hotel. Now go!" David remained motionless in the hallway. His face was still red with rage. "Take off those rubber gloves, put them in your pocket, and use the stairs."

"Dad..."

John closed the door before David could continue, locked it, and walked back into the room. He pulled the gag from Lonnie's mouth and whispered in his face. "I have one more question. Did you feel anything when you shot her?"

"Fuck you! Fuck you both!" Lonnie glared at the man above him. "You know I'll get you. I'll kill you both. If it takes me a lifetime, I'll find you. You can count on it."

"I've already considered that." John walked back to the window and looked out into the rain again. "You know, life's really about alternatives and risks. You haven't left me many alternatives, and I don't take risks, not with my family." John then pulled a syringe from his pocket. "I hear this goes quite well with vodka."

Fifteen minutes later John walked quickly toward David and nodded west down the small narrow street. It was still raining, and the darkness sent a chill up David's spine. "Dad, what happened?"

"Keep walking." The older man walked quickly, his hands inside his trench coat, a brown fedora pulled close over his face.

"What did you do?" David grabbed his father's arm and stopped him in the street.

"I poured half a bottle of vodka down his throat; then I threw him out the window."

David stared at his father in disbelief. "You did?"

"Yes. He left me no choice."

"Good." David searched his father's face for a long time then nodded and started walking more quickly. John hastened to follow. "If you hadn't killed him; I'd have to go back and do it myself."

John glanced at him quickly as they walked on in the rain. Finally he spoke. "I know." After they walked half a block further John continued. "They wanted to kill you, too, David. It's only a matter of time before your version of what happened in Chicago would get out. That could be embarrassing for someone." His voice was soft, almost a whisper in the heavy rain. David was not completely sure that his father was talking to him. Perhaps he was talking to himself. "Our job here is complete. We found him; it's over. Let's go home." Before the older man could continue, David interrupted. "What about Pierre? He's the one who set this up. He's the bastard who ordered the hit. What about him?"

"I'll pay him a little visit. You go on home. Leave Pierre to me."

90

The young man increased his pace as he spoke. "Bullshit!" For a long time the two walked in silence, each searching the other's face, eyes, expression. "Look, I loved Marcia. These bastards killed her. I want to know why. Damn them to hell!" David grimaced as he spoke. "I'm glad you killed him; I wish I had done it myself." David spat the words as the rage in his mind shook his body.

John reached out and put his hand on the young man's shoulder, stopping him beside a dark, deserted building. "I know. I know. But this business will get messy. It won't always be this easy, and who knows, it may not succeed." Slowly the two men turned and continued walking toward a lone street lamp on the corner of the intersection before them. The stoplight changed from red to green, but no cars moved through the wet night. Only the pounding rain broke the silence. As they neared the empty intersection, David's eyes darted left and right up the sidewalks. He stopped briefly while John turned, and checked the route from which they had come. Satisfied that they were alone, the two continued walking through the night. "Dad, I'm glad you didn't just report these bastards to the police. I don't think I could stand to watch some lying lawyer defend the scum who killed Marcia. I just couldn't bear it."

"I know, son. We McClellans have a problem with things like that."

David nodded without looking up, mumbling to himself. "Or have some worthless lawyer denigrate Marcia to save those bastards." John turned to look at the young man as they walked across the empty intersection. David's anger was still brimming.

John spoke slowly, but forcefully. "Can I convince you to go home now?"

"No, not until I know why they did this, and I want Pierre."

John stopped in the middle of the road and turned to the younger man. "I understand. But I think we should stop. Besides, they're looking for you."

"I don't care, I'm going after Pierre, Dad. I know who he is now, and I'll find him."

John tried to measure his son's resolve; he looked into David's eyes, and the rage was still there. He realized he could not dissuade him; he understood his son's anger; they were that much alike. "Then you're stuck with me, but we do seem to make a pretty good team." John continued to study his son's eyes. "David, these guys are serious players, and this is serious business. One rule, I'm in charge; I make the decisions; you do what I say. Agreed?"

"I guess." A slight small smile crept across the determined face. "You surprised me, Dad. You really did."

John turned and looked down the street again. "Did you copy the email list on the flash drive and send the note to Pierre and Collingsworth like I told you?"

"Right, but why didn't we just take the laptop?"

"I need the cops to find that, especially with the notes we sent to the CFT folks. They will find all kinds of leads to keep them busy while we work on the next step in our plan."

"Which is?"

"I'm working on that." The stoplight flashed from red to green again, streaking the dark night with tiny rays of green reflections as two dark figures crossed the wet intersection and disappeared into the darkness of the deserted sidewalk before them.

* * *

The young detective walked into the second precinct munching a bagel in one hand, a large Starbucks coffee in the other. He eyed the older detective seated at the desk adjacent to his own. "Hey Paul, did you see we lost one of the protestors last night?"

"Really?" Paul Hamilton glanced up momentarily then continued to read the sports pages in his hands. "What happened?"

92

"Found his body in an alley. Looks like he got drunk and jumped or fell out of his hotel window." He paused, taking the last bite of his bagel, then mumbled. "Or maybe he was pushed. Either way, we're one moron short now."

"Right." After a moment Paul looked up, putting his paper aside. "Did you say he jumped from a window?"

"Yeah, appears to have been drunk as a skunk. Maybe drugs, too. We'll know soon enough."

"People usually don't jump from windows. They normally climb to the top of the building or jump from a balcony. Windows are too difficult."

"Maybe he leaned out and fell. They found an empty vodka bottle on the floor of his room, and there was a syringe on the table. Both are in the lab."

"Any sign of a fight?"

"No, the room was neat, except for the empty fifth and the syringe. And, oh yes, they found some ammunition in the bedroom."

"Ammunition?"

"9mm—in his dopp kit. There were seven cartridges"

"9mm ammunition?" The older man's interest was suddenly growing.

"Yep."

"Who was this guy?"

"A Lonnie Carver. Michigan driver's license. We're checking further."

The senior detective looked into the distance through a dirty window as he spoke. "I'm concerned about those bullets. Why would a punk protestor be carrying 9mm ammunition?" He turned to look at the younger man. "Did they find a gun?"

"Nope."

"There's an old saying: Where there's ammunition there's bound to be a gun. Or maybe it's the reverse. Let's take a look at that room. I'd like to check out that window."

"And look for a weapon?"

"And look for a weapon." The detective lifted his coffee cup, looked at it momentarily, then sat it back on the desk. He concentrated without seeing the cup in his hand. "Anything else interesting there?"

"No, the hotel's surveillance cameras haven't worked for years, but we did find a laptop in the vic's room. It's in for investigation. Our IT guys have it. I told them to check emails first."

"Excellent, I'd like to see what went in and out of his email for the past week."

"It's on order; we'll have it tomorrow."

Paul smiled at the junior officer. "Great work. If this guy had help getting out that window, those emails just might help us find out who the helper was." He started for the door. "Let's go; I'd like to stop for a real cup on the way."

"Starbucks is just around the corner."

Chapter 8

Morrison, Colorado, May 24, 2017

John sat alone at the table by the window in the small café and played with his spoon as he talked quietly on his cell phone. He was dressed in jeans and a short-sleeved knit shirt that said Maui just over his heart. His hair was trimmed short, and the shirt matched his blue eyes. It was a beautiful Colorado morning with clear blue skies and brisk cool air. The Blue Cow Café was located on the side of Bear Creek in Morrison, Colorado, in the foothills west of Denver. He was frowning, deep furrows forming on his forehead and beside his eyes. "More coffee, John?" The waitress wore tight jeans and a blue T-shirt that was clean but worn. Her hair was pulled tightly back and held in a ponytail by a rubber band. She was in a hurry. He nodded.

"No problem, we'll try again later." There was a slight pause as he turned the iPhone off. "Sure, Jessica. Thanks." He held his cup for more coffee and placed the cell phone on the table. John looked up at the smiling, scrubbed face.

"You don't look very happy. Did she stand you up?" The waitress nodded toward the cell phone.

"Well…" He started to speak, reflected for a moment, then responded seriously as he stared out the window at the mountains surrounding the small town. "Actually, you're right. Yes, I just got stood up." He glanced back at the smiling face beyond the glass coffeepot.

"Sorry, I didn't mean to pry."

"That's okay." He smiled back; her smile was contagious. "It isn't the first time and probably won't be the last."

"Hey, any woman who passes up a great dinner with a nice guy is nuts. And you can tell her I said so."

"I'll do that." He took a sip of the hot coffee while watching her pour more of the steaming hot liquid for the customers at the next table. When she turned back he continued. "She not only missed a great dinner but also a great concert."

"Her loss."

"I guess." He studied her for a moment. John had eaten his breakfast at this restaurant several times each week for about five years. He knew Jessica's first name and was well acquainted with her contagious smile. "Know someone you'd like to take to the symphony tomorrow night?"

She looked at him carefully for a moment. "Maybe, what's playing?"

"It's going to be great. Marin Alsop will be conducting Copeland among others. It should be wonderful."

"Marin? I don't think I've heard of him."

"He's a she. Our conductor is a woman and a terrific conductor."

"Wow, a woman conducting the symphony." She glanced back toward the kitchen and nodded in that direction. Quickly she skirted the tables and disappeared momentarily. When she returned she had three plates of food balanced precariously before her. She served the table adjacent to John's then grabbed two empty plates from the table by the door and disappeared into the kitchen area once more. When she emerged she had a fresh pot of coffee and a plate of food. As she served him she noticed that he was staring at the cell phone. "She change her mind?"

"No."

"Foolish girl."

"Hey, I'm serious about the tickets. If you know someone you want to take I'll bring them tomorrow morning. Doesn't look like I'm going to need them."

"Well, as a matter of fact I do know someone who would just love to hear Marin conduct Copeland, but I'll have to ask him." She looked directly into his eyes. "Well?"

"Well what?"

"Would you like to go to the symphony with me tomorrow?" She was grinning at him, obviously enjoying his surprise. "I just happen to have two tickets promised to me." She glanced around the small café. "And frankly, I can't imagine another soul in here wanting to go to a symphony. In fact, you're probably the only one within miles who even knows where it is."

John looked at her carefully for a few moments then grinned back. "You know, why not? That's a great idea; it would be a shame to waste those tickets. How about I pick you up at six. We could attend the concert and have dinner afterwards."

He watched her eyes light up. "Great, I'd love that."

"By the way, where do you live? Where do I pick you up?"

"Here, just pick me up here."

"Here?" She nodded. "Okay, I'll pick you up here at five. Will that work for you?"

She nodded, smiling broadly, and rushed back into the kitchen. When she was out of sight, she threw her hands into the air in a victory salute.

*   *   *

The curvaceous young woman surveyed the racks of expensive clothes. She was happy; she knew she would someday manage not only this department but also the entire store. She was sure of it, not because she was pretty, not because she was a black female, but because she had brains, a great education, and more class than any of her contemporaries. She smiled to herself. She had goals for her life, and they

97

included the finer things like financial security, success, and, of course, a Lexus.   Not many black girls attended St. Mary's Academy, but those fortunate enough to do so were prepared to succeed. St. Mary's laid the foundation, and the Jesuits at Regis University did the rest. She had dismissed the liberal excuses for failure very early in her life and had decided she would succeed instead. Her goals were set; the path was clear; and she was progressing nicely in her career. She would be of service to others, and in doing so, she would also be of service to herself. It was capitalism at its best. The Jesuits and Milton Friedman would both be proud of her.

Brandy watched the woman nervously checking the price tags on some of the more expensive dresses in the department.   With each assessment, the woman's head drooped further. Brandy moved casually, but purposely, to allow a better view. She assumed the woman to be in her middle 30s. She was poorly dressed and obviously out of place in this expensive store. The woman lifted several dresses, looked at them, and slowly put them back on the rack. As she turned to leave Brandy got a good look at her face. She was somewhere between panic and tears. "May I help you?"

The woman stopped and turned to face her, clutching her worn purse to her bosom. "I'm afraid I really don't know what I want." She looked down at her feet. "Actually, I do need help."

"Well, I'm the best help you can get around here. My name is Brandy. How can I help you?"

"Well, I don't know what kind of dress I need to buy." The woman looked into Brandy's eyes and reached for the only life preserver she could find. "I've been invited to a concert tonight, and I really don't know what to wear." She looked at the attractive woman before her. "Oh, I'm Jessica."

"Do you have any particular preferences, Jessica?"

"I've never been to a concert before." She blurted it out rapidly. Saying it aloud seemed to relax her somewhat.

The young black woman smiled and placed her hand on Jessica's arm. "Well, you're in luck. We have just the thing you need." She stepped back and looked her customer up and down. "Well, you have a great figure; we can certainly work with that." She took Jessica's arm and started for the opposite side of the department. "Now tell me about this concert."

"He just asked me yesterday. His date stood him up, and he asked me to go. He said we'd have dinner and then go to the concert."

"Did he say which concert? Is it downtown or at a university or school?"

"The conductor is a woman named Marion."

"Oh, that would be the DCPA. Her name is Marin."

"I'm sorry?"

"The Denver Center for the Performing Arts. It's downtown. You'll love it; it's wonderful."

"You've been there?" Jessica looked at the young woman with envy. She was dressed beautifully, and her nails were gorgeous. She looked at her own hands unconsciously. Brandy's eyes followed hers. "You have beautiful nails."

"Jessica, these aren't even mine. You can have the same for about thirty bucks. Now let's look at these dresses." As the two women approached a rack of clothing, Brandy turned suddenly. "First tell me about your date. It might affect the dress we choose."

"Well, he's tall, early-forties, some gray, and he's nice looking." Her eyes brightened suddenly.

Brandy thought a moment and wrinkled her forehead in thought. "Can you tell me where he works, his job?"

"Actually I'm not sure."

"Where does he live? What does he drive?"

"He's from Evergreen, and he usually drives a pick-up or an Explorer." She thought a moment and added. "But a couple of times he drove a Lexus."

"Silver?"

"Yes."

"So, he's from Evergreen; he owns three vehicles; and one of them is a Lexus."

"Right."

Brandy looked at Jessica for several moments and finally spoke the question that was on her mind. "Do you know if he's married?" After she said it she regretted the intrusion.

"His wife died five or six years ago. I think she had cancer."

"And he asked you yesterday?" Jessica nodded. "I know him."

Jessica was surprised. "You know John?"

Brandy smiled. "No, not John personally. But I can tell you what he'll wear tonight. He'll be in a blue or black suit, off-white shirt; his tie will probably be some shade of red or maroon. He'll drive the Lexus, and his shoes will be black wingtips that cost more than most of the dresses in this department."

Jessica's eyes were wide with surprise and admiration. "How can you be so sure?"

"That's my job." She lifted three dresses from the rack and smiled at Jessica. "Don't worry, we're going to also make him the most surprised man in Denver tonight." She placed her right hand on her own cheek and stared in the distance for a few moments deep in thought. Suddenly she looked up. She was grinning. "Yes, indeed, the most surprised man in Denver." She placed the three dresses back on the rack and almost danced across the floor. "Follow me. I have a great idea, a simply marvelous idea. This is going to be fun. Yes, indeed." Three minutes later she lifted the phone on the counter by the cash register. "Darlene, this is Brandy. I need your help, and we also need Linda. Are you busy?" As the young woman talked on the phone, Jessica nervously opened her purse and counted her money for the fifth time that day. They were small bills, and there were a stack of them; together they totaled a little over $300. She touched the money, hoping she had enough, wishing she had more. Brandy returned several minutes later and surveyed her new project. "Yes, oh yes. This is going to be great. Follow me Jessica."

Twenty minutes later the two women emerged with arms burdened with dresses. Brandy was bustling around grabbing undergarments to match. She examined several bras and selected the sexiest black lace in the group. She turned to look at Jessica a moment then exchanged it for a size larger. She grabbed a pair of panties to match. Jessica's eyes were wide. "Do you think I'll need those too."

"You never know." Brandy looked at her and the two women smiled together. Now, let's run downstairs. Brenda is the best hairdresser in town. She will do wonders for your hair; Darlene will then give you a facial and apply the makeup. You won't recognize yourself when they finish. Your friend John may not either." She looked at the woman before her and saw the fear in her eyes; quickly she guessed what those fears might be. "Oh, by the way. You're in luck. Today we have a big sale, and the facial and hairdo are complementary. The girls downstairs need to try some new cosmetics they received, so this will be a big help for them." She saw Jessica relax a little and realized she had guessed correctly. Brandy walked back to the counter and fumbled through a crowded drawer. Finally she emerged with a smile. "Here it is, a discount coupon for 50%. Now, let's go do a miracle. Honey, you are going to look divine."

It was a slow day at the store, and the three women became excited with their project as they worked. Jessica sat quietly as the trio did their magic. It was three o'clock when they finished and Jessica stepped before the full-length mirror. The three women did high fives as Jessica stood breathless before the reflected vision. The London Blue dress glimmered gracefully off of her left shoulder as it cut across into a perfect empire waist and fell flowing to the floor. The ladies had picked out a pale gold two-inch open-toed heel and a coordinating clutch purse. Jessica's eyes grew large as she surveyed the beautiful woman looking back at her. Her long hair had been trimmed and curled softly around her face, falling to her shoulders. Her large eyes were highlighted, and her face glowed. The makeup, the dress, her hair, her nails—all were perfection. Only the stiffness of the high heels interrupted the total feeling of joy she felt. Brandy watched Jessica carefully; she saw the tears welling in her eyes. Suddenly Jessica blurted out: "I look beautiful, just beautiful." She turned to the smiling trio. "I don't know what to say. Thank you so much."

Brandy reached out and took the smiling woman's hands with her own. "One thing is missing." She took a simple gold chain from her own neck and placed it around Jessica's. "Now, that completes it. You look gorgeous Jessica. Keep remembering that all night long." Brandy pulled her close and hugged her. "And if you forget, just for a moment, then look into his eyes. That will be enough to remind you."

* * *

The white snowflakes were large and wet as they drifted slowly to the ground. It was one of those late spring snowstorms that are so common in Colorado. The day had been warm and clear, then as quickly as the wind that blew in from Canada, it changed. John drove slowly down Evergreen Canyon and pulled to a stop before the café. He climbed out of the Lexus and walked quickly into the small restaurant. It was the first time he had ever worn a suit in Morrison; he smiled, wondering if the staff and the clientele would recognize him dressed as a successful businessman. He opened the café door and hurried inside, brushing the snow from his hair and his shoulders. It was then that he noticed the silence around him. He raised his head and scanned the room. It was filled with people he had seen many times; however, they were not looking at him; they were staring toward the kitchen. His eyes followed theirs to the beautiful woman standing there, looking at him. John stared at her for a moment, trying to place the face, the hair, the figure. Then suddenly he knew. At that moment, his mouth opened to speak but was silent. He simply stood there and stared at

Jessica. At least he thought it must be her, but he was not completely sure until she spoke. "Hi." She was clearly excited, clearly as surprised as he.

"Hi." John walked toward her slowly and took her hand. "You look wonderful."

"Thank you." He had never seen such a grin; she was obviously delighted with herself, and, he hoped, with him as well.

He stepped back and surveyed her again. "Truly beautiful." She blushed a bit he thought. "Are you ready to go?"

"Yes."

"It's snowing outside, can you believe it? You'll need a coat or a wrap."

The smile vanished immediately, and he felt her disappointment. "Snowing?"

"Yes."

"Damn!" She spoke with conviction.

"Did you bring your coat?"

She looked rapidly around the room as if searching for a life preserver in a swollen ocean. "No, I forgot it."

"We can pick it up on the way."

"No! No, I really don't need it."

He looked at her for a moment then pulled his coat off and gently placed it around her shoulders. "You're right. The car is warm, and we can park in the garage by the concert hall." With a flourish he guided her to the door as the "regulars" in the café smiled and watched.

* * *

The concert was excellent, but John watched little of it. He spent the evening watching Jessica. Her excitement was contagious. She asked questions throughout the evening, anxious to understand the beautiful music that she had previously only heard from mechanical speakers. As the music filled the room, her eyes widened. Then the pianist played the

103

Rhapsody on a Theme of Paganini and tears rolled slowly down her cheeks. Her eyes danced throughout the evening until the music swelled in the final crescendo. When it ended she sat silently staring at the orchestra, mesmerized by the music. It was more beautiful than she had even imagined. All the while, John watched her, enthralled by the beautiful woman by his side. His awareness was heightened by her presence. He saw the eyes of other men glance over as Jessica walked by. He sensed her excitement at the music, and he also became aware of his own heightened perceptions. They ate at a small restaurant near the theater. He smiled at her obvious appetite and watched as she toyed with her food, then noticed the surprise on her face as she tasted the gourmet meal from one of Denver's finest chefs. Her eyes suddenly opened wide with surprise. Finally, she ate with abandon. He ordered a bottle of 2013 Montefalco Rosso from Italy. It was delicious, but Jessica drank very little. She was not accustomed to drinking wine, and she wanted everything to be perfect for the evening.

After dinner, they drove into the mountains and stopped at El Rancho, an historic old lodge off of I-70 for drinks and a chance to talk. Jessica was silent as they drove from the city. As they settled into their leather seats around the fireplace that crackled before them, John turned to her. "What would you like to drink?'

"You order."

"Two ports. Sandeman, if you have it." He turned to Jessica as she sat staring at the fireplace. "Did you like the concert?"

"Oh yes. It was beautiful." She watched the fire leaping into the dark recesses of the chimney. "Thank you, John. This has been a truly beautiful night, one I will never forget."

"Nor will I." The shocking realization dancing through his mind was that he meant it.

She tasted the port. "This is sweet."

"It's great, isn't it?"

"Yes, yes it is." She tasted it again. "Is it strong?"

"If you mean alcohol, a bit, I suppose. But no worry, you don't drink much of this." She sipped her drink and stared at the fire and thought of all she had missed in the years since Sam's death. He had been a good man; he had loved her; he had made her smile. With an effort she put his memories back into the small box tucked in the recesses of her mind. That was then; this is now. Perhaps it was time to live again.

As the evening grew late and the embers in the fire smoldered slowly into ashes, they talked about the concert, about the people in the café, and only a small amount about themselves. But each talked, and the other listened carefully, attentively. It was a relatively short while that they spent together that evening, but in that time a seed of understanding was planted. Mostly they laughed at the mixture of "regulars" in the café, and then she asked more questions about the concert. He answered as best he could and secretly promised himself to get her a book that would do a better job than he could. What she noticed most was how much he smiled at her. What he noticed most was how much he was smiling at her. For the first time in years he was having fun, and it felt good.

* * *

John felt, more than he heard, the vibration of the phone by the bedside. As he reached to stop the incessant ringing he shook his memory to consciousness. Then it all came back. The concert, the dinner, the night together. He smiled; it had been a great evening. How long had it been since he had simply enjoyed someone's company? The phone vibrated again, focusing his attention. It was a voice message from Walter. John rose and started for the kitchen as he placed the phone to his ear. Walter's voice sounded excited; wherever he was, it was not five thirty in the morning. "John, I have some interesting news. I've done a bit of research on the group you asked about. You'll find their org chart, bios, and some other data in your special email. I also tracked their funding. You'll never guess who's financing that group of anarchists—a Saudi Prince, for one. I'll be in Brussels next Wednesday at a meeting that he normally attends. I'll see what I can learn and get back to you if I find anything interesting. Take care. Walter." John erased the message. A Saudi Prince? That seemed strange, but it meant nothing to him.

Chapter 9

Brussels, Belgium, June 6, 2017

Walter entered the room and looked about with the keen scrutiny of an expert. The room was large and filled with well-dressed people chatting and eating exquisite food from lavishly laid tables. White jacketed waiters walked among the delegates with tasty morsels to accompany the glasses of champagne. Walter spent his life tracking money, and he knew most of the wealthy men and women in the room. He wanted to see them, to talk to them, to know them, to understand how they think. The more he knew these people, the easier his job might be some day in the future. He noted each of them, checking against the list that he had memorized earlier in his career. There were men and women of various ages and nationalities in the room, but the one he sought today would be easily identified. How many men would be wearing Middle Eastern robes in a conference on world poverty? To his surprise, there were several.

The CIA agent checked his nametag—Walter Calandra, World Bank. They had seen him here before. He even had an office in the Bank's headquarters in Brussels; no one suspected his real purpose. Carefully he removed a small leather folder from his breast pocket and glanced inside quickly, memorizing again the picture of Prince Fakhir al-Shahri. From the photo he surmised that the prince was in his early sixties, graying, about five feet eight inches tall, and rather plump—the good life had overcome his youthful physique. The prince had not yet arrived, but a phone call had been made when his limo drove away from the Saudi embassy there in Brussels. Walter had been notified, and Walter was a patient man.

The American watched the older man entering the room, finding him to be very amenable and friendly. Just today the prince had agreed to fund the organization's operations for the coming year. None of the pieces fit in Walter's puzzle. It made no sense at all. He had carefully studied everything about the prince's life. He had nothing in his file that would indicate his tendency to support anarchists around the world. Why would this man give ten million dollars to CFT? That was a concern, but there was another, even more disturbing. While tracking the funding for CFT, Walter had uncovered five million dollars that had been sent to an account of a known arms dealer in Moscow. What was that all about?

Walter studied the older man carefully. He had two bodyguards who stood always at his side. Walter wondered if they were armed and had been able to bypass the security measures. Really it didn't matter. He had a plan. He knew the prince's fondness for shrimp, so that is where they would meet. It was imperative that they talk. It was the only way to implement his plan.

Walter's timing was perfect. He turned and collided with the prince just as Fakhir was preparing to bite into a large shrimp dripping with cocktail sauce. The result was a majestic stain on majestic robes that would have pleased any modern art lover. Immediately one of the guards departed for soda to clean the expensive garb. As the other frowned at the American, Walter apologized profusely. He stepped forward with his napkin and began to blot the large red stain. "I am so very sorry, Your Excellency. It was my fault. Please forgive me."

"It is of no consequence. Please, don't be concerned. We are all colleagues in the process of doing good in the world. A bit of cocktail sauce is certainly inconsequential."

"Thank you, Prince al-Shahri. It is an honor to be associated with such a philanthropist. I was especially impressed with your support of the Committee for World Poverty." He watched the older man carefully. "And the Chicago demonstrations." He said it matter-of-factly.

The prince looked up with shock. "I'm sorry, did you say the Chicago demonstrations?" There was surprise in his voice.

"Why yes, the *Citizens for a Free Tomorrow* organization, to be exact." Walter watched the man's eyes. They were wide with surprise.

"I'm afraid you have made a mistake, I would never support such a group. They are an unruly group of uneducated youth."

"I'm sorry. My subordinates must have made an error. But I was sure that they said the funds came from an account with your name on it. There must be some mistake. I apologize." He watched the eyes narrow as he turned to leave. He had made his point, and Fakhir had been truly surprised. The agent smiled to himself. It appeared to be as he expected—one of the younger members of the family was playing tricks on the patriarch. He suspected that the game would get much more exciting when the prince returned home.

Chapter 10

Riyadh, Saudi Arabia, June 14, 2017

The three men sat and talked affably; Fakhir watched his two sons carefully. The room was tall and painted a bright white that shocked the eyes; overhead a large ceiling fan turned lazily in perpetual motion, a vain attempt to control the insufferable heat of the Saudi desert. The room was large but had only one small window for light. Behind the men, opposite the window, hung a large, heavy drape that divided the room. Behind it the servants huddled, waiting, should they be needed. As the afternoon wore on, the older man moved his right hand. The motion was almost imperceptible, but it was instantly seen by a younger man standing discreetly out of sight to his rear. Almost immediately another young man appeared with a tray of strong, bitter coffee for the three. The youngest winced at the strong coffee. "If we were British, this would be brandy. Now that is a civilized drink."

The oldest smiled at the impertinence of the younger man. "But this is not London; this is Riyadh."

The younger man replied with a smile. "Other than a thousand miles of sand, how can you tell the difference?"

The third man watched the other two as they playfully sparred verbally. There was an obvious kinship between the father and his youngest son. The older man sipped his coffee, squinting his eyes, and spoke through the steam to the younger. "I fear you are becoming more European each day."

"I suppose. Even my children. They all want western things: western stereos, western music, blue jeans; my oldest daughter even wants to go to college. What are we to do?"

Finally the third man spoke. "We are losing a war." His voice was soft and barely audible. Both of the other men turned to look at him as he spoke. Perhaps it was to hear him better; perhaps his silence had given his words respect.

"War? With the cursed Israelis?" The older man spoke harshly, eyeing his oldest son carefully.

"No, with the West."

There was a long silence before the younger man set his coffee aside and spoke in a much less joyous voice. "War, my brother?"

"Our children want western toys; they want western products; they want western ways of life. Our own culture is losing the battle. Soon we will be little different from the Egyptians, then the Greeks, then the French. All that is ours today will be gone. Our religion, our way of life, our culture, our beliefs, all will be gone. We will become a country of drunks and womanizers. Our children will watch the sordid movies imported from Hollywood; they will bring drugs and AIDS into our homes; they will turn away from Allah; and He will punish us with the culture of the West." He spoke slowly, softly as the other two men leaned toward him to hear his words.

The younger man's face was almost expressionless when he finally spoke. "But Ammar, what can we do? How can we stop the inevitable changes of the world? Would you give up your Mercedes, your computers, western medicine?"

"Perhaps we cannot stop it, but maybe we can slow it down a bit and give ourselves a respite to find some way of preserving a way of life we believe to be proper and right."

"How?" It was the older man who spoke. He watched the two young men carefully. They were both his sons, but they were so different. The younger was the joy in his life, the one who made him laugh; the older of the two was like his mother, much more thoughtful, more pensive. He loved them both, but

111

he worried about the older son and his radical ideas. Such things could easily be his undoing.

"We must find a way to slow the incursion of international trade."

The older man frowned. "How, by slowing the flow of our precious oil? That would simply doom us. We are not a people of technology. We have never built a car, a plane, a computer, or a cell phone, yet we depend upon all of these. Poor men designed them; poorer men, still, built them. Unfortunately, we have done neither. We simply buy them. The oil is the lubricant that keeps our rather fragile economy moving. Even our misguided revolutionaries must use weapons built by their enemies."

"That is not what I meant, my father. I do not fear the goods we exchange; trade is the purveyor of ideas as well. I do not fear the computers; I fear the ideas the computers bring into our homes, the pornography that debases mankind everywhere. The western idea of entertainment is little more than violence and sex. It is a society of debauchery."

The old man nodded thoughtfully. "Then what can we do, my son?"

"We can attack the institution of international trade itself. We can make people everywhere recognize the threat to their own cultures as well. Did you know, for example, that there are people in the United States who carry on a constant oratory against the United Nations for the same reason? They fear losing their own culture to a world of differences: different people, different religions, different needs."

The younger man watched his father's acquiescence and jumped back into the conversation. "Your words are true, my brother, but what difference can the three of us make? No army in the world could stop the tide of modernization."

"It will not require an army. It will simply require a small amount of money."

The old man's eyes shifted suddenly to his son. "And what will you do with this money?"

112

"We can join the support of causes that further our goals of keeping the infidels out of our land, out of our homes."

"Last month we agreed to contribute twenty-five million each for a list of charities supported by the Committee on Poverty. You are not talking about that money are you?" Fakhir's dark eyes were hard as they focused on the older son.

"Of course not, father."

"Such a thing would have the potential of causing great embarrassment."

"Of course." Ammar stared at the floor at his feet. He could not raise his eyes to those of his father.

"Now, I want to hear about my grandchildren. Enough of the world's struggle." The older man laughed with his youngest son at some antic of one of his grandsons. Inside, however, he was concerned. He knew Ammar was lying. He did not know the size of the lie, but he knew his son was lying about something. Generations of perfecting the art of hiding the truth had also perfected the art of recognizing a lie. He knew his firstborn son. He had watched him grow into manhood from the shaky legs of a boy. Why would his own son lie to him, his father? That was a question that troubled him, but one he would soon understand. Fakhir had many questions, but he was also a very shrewd man. He would have the answers he wanted very soon. Perhaps the man in Brussels who had stained his robe was sending him a message, one he was determined to look into immediately.

Chapter 11

Beirut, Lebanon, June 23, 2017

Ammar sat alone at a small dusty table in the warm sun. Most patrons of the small café had retreated to the cooler confines of the old building immediately behind him. The street was narrow, but most of the windows that lined the wall on the opposite side of the street were closed and shuttered. One need not worry about prying eyes in this area of Beirut. Other than Ammar, the street was deserted with the exception of two men—one half a block north of him and another fifty meters south, just beyond his parked Mercedes. Both men stood silently scouring the street from behind dark sunglasses. Unlike Ammar's traditional robes, they wore western clothes and appeared uncomfortable in the oppressing heat. Ammar glanced at them, then over his shoulder to the third, standing quietly in the shadows of the crumbling building. All three were armed and well trained.

An obviously nervous young man had just delivered a small cup of very strong coffee when the silver BMW-Z4 arrived. As it pulled to a stop the two men stationed down the street turned and began to walk quickly toward the car; both had their right hands inside their coats. A young man climbed energetically from behind the wheel of the new car and squinted into the sun. He smiled at the two guards as they checked the shiny new toy. "Greetings, gentlemen." With a nod he walked to the table and embraced Ammar. He stepped back one step and with a flourish looked at his friend. "You look great my friend. Life has been good to you."

"You came alone, Kahlid? In this area?" Ammar made a mental note of the expensive casual western clothing his friend wore, white linen pants, Italian loafers, and a soft blue silk shirt. Somehow it all seemed appropriate for the BMW.

"No, actually I have a regiment in my boot." Ammar looked at him quizzically. "The trunk!"

"Oh."

Kahlid Bahir nodded to the young waiter. "Coffee...two sugars!"

The two men talked amicably until the waiter had left. Without warning Kahlid leaned forward and spoke in a very low voice. The guards, now only ten meters away were out of earshot. "Did you get the money?"

"Of course." Ammar looked at this friend insolently.

"Good. All of it?"

"All twenty million," Ammar lied.

"Good." Honesty was not a virtue of honorable men in the Middle East; it was the naiveté of fools. Kahlid studied his friend carefully, knowing he had lied. Of course he had; it was to be expected. Silently he wondered how much more Ammar had secured, five million or perhaps even ten? "I had hoped for more, but we can begin. Kahlid rubbed the back of his neck as sweat trickled from his thick, dark hair onto his silk collar. "You have done well. I knew we could count on you. As I have told you before, it is time to move beyond your contributions to the anarchists that plague the West. They are not worthy of the money you have contributed to their silly demonstrations. Now we will do something that will change the world."

Ammar smiled. "Of course." He studied the handsome young man before him. Their friendship had spanned many years, yet he still felt uncomfortable around Kahlid. Was it the fact that Kahlid's parents had been poor while royal blood flowed in his own veins, or was it the fire that burned in his eyes? Something about Kahlid both repelled him and seduced him. He could not define it, but somehow Kahlid always seemed to control the moment.

"You still have guards?" Kahlid sat back into his chair as his coffee was placed before him.

"There are those who don't care for rich Saudis here—especially from the royal family."

"There are nuts here who don't like anyone—their own mothers are not safe around them. Beirut has become a wasteland."

"Thanks to the Americans and the Israelis."

"Thanks to the fools who blame everyone else for their own failures." Kahlid frowned, small lines etching themselves across his handsome face. "Men who live lives of excuses deserve their fate. They haven't the courage to face the truth of their own failures."

"Don't you believe in anything Kahlid? Don't you care?"

"I believe in two things my friend, money and power. Both of those are best earned, not received as gifts." The insult was clear, but Ammar ignored it. He and Kahlid had discussed this issue before. "These allow me to drive that beautiful machine over there," He nodded to the BMW. "To ski in Switzerland in the winter, and to live a life of luxury in a beautiful home with air conditioning in this hell hole."

"You are no better than the Americans."

"True, I believe in the finer things in life. But enough small talk. Listen carefully. I've made a contact in Russia. What we want is available, but the price is high. They want two hundred fifty thousand, US, just to meet with us."

"For a meeting?" Ammar wondered what the real price might be.

"There are risks for them, too. Plus it shows we are serious." He paused and added. "It also indicates we are not from the internal investigations office in the Kremlin. They don't have that much money."

"Tell them one hundred thousand."

"No, their price is two hundred fifty. Either we're serious or we aren't. Where else can you go to purchase a nuclear weapon? Not here in the Middle East." Kahlid smiled suddenly. "Well, maybe that is possible, but I doubt the Israelis will sell you one of theirs. Besides, what is that to a rich man like you?"

Ammar sat silently for a few minutes, stroking his moustache and staring into the distance. He had practiced this serious demeanor carefully. Finally he spoke, "Alright, but we need the meeting soon."

"Good." Kahlid reached inside his right pocket, withdrew a small sheet of paper, and studied it carefully. "Here is the account number. When will the deposit be made?"

"Before you arrive home."

"We are in business, my friend. I'll alert the Russians, transfer the money to them, and arrange the meeting." Kahlid finished his coffee and rose to leave.

"May Allah bless our purpose."

"Right." Kahlid nodded sarcastically to the guards and walked briskly to his car. With a wave he was gone.

Ammar signaled for another cup of coffee and waited patiently for it to be delivered. Why did he dislike Kahlid so much? Yet he admired his panache in life. Even as boys it had been so evident. Maybe when one is born poor, he must become tough. But tough really was not the word for Kahlid. What was it the Americans called it, "street smart." He finished his coffee slowly and rose, it was important that he give the impression of being in control, mostly for himself. His guards joined him in the Mercedes as Ammar studied the phone numbers in his iPhone and began dialing. "Hello, I have the account number we discussed. Are you ready to copy?"

As the large expensive car pulled away, one last picture was taken from the dark room on the second floor of the building across the street from the small café. A small hole in the left hand corner of the wooden shutter was sufficient for the sophisticated equipment and the expert who was using it. There

117

was a slight smile on the photographer's face as he handed the nervous homeowner several large bills and began packing his equipment to leave.

* * *

Kahlid sat back into his comfortable chair and sipped from the green Heineken bottle as he dialed the phone. There was a large grin on his face. He was very pleased with the day, very pleased with himself. Once again he had used Ammar to get what he wanted. Ammar, the slow, somber Ammar. Kahlid reflected on the injustice in life. Ammar was wealthy beyond counting, and all he did was get born into the right family, while he, himself, had been born into one of the less privileged families in Saudi Arabia. How unfortunate—or was it? He looked around at the beautiful apartment, well-furnished and sparkling. He had one thing that even Ammar didn't have, anonymity. He could walk the streets of any city in the Middle East without the need of guards. That was worth a lot, especially for his lifestyle. This thought led Kahlid off on other tangents. He had something else that Ammar had never experienced and likely would not for a long time—independence. Ammar was still a boy, still under the constant control of his father. Ammar had to maintain the family name. That was a burden that Kahlid did not want. In his family it was Kahlid who provided the financial support; it was he who gave the orders, not his father. Kahlid laughed to himself. How shocked Ammar and his father, old Fakhir, would be if they had seen the party Kahlid threw at his apartment last week. It was, as the Americans would say, a badass party. Booze, broads, even drugs. Yes, it was nice to have the freedom to live his life as he wished without the burden of answering to someone else. He had always used Ammar and therefore held little respect for him. Now he actually felt pity for him. He reflected on that as he gazed into the clear blue Lebanese sky. Perhaps pity was even worse than disrespect. He sipped the cold beer and thought about how appalled Ammar

118

would be if he suspected his true feelings. Oh well, when this deal was complete he would have sufficient funds to live as he pleased for the rest of his life. He would have no further need for Ammar. He would leave him and the rest of the fools in this part of the world and move to England, France, or perhaps even Switzerland. It would be nice to stay close to his money. That thought made him smile again.

Kahlid was just ready to snap the cell phone closed when the call was answered. "Swiss commercial bank, Gerhard speaking. May I help you?"

"Gerhard, old friend, it is Kahlid. I just wanted to check to see if the deposit I mentioned has been made into my account."

"Yes, sir. It has. It arrived about half an hour ago."

"Thank you, Gerhard."

"Thank you for your business, sir."

Kahlid lounged in the large soft chair and smiled. *How differently people treat you when you are rich*, he thought. *When one is poor he is ignored; when one is rich he is addressed as "Sir."* He drove a German car, used an American computer, drank Dutch beer, and spoke on an iPhone. Only the best! Kahlid definitely preferred being rich. He stood slowly and looked out at what remained of a once prosperous city. Now, he reflected, it was time to move west. Paris might be a good place to start. A multimillionaire could live well there, or anywhere else for that matter.

The hot sun shining through the seventh floor window burned his face and caused him to back into the shadows. He looked at the dark drapes but decided against them; he wanted to see the city. Perhaps someday it could be returned to its prior glory; perhaps not. Kahlid dialed his phone, and it only rang twice before it was answered. "Vasiliy."

"Hello, my friend; it is Kahlid. I'm glad I could catch you today. I just returned from a very important meeting. It seems I have a rather large order. Perhaps you could help me fill it. You may recall we discussed this possibility last month in St. Petersburg."

"Yes, I recall." There was a short pause before the Russian continued. "Are you quite certain? There is considerable risk with this client. I don't want to pursue a vapor contract."

"This is for real, my friend. I have the funds in the bank as we speak."

"That is excellent news. In that case I'm sure I can help you. When would you like to place the order?" The excitement in Vasiliy's voice was apparent.

"Immediately."

"Immediately?"

"Well, I recognize this may take a little time, but as soon as possible."

"I'll get back to you within a few days."

"Sounds good. I'll talk to you then." Kahlid tried to imagine Beirut with green grass and boulevards lined with tall trees. He downed the rest of his beer and quickly closed the drapes. He had a lot of work to plan. He was concerned as he walked to the refrigerator to select another beer. He had known Vasiliy Petrovich Kirzanov only a short while. In this business, it was good to have more information about one's contacts. Unfortunately, Vasiliy was the only contact he had, and the money was ready. It was a risk he had to take.

Chapter 12

Dubai, United Arab Emirates, June 26, 2017

Ammar's large black Mercedes eased carefully through the traffic in Dubai. The passenger compartment was separated from the driver by a thick glass window. The uniformed driver could not see the nervous young man in the back seat, nor could he hear the conversations that would transpire there. Only when the button in the rear was pressed and the red light illuminated on the dash could he hear the directions of the wealthy and powerful men who sat in the rear. That was the normal operation; tonight would be different. Under his seat was a small tape recorder that would record everything that was said in the car. The driver, Pitong Kirat was Filipino; he was afraid and sweating profusely. What if he were discovered? If so he would be sent back to Manila immediately or perhaps even killed in the back streets of this city he loved. He had worked very diligently to achieve his position in Dubai. He had even taken the job as chauffeur in spite of his physical limitation. His employers did not understand his name; they were either too stupid, too lazy, or they just didn't care enough about people like him to learn even a small bit of his background—especially his language. The fact that he could only see partially from his right eye was a secret he could keep; though it did require that he drive slowly and very carefully. Originally he had been called simply Pito; then as his eyesight faded, the villagers had changed his name to Pitong Kirat—Pito with one good eye. The Filipinos laughed at the joke the Arabs never understood.

Pito was afraid tonight; the directions he had received had been clear. Whenever another man entered the car, touch the small green button on the machine below him, and then continue as if nothing were amiss. If discovered in any way, he was to deny any knowledge about the recorder. His boss would support him and promise an investigation. But Pitong Kirat was no fool. He knew if the recorder were found his future would be bleak. He understood this clearly; those instructing him were well aware that he knew. That ensured that he would succeed; they had planned well. Suddenly the red light flashed before him, causing him to jump. "Driver, proceed to the open air market. When I flash the red light, stop. When I flash it again, you may proceed to the hotel. Any questions?"

"No, Excellency."

The trip to the market was no more than ten minutes. In Dubai everything is close. It is a remarkably beautiful city in spite of the desert upon which it was built. Pito drove slowly in the comfortable air-conditioned car. Even inside the Mercedes he could smell the fish in the market place as they approached. Not sure of which direction to proceed, he entered the market area and turned right toward the large tents with fresh fish and vegetables. He was just beginning to ponder his directions when the red light flashed on the dash of the car. He checked his rearview mirrors and braked to the right side of the narrow road. Three men were standing there in western clothing. The man in the center walked directly to the rear door, which one of the other men held open for him. As the tall man entered, he spoke. Pito recognized the accent; he was Russian. Quickly, Pito reached below the front seat with his right hand and pressed the green button on the small recorder. The perspiration on his forehead beaded and merged into a small rivulet that ran into his eyebrows and then across his cheeks. He mopped his face with his handkerchief and stared straight ahead. The door closed quickly as the two remaining men peered at the crowd for prying eyes. The red light flashed again, and the large car pulled back into traffic and headed toward the royal six-star Burj

Al Arab hotel, arguably the most beautiful hotel in the world. The chauffeur drove carefully as he pulled onto the bridge that led from the mainland to the small man-made island in the Persian Gulf where the hotel had been built. From a distance it appeared to be a large sail caressed by the winds and the tides. In reality it was a remarkable and very expensive hotel where the wealthy of the world congregated, especially those from the Middle East who had made their fortunes by allowing others to extract the black oil that oozed from the sandy soil of their desert homelands. The Mercedes S-Class Maybach pulled to a smooth stop before the large building and was immediately surrounded by the hotel staff, Indians who were well trained to indulge the wealthy patrons. Two uniformed doormen held either door as the two men climbed from the back of the car and walked casually into the hotel. Pito pulled the car to a parking area on the side of the building and joined the other chauffeurs there waiting for their bosses to call for their next destination. It was hot outside, and strangely humid for a desert locale, so he left the engine running. After all, fuel prices were of no concern to the men who owned the waiting limos.

Cursing silently, Pito remembered the recorder and quickly reached under the seat and switched it off. Then he carefully unplugged the machine and placed it in his right coat pocket. Twenty minutes later a small, well-dressed man walked to the car smoking a cigarette. "Excuse me, is this the car of Sir Richard Harris?" He looked around carefully as he spoke. It was dark but the lights of the hotel shone around the building with the intensity of daylight. The sweating driver quickly opened the window and handed the man the recorder. The man spoke very slowly as he peered carefully around the parking area. "You are to speak of this to no one. You understand? This never transpired."

"Yes Sir."

The man dropped a fat envelope inside the car then nodded and turned and left. As he walked quickly toward the hotel entrance, he placed the small machine inside his breast pocket. Two more men emerged from the shadows and joined him as the three entered the large, beautifully ornate lobby.

Chapter 13

Moscow, Russia, September 7, 2017

General Ivan Sergeevich Turgenov was a short and balding man in his late fifties. He was resplendent in his uniform with rows of medals on his chest and epaulets hanging from both his shoulders. His military hat, like those of all Russian generals, looked ridiculous perched atop his short frame. Turgenov's gift in life had not been his stature, rather it was his keen mind and iron will, both of which were well known and celebrated in his country. He was secretly proud that his promotions were not political; rather they came from hard work and demonstrated courage. Politics, he decided, were far too fickle. Performance, on the other hand, was measurable, and for him the measure was great. That was before; now everything had changed. He found himself immersed in a world that was confusing. It was changing fast, and the strict discipline of the old Soviet Union was crumbling against the modern technology and the freedom of the West. His military equipment was not only inferior, but so, too, were the indolent youths they sent to maintain it. The lethargy of socialism was firmly established in Russia and had become a stained reality of sloth and dependence. Détente had given him a glimpse of the other side of the fence. How had the West progressed so fast? How had the Soviets fallen so far behind? He had attended a meeting in Vienna as the Soviet Military Representative—what a city! Ordinary people on the streets dressed well and carried cell phones. How could that be? For the first time in his life he was totally confused. He sat in a meeting and watched sergeants typing notes on laptop computers. He wanted one. They were thin, sleek, and beautiful. They were objects of desire. And the men operating them were sergeants from the Bundeswher. Weren't they the ones the Russian Army had defeated? Who really won the war? Even the German cars were smooth, fast, and powerful, far better than any in the Soviet Union. The hotel's Mercedes even had leather seats. Leather! And the food. It was all such a shock. Ivan Sergeevich had never known lust before—not for machines, cities, hotel rooms, or computers. It was simply overwhelming.

Then three months later he awoke in the middle of the night with intense pain in his chest—then his left arm. It had eventually subsided but not without leaving him terrified, sweating in his bed. And that was the general's epiphany. A close brush with death causes most men to measure their past and the lives they led.   Ivan measured, instead, the days remaining. He was a military man, a practical man. Religion was never a part of his life. He had seen men die and never felt a presence of anything immortal, only the void of life. Funny, he thought, that a man at twenty-two with most of life to live will risk it without a thought while a man approaching sixty suddenly values life above all else. How many years were left? Two? Five? Ten, maybe? Well, if the government he had lived for was gone, what would he die for? What good were all the years of service? The pain in his chest was now like an old friend; it visited him often. But, unlike an old friend, the visits were filled with fear, and finally, resolve, resolve to live his remaining days for himself and his family. He had dedicated his prior life to leaders who deserted him, deserted the entire Motherland. Now his only loyalty was to himself for whatever days remained. And he wanted a laptop like the ones he had seen in Vienna.

* * *

Vasiliy Petrovich Kirzanov pulled his car into the muddy parking lot, vainly trying to dodge the largest puddles of water that impeded his progress. The rain had ceased, but the air was heavy with moisture as the arms dealer parked before the low, decrepit building. It was a wooden structure; there were two small windows in the front of the building, and only one light hung suspended above the door. Vasiliy surveyed the building, the parking lot, and the forest surrounding it as he climbed out into the evening mist. No one was in sight, but there was one ancient truck parked beside the front door. The color of the truck had long since faded, and one of the doors, like the fenders, was missing. Vasiliy was a tall man and powerfully built. Still, he was nervous as he approached the door. This was, perhaps, the most dangerous part of the work he had chosen— the initial sale. He was vulnerable here. He could be arrested at any moment should the deal go sour or if he had been set up by the authorities. How could he compete with the word of a general should this be a "sting" operation. His apprehension increased as he opened the creaking door and walked inside. In the twilight of the bar he surveyed the wall before him and a varied assortment of tables and chairs strewn around the room. The bartender was stacking glasses on a shelf as he eyed the new customer. Two older men sat at a table in the corner to his left talking quietly and laughing often.

"Vodka."

The old man behind the bar grunted when Vasiliy threw several rubles on the bar. As the drink was served, the arms dealer quickly checked the room for exits. Other than the front door, there was one more beside the bar that he assumed led to the back of the building, but that was an assumption, and arms dealers did not like to operate on assumptions. Vasiliy had no weapon; he didn't like guns, much preferring flight in times of danger, though he was skilled at hand-to-hand combat if it became necessary. He rubbed his hands together, hoping that

127

it wouldn't come to that. It was the only thing his years in the army had taught him that he considered useful—other than the fact that he didn't intend to spend the rest of his life in the Russian army taking orders from men with only one goal in life—their next promotion.

Vasiliy let his mind wander to the profits he could make on this transaction—a fortune, even by western standards. But he had to be on guard, and he had to plan this carefully. The money would be the key. How could he hide millions of dollars? Switzerland?

The shriek of metal hinges was followed, almost immediately, by the crashing of the door against the wall. All eyes in the bar turned to see a tall major standing in the doorway, his hands on his hips, his feet spread apart as he surveyed the room. The major was a large man, powerfully built. His camouflage uniform was freshly pressed and a black beret was pulled close above his eyes. He pointed at Vasiliy and motioned for him to come. Vasiliy felt a sudden surge of adrenaline course through his body, tensing every nerve. Rapidly he downed the last of the vodka and turned to obey. The drink was a cheap, coarse variety, but it helped settle the fear that was settling in his stomach. "Vasiliy Petrovich?"

"Yes."

"Follow me."

He watched the major carefully. There was no expression on his face—neither threat nor complicity. Finally he summoned his courage and resolved to assume the best. "Will the general meet me here?"

"Not here. He's in the car." The soldier nodded toward an official car parked off the main road one hundred meters away. They walked in silence through the mist. Vasiliy wore his best clothing and shoes. He wished he had his old boots now. It would take much effort to remove the mud from his newly imported Italian shoes. He could feel the moisture soaking through his socks; it was not comfortable, but it was necessary. If this worked he would never again have cold, wet feet. He and his wife would live in luxury. He pushed the thoughts of Lidiya from his mind and concentrated on the car he was approaching. He was soon to meet the famed general. What kind of man was he? His contact had given him a description—not of the man's physical structure, but of his great courage and unbendable will. Vasiliy imagined him tall, broad shouldered, and gray. His contact, Oleg Golovan, an old friend from his army tour, was now a senior sergeant and mistakenly considered Vasiliy rich. Comparatively, he probably was. Oleg, like Vasiliy, wanted the things of the West with its great productive engine. If he could help Vasiliy, perhaps he, too, could earn enough to resign from the army and find an apartment. Then he could marry his Valentina and have a family of his own. It was certainly a dream worthy of risks.

The major stopped twenty meters from the car and turned to Vasiliy. "Arms up!"

"What?" The shaft of fear returned.

"Arms up. I must check for weapons."

"Oh." He extended his arms while the major patted him down. When satisfied, the officer turned and walked rapidly toward the car. Vasiliy followed closely behind. The major opened the rear door of the Volga and motioned for Vasiliy to enter. Several drops of rain splashed against the roof of the vehicle as Vasiliy bent to climb in. What he found inside surprised him. The general was neither tall nor gray; he was younger than Vasiliy had expected. The uniform, however, was impressive. Like generals the world over, the stark brown uniform had its own array of colored ribbons to impress both military personnel and civilians alike. It crossed Vasiliy's mind that the man was almost humorous, a short, fat, bald toy dressed for a show. The slamming door behind him brought him back to the task at hand. "Good evening, General."

"Good evening, Vasiliy Petrovich; I understand you want to talk to me."

"Yes." Vasiliy fought the urge to add a "Sir." "I have a friend who would like to meet you. He is very wealthy and has asked for the opportunity to discuss mutual interests." Vasiliy was speaking slowly, choosing the words carefully. It was obvious that he was skirting the real issue of his inquiry. It was also obvious to the general that he was nervous.

"Your friend wants to buy a bomb?" The general watched the expression on Vasiliy's face turn to shock, then relief.

"That may be a possibility, but I cannot be sure."

"It can be done if the price is right." The shorter man said it flatly, without expression.

"I see."

"When does your *friend* want to meet?"

"Soon. He sends this to demonstrate his sincerity in completing this deal." Vasiliy reached inside his breast pocket and extracted a very thick envelope. He handed it across to the general who quickly shoved it into a small, worn leather briefcase at his feet. As he did, he glanced at the major, still standing in the rain in front of the car, facing the road to guard the two men inside.

"How much?"

"One hundred thousand, US."

The general's eyes widened. "For a meeting?"

"As I said General, my client is wealthy and a serious buyer."

"Very well. That is good; I am a serious seller."

"The building blocks of business." Vasiliy was beginning to relax.

"The essence of the new capitalism." The general smiled and then added in a more serious voice. "Sergeant Golovan will notify me of the time and place?"

"Or you can dictate the time and place that meets your schedule if you desire, through Sergeant Golovan."

"That would be wise. Our business is finished for now. You will hear from me within a week."

Vasiliy climbed from the cramped car and stood in the rain as the major got in and drove away into the night.

Somehow the rain and the cold seemed insignificant, but he knew he suddenly had to pee. As he urinated beside the roadside, he considered that he had just earned fifty thousand dollars. He was now a wealthy man, and more, much more, was on the way. As he trudged through the mud toward his own car he smiled and resolved to do two things tomorrow. He would buy a bottle of the best vodka for himself and then take Lidiya to the finest restaurant in Moscow for dinner. Yes, success was finally his, and it was intoxicating.

* * *

Slowly the incessant ringing of the cell phone penetrated his mind and awakened his consciousness. Vasiliy Petrovich dragged himself from the depths of sleep to the cold consciousness of the Russian night as he struggled with the small cell phone in the dark. "Vasiliy." He knocked a handful of rubles from the small table as he grasped for his watch. It was almost two am.

"It is done. The arrangements have been made."

Vasiliy's trip to wakefulness moved rapidly. "You're sure?"

"The remaining funds are in the bank. We're in business my friend." The voice was light; Kahlid had been celebrating. "When can we proceed?"

"I'll have to check with the..." Vasiliy paused. "...the client."

"Right. Call me tomorrow at the office. Can you make two o'clock?"

"Give me three days; I need to make arrangements."

"Till Thursday." The phone clicked off.

Vasiliy sat on the edge of his bed and looked at the woman sleeping beside him. Even in her sleep she was beautiful. Now he would be able to buy her the things he wanted her to have. Now their children would have the same opportunities as the wealthy and the corrupt. So this is how you make money, he thought. It certainly beats working like his father who had died in the mines at fifty-seven. Vasiliy rose quietly and walked through the small apartment to the bathroom. He accidentally kicked a small toy in the dark then stood quietly to see if he had awakened anyone. Finally he found the toilet and sat to pee. It's quieter this way, he thought. Soon, however, I will have a large enough home where my family can sleep while I piss standing in the dark. He was smiling as he climbed back into the bed and snuggled under the heavy down comforter beside the sleeping woman. Instinctively she reached for him and snuggled into his arms without waking. He considered waking her but decided against it; the morning would come soon enough.

Life is good, he thought; it has infinite possibilities for those who dare to take risks. In minutes her slow breathing matched his own, and, like Lidiya, he was lost in dreams of tomorrow.

Chapter 14

Madison, Wisconsin, September 29, 2017

Hamad Al-Falani sat patiently in his CFT office, waiting. For almost half an hour he had worked on a report that was due tomorrow, but repeatedly he would stop and glance at the phone. He was not so much anxious as he was curious. A gruff voice on his recorder earlier in the morning had promised information regarding Lonnie's death. Hamad recognized the voice immediately; he had hired Willie Thomas before. In his business, one always had need of a good private investigator now and then, and Willie was one of the best. When it finally rang, Hamad was engaged in a discussion with one of the young demonstrators. She was pretty; she was also high on pot. "Hamad."

"Hey Man, it's Willie. We need to talk."

"Hold on." Hamad ushered the girl into a nearby office then returned quickly to the phone. "What do you have?"

"Not much. Lonnie fell eleven floors from his hotel room to a paved alley. His body was found the next morning by a deliveryman bringing food service items to the hotel. He appeared to have consumed a lot of vodka, and a syringe was found on the floor. As of yet, the contents of that syringe are still under investigation."

"Do you know if he was using drugs?"

"Not yet, but I'll know in a couple of days when the cops get the report."

"Any sign of a struggle? Could he have been pushed?"

133

"It's possible, but it's hard to tell. He was in pretty bad shape after that fall. He landed approximately three feet from the vertical plane of the window. The trajectory appears to be a fall, but that's inconclusive since he exited a window."

"What about the room?"

"I talked to the police; they said the room looked normal, no signs of a robbery or foul play." There was a long pause while Willie waited for more questions. When none followed, he continued. "I checked the room myself. Everything looked okay. I also checked around at the hotel. The last folks to see him alive said he was drinking in the bar with two white dudes."

"Any description?"

"Yeah, the older man looked to be in his late 50s and the other much younger, with blond hair."

"Well, if they were with the demonstration, someone around should know them."

"I've already checked that. One of the team leaders said they were AFL/CIO reps."

"What were they doing?"

"Just drinking together. Everything seemed normal, so I'm told."

"Well, see if you can locate the two union guys. Maybe they'll know something. What was his mood? Was he upset? Was he in trouble? How drunk was he when they last saw him? That sort of thing."

"I'm looking for them already." Willie's professional pride was hurt. He didn't need Hamad to tell him how to do his job.

"No luck?"

"Not yet."

"Keep looking. I'll call the union. Maybe they can help us locate the pair." Hamad thought a moment then closed the conversation. "Look, I've got an important meeting. Keep in touch."

"You got it man."

134

Chapter 15

Morrison, Colorado, November 17, 2017

Jessica Hanagan stood in the warm sunlight and smiled as the cool wind blew across her face. It was early, and the sun had just broken over the ridge behind her. The lingering crispness of the fall season surrounded her, but the chill of the coming winter was apparent in the breeze. She watched the man seated at the old picnic table by the creek, his back to her. She recognized the head, the short cut hair, the shoulders. He was sitting motionless, staring at the creek that crashed along the large boulders below him. There was ice covering much of the creek, but the water remaining crashed viciously against the rocks. Even the large cottonwoods that lined the creek seemed to be waiting—waiting for winter's blast. The small restaurant was not yet open, but there were smells flowing from the small window in the back of the building; the distinct smells of coffee and bacon wafted across the small parking lot. Jessica watched the man for several minutes then turned, walked thirty yards to the front door, and entered. Five minutes later she emerged, two cups of coffee in her hands. She walked toward him; he had not moved, his gaze still locked on the creek below. As she straddled the seat on the table she slid the coffee before him and placed a hand on his shoulder. "You look like you could use a cup of coffee."

John turned and looked at the familiar face. "Thanks, Jessica." He took a long sip of the black liquid. "Perfect."

"Hot and black." She watched him for a long time. "How are you doing?"

"I'm okay." He didn't sound convincing.

"You look like you've got a lot on your mind."

He looked at the woman before him. She had a scrubbed look, he thought, a pleasant face with no makeup at all except for very light lipstick. He looked at her for a long time and decided that actually she was pretty. Her brown hair was of medium length and extremely full. Her smile was accentuated by even, white teeth. John reflected that Jessica smiled a great deal. "Yeah, I guess I've been worried about..." He thought a moment. "Work; I've been worried about work." Jessica looked at him, really through him, he thought. He suspected that she knew he was lying, but she said nothing. She simply sipped her coffee and watched the man seated beside her. "It's been a rough week."

She nodded. "You haven't been around for a couple of weeks. Where have you been?"

John looked at her carefully before answering. "Seattle."

"You travel more than anyone I know."

"It's just work." John felt her smile penetrate his gloom, and like the rising sun over the ridge above him, it warmed his soul.

"Where are you going next?"

"I don't know; I need a break from work. Maybe I'll go to Hilton Head or someplace warm." He turned away from her and looked again at the rushing creek below them. "My son is going to spend some time..." John paused a moment then continued, "with a friend in California, and I just want someplace warm with a beach. Maybe I'll fly down next week."

"I understand." She reached and placed a hand on his arm. "Hilton Head? What is that?"

"Hilton Head is a beach in South Carolina."

Jessica looked through the steam of her coffee at the sun rising over the ridge beyond the creek. "A beach. That sounds fun."

John watched her shading her eyes, staring up at the mountain. He automatically followed her view. "Do you like beaches?"

"I don't know. I've never seen one."

"Never?" There was incredulity in his voice.

Jessica's gaze dropped to the tabletop before her. "Want some breakfast?" She stood and turned to leave. Her embarrassment was evident.

John did not recognize the voice as his own, but he felt his lips moving. "Hilton Head is a beautiful place to spend a weekend. Want to come along?"

Jessica had taken a step toward the restaurant but stopped abruptly. Slowly she turned and looked at the man seated at the table. There was shock on her face. "Did you just ask me to go away with you for a weekend?"

John's face was also one of total surprise. He looked at her for several moments, speechless. Finally he spoke. "Yes, I guess that's what I just said." There was obvious discomfort in his voice. Jessica's eyes were locked on John's. Slowly a large grin crossed her face. "I'm sorry Jessica. I didn't mean that the wrong way..."

She stepped to him and placed a finger on his lips to quiet him in mid-sentence. She spoke very slowly, very deliberately. "John, I'd love to go to the beach with you." Her smile grew even larger. "Are you sure?"

He stammered slightly as he answered. "Well, yes. Yes."

"Great. You can tell me tomorrow when we will leave." Smiling broadly she turned and walked into the café. "I've got to get to work; I'll talk to you later."

John rose, smiling also, and followed her into the small restaurant. "I'll have my regular order." He could hear the mirth in her voice as she shouted over her shoulder.

"Blueberry pancake, one egg over medium, and bacon—coming up!"

Chapter 16

Savannah, Georgia, December 8, 2017

The rental car passed the bed and breakfast and pulled around the corner to the small parking lot in the rear. It was a gracious old building, like so many in Savannah. The front stairs climbed to an abundant porch and a glass door that, like the large windows across the brick edifice, was opened to illustrate the warmth emanating from inside. In the middle window of the old house they could see the bright lights of a very large Christmas tree welcoming travelers. There was no porter, so John carried the two bags while Jessica followed with a small satchel.

John opened the door to their room with a long metal key and motioned for Jessica to enter. As he did, he watched her face. It was filled with excitement. The room, like the old hotel, was soft, warm, and inviting. The bed was covered in coverlets and five large, colorful stuffed pillows. On the antique chest was a large green vase filled with flowers of all colors and sizes. The room was a light shade of green except for the wooden floor that was partially covered with a large brown and beige rug. There were four pillar candles scattered around the room—all lit. Directly opposite the door was another leading onto a rear porch. To the right of that was yet another leading to a bathroom; to the left was a small fireplace with an old gas insert. It, too, was lit. Immediately inside the room to her left was another Christmas tree decorated with large multi colored lights. Jessica stood in the door for several minutes taking it all in. John, suitcases in hand, stood behind her, watching her, smiling.

"It's beautiful, just beautiful." She turned, noticed him standing behind her, and moved quickly into the room. He followed and put the bags beside the bed.

It was dusk, and darkness was slowly filtering through the old oaks and the heavy gray moss that hung from their limbs. Jessica stood on the upstairs porch and savored the soft warm evening air. Unlike the crispness of the Colorado breezes, the air caressing her face was soft and moist and filled with the scent of food cooking in the kitchen below.

John watched her, uncertain of his next move. He was nervous. He had always known what to do in his world. He was a pro. Now he was uncertain. With Sybil it had been so easy, so predictable, but now he stood in a beautiful room with an attractive woman with whom he was going to spend the night, and he was nervous. He wondered about Jessica. Was she as uncomfortable as he, or was the excitement of the Briarwood that encompassing? Should he go to her and put his arms around her? Kiss her? What would they do about the bathroom? He glanced at the bed and perspiration began to bead his forehead. It had been so long...

Jessica walked back into the room. The excitement and the smile on her face warmed him and banished his thoughts momentarily. "John, it's gorgeous." As she spoke she turned and entered the bathroom. There was a large freestanding tub in the rear with a bright colored shower curtain tucked inside. Before the large wood frame mirror was another beautiful candle reflecting the soft light across the room. She looked over her shoulder to see John watching her. "Thank you, John, this is lovely."

He glanced at his watch, smiling. "Dinner will be served downstairs in half an hour. I need to get the map from the car. Why don't you freshen up and then meet me downstairs. We'll have a drink before dinner."

"Great." She looked at him for a moment then turned back into the bathroom, closing the door behind her. John walked slowly down the creaky stairs, wondering about his decision to bring Jessica on this trip. Why had he done it? Was it loneliness? He had always thought her attractive, was that it? Was it a chance to show her a world she had not known, one she had been unjustly denied? If so, was that fair? John walked into the small bar and turned left into the men's room. Later he was seated on an overstuffed floral couch opposite the darkly stained bar drinking a beer when Jessica entered the room. John rose, guided her to the couch and sat down beside her. "Would you like something to drink?"

"Sure." She looked at him momentarily. "Wine."

"White or red?"

"You choose."

"We'll split the difference." John motioned to the waiter. "White Zin please."

More people entered the room as magnificent smells drifted from the kitchen behind the dining room. At seven o'clock the hostess welcomed the assortment of guests as they seated themselves around the long, elaborately adorned dining table. Like everything in the old home, the furnishings and the furniture were old and elegant. The dinner was grand. First came the shrimp cocktail and a fine German Riesling. That was followed by a large bowl of pumpkin soup and a beautiful salad of green and red, covered with a tasty goat cheese dressing. Then came the main course of Veal Marsala and more wine, a cabernet from Washington State. Dessert was authentic Georgia pecan pie served with strong hot coffee. Finally the hostess produced a bottle of Watchtower port and a tray of small glasses.

John had watched Jessica throughout the meal. She had enjoyed it as much as he and had marveled at every course. "Wow, I'm stuffed. I could use a walk."

John rose from the table, taking Jessica's arm. "Great idea. It's not too cold out; let's walk down the block."

141

The evening was pleasant, and the evening breeze had not yet turned cold. Jessica threaded her arm through John's as they strolled before the old brick homes hidden behind the thick growth of trees and shrubs. The antique streetlights cast small pools of light through the evening and reflected from their faces as they walked. In the distance the soft glow of Christmas decorations shone in the night. Somehow it felt so natural John thought—two people strolling arm-in-arm in a pleasant evening.

At his side, Jessica felt the stiffness in his body relaxing as they walked. She had watched him carefully during dinner. He was trying so hard—for what? To make her feel at ease? Did he regret bringing her? Did she regret coming? Was he nervous about their night together? Her mind reflected back to the beautiful room. It was like a dream. It was the most beautiful room she had ever seen. She smiled to herself and glanced up at the man walking beside her. She had seen him glance at the bed; she had also seen his reaction. He had been clearly nervous. Somehow that had pleased her. He did not appear to be a man who took this lightly. No, he had been nervous. She was sure of it. But he was finally beginning to relax. She had noted that John had finished her Port as well as his own. Jessica looked up though the hanging moss at a lone light in one of the old homes. She wondered who lived there. Were they as happy as she, or as unsure? Like John, she was nervous about that bed, too. It had been four years since Sam's death and only once in all those years had she succumbed to the flames that still raged in her body. It had been disastrous. She still remembered the regret the morning after. She pulled closer to John and wondered what she would feel tomorrow. John is different she kept telling herself. He has to be.

When they walked into the room, Jessica could feel the tension returning in John. She smiled and immediately walked toward the porch. "Why don't you take the bathroom first; I want to enjoy the evening a bit longer." With a quick smile she walked outside.

John stood before the mirror and apprised the man staring back at him. He had the physique of a man ten years his junior, but the gray at his temples was beginning to spread slowly throughout his brown hair. And there were wrinkles that set off his face, outlining his forehead and the large hazel eyes. John had never thought much about his looks; somehow they had not been important for years. But tonight he cared. He looked into the mirror and sucked in his stomach. Then he smiled. He was forty-two years old and acting sixteen. Perhaps that is good, he thought, perhaps.

After John exited, Jessica took her small suitcase into the spacious bath and put it on a wooden chair beside the old open armoire filled with green towels. She surveyed the room; John's dopp kit was lying on the small stand beside the lavatory. A profusion of small bottles of shampoo, conditioner, bath gel, and even mouthwash were arranged in a basket beside the bath. She longed for a long hot bubble bath in the beautiful tub. Her own small bath had only a shower. After burying her husband Jessica had been penniless. A friend had given her a job in the small café and helped her find a room nearby. It was a convenient arrangement; she lived with George Eldridge, an eighty-nine year old man, and took care of him and his house. Eventually she became the daughter he never had. Being childless he had never envisioned a permanent resident like her living in the upstairs room. She thought of the old man, alone, and worried about him and about what he might think of her. He had not asked with whom she was traveling, but she suspected he knew she was with a man.

Jessica turned the handle and watched the hot water spray against the shower curtain. Somehow she felt a sense of urgency. It was as if she were afraid when she entered the bedroom John might be gone. Perhaps he would interpret delay on her part as reluctance. She stepped out of her clothes and stood before the mirror in her panties and bra. She was not a young woman at thirty-seven, but she looked younger than her years. She glanced at her stomach and wished that she had

143

eaten less at dinner. She stood straight and pulled in her stomach. Her breasts were large, her hips and legs muscular. She looked at the muscles in her thighs. Too many years of waiting tables and riding bicycles she thought; I look more like a soccer player than a soccer mom. But overall, the image pleased her. Looking back at her was a beautiful woman. Only the tiny wrinkles around the corners of her eyes betrayed the years of hard work and lonely nights. She brushed a tiny bit of makeup around each of her eyes as Brandy had demonstrated. She checked it in the mirror. Yes, it worked! The wonder of cosmetics! Jessica watched herself as she unhooked her bra and dropped it to the floor. Then she slowly slid her panties down over her thighs and let them drop to the floor. She smiled at the woman reflected back at her and climbed carefully into the bath.

John sat in the large bed and listened to the shower in the next room. How many times in his life had he done this before? He could never remember being nervous waiting for Sybil to enter his bed. But they had been married almost fifteen years. One tends to relax into marriage in that period of time. The shower stopped. John wondered about Jessica. What did he really know about her? In the three years they had been acquainted he had never seen her sad or angry. She was always smiling. He thought back on his last year with Sybil as the cancer slowly ended her life. It was too painful; he refocused on the woman moving about in the bathroom. She was attractive; John had noticed her figure in the tight jeans and flannel shirts. The night at the symphony had shown him yet another side of this intriguing woman. What would he learn of her tonight? He knew she was trying hard to please him. He had discovered the loneliness in her life during their evening together at the concert. Perhaps she needed him as much as he needed her. The honesty of the thought surprised him.

He watched the faceted glass door handle flash in the dim light as it turned. He was trying to steel his resolve. John wanted her to feel beautiful; he wanted her to feel wanted. The door opened and Jessica walked into the room. His eyes were

144

wide as he stared openly at the woman before him. She wore a black silk nightie. Underneath was a matching pair of black panties. She was beautiful. John sat upright in the bed and dropped the magazine in his hand. Neither of them noticed as it slid across the bed and fell noisily to the floor. Her eyes were locked on his as he stared at her. As she walked to the bed he finally spoke. "Jessica, you're beautiful."

Her crimson cheeks darkened slightly as she crossed the room. When she spoke it was barely audible. "Thank you, John."

The fears, the doubts, the confusion vanished in his mind as he watched her approach. She stopped, turned from him, and carefully slid the black nightie over her head. He watched as she neatly folded it and placed it on the stuffed chair by the window as if it were something of great value. Blushing slightly she stepped from her panties and folded them beside the nightie. Finally she turned to him blushing and unsure. She looked down at her body briefly and then back at John. She watched his eyes as they found their way back to her own. She saw both the surprise and the joy on his face.

He reached for her hand and lifted the sheet as she crawled into the bed beside him. As she did he heard her inhale deeply, and he felt the tremor move gently through her body. John started to speak, but Jessica's index finger touched his lips and silenced him. Then she reached both hands to his face and kissed him. They both had waited for this night for many years. It was one they both would remember with smiles for the rest of their lives.

* * *

Jessica was leaning on her elbow looking at the sleeping man beside her. He was lying on his back, spread across the bed, snoring softly. Obviously he was a man accustomed to sleeping alone; he had left little room for her in the large bed. She studied him carefully. Like her, he was naked, the sheet tucked loosely around his waist. He was surprisingly muscular for forty-two. That thought made her smile, thinking of the events of the prior evening. His thick brown hair was shaded with gray; even the hair on his chest had streaks of gray. She wanted to touch him, perhaps to reassure herself that the dream was real, but she resisted and continued to study him carefully, memorizing his face, his body, and even several scars that puzzled her. She was still looking at him when she realized his eyes were open; he was smiling, watching her.

"Good morning." He rubbed his face with his palms as he spoke.

"Good morning, sleepy head. I thought you'd sleep all day."

"I was dreaming."

"About what?"

"About you. About last night." He reached for her and pulled her to him, kissing her softly. The tenderness of the kiss surprised her; her response was immediate and equally pleasing to him. "Do you always smile in the morning?"

"Only when I'm happy."

"Are you happy?"

She looked at him for a long time. "Oh yes." She lay her head on his left shoulder and snuggled close as he held her.

"I love it when you smile." John had forgotten that such joy existed in the cold world outside his barricade of pain and memories. He closed his eyes and with fear tried to remember the last time he had felt such joy. His mind balked, but he urged it on. Quickly he scanned back over the years. The lake! It had been in the cabin by the lake. How many years? How much pain between? Slowly he allowed, no, demanded, that his mind open that door. He looked into her face—Sybil's face. It was before the cancer, before the pain, the loss. He felt his body tense, the perspiration flowed from his pores, but he moved forward; he had to know. She was smiling; he knew the expression. "It's

146

okay John. It's time." As the tension drained from his body a small smile crossed his face.

Jessica didn't understand the demons in John's soul, but the sudden tension and the expression in his eyes were obvious. She held him closely as the unseen battle raged in his mind. She didn't understand the specter that haunted this man, but she feared it. She feared what it might mean to this new joy she had found. Somehow she guessed its source. Hadn't she fought a similar ghost? She didn't look up at his face. She simply held him as tightly as she could.

Jessica's grip around his chest was the first thing he was aware of as he opened his eyes to the ceiling. Somehow he understood. Slowly he sat up and pulled her to him. He kissed her and said nothing. It was the first time he had seen her without a smile on her face.

"Are you okay, John?" It was the small voice of a child, not the woman in his arms.

"Yes, I'm fine." He lifted her chin and looked into her eyes. "I cannot remember being this happy in a long, long time." He gently moved strands of hair that fell across her face. "What time is it?"

"It's seven fifteen."

"Good." He looked at her with a big smile. "Breakfast is at nine." His smile beckoned hers as the morning sun peeked into their room, into their lives.

* * *

The smiling pair walked into the dining room at 9 o'clock and ate hungrily. Fruit bowls, eggs Benedict, grits, biscuits and gravy, and ham were consumed slowly with orange juice and cups of hot, strong coffee. Finally satiated, they departed for their drive to Hilton Head.

The drive to the beach was filled with excitement for Jessica, and her enthusiasm spilled over to John. The roadside stands filled with fruit, the moss covered trees, and the thick growth beside the road finally gave way to boats and great expanses of water as they drove across long bridges spanning the inland waterways. When they pulled up to the beautiful hotel, Jessica just sat staring at the flowers and the landscaped lawns. John took her hand and walked through the impressive lobby out to the pool area behind the hotel. There were three pools of various sizes. The largest had a large man made waterfall cascading from a rock structure that looked like a giant cliff beside the pool. He watched her eyes as they surveyed the pool area and the laughing people there. Almost immediately, however, she looked beyond the beautiful pools to the dark waters of the Atlantic. John could sense her excitement. "Let me check in, and we'll go straight out to the beach." As he turned to leave he was aware that she was still watching the waves and the excitement around the pools.

"It's all so beautiful."

"We'll try the ocean first if it's not too cold. Then we can try the pools. One is heated." As he took her hand and walked back into the hotel he noted that her eyes were still turned toward the ocean. He smiled broadly. The sun was shining brightly; there were no clouds in the sky; it would be a wonderful day, and he knew just the right restaurant for a great dinner by the ocean. Both were smiling as they hurried to their room to don their swimsuits.

* * *

He stood and watched her carefully as she sat in the sand staring out at the broad expanse of water before her. They would leave tomorrow morning, and she had been quiet all day. It began at lunch and had continued into the afternoon. She sat silently staring into the sunset, her chin resting on her knees. It had been such a beautiful trip, so filled with surprises for both of them. Her excitement and delight at the ocean and the beautiful resort had pleased him. It was all so new to her, adding even more to the experience. Her excitement fed his own—the

148

thrill of watching a grown woman laugh at a sand crab, or eat over a dozen shrimp at one sitting, or run into the ocean with abandon. There were so many new adventures for her, and he experienced the old anew—through her. She had laughed, and he laughed. She smiled, and he smiled, and somewhere deep within his scarred soul he found a small spark he had long thought dead. Her warmth fed the spark, and it exploded into flames of joy, an inferno of excitement he had long forgotten. The flames warmed his cold heart and melted the years of sadness. John McClellan laughed, smiled, and, in time, learned to love again.

As he watched her he struggled with the structured organization of his man's mind. Why was she suddenly sad? Carefully he traced the trip to this, the last day. Tomorrow they would rise early and drive back to Atlanta and then fly to Denver. Of course, he finally understood. It was their last day, and it had been a magical four days. Perhaps she was sad to leave the ocean. She had loved it so. Perhaps it was more; he prayed it would be so. Perhaps she was sad that their time together was over. Didn't she understand? John rubbed his forehead with his fingertips and walked slowly toward the woman he watched. As he sat beside her and pulled her to him on the sand, they watched the waves crash onto the shore and race toward them, only to retreat ten yards away. He finally spoke first. "It's been such a wonderful trip."

"Yes it has."

"I hate to leave."

She turned to face him, a small smile on her face. "Me too."

"I'm sorry I was late coming down."

"That's okay." She placed her arm around his shoulder but continued to stare at the horizon.

"I had to check with a hotel in Key West for reservations for our next trip." She turned quickly to look at him. She said nothing but her face was filled with surprise. "Think you could take a few days off from the

149

café end of next month? We'll be playing in the ocean while it is snowing in Denver."

"Are you serious?"

"Yes, I've never been more serious in my life. I hope you don't think you're going to get away from me easily." He looked into her eyes as she nodded. "It's been fun, Jessica. I had forgotten what that felt like." He kissed her gently. "Thank you for reminding me what life's all about. I fear I had forgotten."

A small tear welled into her left eye and winked quickly at him. Soon it was overwhelmed by others as they raced down her cheek, dancing with gravity in the fading light. She said nothing, nothing at all. She simply kissed him long and passionately. They sat quietly in the sand, holding each other, watching the daylight fade into a memory of one of the happiest days either had known in a very long while.

Chapter: 17

Denver, Colorado, January 4, 2018

The two men sat alone in the back of the small Starbucks shop, drinking their coffee. It was hot and strong, just the way John liked it. David added enough cream to change the color to a pale brown and then dumped in two spoons of sugar. John winced as he watched, thinking that it looked more like the Altamaha River than coffee but said nothing. "How will we find Pierre? He could be anywhere. We don't even know what country he lives in."

"We'll find him." John leaned back in the comfortable, over-stuffed chair and studied his son.

"He may be at the CFT headquarters, but more likely not."

"I'll have his location in three days."

"How?"

"I have some friends who know how to do these things." He said it simply, without elaboration.

"Friends?"

"Just some guys I work with. One used to be a cop."

The young man looked at his father for several moments, started to speak, then stopped short. Finally he spoke. "I want to know who made the decision to have Marcia killed. Do you think it was Pierre?"

"I doubt it."

"How high up the organization do you think this will go?"

"I have no idea. But I intend to find out." John savored the hot liquid and watched the young man across the table. "David, how far do you want to take this?"

David looked at the man he once thought he knew but now realized he did not. "We've discussed this already, Dad." He watched John and then continued. "We both know Lonnie was little more than a dumb punk. Someone else made the decision to have her killed. That's who I want, and I want to know why."

"I agree. This whole thing certainly makes no sense at all. But we'll find out." He said it with a resolve David had not expected. John looked into his coffee cup and studied the black liquid there. When he raised his eyes they were cold dark slits. "We'll find out. Those bastards chose the wrong girl." The two men sat in silence for a few moments; when John spoke again, he spoke quietly and in a tone that surprised his son. "David, we can quit whenever you're ready, but as long as you pursue this, I'll be there with you." He paused briefly in thought. "But we know they are after you now, so we have to be very careful."

The young man's face hardened visibly as he spoke. He turned his eyes from his father and focused somewhere into the distance. "Maybe you're not where I am in this, Dad, and that's okay. It's just not over for me. I want the men who ordered this even more than I wanted the one who pulled the trigger. Does this make any sense?"

"Yes, son, I understand where you're coming from." John's eyes looked off into the direction where David was staring. "I don't know why they wanted to kill Marcia, but I have a pretty good idea why they now want you dead." John looked back at his son. When he spoke, he spoke to no one, perhaps only to himself. "These men have crossed a line." He thought a moment then continued. "No, they crossed two lines."

"I still can't fathom why they wanted to kill her. She was just ..." David's voice trailed off in a mixture of pain and frustration. "I loved her Dad. I had planned to spend my life with her and give you lots of grandchildren. I just don't understand all this."

John nodded without speaking. Finally he rose and dropped his paper cup into a receptacle near their chairs. "I'll know on Thursday. I'll know how to find Pierre by then." As he turned to go he leaned toward his son. "We'll need a plan. I'll have some ideas to run by you Thursday evening." Before the young man could speak, he turned and was gone.

An hour later John dialed his phone and waited patiently as it rang four times. He immediately hung up and redialed. After two rings he hung up again and redialed. It was answered on the first ring; he recognized the voice. "Walter."

"It's John. I need some information and thought you might be able to help me." Little did he know that the door he was opening would lead to a web of intrigue he could not even envision.

* * *

It had been difficult to leave without David's knowledge now that the two of them were living together. John had not allowed David to return to his apartment in Wisconsin since the discovery of the pictures. He was worried. He knew that he was dealing with pros. The weapons and the planning had been handled well. These guys knew what they were doing. Killing Marcia had not been enough; now they were after his son. The question that still plagued his mind was *why*. Why they wanted to kill David was clear — David knew Marcia had not been killed by the police but by someone among the demonstrators; for all they knew he might have seen the killer.   Someone didn't want that information in the papers.   But why did they want to kill her? Was there something about Marcia that John did not know? Had she ever been involved with drugs? Who was her father? John selected a seat in the concourse away from the other passengers awaiting the flight to Pittsburgh and opened a manila folder he had tucked inside his briefcase. At least he had

153

the information about Marcia's family. It had arrived in the mail just the day before. He glanced around to ensure he was alone then opened the folder and read quickly. Father – dead eight years. Mother – single widow, successful actress. Siblings: One brother, nine years old. John stopped reading, folded the papers, then replaced the folder into his briefcase. He made a mental note to check on Marcia's mother. Did she need any help? How was she handling the loss of her daughter? Then he realized what a ridiculous question that was. How does any parent handle the loss of a child? He caught the movement with his peripheral vision and turned quickly to the approaching man. It was David; he was frowning at his father as he sat next to John without a word.

"What are you doing here?"

"I'm going with you."

"No, you're not. And how did you know I was on this flight?"

"I'm a computer whiz, remember?"

"You hacked into the United reservation system?" John turned to look straight at his son, incredulous.

A small smile crept across David's face. "No, the airline called to let you know that the plane would be delayed just after you left. Besides, I heard the garage door; it wasn't hard to know where you were sneaking off to." The older man frowned at his son. "You should have just told me you were going out with Jessica and left last night."

John's frown turned to a small smile. "That would have worked, huh." The two men sat in silence for several minutes. Finally John spoke. "David, there's a reason I wanted to do this alone. I've been thinking...I don't want you involved in all this. Let me handle it."

"You don't think I can handle myself?" David's face was turning a darker shade as his voice raised above the din in the waiting area. John motioned for him to hold his voice down.

"You know that's not it."

"Sure it is. You still think I'm a kid. Well I'm not. I'm twenty-one. Grandpa went to war at eighteen, and you were just a little older when you were in Nam."

"That was different."

"Oh yeah, how?"

"It was just different."

"Right."

John ran his right hand through his thick hair while staring at the floor. "Look, David, this isn't a war. We're talking about going after some murderers here. These guys know what they're doing. It could be dangerous."

"Sure, and fighting in Vietnam was a picnic, right?"

"It was different." John desperately searched his mind. How could he communicate with his son? It was always the same. He secretly pleaded with his dead wife, entreating her assistance with this child he loved but could not understand. "What did you do for a ticket?"

"Carl, the AFL/CIO rep. Remember?"

"David, this could get messy. Just let me handle it. I'll take care of these guys."

"You might need my help. Did you ever think of that? What if there is more than one of them? You're not as young as you were in the jungles of Nam. It's not like you're a cop or something."

John looked at his son's face and saw something that he had not recognized before. David was worried about him. David felt the need, in some way, to protect his father. It made John want to smile, but he knew he could not. "I'll be okay. I'm really quite capable of taking care of myself."

"I'm going, Dad. I'll never quit until we find them all."

As the young man spoke, John's mind flew back over the years to the day he kissed Sybil for the last time. He remembered the crushing pain, the total loss. How was it different for David? He had held Marcia's blood spattered body. He had looked into her lifeless eyes, and he had not had a year to prepare as John did. What a shock that must have been. His

155

heart wanted to cry out for his son, for his suffering. Without even thinking he extended his hand to the young man beside him. "I can understand that." David took his hand without smiling. "But remember, I'm still the lead."

Chapter 18

Pittsburgh, Pennsylvania, January, 29, 2018

Pierre opened the door to a cold Pittsburgh evening and two men he had never met before. "May I help you?"

"Good evening Pierre, I'm John and this is David. Dr. Collingsworth sent us. You may be in trouble."

"I don't think I know you. Lawrence never mentioned you gentlemen."

"Dr. Collingsworth never mentions us." John stepped into the room pushing Pierre from the door. "And we are hardly gentlemen." John walked into the back rooms of the apartment and checked them in a cursory fashion. David stood squarely in the door as Pierre followed John.

"What the hell are you doing?"

"Making sure you're alone so we can talk."

"There's no one else here."

"Good." John motioned to David who entered the room after checking the hallway carefully. He closed the door behind him. "Sit down." John pointed at Pierre who watched him carefully.

"I don't take orders from you."

"You do if you want to stay out of prison."

"What are you talking about?"

"Lonnie. You picked the wrong guy for the job." John watched the man before him and waited until he was sure that Pierre was unsettled. "You screwed up, Pierre. Collingsworth is pissed. Did you know that Lonnie left a note?"

"What note?"

"That's what Dr. Collingsworth wants to know."

"Then why doesn't he just call and ask?"

"He won't call. No one will until we know what's in that note. There's a rumor Lonnie mentioned you."

"Me?"

"That's right. And Collingsworth wants to know how much you told Lonnie. What are the chances there might be other names in that note, like *his* name. We need to know how much trouble we have to take care of."

Pierre sat slowly on the couch. The gravity of the information was settling in; his face was one of shock. "That dumb bastard left a note?"

"How did you pick such a dolt?" Pierre looked up without speaking. "There are a lot of questions being asked; it is imperative that we know just how much you told Lonnie." John leaned menacingly toward Pierre. "And you'd better tell us the truth. It could protect your own dumb ass as well as others."

"He didn't know much. I didn't tell him much at all."

"Good. Now, first question." He looked directly into Pierre's eyes. "Did you kill Lonnie?"

"What?" The question startled the man, as John had planned.

"Dr. Collingsworth thinks, and I suspect, that Lonnie did not jump from that window after all. He may have been pushed." John thought quickly but spoke slowly. He was watching Pierre's face carefully. It was revealing a great deal. Pierre was shocked and frightened. "Actually, Collingsworth thinks you may have been involved in Lonnie's death. And be assured that he really doesn't care, except that he is quite concerned about the rumors of the note Lonnie left behind." He watched as the man absorbed the information. "If you did kill him, just assure us that there was no note, and all will be satisfied, even relieved."

"Dammit," Pierre began to nervously run his fingers through his hair. "I didn't kill him. I have no idea who did, or even if he was killed. For all I know he jumped."

158

"Why would he have done that? There was no evidence pointing to him, and I doubt he had enough conscience to feel any guilt. Why would he have done that?"

"I don't know!" Pierre was clearly confused.

"We need to talk to Hamad again. Perhaps he can give us some information." John looked at David who sat silently watching the unfolding confession. "David, do you have Hamad's phone number? I left it in my laptop in the hotel."

David scratched through his pockets for several minutes. "Damn, I didn't bring my phone with me, but I can get it on the internet." He turned to Pierre. "Do you have a computer here?"

Pierre was staring at the floor, lost in his own thoughts. There was perspiration on his forehead. "Sure, back room on the right." As David rose, Pierre pointed toward the desk by the door. "But if you need Hamad's new number, it's in my address book by the door."

"Thanks." David rose and retrieved the thick leather notebook for Pierre.

Pierre thumbed through the pages quickly as he spoke. "This note. Where did the rumors come from, and what is it supposed to contain?"

"The Seattle police. We have friends who keep us informed."

"Shit! Fucking idiot! A note? I didn't kill him, but if he were still alive, I would choke him with my own two hands."

"As I said earlier, he may have felt that his life was in danger, and perhaps that was his insurance policy." John glanced at David who was now standing behind Pierre, holding the Daytimer. There was a small smile on his face. "You'd better hope this rumor isn't true. If it is, you may be in a lot of trouble. But that's why we're here—to get to the bottom of this. But let's go back to my original question. What did Lonnie know? All of it."

"Nothing. I located him through a friend. I gave him ten thousand before and promised fifteen thousand afterward. That's all he knew, I swear it."

"Who was the friend you mentioned? That could be important."

"Hamad, Hamad Al-Falani; he's been in the organization since the beginning."

"Is that the Hamad Collingsworth speaks of?"

"Probably. They're long-time friends, I think. Collingsworth knew him at Florida International University. They taught there together once."

"Who picked the girl? Was that you or Lonnie?"

"Hamad did. He thought she was beautiful and the daughter of an actress; that would get more publicity. He thought that would get the press involved very quickly. We needed them, and they were sitting on their hands. He figured they would go nuts and give us all the coverage we needed after that. He was right, you know. Lawrence should be happy about that. We're on the map now; before we were nothing."

John watched as David turned his face from Pierre. He suspected he knew what was going through David's head, much the same as was raging through his own. "Hamad picked her and gave you the go-ahead; you hired Lonnie, and he did the work. Who else knew about this?"

"Only Silvia."

John stood slowly and paced the room in thought. He had studied the list of names on the CFT organization chart so that he could appear to be inside the group. He had expected many names, but this was one he did not know and had not expected. "Sylvia?"

"She is of no concern. She surely didn't kill Lonnie."

"Collingsworth wants all of the information, everything. He will determine what we do with it." John thought a moment then continued. "One last thing. Collingsworth was pissed that you didn't clear this through him. Why didn't you do that?"

160

John was taking a risk, but he needed to know if Collingsworth was involved.

Pierre was staring at the floor. "Why would he expect me to do that? That's Hamad's job. I just carry out their orders."

"Then perhaps Hamad did relay the plan to him?"

"I don't know what they told him. They never kept me in that loop."

"Then all we have to do is protect you and Hamad."

"I suppose."

John nodded. "Oh yes; before we rule out Sylvia, suppose you tell us about her involvement. Collingsworth didn't mention her to me."

"She couldn't have been involved. She's merely a secretary; she got the info on the girl. Only later did she figure out the facts."

"Did she cause any problems afterwards?"

"No, she was never sure we were involved in the girl's death, but I think she had suspicions; she quit and left. Hamad wanted to talk to her, but she left before he could."

John rose and stretched his back as he spoke. "What about the kid? The one who was with the girl? He probably knows the CFT report wasn't right. He could be a problem."

"Yeah, that's what Hamad said. But I'll take care of that."

"How, Lonnie's dead."

"I'll find someone."

John's face was filled with rage. He turned to face the man seated on the couch. "The girl, what was her name, Pierre?"

"I don't recall. Why?"

"Marcia. The girl's name was Marcia." He looked at the man seated before him. "Didn't you even know her name?"

Pierre looked at him, puzzled. "Why should I know her name? Why would I care?"

"Because she was a beautiful young woman. There were people who loved her." Pierre sat back slowly. His eyes grew wider. "Was that all she was to you, a way to get TV coverage?" John's voice shook with rage. "You took her life for that? For five minutes of TV coverage? What kind of man are you?"

The shocked man started to rise, but John's right fist caught him in the process and knocked him across the couch. As he struggled to stand, David repeated the attack with a sharp blow to his chin. When Pierre fell to the floor, he did not rise. David quickly turned to locate the computer in the back room. When he finished twenty minutes later he carefully took the CPU and laid it on the floor by the desk as John had directed him. He then smashed the monitor beside it and threw the modem and speakers across the room. Then he emptied all the drawers in the room, scattering their contents across the floor. He did the same in the adjoining room, then joined John as they ransacked the living room. Finally John poured a white powder onto the floor and then dropped the remaining drug pack beside the spilled cocaine. Pierre lay on his back by the far wall, semiconscious. John peeked out the front window and then shoved David out the door. "Don't start the car until I get there."

Pierre had risen to a sitting position as John screwed the silencer onto Lonnie's pistol. "Do you recognize this gun, Pierre?"

"No." Pierre was watching him carefully. There was fear in his eyes.

"Well, let me tell you where I got it. This was Lonnie's gun, the one that killed my son's fiancée. Tonight I'm going to use it to avenge that murder, and you can go straight to hell where Lonnie is waiting for you."

Chapter 19

Madison, Wisconsin, January 30, 2018

The phone rang repeatedly before Hamad finally turned from his computer and lifted the receiver. He was still studying the monitor as he answered. "Hamad."

A deep voice boomed over the phone. "Just wanted to let you know that Pierre was killed last night."

"What?"

"His body was found this morning. His entire apartment was ransacked. Police assume he knew the killers; there was no sign of forced entry."

There was a long pause; finally Hamad spoke. He was obviously shocked and upset. "How was he killed?"

"It seems he was beaten then shot at close range."

"Pierre had nothing of value; who would rob him?"

"Someone who was either desperate, dumb, or both."

"When did it happen?"

"The police aren't sure, but it appears to have transpired early last night."

"Didn't anyone hear the gunshot?" Hamad's voice reflected his impatience and also fear.

"Apparently not."

"Didn't he live in a town-house?"

"Yes."

"And no one heard the gunshot?"

The voice suddenly turned thoughtful. "No, no they didn't."

"That's strange." As he hung up the phone, he stared blankly ahead, his mind weighing scenarios he had not allowed it to consider before.

The next morning, Collingsworth walked into Hamad Al-Falani's small and cluttered office, not what one would expect from a man making over two hundred thousand a year. "I guess you've heard about Pierre."

"Come in, and close the door." Hamad was a harsh looking man. He was only five feet six inches tall, but he was powerfully built for a man in his early forties. His face was perpetually expressionless, but his dark eyes shone with an intensity that would cower most men. He pushed away from the small desk and leaned back in the large leather chair that was obviously the most expensive piece of furniture in the entire room.

Collingsworth was a thin man, approximately six feet tall. He had a large forehead accentuated by a receding hairline. His face had a nervous look that seemed perpetually frozen in place. "What the hell is going on? Did his murder have anything to do with CFT?"

"No. Pierre was an idiot. He should have stayed away from the drugs."

"Drugs? Pierre was into drugs?"

"The police report stated that drugs were found on the floor of his room. They surmise that he was killed in a drug deal gone bad."

"Pierre? Drugs?"

"Who knows, but it looks that way." Hamad watched Collingsworth pace up and down in the small room. "There are some strange things going on in CFT. Remember, they found drugs in the room of one of our security guys, the one who jumped out of a hotel window." Hamad watched with satisfaction as Collingsworth's eyebrows knit in concern. "Perhaps we have a drug problem within the organization."

"Could that happen, a drug ring inside the organization?" Collingsworth was getting more anxious as they talked.

"Sure. Anything is possible with the conglomeration of knuckleheads we've accumulated. I suspect most of them are on drugs of some kind. We really don't have any mental geniuses here, do we?"

"Then the drug thing is a possibility."

"It's a possibility." Hamad looked into his coffee cup and quickly returned it to his desk. "We also had something unusual happen with some union reps."

"What happened with them?"

"I was told that Lonnie was last seen having a drink with them. I was going to call to see if they had any information on him, but our crack secretarial staff had lost their paperwork, so they called to request that it be resent."

"And?"

"The union couldn't find any record of the two men in question."

"Who do you think they were?"

"Could be press; could be FBI; could be AFL/CIO. Who knows? They might even be narc agents, or even drug dealers. Or, perhaps the AFL/CIO staff is even less efficient than our own. Maybe Pierre and Lonnie were dealing drugs. Maybe our guys didn't understand that drugs aren't donations. These bleeding liberals seem to think that everything is free. Maybe Pierre forgot to pay his bill. Maybe someone was simply collecting a debt. Who the hell knows?"

"Can the unions re-check the two reps?"

"That's in progress. Shit, it's been in progress for a week now. Do you know how easy it is to get information from the AFL/CIO? It's a damn good thing those idiots don't try to manage anything but their own fucking union. They couldn't find their ass with both hands."

"Well, keep me informed." Collingsworth rose slowly and walked down the hall.

Hamad noticed that his boss's head was down, and he was leaning forward more than usual. The pressures of the job were showing. He was careful to insure that Collingsworth wasn't aware of anything but his own memoirs and his esteemed place in history. Hamad smiled, maybe Collingsworth could get a job with the unions. If he left here and joined the AFL/CIO it would most likely improve the average IQ in both places. Hamad's smile slowly faded. He didn't tell Collingsworth anything unless it required his signature for a check. Hamad peered into his coffee cup as he reached for his phone. "Bill, I want copies of all of Lonnie's emails this afternoon." He started to replace the phone then quickly added. "I also want copies of Pierre's as well. And I want you to arrange a bodyguard." He waited impatiently while the other man replied. "Right, for me." As he stood and poured the remnants of his coffee into the trashcan by his desk a dark thought crossed his mind. If the police had Lonnie's and Pierre's computers, they would also have their emails. He needed to see those immediately. Hamad slammed his cup on the desk, breaking it. "Dammit; who hired those fools?"

Hamad leaned back in his expensive chair and opened his CFT emails. He sat up abruptly and cursed as he saw a new email from Pierre titled: *Need more money; the delivery was late.* He checked the time on the message. It appeared to be about the same time as his death. "Son-of-a-bitch!"

Chapter 20

Moscow, Russia, February 7, 2018

Vasiliy stood in the cold hallway and dialed the cheap "burner" phone he had purchased the day before. He waited patiently, hoping the phone would work. It did. "Yes?" The voice was soft and quiet.

"I'll have the time and the place for the meeting within a week."

"Good. But first we need to discuss the arrangements."

"Of course."

"You'll receive instructions tomorrow."

"Excellent." Vasiliy listened to the click on the other end of the call and then carefully wiped the phone clean. He then placed it on the floor and stomped on it several times. As he walked to his car he tossed the mangled phone into a trash can. As he drove away he watched his rearview mirror carefully. There could still be danger, though he expected none. It was just better to be careful. As he drove he smiled to himself. Flowers, he must not forget the flowers. They would be expensive with snow on the ground—an even more important reason to buy them now. Lidiya would be impressed.

* * *

Vasiliy sat in the first class section of the Lufthansa flight and sipped the fine German Spatlese with appreciation. It was a 2015 St Urban's Hof, and it was excellent, as was the food—so unlike the Aeroflot flights he normally took. He was excited. His heart raced as he considered the future. He would soon have several million US dollars. That would certainly change his life. What would he do with so much money? Would he remain in Moscow or move to Prague or Frankfurt—maybe even the US. It would all be possible with such wealth. He glanced around the aircraft at the men in first class. Who were they? What did they do to earn the money for such luxury? How many of them were millionaires? Vasiliy smiled. He might well be the richest man on board—or at least within a month or so. His thoughts wandered to Lidiya, his beautiful Lidiya. Would she find it difficult to adjust to the changes that awaited them? He smiled. He'd guide her. How she would admire her rich husband, her millionaire husband.

Vasiliy's reverie was interrupted by the flight attendant refilling his wineglass. He smiled at her, and she returned the warmth. *People treat you differently when you fly first class, when you are rich,* he thought. The wine was slowly clouding his mind, but he forced it to concentrate, to abandon the dreams that suddenly looked possible for the first time in his life. Prague had been such a delight.

The meeting had been short, but obviously well planned. He had asked for twenty five million for the nuclear bomb. They had countered with fifteen. He followed his strategy completely. When they made their offer, he had simply gathered his things and started for the door. He would never forget the look on their faces—shock, disbelief. They had expected him to bargain, not walk out. It had worked; they had agreed to his price. They had obviously not seen the sweat stains under his coat.

Chapter 21

Seattle, Washington, February 7, 2018

Paul Hamilton walked into the office of his lieutenant and waited until the older man looked up from the sports pages he had been studying. "I miss football."

"You bet. We have a long wait for next season. I guess we'll just have to concentrate on work for a while, or are you part of the boycott?"

"I lost some friends in Afghanistan. They were *real* men, not spoiled boys playing a game. I boycott for them."

"I understand. I haven't watched a game in years myself."

The thin detective lifted the news and thumbed toward the back of the first section. "Speaking of work, did you see this little article?" He laid the paper across the open sports pages. "Seems another CFT staff member was found dead." He waited for a comment. When there was none, he continued. "Only this one was murdered." That pronouncement elicited the response he had desired.

The older man scanned the article quickly. "I'll be damned. You think there could be any connection to the one who died here?"

"Look at that name. Ring any bells?"

"Not offhand." The captain looked up patiently, waiting for the connection to be explained.

"Remember that laptop we retrieved from our jumper's room?"

"Yes, now that you mention it."

"Well, guess who the last email was sent to."

"This guy?"

"Right."

"What did it say?"

The detective pulled a folded sheet from his coat pocket and began to read. "Hey man, what's going on with my bread. I'm still waiting for the rest you owe me, and you owe me big time. I delivered like you asked, now get me my money."

"Any idea what that means?"

"It means these two knew each other, and it also means that they were into something together, something that involved money."

"Dope?"

"Most likely. We found some at the apartment. I'll give Pittsburgh a call and see what they have. I wonder if this Pierre's computer was found. I'll ask them to check."

"If you need to fly out, let me know. I might have enough budget to cover that." He was smiling as he pushed the news aside and continued his perusal of the sports pages.

"Thanks boss. I'll keep you informed."

Chapter 22

Frankfurt, Germany, March 5, 2018

Walter sliced the envelope with a very sharp letter opener and withdrew the stack of paper. There were over thirty pages of material; that surprised him; he had expected less. Thirty pages for Walter, however, represented less than fifteen minutes of reading. He rose, stretched and walked into the new office suite for a cup of coffee. He poured out most of a cup of cold black liquid and replaced it with a fresh, hot brew and then returned to his desk. Carefully he began to study the material. The first two pages were simply names, addresses, and phone numbers. He pulled a crumpled sheet from a file in his top drawer and compared it to the list in his hand. They matched. He scanned the addresses quickly then turned to the third page. It began with the dossier of one Hamad al-Falani. He scanned it briefly, then read it again more carefully, then put it aside. He was on page twenty-eight of the second report when the number jumped out at him. Walter was an agent for the CIA; he was trained in many skills, but accounting was his specialty. The Agency had learned many years ago that money, like men, leaves a trail, a trail that is often far easier to track than that of the men they pursued. Walter had graduated in the top five percent of his class at the University of Chicago; he had been selected to join the second largest accounting firm in the states. Then he had been recruited by "the company." If there was one thing Walter understood, it was numbers, and the last five numbers on the Swiss Account in the report practically leaped from the page. He had seen that number before, recently. He placed the scarred coffee cup on his credenza and began sorting papers in a file from a locked drawer.

His elbow rested on the desk. His left hand supported his head as he scribbled numbers onto a pink form. When finished, he slowly rechecked the numbers and dialed for his colleague sitting outside at the reception desk. "Ronnie, I have an account I want you to check. It was one of forty-seven transferring funds from the Middle East to Swiss bank accounts. Check forward and backward; I want a list of all money into and out of this account. Who owns it? How much money transferred, from whom, when? Everything." Two minutes later an attractive young woman walked into the room, took the form, and left. An hour and forty-eight minutes later she returned and laid three sheets of paper on the agent's desk. He looked up from his phone call, smiled, and took the sheets. She had barely left the office when he abruptly ended his phone call and rose, waving at her. "Damn! I knew it!" As the young woman walked back into the room Walter grabbed a large black pen on his desk and began scribbling notes. He was clearly excited. "I think we may have found something important. Are you ready to do more research?"

Chapter 23

Denver, Colorado, March 7, 2018

John looked at the young man before him. He studied the young face; it was not at all like Sybil's; David was his father's son. He was not what one would call handsome, but he might be called good looking. His eyes, like his hair, were dark, yet his complexion was relatively light. He had John's square chin and Roman nose. He was so unlike Marcia, whose blond hair and blue eyes reminded him so much of his deceased wife. John was suddenly aware of the pained expression on his own face and the concerned look on the tall young man before him.

"Remember, we still need to know about Collingsworth."

"He's such a fraud." David's words were barely audible.

"And he has a lot of crazies following his orders now."

"How does he do it? How can you convince so many people to demonstrate about something they don't even understand?"

"Money, David. Money. How do you think he got all the unions and environmentalists and the college kids to fly to Chicago or Seattle? That's not cheap. Somebody had to finance a lot of airline tickets and a lot of hotel rooms."

"Money applied liberally in the right places?'

"Right. Add in a lot of TV cameras and unsophisticated people and you have the makings of a demonstration. Plus, of course, a good sprinkling of nut cases." John finished his coffee. He paused a minute then continued. "You know, there is one

173

other factor that contributes to this mess. For years my generation got up and went to work each day to build a better life for our families, and all that time much of the education system was pouring leftist propaganda into our kids' minds. We finally discovered the liberal progressives had infiltrated our schools, largely through the unions, but by then the damage had been done. We failed all of you, and it's our fault. We weren't vigilant enough. We are leaving you with a crushing debt and a system of political correctness that may well destroy much of the freedom many of us fought for. And also, while people today are debating who can use various toilets, your competition in Asia are studying physics, math, and history. Then our enemies within struck one last major blow, they embraced drugs and made millions destroying the intellect of our children. They've methodically weakened the competitive spirit that made America great. The "Nanny State" is here, and it's dragging the nation down."

"Not very encouraging is it?"

"No they've consolidated their hold on academe. They've systematically removed most conservative professors and practically all conservative thought. Freedom of speech is dead if you're not a liberal progressive or outright communist." John paused and changed the subject. "But back to Collingsworth, someday I might just do a bit of research into his operations. I wonder how a professor could manage to secure millions—and we are talking millions—for his organization. Tenured professors are paid well, but not that well. Somebody's financing this; somebody always does."

"That's interesting. Where do you think the money came from?"

"I think I know where it came from. Most of it probably came from a very liberal billionaire in Europe. His name is Gavalas, and he is known to finance such things. He may well be involved. I might just pose that question to a friend of mine."

"Government?"

"Sort of. If he has time he may get some information for us."

"Why do we really care?" David's face was blank, free of emotion.

"Collingsworth may, or may not, be clean regarding Marcia, but he organized the bastards who killed her. He's not getting off scot-free. Plus, I enjoy embarrassing stupid ideas and arrogant people."

David looked down at the table and spoke in a soft whisper. "Ideas that even smart people sometimes buy into."

John looked up suddenly. He instantly recognized the source of the pain in David's voice. "Marcia was young, David. She would have figured it out."

"Yeah, she was smart."

"Yeah." Both men looked at each other in silence. Finally John spoke as he placed a small notebook on the table. "Now, thanks to Pierre we know everyone involved. And," he forced a small smile, "with a little help from my friends, we now have addresses to match those phone numbers. Are you ready for a little surveillance?"

"You bet."

"Good. We leave next week."

"That gives us time to plan."

"Right." John rose to leave, tossing several bills on the table. "Planning is the key to success."

"Dad?"

"Yes?"

"Did they really kill her just for press coverage? Just for TV time?" David's face was stoic, but a tear brimmed in his left eye.

John stepped forward and, for the first time in many years, put his arms around his son's shoulder. "We're going to get these bastards, son, every last one of them." David watched his father's face brighten quickly. John turned to him and smiled. "But in the meantime, I'm taking Jessica skiing tomorrow. Care to join us? I'm not a very good teacher; perhaps you could help. She's a quick learner."

The grimace on David's face slowly turned to a smile as he nodded to his dad. "Sure, sounds fun. It's hard to beat spring skiing in Colorado."

Chapter 24

Chkalovsky Military Base—Near Moscow, March 13, 2018

The crowd of highly decorated officers and their guests watched carefully as the huge "Tjorny Aryol" (Black Eagle) tank lumbered into view from behind two small hills to their left. It sped toward them at over fifty km/hr, stopped abruptly thirty meters away, and swung its large 125 mm cannon rapidly toward two targets to the north of the group. As planned, the sheer size of the tank was intimidating to anyone that close to the fifty-ton monster. It had barely stopped moving when the first shot boomed out of the long steel barrel. Almost immediately the first target, one of two shacks filled with barrels of gasoline to make the explosions even more dramatic, burst into flames 1500 meters downrange. Before the group could refocus, the second target exploded over 2000 meters away. As quickly as the tank had pulled into position it left, leaving a large cloud of tan dust following the green machine. When the three generals began applauding, the others followed suit. The timing had been excellent, the results as expected. The foreign customers would be impressed, and another sale was practically a certainty.

The crowd of men walked slowly from the dusty field to the warmth of their waiting cars. It was March in Russia, and it was still bitterly cold. The government officials hosted their guests while each of the general officers had his own car and driver. Major Simkov joined his general for the drive to the officer's club and lunch. As they climbed into the car the general quizzed his adjutant. "What did you think of the demonstration?'

"The shooting was excellent."

"But?" Turgenov recognized the hesitation in the major's voice.

"If the risk of a miss were less, it would have been far more impressive if they could have fired that accurately while moving at a high rate of speed."

"Like the Americans?"

"Like the Americans."

"It is good that we are no longer enemies."

"Yes sir, I agree. My guess is that we will soon be allies."

"I think you may be right, Major. I certainly hope so. The Americans are sometimes difficult, but they are at least predictable. That is important in any adversary."

The five cars pulled into the crowded parking area together. Four young soldiers removed the barricades from the reserved parking places and saluted as the senior officers climbed from their cars. As the young driver scrambled out of the car and raced to open the general's door, Turgenov placed a stack of papers in the major's lap. "Careful with the one on bottom. It's for you. Open it later." He looked into the major's eyes with a smile on his face. "It's a down payment from our new friends." Simkov felt the envelope on the bottom of the stack and bent forward slightly as he carefully slid it into the inside breast pocket of his military tunic. "Thank you, Sir."

"It is the first of many."

The smell of food wafted from the building and hastened the footsteps of the distinguished team as they proceeded into the dining area. The government officials would consider the appointments in the room to be Spartan. There were long tables covered with white linin tablecloths and chairs arranged in close order. To the army officers entering the club, it was ornate. These were military men who spent much of their lives near the fields of battle, sleeping in snow or mud. They cared little for the appointments in the room; they savored the food. Battlefield rations are sufficient to allow a man to fight. Gourmet is a word they seldom use. The vodka was cold and the food hot. General Turgenov and his major ate with relish. Both men seemed particularly hungry as the group enjoyed their lunch.

* * *

Major Rodion Mikhail Simkov was ignoring his wife as they sat at their dinner table in the cramped apartment. He had just been promoted to major, and his salary and housing allowance were still in the update cycle. He was not watching her but rather thinking of how to steal a bomb; actually he had decided that would be easy. Concealing that fact from future inventories would be the key, and that would be difficult. He was staring at the bowl before him when his wife interrupted his thoughts. "Rodya, don't you like the borscht?"

"Yes, dear. I love it; I'm sorry, I was thinking of work."

"You always think of work." She said it playfully, smiling. "Now eat your dinner—and think of me." She was a plump woman and pretty. Rodion adored her. What should have been a marriage of convenience had blossomed into one of passion and deep affection.

"How do you know that I wasn't really thinking of you in our bed?"

"You were frowning. You never frown in our bed." She rose, smiling and walked to the small stove with the large simmering pot, pouring more hot soup into her bowl over a large piece of coarse, black bread. "More borscht?"

Rodion watched his wife attentively. "No; maybe later." He smiled as she walked slowly, balancing the full bowl, until she was seated. Finally he reached for her hand. "Nina how would you like a baby?" His voice was soft, but serious.

She sat her spoon down and looked very hard at her husband. "I thought we had discussed that. You said we could

179

not possibly afford a child." There was a pained expression on her face.

"Suppose we could?"

"But we can't." Nina Sergeevna was near tears. She was thirty-seven and had recognized the few years left for such things. Her internal reproductive clock was ticking; and somehow she felt it was running out.

"Yes we can...well, maybe."

"How?" A single tear escaped her left eye and rolled quickly down her cheek.

"I'm working on a top-secret project for the Army. Top-secret! It cannot be discussed, do you understand?"

"Yes, of course."

"If it succeeds we will be well rewarded, more than enough for a larger apartment and a little one's needs. They even gave me a "bonus" for the work thus far." He placed a large stack of rubles on the table. It was a very large stack.

Nina's eyes were wide at the sight of so much money. "Oh Rodya, babies need so little." Tears were streaming down her face as she turned to her husband. He had recognized the longing and the empty spot in his wife's heart. He had seen her hold the children of other couples. She wanted a baby; she needed one. He wiped a tear from her cheek. A son? A daughter? Nina pushed her soup aside and smiled at her husband. "We have work to do. We could start now." She was grinning through her tears.

"You call that work?" He smiled as she laughed softly. "We may even need to try again tomorrow morning."

"And tomorrow night, and the next." Together they rose from the table and rushed to their small bedroom. They were laughing as they began throwing their clothes to the floor.

*   *   *

Simkov stood uncomfortably on the cold platform, waiting for the train to Moscow. He was wearing civilian clothing that clung to his body like the old suit that it was. The trousers were too tight and the coat seemed a bit short. Mostly it was the shoes that bothered him. He much preferred the warmth of his military boots. The small station was crowded with young people on their way to the university he assumed. His eyes automatically turned to a very young couple with a small baby. It was crying softly; the girl, for she was really little more than a child herself, was cooing to it. Rodion watched her face, a mixture of pride, love, and awe. They were dressed poorly, but they seemed very happy. He wondered where they were going, perhaps to see grandparents. What a happy reunion that would be. He imagined his own wife holding a child for her sisters to see. It almost made him laugh. She would be unbearable. Certainly the child would be spoiled, but it would be the most beautiful in all of Russia, so spoiling would be appropriate. To his left, far down the track he spotted the engine of the train as it climbed a small hill into the town. Thirty-three minutes late—that was good; he would still have time to reach Moscow, find an appropriate meeting place, and arrange the rendezvous. It would be a short meeting, less than ten minutes. He would meet with the one man who could manipulate the giant military inventory computers, explain his task—to remove one nuclear bomb from the inventory—and then give him the money. It was that simple. He and the general would sell something that did not exist. He patted the breast pocket of his coat; the large envelope of money was still there.

The train struggled slowly up the hill toward the small station, its slow pace juxtapositioned against the major's racing thoughts. He quickly reassessed his plan one more time and then stepped aboard the rail car for the trip to Moscow.

Chapter 25

Morrison, Colorado, June 2, 2018

  George Eldridge stood at the foot of the two flights of stairs that led to Jessica's small room and studied them solemnly. They might as well have been Mount Evans he thought. He took several deep breaths and looked down at his withering body. George knew he was losing weight; he also knew he was getting weaker. The steady rhythm that had beat in his chest for over eighty-nine years was no longer strong. At times it even skipped a few beats and forced him to sit lest he pass out. He looked again at the stairs and placed his right foot on the first step. Slowly he pulled his body onto the step and then placed his left foot on the next. He stopped and admired the railing that he, himself, had built over fifty years ago. That was when he was young, when he could easily run up the stairs to join his Maggie in their tiny little bedroom over the creek. So many nights they lay there together, listening to their hearts beating wildly after making love, and always there had been the splashing of the creek's clear water over the large rocks below. How quickly those days had run their course. He pulled his weight to the next stair and stopped to rest. He could feel the weakness in his breast. It had been a good heart. It had loved so deeply; it had borne such pain when she was gone. How many years had Maggie been gone? Twenty? More? Funny, he still missed her, still missed the long talks they had shared by the creek or over on the mountain trails beyond the small house he had built. Mostly he missed her smile. He looked again at the railing and then at the small window at the top of the first flight of stairs. He could still remember installing it wrong. Maggie had laughed at him as he cursed the window then put it in again—this time correctly. It had been their room. Now it was Jessica's. He thought about Jessica. She was a good woman. Like Maggie, she understood him. Sometimes George felt they both could see right into his soul; women had a way of doing that. Jessica had come along at a specific moment in his life, one he would never forget. He had been eighty-four when it happened. It had not been dramatic; he simply got up one morning and realized that he could no longer live alone. He needed help. His mind was still sharp, but the once young body was giving out. Used up, he liked to think. Not wasted on life, but used up; that was different. One more step; how many more to go? Fourteen? Could he make that today? Once last week he had given up half way and had climbed back to his easy chair for a nap. Not today. He would succeed; he had a mission, and at his age there were few missions left. His right foot struggled for the next step, and he would have stumbled had he not caught himself on the sturdy railing. George stopped to rest for a few minutes. The landing was so close now. His mind roamed back to sunny days and a young woman with sandy hair and a perpetual smile. Maggie had always been so happy. The only time he had ever seen her cry was the night she lost the baby. It had taken her almost a year to recover from the loss. They tried, but she never got pregnant again. She always said, "Maybe next time." There was no next time, but somehow she managed to smile through a sadness that permeated her soul. He had spent his life trying to make it up to her. He tried, and perhaps it had helped.

George struggled up several more steps and finally reached the small landing. He wished there were room to place a chair there. It would be a good resting place. Funny, he had never thought of that so many years ago when he had built the house. He looked up the stairs and counted again, though he knew the total count for each level was nine. It had always been nine. He knew; he had climbed these stairs so many times. Old eyes looked at the large watch that he pulled from his pocket. It was just after ten in the morning. He still had plenty of time. Jessica would not return from the café until after two. He could surely climb nine steps in four hours. Summoning his strength, George stepped on the first step of the second flight of stairs. He was breathing steadily; his heart seemed ready for the challenge. He knew he would make it. As he neared the top of the stairs he could smell the odor of a woman in his house, the scent of perfume. How strange, he thought, that so many senses had been dulled over the years, but his nose was still his guide to so much of life around him. Jessica, she had needed him as much as he had needed her. After her husband had rolled his tractor-trailer on interstate 70 she had been inconsolable for a week, then she had walked into the café one morning and announced that she needed a job. It had cost everything she and Sam had saved to bury him after the accident. She had no place to live and no money to even feed herself. Mildred owned that café and had fed her, given her a place to sleep for the night and most importantly, she had given her a job, one that not only earned a small amount of money, it also kept her mind and body busy through the difficult days and nights after Sam's death. Mildred had a house full of children of all ages to raise; it had seemed better for all if Jessica would live with George. She could cook and clean house when she wasn't working in the café, and she would have her own room upstairs above the creek. He had wondered if he could live with another woman under his roof after so many years of living alone. Surprisingly it had been easy. Jessica seemed to understand him, and over time he began to understand her. She became the daughter he had never had. One more step; George stopped suddenly and leaned against the wall. He felt the sharp pain in his chest. It did not frighten him; he had felt these for years now. But it did alert him to slow down and rest. He looked at the chair across the room. One step up and ten feet to cross. It might as well have been a mile. He leaned against the wall and looked into the room. It was neat, like a woman's room. There were flowers stuck into a

184

small jar on the dressing table, and the bed was covered with pillows. Now why would someone want so many pillows, he wondered. You can only sleep on one at a time. He smiled, thinking of the times she had surprised him on his birthday and on Christmas. His first Christmas with Jessica had been the first he had celebrated in over twenty years—since Maggie died. Jessica had gotten a tree and covered it with small balls and lights from the grocery store. It had been grand. They both laughed then grew silent. He knew what she was thinking, so he tried to make her happy. He took her into town for dinner. It was the first time either had eaten at a fine restaurant in many years. It was a wonderful dinner at a large cafeteria on Wadsworth Boulevard. They ate so much that she forgot her sadness for a short while. George understood. Jessica was struggling with the first year after Sam's death. He dared not tell her that he still struggled with Maggie's death, and it had been so many more years than that.

With his strength waning, he took the last step and stood finally in Jessica's room. He looked about. There was what he had come for. There on her table was a large jar half full of money, her tip jar. There were ones, change of all sorts, and one five-dollar bill. George looked carefully at the five. Now who would have given that kind of tip in Morrison, Colorado? Must have been a tourist, or one of those folks from up in Evergreen. They were supposed to have money he had heard. His eyes moved from the jar momentarily to the perfume bottle standing next to it. George smiled. He suspected that he smelled a change in Jessica. He might be nearing ninety, but he could still recognize a woman in love. He had noticed the changes in her hair, the new lipsticks, the color in her cheeks as she raced about the house. And the smile; it reminded him so much of his own Maggie. Yes, something was changing in this young woman, and he suspected he knew what it was, a young man somewhere. George reflected on the various men who frequented the café. Which one could it be? It didn't matter; she was happy. A sudden thought flashed through his mind.

What if she fell in love and left him alone. It was a bittersweet notion. It would bring him great joy to see her smiling, happy, in love. And what the heck, he wouldn't need her much longer anyway. He felt the cold hand of time touching his shoulder. He could leave happy if she were cared for by someone who would love her, as he had loved her. Yes, as he had loved Jessica, as a friend, and then like a father. The smile was still on his face as he rustled through the contents of his pockets. There were three ones and two quarters. Yes, perfect. He dropped them carefully into the jar, careful not to disturb anything in the room. It was not a great deal of money, he knew, but to him it was most of what he had left at the end of the week. He didn't need things, but women did. Maggie had, and Jessica was so like Maggie. George turned to the mocking stairs; now for the trip down.

Chapter 26

Morrison, Colorado, April 4, 2018

The phone rang several times before a sleepy voice answered. "Yes?"

"Jessica, it's John. How long before you could be packed for a week-long trip?"

"A week?" There was both surprise and excitement in her voice. "Where are we going?"

"It's a surprise." He thought a moment. "Well, you'll need two swim suits, some shorts, and some tops. And oh yes, lots of sun lotion."

"The beach!" The excitement in her voice abated abruptly. "Gosh, John, Mildred needs me. A whole week? And what about George?"

"I already talked to Mildred. She says she can call someone else for the café, and she also volunteered to check in on George to make sure he was okay."

"You already talked to her?"

"Did you know that she loves you like a daughter?"

"Of course. That's why I worry about leaving her."

"Trust me, she's okay, and you know she'll take good care of George."

"Well, in that case about twenty minutes." The excitement had returned to her voice.

"That's close enough. We're leaving at 8:27 tomorrow morning. I'll pick you up at five."

"Are we going back to Hilton Head?"

"It's a surprise, remember. And don't forget your sunglasses."

*   *   *

John and Jessica walked onto the United flight and sat in the second row. She was by the window. John had kept her away from the gate until time to leave, so she still didn't know where they were going. When the flight attendant announced the flight was to San Francisco, Jessica looked at him suddenly. He could see the clear disappointment in her eyes. "California?" was all she said as the drinks were brought around by a smiling blond flight attendant. As the plane climbed through the clear morning sky, Jessica looked down at the snow-capped mountains below and the excitement returned. John watched her with amused excitement. He had forgotten the beauty of the Rocky Mountains from over thirty thousand feet. But Jessica reminded him of the excitement in life that had faded from his memory so long ago.

The flight to California, like the meal served in first class, was unremarkable. The pair exited the plane at San Francisco International airport and began the trek to their next gate. John studied the airport video displays carefully then led the way as the two walked briskly down the concourse. He watched her as she walked beside him, stride for stride. Her brown hair bounced across her shoulders and the tan top she wore over the brown skirt. She was wearing leather sandals; he noted that her nails were freshly painted and matched the small necklace she wore around her neck. He smiled to himself, wondering how many men would even notice the necklace hanging over the stretched tan top. She looked up and saw him smiling at her. She grinned back. "Where are we going?"

"I told you it was a surprise."

"That wasn't what I meant. You just passed the exit to baggage."

"We're not going to pick up our baggage here. We're connecting to another flight.   Gate 88."   He smiled as he watched her eyes.

"Oh."

The crowds were thick as the pair walked along, oblivious of everyone else in the terminal. Ten minutes later they turned into the Red Carpet Club. "We have half an hour before boarding. Would you like anything before we take off?"

"I'd like to step into the lady's room."

"I have a few phone calls to make. I'll wait here." He motioned to two seats as he pulled his cell phone from his belt. She walked toward the restrooms, stopped, returned and kissed him on his cheek, then turned again for the lady's room. He smiled as he dialed the phone. When David answered, his face turned suddenly very serious again.

* * *

"Lihue California? I've never heard of it."

"It's not in California."

"It's not?"

John turned and looked into her eyes. He didn't want to miss this moment. "It's on one of the Hawaiian Islands."

Her eyes were suddenly wide. She looked at him in total shock. "Hawaii?"

"Hawaii."

She whirled instinctively and looked out the small window of the large plane. All she saw was water below. Quietly she mouthed the word again. "Hawaii." She turned to John and grasped his right hand. "Oh John, I'm so excited. Hawaii. I've always wanted to go there. Now I am."

"Yes, you are. It is truly one of the most beautiful places on earth." He watched the sparkle in her eye. "And we are going to the Princeville hotel on Hanalei Bay, one of the most luxurious in the islands. It will be beautiful."

She spoke softly, looking at her own hands cradling his. "You've been there before." It was not a question.

"Yes, long ago. I thought I'd never go again." He looked at her and pulled her hand to his lips. "Thanks for giving me reason to want to go back." Her smile warmed him, then she turned back to peer out of the small window. He watched her closely; he could see the small beat of her heart in the jugular vein along her neck. It dawned upon him how precious was that life that surged through her body. It had renewed his own. He had never realized how lifeless his own existence had been until she had entered his drab life and given it warmth and light. Without thinking he reached and touched her hair. She turned and saw him looking at her. In that moment what she saw in his eyes confirmed every hope she had been feeling for the past few weeks. He was in love with her; she was sure of it. She could not remember such happiness in many years. Now she knew; he loved her too.

"Pardon me, would you care for anything to drink?"

John turned to the woman standing beside him, her apron, like her hair, pulled tightly and tied behind her. "It would only seem appropriate that we start this trip with Mai Tai's."

"I'm sorry, Sir, we don't have those. It's probably illegal to try to mix one unless on an island."

"I agree, then how about cabernet sauvignon. Chilean if you have it."

"Certainly."

Chapter 27

Hanalei Bay, Kauai, Hawaii, April 5, 2018

John awoke suddenly. It was not a slow leisurely journey to consciousness, but rather a rapid awareness of something exciting that was to happen. His left arm was extended across the bed. It was empty; he was alone. He was immediately aware of an unknown roar that invaded his awakening consciousness. Hanalei Bay was just outside his window. John loved the Princeville hotel. It was hard to imagine that this valley had once been taro fields, then cattle ranches, silk worm farms, and even a coffee plantation. Today it was one of the premier vacation spots of the world, known for its beauty and the peaceful setting it offered. He had stayed here once before, with Sybil. It had brought him great joy then, surprisingly, that same excitement still remained today. He leaned up and searched the room for Jessica.

She was standing at the window, staring out at the scene before her. She was silent and motionless, as in a trance. The roar of the surf crashed across the entirety of Hanalei bay and echoed back from the mountains that rose majestically from the ocean below. It was a cloudy day; the mountains stood like giant gray sentinels in the morning mist, a dark contrast to the whitecaps of the waves crashing onto the beach below. Several miles across the bay, black shadows of tall trees drew the outline of the curving bay and the ocean that surrounded it. Across the bay the mountains slowly eroded into the sea, with one lone peak standing defiantly as the final guard of the gray giants behind. The large sliding windows were open and there was a mist in the air; John pulled the covers close to ward off the early morning chill as he watched her. At that moment she inhaled suddenly, clasping both hands before her as if in prayer. She stepped closer to the window in excitement. John sat up and leaned to see what had caught her attention. It was a rainbow. It spanned Hanalei bay and arched off into the Pacific to the northeast. Like her, it was a moment of joy in his morning.

*   *   *

It was getting dark as John and Jessica trudged through the sand toward the rental car; two things caught John's attention in the fading light. There were only two cars in the small parking lot—theirs and another parked immediately behind it, blocking its exit. The gray sedan behind the Pontiac contained three men who were watching them carefully. Red flags were filling his mind with warnings as he slowed his speed somewhat and studied the men. Jessica, sensing the sudden silence and the change in his step, looked up just as two of the men stepped from the car.

The couple stepped onto the asphalt forty yards from their car when the two men turned suddenly toward them. John noticed immediately that they were young; one had a pistol; and both were nervous. The third man sat in the large gray car and watched. John's mind raced rapidly. He was in swim trunks and had few weapons available—three that he could immediately identify: sand at his feet, a ballpoint pen in the pocket of the man with the gun, and the gun that grew more ominous as the men approached them. John considered a fake fall for a handful of sand but decided against that. A fake fall might startle these goons into doing something rash, plus he and Jessica were well onto the asphalt and very little sand remained. Jessica sensed John's concern; then she saw the gun. "John!"

He stepped in front of Jessica as the duo approached and suddenly realized that he might have yet another tool. It was late and the growing darkness made it difficult to see at a distance, especially under the overhanging Kamani trees. There were no lights in the parking lot; for that he was thankful. He spoke quietly to Jessica as they approached; the urgency in his voice was apparent. "Jessica, listen carefully. Walk directly behind me, and stay close. Undo the top of your bikini. When I step abruptly to my left, pull off your top and step sharply to your right. This is important. Understand?"

"Yes." There was a nervous energy in her voice. "I understand."

The two men approached to within ten feet of the two beachcombers, scrutinizing them carefully in the fading light. "It's him, alright." At that moment John stepped left; Jessica stepped right, releasing her top and dropping it to her feet. She watched the two young men; her figure worked its magic. Both pairs of eyes snapped immediately to her body. John was watching the eyes of the man with the gun. The momentary diversion was just enough time. He lunged for the gun, grabbing it and the man's wrist as he rammed his head into the startled man's face. Swinging the gun, John managed to pull the man's finger and loosed a shot. It hit the second in the stomach; he grimaced and doubled up, falling backward onto the pavement. The head butt and the sound of the pistol stunned the gunman momentarily, but adrenaline and fear took over, and he recovered rapidly as John chopped his wrist and slung the pistol across the asphalt. The assailant was strong and shoved John backward onto the parking lot. He then dived for the pistol, with John chasing him on all fours across the rough surface. As the two men grappled for the weapon, Jessica ran forward and kicked the man in his side. His reaction was rapid and furious, he kicked John away and grabbed Jessica's ankle as he rolled across the pavement, dragging her to the ground. Securing the pistol, he rolled atop Jessica and raised his hand to strike her with the butt of the gun. She watched in horror as his hand cocked above her head with the weapon. Her eyes were wide as the arm swung back with the cold metal aimed at her head. Suddenly it stopped in its arc high above the man's head and began to tremble momentarily. Then it fell limply by the man's side, blood dripping from his nose and mouth, puddling on the warm pavement beside her. Jessica screamed and pushed the body from her own. It fell lifeless beside her, a ballpoint pen protruding slightly from the man's left ear. John held the man's arm and wrenched the pistol from the limp fingers.

The roar of the engine startled them both into reality; John shoved Jessica aside as the gray sedan accelerated past them. Slowly he stood and aimed the pistol as the car sped from the parking lot. He fired once. The car continued to drive forward, but John lowered the gun and watched the fleeing vehicle. In shock Jessica looked up at John as he stood relaxed, watching the car race toward the exit. But the car did not make the turn onto the roadway; instead it continued across the intersection into a large Australian pine and crashed. It had barely come to rest when John ran, sprinting across the distance to the wrecked car. He returned a few minutes later with a wallet, another pistol, and a partial box of 9mm shells in his hand. He threw the wallet to Jessica. "Keep this, and get his wallet too." He motioned to the dead man bleeding onto the pavement. John's voice surprised her. It was as calm and cool as when he had ordered a special Australian wine at dinner. No, actually, it was even more cold and determined. It frightened her. As she pulled the wallet from the dead man's pocket she watched as John leaned over the wounded accomplice. His voice was low and unemotional. "Okay, let's talk."

"I'm shot. I need a doctor." The man was practically crying as he spoke. "Help me."

"Who sent you?"

"For God's sake, get me to a hospital." John hit the man across the face with the pistol; he screamed in pain.

"Who sent you?" John raised his hand to strike the man again.

The young man spoke quickly, his voice tinged with pain and fear. "Boone! It was Boone that set this up."

"Boone who?" John leaned close to the man. There was a trace of blood flowing from the corner of the young man's mouth.

"He's the bouncer at the Jetties."

"What were your orders?"

"To find you and kill you. But he didn't say anything about her. We found your car; we thought you were alone. When we saw a couple, we weren't sure it was you in the dark."

"Your mistake." John stood a moment in thought then knelt again beside the young man. "Were there just the three of you? Are there more?"

"Boone hired us, that's all I know."

"Where did Boone get his orders?" John watched as the man's eyes suddenly grew large then slowly rolled back into his head. Slowly John rose and stretched his legs and back. He looked into Jessica's eyes as he did. There were a thousand questions there. She was frightened and near tears.

Jessica watched the man before her, the man who had marveled at the beauty of a sunset, the exquisite art of a hibiscus, the man who had held her tenderly and had loved her in ways she had not known existed. Who was this man? She had watched in fear and horror as he killed with a skill and precision she would never have attributed to him. Coldly he had fired one shot and had killed the driver at over 200 feet as he drove away in a speeding car. "Why did these men want to kill you John?"

"Cheap muggers I guess."

"No, that one said someone named Boone hired them to kill you. You! Who is Boone?" The tears were beginning to flow. He reached to embrace her, but she pushed him away, her eyes large and overflowing now. "And why would anyone want you dead?"

John looked at her for a moment then scoured the deserted cove with his eyes. Only a solitary rooster and several brown hens remained on the beach. "Jessica, we've got to get out of here."

195

"No, tell me what's going on John. I have a right to know."

He reached for her and put his arms around her in spite of her protests. When he finally spoke it was calm and measured. "Jessica, I work for the government in a job I really can't explain right now. You have every right to know, but for now I can only ask you to trust me." He held her close as she sobbed against his chest. "When the time is right I'll explain everything, and that will be soon, I promise." He pushed her toward the Pontiac, "But we've got to get out of here. There may be others out there. Please."

"Okay." She slid into the passenger seat as John wiped the first gun then placed it into the hand of the man with the ballpoint pen protruding from his ear. He put the dead man's finger on the trigger and carefully pulled it, firing the gun into the sea twice. He looked to see Jessica's face, terrified. He had forgotten to warn her. He stood, scoured the darkness for lights then jumped behind the wheel. "Why did you do that?"

"To make sure he has gun powder on his hand. It'll look like he shot the other two."

"Oh."

"Wait, I might need that gun." John spoke to himself as he retrieved the pistol. It was a wise decision

* * *

John pulled into a small motel near the airport and rented a room under the name of John Smith. No questions or ID's were needed. The owner had seen many men and women move in for the night under the same name. "John Doe" was also popular. The rooms weren't first class, but they were clean, and no questions were asked. The owner made a good living by being discreet. Once inside the room John paced for a few moments then finally turned to Jessica. "Look, you'll be safe here, but I've got a limited window to stop this madness." He looked at her sadly. "I'm sorry, Jessica, but I've got to go out for a few hours."

"Do you have to?" She was not crying now, but she was near panic. He could sense it. She was working hard to control her emotions. "Must you?"

"Yes."

"Will you be safe?"

"If I don't go it will be worse."

"Can I go with you?"

John looked at the worn linoleum floor. "No, I've got to do this alone." He looked up into her large eyes and felt a sudden weakness. Quickly he turned toward the door. "Keep this door locked." He turned back to her. "If I'm not back by morning, go to the airport and tell them you need to go home early." He fished in his wallet and gave her four one hundred-dollar bills. "This should cover any change fees for your ticket and some clothes. Don't; don't go back to the hotel. Do you understand?"

"Yes." Her voice was small and shaking. The tears had returned to her eyes. She suddenly ran into his arms. "John, I'm so afraid." She clutched him as she cried. "I've never known a person could be as happy as I've been these last few weeks. Now I'm so afraid I'm going to lose you."

"You won't." He raised her head and looked down into her eyes. "These weeks have been magic for me as well. I had forgotten how it felt to laugh and to want to sing. I had forgotten what it was like to care for someone other than myself. Now that I've found you, you don't need to worry about losing me. You won't." He wiped the tears from her eyes and watched them slide across her cheeks, glinting in the dim light in the small room. "I've got to find this Boone and discover who paid him. If I don't, this will go on forever."

"John, is this about your work, really? I'm so afraid."

John stroked several stray strands of brown hair from her face. "It's okay, Jessica." He watched her eyes. "Look, I know what I'm doing."

"Sure you do. That shot back on the beach...It wasn't just luck, was it?"

"No." John stepped back from her and peered out the dirty window briefly.

"What do you really do, John? I've suddenly realized that I don't know much at all about you."

"It's government work, Honey. I can't explain the details now." He turned to face her. "But I will—soon."

Jessica looked into his face for a long moment. She was thinking, measuring her response. "I understand that you don't want to talk about this. I can live with that." She walked to him and reached to touch his face. "What I can't live with is the thought that I might lose you."

As he looked at her, a small smile crept across his face. "You're amazing."

"There's never been anything in my life like what I've felt these past few months. I'd rather die than give you up." She walked back into his arms.

"It won't be long. I promise."

"Here." She handed him a note on hotel stationery. "Boone."

John looked at his own quickly scribbled note and began shredding it into small pieces. "Forget that name."

"He sent these men?"

"Yes."

"When you find him, spit in his face."

"Spit in his face?"

"Yes, he ruined a beautiful evening."

John smiled into the frightened face that was so close to his. "I'll just do that."

"What will you do if you find him?"

He looked at her for only a moment, stuck the pistol in his belt, then turned and peeked through the blinds. His last words to her as he slipped out were: "lock the door."

* * *

John drove across the bay and stopped at a 7-Eleven store. He made two calls. The first was to a number seldom called and known to only a handful of men, men like himself who "worked for the government." He spoke a special code word and in twenty minutes room fourteen at the Wayside Hotel would be guarded until his return. The second call was to the Jetties. John held the driver's license in the dim light so he could read the name. A young male voice answered. "Yeah Dude, you got the Jetties."

"This is Mckinney, got a message for Boone."

"Say again; can't hear you man. Speak up Dude."

"Shut up and listen carefully or I'll come down there and kick your ass all the way to Hanalei bay."

"Hey man, take it easy. You're hard to hear. It's loud in here."

"Look man, I can't shout here. Got that? Now listen carefully. Tell Boone the job's done, but there was a woman there. What do we do with her?"

"Hold on."

Several minutes later the man returned to the phone. "Hey Dude, Boone says the same as the guy, whatever that means."

"Listen carefully, you go tell Boone no deal. Women aren't in our contract. Tell him McKinney said for him to meet us at Ha'ena beach, it's near Tunnels Beach and the Wet cave, then we'll let him take care of this business."

"Hold on." A while later the voice returned. "Boone says he can't make it until two am."

"Tell him we'll be there." John waited several minutes then made another call. "David, it's me. I only have a few minutes so listen carefully. Someone tried to kill me tonight. They were after Jason Kinkaid, my AFL/CIO alias. Did you book your flight yet?"

"No. Are you all right?"

199

"I'm fine. Now listen. Both our aliases just disappeared for good; Kinkaid and Carl Johnson no longer exist. Understand? And destroy that credit card."

"Gotcha."

"Standby for a change in plans. For now just sit tight, and be very vigilant."

"How do you think they tracked you?"

"Airline ticket, rental car, hotel. It's hard to say." He paused a moment then added. "It does tell us we're dealing with pros, however."

"I guess."

"Take care; I'll keep in touch."

"You be careful too."

"I'm always careful." John hung up the phone and walked quickly back to the rental car.

* * *

It was one forty-five in the morning when the big black Cadillac convertible pulled into the parking lot by the beach and stopped in a pool of yellow light from an ancient bulb hanging from an old phone pole. A large man, six foot three, two hundred sixty pounds, crawled from behind the steering wheel. He was alone. Carefully his eyes searched the sandy parking area that was empty. He checked his watch, walked to the front of the car, leaned against the hood, and proceeded to light a cigarette. In the distance the pounding surf reflected in the pale moonlight. He glanced around again and exhaled a large cloud of gray smoke into the night air.

"Those are bad for your health; they can stunt your growth." John stepped into the edge of the dim light.

The man looked at him quizzically. "Fuck you." John walked slowly to within twenty feet of the large man; he was wearing a blue windbreaker, dark trousers, and his head was covered by a black watchcap. Instinctively the man's head jerked up; he instantly recognized the threat. Boone flipped the cigarette in a high arch. It hit somewhere to his right in the parking lot. "Who the fuck are you?"

"The man you ordered killed tonight." The big man immediately stood away from the car, alert. "You sent a bunch of amateurs, Boone."

"Where are those idiots?"

"They're all dead." He held up the pistol. "Recognize this?" It took a moment for the message to sink in.

"Fuck you." It was obvious that he did not believe John.

"No, Boone, I'm afraid you've got that backward. It's you who is going to get fucked tonight. Now, how about we talk." The large man lunged toward John. Somewhere in mid stride a 9mm bullet ripped through his left leg just above the knee. He fell like a sack of rocks and lay on the ground writhing in pain. John's foot caught his head; the kick lifted him from the ground. Stunned he lay back on the asphalt as John frisked him quickly, removing a cellphone and his wallet from his pockets. "Stupid big guys always think their brawn is enough." John backed away from the prostrate figure, his gun leveled at his target. "Were you really going to kill the woman?" Boone fought the pain and forced his mind to assess his situation. The gunshot had been quick and accurate. The man standing over him was a good shot. He cursed himself in his pain. It appeared he had gone after a pro. It was so easy with the average Joe. But this was no average Joe. "Who paid you?"

"I don't know what you're talking about." The sound of the pistol echoed across the beach and was almost instantaneous with sudden excruciating pain — this time his right knee.

"Okay, you're practically an invalid now. I'll ask you again. Who paid to have me killed?"

Boone writhed in pain and shock. Finally he spoke between gasps for air. "Some guy called and said he needed a job done."

"Who was he?"

"Shit, I don't know. He didn't give me his name."

201

"Wrong answer Boone." John aimed the pistol at the man's groin.

"No wait. He really didn't give me his name—just a number to call when the job was done."

"Give me the number."

"It's in my wallet." The large man was rolling back and forth in pain.

"You'd kill a man on no more than that?" John was incredulous.

"He said Manny would vouch for him."

"Who's Manny?"

"He owns the club."

"And did Manny vouch for him?"

"Yeah, He said he was okay."

"One last question, would you really have killed the woman?" The large man said nothing. "You really are scum. But I think a lifetime in a wheelchair will be enough time to think about it." John turned slowly and began to walk away, but the familiar sound of the switchblade opening shocked him into immediate action. He dropped to his right, spun and fired as the large man sat upright and threw the knife with amazing accuracy. It passed just over John's right shoulder. The bullet, however, did not miss. It was fired quickly and struck Boone in the middle of his chest. John readied the pistol for another shot, but that was not necessary. The impact of the round knocked Boone backward onto his back. He lay there, staring blankly into the dark sky. John made a mental note to do a better job of frisking his victim in the future. The knife must have been in his boot.

A quick search of the Cadillac produced a .38 pistol under the front seat. He pocketed that and a handful of shells before leaving. He hoped the gun would be licensed to Boone, but that was doubtful.

*   *   *

The phone by the bed rang several times before Manny De Franco finally reached over the young girl asleep beside him and picked up the receiver. "This had better be good." He was angry.

"Boone's dead."

"What?" Manny looked at the phone in his hand in disbelief. "Who is this?"

"Look on the front porch." The phone clicked off. Manny lay back a moment, trying to place the voice. He couldn't. Finally he stumbled out of bed. The cold voice didn't sound like a prank. Besides he needed to pee. He stumbled into the bathroom and switched on the light. He fumbled with his shorts and finally secured what he was looking for. As he stood there, relieving himself, the girl mumbled in her sleep. Manny spoke over his right shoulder. "Go back to sleep." The voice on the phone intrigued him. He finished and turned to walk down the hallway toward the living room of his large mansion. He could feel a tingling in his stomach. Boone had not come back to the bar, and he had not checked in as was his custom. He looked at the clock on the microwave as he passed the kitchen. It was 3:17 in the morning. Manny peered out the front window into the darkness. From the hillside he could see the ocean below, and he could hear the crashing waves against the lava cliffs along the shore. Then he saw Boone's large shape swinging in the moonlight in the swing on the far end of the porch, the metal chains groaning with each arc of the swing. Smiling, Manny switched on the light and stepped from the front door. He started to walk toward the large man, cursing him with a sardonic smile. He stopped suddenly in horror as Boone slumped to his left then fell forward onto the porch.

"Now it's our turn."

Manny spun around to see the man in dark clothes standing behind him with a pistol pointed at his head. "What the hell is going on?"

203

"Well, for beginners, four of your goons are dead, and you may well be next." Manny glanced around quickly. "Don't even think about it. I could nail you at five times this range if you were riding a horse—or fucking that kid in there."

Manny relaxed a little. "Okay, how much do you want? I've got fifty grand on my desk in a briefcase."

"Actually, all I want is some information."

"What kind of information?"

"You arranged a hit. Boone was to take the guy out. I want to know who ordered it."

"I don't know what you're talking about."

"Shit, do I have to go through this every time?" John moved the .38 rapidly and fired a bullet through Manny's left knee. The man screamed and crumbled onto the porch. "Shut up, you'll wake the girl. I expect she's tired and needs her sleep." John leaned closer to the moaning man. "Now talk, dammit."

"It was Al-Falani."

"Why does he want me dead?"

"You?" Manny was talking between groans and great gulps of air.

"Right. Now answer my question."

"I don't know. We did some work together in the past. He asked me to vouch for him."

"Who else knows about this besides you and Boone?" Manny moaned as he clutched his left knee, blood flowing over the porch. John hit him on the side of the face with the butt of the gun. "Answer me, dammit."

"No one. No one."

"Good." John struck the prostrate figure in the back of the neck with the pistol. The sound of the blow was a loud crack; immediately Manny went limp. John checked him quickly then slipped into the house, checking to be sure the girl in the other room was still asleep. He heard nothing, so he took the money from the briefcase and stuffed it into his shirt and pants. He scattered a handful of the money around the back of the desk, broke a small plastic pouch of cocaine and sprinkled it on the floor in front of the desk and also on the corner of the desk. He left the briefcase open in plain sight. Finally he reached into his pocket and retrieved the wallet from one of the men he had killed at the beach. It was worn and held the man's driver's license and fifty-five dollars. John then took Boone's wallet, removed the credit cards, and placed them inside the worn wallet. He then placed it carefully under the desk and quietly slipped outside the door and replaced Boone's empty wallet into the large man's hip pocket. Finally he stopped in the light of the porch, pulled a yellow slip from his pocket and called the number he had found in Boone's wallet. He covered the phone with his handkerchief and whispered "Mission accomplished. Send money as agreed." He then re-entered the house and placed a call to the local police from the phone on the desk. "Help me, please," he whispered. "I've been shot; Manny shot me! Hurry, please!" He did not hang up but left the phone dangling beside the desk. That would give the police the address they needed. He walked back onto the porch, wiped the 9mm pistol carefully, and placed it in Manny's hand. John then aimed the pistol in Manny's hand toward the ocean and fired two shots into the distance. Finally, he took Boone's .38 and placed it in Boone's hand and fired once into the ocean. "Well my friend, this will give the police reason to inspect this place very well. I suspect what they find will be very interesting." As he ran down the hill toward the gate he saw lights go on in the bedroom, then the rest of the house. Finally the porch light came on followed by a young girl's scream. He had just enough time to exit the area before the police arrived. He accelerated as he raced toward the motel and Jessica.

It was ten before five when John walked to the parked car with the two men watching the motel. He spoke briefly before going into the motel room. When he quietly stepped inside the lights flashed on immediately. Jessica sat up in the small bed, a sheet pulled up to her neck. Her tear-streaked face broke slowly into a smile. "You're safe."

He went to her and held her in his arms. She was naked. He looked at her and smiled. "Waiting for someone?"

"Well," she spoke through her sobs, "I couldn't just sleep in my wet swimsuit."

"Why not? There's not much there to get in the way." He was smiling. She hit his shoulder playfully then hugged him.

"I've been so afraid."

"Come here." He turned off the light and led her to the window where he held back the curtain a few inches. "See that car over there, across the road?"

"There are two men inside!" She tensed immediately.

"Don't worry; they're friends. They've been there since ten minutes after I left."

"Are we in danger?" She looked up into his eyes. There was fear on her face.

"Not now. All the bad guys are gone—picked up." He lied. "We are absolutely safe now." He led her to the small, uncomfortable bed. "I'm beat. I need some sleep, and I suspect that you do too." He hugged her to him and was asleep in three minutes.

* * *

John walked across the road and talked briefly to the two men in the sedan as the sun crept slowly overhead. They nodded and drove off toward the city. He returned smiling. "They'll pick up our things at the Princeville and have them brought to us."

"We can't go back to the hotel?"

"It's probably okay, but I don't like to take chances."

"Are we going home?"

He searched her voice for disappointment or relief. He found neither. "No, we have four days left in paradise. We're just going to another corner. I happen to know a B&B that rents tree houses." He watched her face. "No, really. You can rent a house on stilts in the trees in a jungle setting beside the Pacific."

Jessica watched him, excitement growing on her face. "It's very romantic. They actually have hot tubs on the lanai overlooking the ocean. You'll love it. The neat part is that we are going by boat."

"By boat?"

"I want to make sure no one is looking for us at the airport." He watched her eyes. "Just to make sure."

"Where are we going?"

"To a beautiful place named Hana."

"But we're going by boat?"

"Those two "friends" out there will make the arrangements. We simply need to pick up a few things at a general store—like a razor for me and some new clothes for the trip. Then we're off."

"John, are we safe now? Are you sure?"

"For the time being I think we're okay." He held her close and looked into her eyes. "I've got some more work to do when we get back to the states, but for now we're fine."

She looked at him and nodded. John peered through the blinds for several minutes, placed a nice tip on the bed, and then the two stepped out into the bright sunny morning and drove away.

* * *

Billy Wong had been a detective for over fifteen years. He had been a cop on the beat five years before that. He had seen it all; he had investigated murders of passion and murders of convenience. These killings were obviously professional. Both men were shot at close range and apparently with the intent of more than simply killing them. The shots to the knees were similar for both; someone wanted information and knew how to get it. Billy wondered if the killer got that information and what it might have been. Whatever the information, it had obviously been important. But that made little sense since both men had weapons in their hands. Forensics would probably prove that each had shot the other. How could that happen? They worked together, and how could two men shoot each other with such precision at the same time? It made no sense at all, and it also appeared that drugs were involved; these days they almost always were. There was money spilled on the floor as if someone left in a hurry—probably leaving with a lot more than what was found behind the desk. Small amounts of what appeared to be cocaine were found on the floor—the lab would have that report before the day was over. It had all the markings of a drug deal gone bad, as so many of them did. But then there were other discoveries that as of yet didn't make a lot of sense either. Boone's wallet was empty—no money, no credit cards. Then those very items were found in a wallet found under the desk—the wallet of another man who looked familiar. He must have been a local. Billy made a note to check this man as soon as he returned to his office. He watched as the coroner bagged the two bodies for the trip to the morgue; the young assistants struggling with the weight of the large bouncer. Manny's neck had been broken. Boone was clearly capable of that. Billy knew both of the men; the island was small, and they had all grown up together. He despised them both. For years he had suspected that they were involved with the mob or some other criminal connections, but they always managed to stay a step away from his inquisitive eyes. He smiled secretly to himself; he had once fought Boone in high school. The bigger man had won, but he had also learned to respect the smaller Wong who had gotten in his fair share of good licks. Boone had never crossed him again; even bullies stay away from those who fight back. Manny was different. Boone was a simple man, his main asset his brawn. Manny, however, was smart; he was the more dangerous of the two. Billy patted his shirt pocket for a cigarette. He had quit several weeks earlier, but for some reason he desperately needed one now. As he walked toward one of the uniformed officers to bum a smoke, he wondered how much money had been in that briefcase—probably more than he made in a year. Oh well, he thought, it won't do Manny any good now. He watched the body bags being loaded into the van for transport to the coroner's office. There was little he could do now except check for any evidence that might be present. In time it would make sense. At first blush it looked like Manny had shot Boone. Then if Boone had help, perhaps one of them killed Manny and made off with the money. Perhaps the wallets might give some clues. If there were others involved, Billy probably knew them. In fact, he already had a few suspects in mind. Maybe it was time to clean out the nest of vipers he had watched from a distance for too long. He smiled to himself wondering if he could confiscate one of their cars. Yes, that would be nice. He was thinking of this when his cell phone rang. He placed it to his ear and listened. He was tired, but the fatigue evaporated rapidly. "Wait, slow down. Three bodies at Ha'ena beach?"

Chapter 28

Hana, Maui, Hawaii, April 10, 2018

The silver Pontiac Grand Am turned left off of the main road and began the descent toward the small harbor. It was a compact harbor, a small bay protected on the north by a large promontory that rose several hundred feet out of the dark blue ocean. To the driver's left the bay curved lazily along for about half a mile then reached again into the sea with dark black volcanic rock, spewed there many millions of years ago as the earth thrust upward from the depths of the ocean, reaching for the light and the life sustaining atmosphere above. The driver pulled slowly into the parking lot behind the short expanse of sandy beach. Off to his right he could see the concrete pier that extended several hundred feet into the bay. Like a large "L" it ran from the tree-covered mountain at the north end of the bay and then turned abruptly to the east toward the ocean. The road ran along the beach toward the pier; behind that was a large green building with a small restaurant and public toilets catering to the tourists and those enjoying the beach. After several minutes the driver locked the car and walked casually over to the large trees that flanked the beach and offered some respite from the afternoon sun. He was carrying a small blue sport bag by his side. Finding an empty picnic table, he sat down and surveyed the harbor. He looked at his watch; it was 1:32 in the afternoon. As planned, he was early. That gave him time to survey the site.

It was almost quarter past two when the large motorized boat pulled slowly into the harbor. It was a beautiful boat, over forty feet long and strangely with no markings whatsoever except for an American flag flying from a small staff on the stern of the vessel. The captain carefully maneuvered the craft to the pier, and two men jumped ashore to secure the boat. A tall man stepped onto the pier then turned to assist a woman. In seconds the couple were walking toward the beach area.

The man sitting on the picnic table rose slowly and watched carefully as the boat discharged the two passengers. He glanced around and then carefully reached into the small blue bag. Everything was carefully concealed inside, a 9mm pistol and two boxes of ammunition. Fishing in his pocket he found the keys to the rental car, tossed them inside the small bag, then rose and began walking toward the crowded building where laughing people waited in line for their hot dogs. He arrived at the building before the approaching couple and stood aside, watching from under the long bill of his cap.

John walked briskly with Jessica beside him as they approached the large green building. He was relaxed; he was also alert. "Isn't this beautiful?"

"Oh yes. It's gorgeous!" She was watching the sweep of the beach, the palm trees along the bay, and the flowers that bloomed profusely.

"Would you like a hot dog or a drink?"

"A Coke would be great."

John reached in the pocket of his shorts and handed her several dollars. "I'll be right back." With a smile he turned and walked into the men's room. As he did, the man watching from across the small road turned and followed him.

In contrast to the sunny day outside, the restroom was cool and dark. John walked inside and carefully bent over to see if there were any feet in any of the toilet stalls. There were. Someone was occupying the second to his left. He stood patiently at the sink until the man with the sport bag entered. John nodded toward the second stall. The other man nodded, handed him the sport bag and turned and left. As John followed

211

him out the door, the man spoke quietly. "Silver Pontiac. Last three are 1-8-7."

"Thanks."

"Remember, you're alone out here. We're at least a couple of hours away."

"Did you bring the ammo?"

"9mm; it's in the bag."

"Thanks, we'll be okay."

The man turned to his right and walked down the roadway then casually down the long pier. He reached down and untied the boat that was docked there, then stepped aboard. The loud roar of the boat motors interrupted the peaceful afternoon as it turned toward the ocean and disappeared around the mountains on the north end of the bay. As most of those on the beach watched the raucous boat, John and Jessica climbed into the Pontiac and turned up the hill toward the main road through Hana.

* * *

The phone rang only once and a young man answered. He was upset, and it was evident in his tremulous voice. "The Jetties."

"Let me speak to Manny. Tell him Hamad is on the phone and that I owe him one."

"I'm sorry that won't be possible. He's dead."

"What?" There was obvious shock in the voice. "He's dead?"

"He was robbed or something last night." The young man's voice was thick with emotion. "Somebody shot him."

"He was shot?"

"Yes; he's dead."

There was a long pause on the phone. Finally the long-distance voice responded. "Is Boone there?"

"No, sir. He was shot last night too." The young man was obviously frightened. "He's also dead."

A voice in the background interrupted the young man. "Who is that?"

"Just a minute, officer." The young man turned again to the phone in his hand. Who is this?" There was no response; the phone connection was dead.

Hamad Al-Falani sat looking at the phone that he had just placed on his desk, his mind rapidly recovering from the shock of the information he had just received. Boone and Manny were dead, both killed by someone. Who? The man he had ordered killed? Jason Kinkaid? Whoever it was had proven himself a capable killer, hardly an AFL/CIO delegate. But hadn't he already received a message confirming the hit? Kincaid was reported dead. He had even sent the money based on that report. Could there be problems among the troops he had sent to do the job? That didn't seem like an operation that Manny would run. Manny was a pro. He had taken care of a number of problems for Hamad in the past. Their dealings had always been professional. What was going on out there? Hamad looked out of the window into the night's darkness and weighed the facts. First, someone had called to say the hit was completed and to send the money. Then, Manny and Boone were taken out. This raised several issues. Had the hit actually been completed as reported? If so, Kincaid could not have killed Manny and Boone. But the two men who could confirm that Kincaid was eliminated were now dead. He had no idea why the murders had occurred or who had been responsible. Maybe the two had gotten involved in a local turf war. Maybe not. He made a note to discover what the local police had found. Maybe that would be helpful.

Hamad rose and walked to the small bar and poured himself a glass of scotch. He knew he was operating in the dark in more ways than one. He lacked necessary information. Was that a coincidence, or had it been planned that well. There was only one option remaining—he would send one of his best men to Kauai to find the truth. If the hit had not been made, and if there were no plausible explanation for Manny or Boone, then

213

Hamad knew he had a big problem on his hands. Someone was killing off his troops, and he had no clue as to who or why. Whoever it was, he, or they, were pros. He had to acknowledge that. He surmised that they must be government agents or hired guns. Who else could pull this off so well? He took a sip of his drink and sat down again at his desk. He knew he had to face the dark specter that waited in his mind. He knew it was there; he knew it was waiting for his analysis. "Could it be possible—possible—that someone inside the CFT organization had ordered the hits. He had heard the rumors of the emails from both Lonnie and Pierre. He had even seen one himself. Was it possible that someone inside the circle was eliminating assets no longer needed or perhaps even dangerous? Or could he possibly be dealing with a killer so cool and so professional that he was poisoning the group against each other as he killed them off systematically. The killings had the earmarks of a professional or perhaps someone with military training. It was well known that the "left" didn't support the military. Benghazi had demonstrated that rather emphatically. Could someone be eliminating CFT leaders as retribution? Finally, mentally exhausted, he reached for his cell phone and dialed a number long since committed to memory. "Tony, it's Hamad. I need some help."

* * *

The car drove slowly through the thick jungle growth toward the roar of the surf in the background. Jessica sat silently looking at the bright profusion of flowers along the narrow road. There were hibiscus of various shades of red and yellow, large white angel's trumpets drooping toward the ground, orchids of many shapes and sizes hanging from the trees, and the sweet fragrance of plumeria that enveloped the afternoon. It was so different from Colorado's majestic mountains. The frightening reality of the encounter at Kauai was quickly dimming in her mind as the beauty of Hawaii worked its spell. Finally John pulled to a stop and slid from behind the wheel. They had driven less than twenty minutes from the harbor when they reached their destination. Finding the entrance through the lush growth had been difficult, but the two stone pedestals with Balinese monkeys helped John locate the small road into the thicket. Jessica got out of the car and looked up in surprise at the tree house before her. It was over twenty feet in the air and supported by the trunk and limbs of a large Banyan tree and several tall beams that were there for insurance. The stairs leading up to it were guarded by "Honeyboy," a large orange Tabby that eyed them suspiciously. The path wound past several banana trees and two papaya trees as it led to the steep stairs. Jessica's eyes were wide as she looked at the fresh fruit hanging in the trees around the entrance. Like Jessica, John's excitement was also growing. "Come on. Let's see what's up here." The two climbed the stairs quickly, followed closely by the orange feline proprietor. A note was taped to the door by the proprietor; meals could be delivered if desired, and the key was in the door. As they entered John looked quickly around and then stood watching Jessica's reaction. The room was approximately thirty feet square with a large bamboo bed hung with mosquito netting as drapes at all four corners. It was centered against a fake wall. Behind that wall was the bathroom, a narrow hall, and a small kitchen. Opposite the bed were two large glass doors that opened onto a screened porch that ran the length of the building and was twelve feet wide. On the right side of the porch were several large cushioned bamboo chairs and a table. On the left, behind a screen, was an outdoor shower/Jacuzzi. High overhead, hanging from the beams of the tall peaked ceiling, a large fan cooled the room. Facing forward on the porch, one could see the beautiful coast with waves crashing against the volcanic rock shoreline about a hundred yards away. Only the large swaying palm trees interrupted the vista of the ocean and the shore. Jessica stood silently looking at the view. John watched her, smiling. "It's beautiful, isn't it?"

"John, it's unbelievable."

"And we are less than ten minutes from Hamoa beach—one of the most beautiful in the world." He pulled his right hand from behind his back. It held several plumaria flowers that he had picked up on the way in. "Put one of these behind your left ear."

"My left ear?"

"That means you're taken. The right ear means you're available."

She turned and smiled up at him as she hugged him. "I'm taken."

"Yes you are." He held her close and kissed her very slowly. Sensing her excitement he reluctantly released her, pulled his phone from his belt, and dialed a number written on the note from the front door. "Good afternoon. I'd like to make a reservation for two for dinner this evening." He listened as he watched Jessica. "Seven thirty; Mark Johnson. Mahalo."

John sat slouched into one of the large bamboo chairs on the porch, the giant cushions collapsing around him. Ostensibly he was rereading Mitchner's *Hawaii*. In reality he was watching Jessica as she surveyed the small tree house. She walked around slowly with her hands grasped behind her back, much like an overly critical supervisor inspecting the work of her team. She looked at everything quietly, touching everything unconsciously, lifting even the decorative shells on the nightstand. She studied them closely then put them back. When she finally turned toward him he noticed there were small tears in her eyes, though she was smiling. "I never knew places like this existed. It's so beautiful."

"Neither did I until yesterday."

"You've never been here before?"

"No." He closed the book, placed it beside the chair and looked up at her. "A colleague in Europe recommended it. He owed me a favor."

"Good. Then this is our place." She turned and walked back into the bedroom/dining area/kitchen space and began unpacking her bag. She seemed to be searching for something.

"Oh, good. Here it is." She rose triumphant, a small glass container in her hand. John looked at it, puzzled. "It's our candle. Our very own candle, for our very own tree house." She studied the room carefully before finding just the right spot.

John found the stereo and selected one of the many Hawaiian CDs there. As the soft island music flowed through the secret hideaway, John turned to the busy woman before him. "What do you think about the outdoor bath?"

Jessica stopped her unpacking and walked back onto the screened porch and surveyed the large shower behind the bamboo room divider. "It's a bit public, don't you think?" She was smiling as she walked back into the room.

"Could be interesting." He smiled back at her, still watching her every move. "Is the shower big enough for two?"

She grinned at him broadly. "It'll be tight, but yes, I think so."

"Good." He moved to her and took her in his arms. He carefully wiped a small tear from her left cheek. "Are you sad?"

"I've never been so happy in my entire life." She backed away from him one step. "Or so confused." She thought a moment. "I'm also afraid of all the things I don't understand."

"I won't let anything happen to you; I promise." He stepped forward and pulled her to him once again.

"I'm not worried for me. I'm afraid for you." She buried her head in his chest. "I'm afraid for us. I'm so afraid I'll wake, and the dream will be nothing more than a dream."

John lifted her face to his own and kissed her gently. "I'll be here for you forever. You'd better get used to me. Nothing, nothing will change that." He hugged her to him. "We've certainly had our share of hurt and broken dreams. Now, dammit, it's our time for joy, for love, and nothing will change that. I won't allow it." Behind them the sun began its slow plunge into the dark waters of the Pacific as the two silhouettes clung to each other high above the evening sounds of the tropical jungle below.

The young Hawaiian sat uncomfortably behind the wheel of the red Pontiac Grand Prix. It was the first time he had worn long pants in months, and the brightly colored shirt made him look like a tourist instead of a life-long resident of Maui. He had even traded his flip-flops for an uncomfortable pair of leather shoes, but he had drawn the line at socks. That was something he could not abide. He watched the crowd exiting the protective shade of the Kahului airport entrance and squinted into the sun, searching for someone he did not know and therefore could not recognize. The man he was meeting would be looking for his car, the fastest on the island. James knew that to be a fact; so did every other hot rod on Maui. It did not appear to be a road rocket, but it was. James had made sure of it. Affectionately he ran his hand across the dashboard, diverting his eyes only momentarily from the smiling tourists pouring into the parking lot.

The overweight man shifted his weight behind the wheel of the Grand Prix and pondered his assignment. Carefully he leaned to his right and reached under his seat. The package was there, as ordered, though it made him nervous to have a gun in his car. The Red Dragon was well known and had proven to be a speeding ticket magnate for the local police. He was just making a mental note to alert his contact of this fact when a rap on his window caused him to jerk around in surprise. The man standing beside his car was not at all what James had envisioned. He was younger than expected, tall, and good looking. He was dressed casually in khaki trousers and a dark blue golf shirt. His eyes, like his hair, were dark brown. Instantly James decided he had seen too many Mafia movies.

"James?"

"Yes." The Hawaiian leaned away from the window to get a better view of the man standing outside. After a moment of shock he lowered the window.

"Waiting for someone?"

"Frank from Pittsburgh."

"It's Frankie Joe. Thanks for picking me up." The man walked around the car and got into the passenger seat. He threw one small handbag into the back seat. As the red Pontiac pulled from the parking lot, the Hawaiian nodded toward a police car parked alongside the road. Frankie Joe smiled. "From the sound of that V-8 I suspect every cop on the island knows this car."

"It's the fastest on the island. That's for sure."

"Turn right, here." The man from Pittsburgh pointed toward an Avis lot. James did as he was told, but with a puzzled look on his face. "Sorry James, your car is a beauty, but I need one a little less conspicuous. Understand?"

"Damn, I'm sorry. I didn't think of that. Shit!"

"No problem. You were trying to help, and I appreciate that." As the car pulled up to the office area, Frankie Joe retrieved his bag then turned to James. His handsome face was suddenly serious. "You got my piece?"

"Yeah, it's under my seat."

"Let me have it." The big man grunted slightly as he bent to retrieve the brown bag under his seat. ".38?"

"Yes."

"How many bullets?"

"A box, like you said."

"Good." Frankie Joe opened the bag carefully, reached inside and caressed the weapon. "Good." He reached across the seat and dropped an envelope into James' lap. "One more thing, Kinkaid's location."

"Somewhere around Hana in a Silver Pontiac, license PBY-187. It's a six; can't be too fast."

The handsome man smiled. "I'll keep that in mind." Placing the brown bag into his handbag, he glanced around the rental lot quickly then stepped out of the car. "Thanks again; now beat it. I'll give you a call if I need anything."

James was smiling as he pulled into traffic. He lifted the envelope and measured its thickness with his fingers. It was thick. Best of all, he got it without having to risk his baby. He really didn't like other men driving his car.

* * *

John and Jessica were lying on the sand on Hamoa beach, basking in the sun and enjoying one of the most beautiful beaches in the world. A hundred yards from where they lay, a large monk seal flopped lazily onto the beach to join the people basking in the sun. One of the lifeguards hastily ran over and placed small yellow signs around him in a thirty-foot radius warning the tourists not to disturb or hassle the animal. The sound of his phone startled John. He had forgotten that he had even brought it along. Reluctantly he reached and keyed the phone. "Yes?"

"You need to be aware of an incident in Kauai."

John sat up abruptly, instantly alert. "Go ahead."

"There were questions at the Princeville. Some guy wanted to know about Jason Kinkaid. Seems he tried to track Jason's bags."

"And?"

"We know he left. We don't know what information he got or when or how he left." There was a long silence. "We left a rather large tip with the concierge, and it paid off. At least we know they're checking."

"When did all this happen?"

"Last night. We just got the phone call."

"Thanks for the alert."

"Can we do anything for you?"

"I'll let you know if I need any help. In the meantime I'm changing venue."

"Give us a call when you get situated."

"Thanks, I appreciate your concern."

"We good guys have to stick together."

"Right." John scanned the beach as he reached carefully and felt for the hard bulge in his small blue bag. It was still there. He nudged Jessica. "Jessica, we've got to leave."

"Must we?"

"Now!" There was urgency in his voice. "Seems there was someone checking on what happened to our baggage at the Princeville."

Jessica sat up quickly; there was fear on her face. Without saying a word she started to pick up their things and roll them into the large beach towel that she had been laying on. Finally she looked up into John's face. She saw him scanning the beach and checking all of the faces that had just been faces until now. "Are they here?"

"I don't know, but we're leaving. I'll book us a flight to the big island. We can hide out in Kona."

"Maybe we should go home." She was frightened and appeared close to tears.

"It's okay. But let's hurry just to make sure."

"Alright."

Thirty minutes later the gray Pontiac pulled from the tree house and turned onto highway 360 heading west for the Kahului airport. John drove rapidly toward the small town of Hana, passed the Hasegawa General Store and was soon navigating the famous road to Hana. There were over 600 hairpin curves and 54 one-lane bridges along this famous stretch of road. It was difficult, even for a good driver. They had driven barely fifteen miles when a dark green sedan passing in the opposite direction braked hard as they passed. For an instant John looked directly into the man's eyes. Somehow he knew this was the man who was searching for him. When he heard the car brake behind him and initiate a U-turn on the roadway, he was sure. Instinctively he reached under the seat and retrieved the 9mm pistol. Holding it before his eyes so that he could see it and drive at the same time, he checked it for the second time in the last hour. "Jessica, quick, crawl over the seat and lie down in the back floor. Do it. Now!" Her eyes were large as she looked at him for only a moment. Then she obeyed and climbed over the seat. "Stay there unless I tell you. Understand?"

"Yes." A few seconds later. "John, what will we do?"

"Don't worry, I've got a plan. This guy gave himself away too quickly. He's no pro, but he damn sure knew this car." He swerved the Pontiac around a sharp turn as he accelerated along the narrow road. "Just keep down, honey." John watched in the rearview mirror as he rounded the curve. The dark green Chevrolet was accelerating, closing the distance between them. As he approached a one-lane bridge, John slowed as an oncoming vehicle entered the bridge from the opposite direction. It delayed him, and the green sedan sped closer. When the oncoming van full of kids crossed the narrow concrete bridge and passed him, John quickly raced across and started up a small incline toward a curve to the left around the mountain. As he rounded the corner John saw the driver lean from his vehicle and fire at him. The bullet crashed through the rear window, sending glass flying through the car. "Shit!"

"Are you okay?" There was terror in her voice.

"I'm fine. But he's a better shot than I guessed. Stay down." John sped away from the chase car and swerved around the next curve. He crossed another small, one-lane-bridge and turned sharply right, following the terrain and looking directly across at the shooter as they raced along on opposite sides of a large creek falling toward the ocean below them. The man fired again but missed as John swerved left around the next curve and was again protected by the mountain. He studied the car following him in his rear view mirror as he accelerated along the highway. The man following him was a very good shot, but he was not an accomplished driver. He filed that in his mind; it might be an advantage later. As the road turned left into a small mountain cove, John saw a large truck about half-mile away approaching a narrow bridge between them. He stepped on the accelerator and swung the car recklessly around the curves between him and the bridge. He watched the truck approaching and timed his approach carefully. He arrived slightly before the truck and entered the one-lane bridge. The truck jerked to a stop and allowed him to cross. As John accelerated from the bridge and around the curve, the truck slowly lumbered onto the bridge and began to cross. On the other side the green sedan skidded to a stop, waiting for the truck. Finally it passed, and the sedan raced across the narrow bridge in hot pursuit. The driver knew he had lost precious minutes waiting for the truck, so he accelerated quickly to catch his prey. He followed the same path as the Pontiac and slowed only slightly as he turned left around the sharp curve on the mountain. As he cleared the green lush vegetation accelerating into the turn he suddenly saw the Silver Pontiac directly in front of him—parked in the middle of the road. The driver was caught completely by surprise and instinctively slammed on his brakes, swerving hard to avoid the car in the middle of the highway. It was then that he saw the man standing near the side of the road with the weapon. As the Chevrolet braked, John raised the pistol and fired twice. The brakes on the green car ceased their screaming as the vehicle swerved sharply to the right and crashed into the small stone wall and thick brush beside the road. Before it had even stopped, John sprinted toward the car, his pistol raised and ready. The driver had been hit and was leaning against the steering wheel. He was moaning when John grabbed his hair and jerked his head back. "Who sent you?" The shooter moaned loudly then jerked away, reaching for his pistol that lay in the passenger seat beside him. John fired quickly, hitting him in the right shoulder. Very quietly he spoke into the wounded man's left ear as he jerked the shooter's head back into the headrest. "I said who sent you?"

"Fuck you!"

John fired another shot, this time into the man's right arm. The man screamed in pain. "I said, who sent you." John placed the pistol to the side of the man's head and pressed it into his left ear. "You've got three seconds. One...two..."

"Tony! It was Tony."

John smacked the man in the face with the gun. "Tony who?"

"Valanetti. Tony Valanetti." The man spoke quickly, spitting blood as he spoke. John's face was one of surprise.

"Tony Valanetti?"

There was a slight smile on the bloody face. "That's right. And you're a dead man."

"Really? Then he'd better send better men than you." Watching the man carefully, John walked around the car and reached inside to retrieve the man's pistol. He then looked over the mountainside at the dark blue waters of the Pacific, checked the car's location, and then ran back to the Pontiac. Quickly he backed the car beyond the wrecked sedan and then slowly drove forward, bumping the damaged car. Slowly he pushed the car until it was balanced over the precipice; finally it fell, plunging several hundred feet into the azure sea below. John got out of the car and walked to the side of the cliff. He looked over for several moments, watching the sedan slowly sinking into the Pacific. As the car disappeared into the dark water below, John threw the assassin's .38 after it. Finally satisfied he walked back to the Pontiac, waving Jessica from her sanctuary behind a large eucalyptus tree. "It's over." He said it without emotion. "For now."

They drove for fifteen minutes before she spoke. "John, let's go home."

"I think that would be a good idea." He looked at her and spoke quietly. "But if we do, you'll have to promise to return with me when all of this madness is over." She nodded without speaking. "Jessica, I'm really sorry that you got involved in all of this. I told you I would explain what's going on. I promise I will, but can you wait for just a while longer?"

"I guess."

"I can promise you that you'll be safe as soon as I can get you home."

"Who are they, John?"

224

"Trust me. They don't even really know who I am. They're chasing an alias. Me and David." He suddenly pulled the car to the side of the road. "Oh shit! David!" John pulled his phone from his belt and dialed a series of numbers. "David?"

"What's up?"

"Damn, it's good to hear your voice. Any action there?"

"Quiet as a church mouse, Dad. How about you?"

"Three alarm every time I turn around. Somebody's serious. They don't seem to like union reps."

David's voice lost its friendly tone. "You okay?"

"Yeah, but stay low. The plan is changed; we're not going to Singapore. I'll explain when I get back."

"Sounds fine. Take care." David paused slightly. "Dad, be safe."

"You do the same." John looked relieved as he clicked off the phone and reattached it to his belt. He looked into Jessica's face and saw only confusion there. He reached and pulled her face to his and kissed her. He looked into her eyes for a long time then spoke very deliberately. "I love you Jessica Hanagan. I'm going to take very good care of both of us. I intend to spend a lot of years enjoying your company. I don't intend to get myself killed by some of these punks first."

"I love you too, John. I'm just so frightened. I don't understand any of this."

He pulled the Pontiac back onto the road and continued along the narrow highway. "Check the outside pocket of my blue bag. There should be several drivers' licenses there. Read me the names."

Jessica turned and reached into the back seat. After several moments of struggle she retrieved the small blue bag and began searching through the small zippered pocket. "Frank Ziminsky and Sarah Ziminsky, Charles and Lillian Thompson, Henry and Dottie Bergonz." Her eyes were wide as she looked at her own picture on half the ids. "Where did you get these?" Before he could speak she answered her own question. "Your friends on the boat."

"Actually it was the one who brought the car." He looked at her as she studied the fake licenses. "Well, Sarah, where are we from?"

"Illinois."

"Arlington Heights."

"Arlington Heights?"

"Arlington Heights, Illinois. That's our cover story." He focused on the road and the cars they passed as he navigated the narrow curves of the winding road. Several miles later he found a secluded pull-off and began searching for a suitable rock. With Jessica standing aside watching, he carefully bashed the window where the bullet had penetrated. "Mustn't look like a bullet hole." John cleared most of the glass from the car then reached for the blue bag. He studied its contents carefully. "White hair dye for me—the three day variety, I hope. Aha, even a neat moustache." He turned to the woman watching him. "Ever wonder what I'll look like when I'm older? Well, you're going to find out." He cranked the car and backed carefully onto the roadway. "We'll stop and get a blonde wig for you in Kahului, plus some weak reading glasses."

"What about the driver's license? What color hair do they have?"

John checked his carefully. "Yep, gray hair. They don't miss a thing." He looked at her license. "Well, well. Forget the blond wig. You'll be a redhead."

She held a small bottle of red dye in her hand. "You'd better be right about the three days."

"I've always wanted to sleep with a redhead." He smiled as she hit him playfully on the shoulder.

At 11:15 that evening the Ziminsky's boarded a flight for San Francisco, their destination. At eight fifty the following morning Charles and Lillian Thompson boarded a flight from San Francisco to Denver. By noon John and Jessica were safely back in Colorado.

Chapter 29

Denver, Colorado, April 25, 2018

The two men sat in the neighborhood restaurant in the western suburbs of Denver and enjoyed the fine Italian dishes. John completed his "Bob's Special" and laid his fork down appreciatively. "That was fantastic; the wine was great. I love this place."

"So do a lot of other people. If you don't get here early, you'll end up standing outside waiting in the cold." David downed the last of his wine.

"Such is the price of excellence. Even the masses recognize excellence when it has to do with food."

"So they sent a backup. These guys sound serious." The younger man leaned toward John as he spoke quietly.

"I think they're getting nervous. Those email messages must be having an effect."

"Do you think they know why we're after them?"

John considered the question for several minutes as he ordered two coffees from the young waitress. She was attractive. John smiled to himself as he watched David's gaze shift to her as she approached the table. He was beginning to enjoy David's company. "No, I don't. My guess is that they're in a great deal of confusion right now. They probably think we're quasi-government or a bunch of right wing nuts—or, if they've seen the emails, they may think the danger is from inside their own group."

"Maybe hired hit men from the mob."

"No, that's who was chasing me out of Hana. Only one thing didn't fit."

"What was that?"

"He was alone. Usually they show up in pairs." John paused while the coffee was delivered. It was hot, black, and strong. He watched David's eyes flash to the young woman again, then back to him. "If he came alone he must have been good." He sipped his coffee and quickly scanned the room. "Based on his shooting skills, he was."

"That was a great idea about leaving the car in the middle of the road on a blind curve."

"It had its risks, but I knew he'd be in a hurry. The truck on the bridge gave me just enough time to set it up; it also caused him to drive as fast as possible when he approached that curve." John watched the excitement in the young man's face. "Can you evaluate the risks? Everything rides on the risks."

David thought for a short time then leaned close, speaking quietly. "The largest was Jessica."

"Why?"

"If the shooter managed to stop and get out shooting, you've got the handicap of protecting her."

"Good, but the road was a very sharp curve. I knew he'd never see the car until he was on top of it. I had Jessica hiding behind a very large tree just down the road. Go on."

"Let's see." David looked off into the distance as he thought. "Another driver could appear in either direction."

"That, to me, was number one. I was lucky there. I was also lucky to have found a place where oncoming traffic could see the car with plenty of time to stop; the danger would only be for any vehicles coming from the direction of Hana, and I knew his was the next car coming from that direction."

"You still had to worry about gunshots and innocent drivers."

"True, what else?"

"He might have crashed into your car. Then you could have been tied to his death."

"Right, but how could that be handled given that there were no other drivers there to witness the event."

David's face lit up. "Damn, you'd actually thought about this, hadn't you? That's why you pushed the car over the cliff."

"Right. It was convenient. If he had hit the Pontiac it would have given me ample time to disarm him. That's what I wanted. So you see, in a way I failed. When I realized he would actually avoid the car I had no choice but to shoot him."

"That was a damn good plan, and I'd say it was executed well, too."

"Good choice of words." John sipped the coffee without smiling at the pun then added. "I just wish I had had more time to interrogate that goon, but my guess is he wouldn't talk much anyway; probably he had nothing to add. Chances are good he was simply given an assignment from some mob lieutenant."

"And Jessica was there."

John's face brightened. "Yeah, I thought of that."

David looked at John a long time in silence. Finally a small smile crept across his young face. He looked directly into John's eyes. "You're in love with her aren't you?"

John toyed with his coffee cup without looking up. "Yes." He slowly raised his face and looked into his son's eyes. "Yes, I am."

"Oh man, that's great. That's so good to hear." David's face was serious, but there was also a small smile across his lips.

"Well, I'm glad to have your approval." There was a small smile on John's face too.

"No, not like that. I mean—it's great. You've fallen in love again."

John looked up, directly into David's eyes. He thought carefully for several minutes before speaking. "And so can you, David. So can you."

"Yeah, someday." There was sadness in his voice.

"David," John's voice, like his face, was suddenly serious. "Jessica doesn't know everything, but she does know you are involved. She thinks this is some government thing. She doesn't even know who these guys are. I'd like to explain the truth when the time is right." He looked away suddenly. "And maybe I'll never tell her the real story."

"I understand."

"Good, now let's reassess where we are."

"Right."

"Lonnie did the shooting. He was under directions from Pierre."

"Two down." David watched his father carefully.

"It was all Hamad's idea—the son-of-a-bitch."

"He's next; he approved it all. He also apparently called in some "friends." Or do you think the shooters were inside guys."

"Outside. Even Lonnie was essentially outside. They're buying the firepower."

"What about Collingsworth?"

"I tend to believe that he was unaware, but I could be wrong. It was far too risky for an academic. I would like to think that even an egomaniac like him would have balked at murder."

David repeated his earlier question. "Who's calling in the guns?"

"Manny said it was Al-Falani. But he may not be working alone. I suspect they're all pretty worried about those deaths. They probably figured out by now that something is wrong. I'm hoping they thinks it's drug related."

"Drugs?" There was surprise in David's voice.

"I left small amounts of cocaine at both Pierre's and Manny's houses —packaged." He glanced around carefully. "Plus I lifted a sizable amount of money from Manny's desk. Somebody had to know about that much money. It could appear to be a simple robbery or a drug deal gone bad."

"Sounds confusing."

"Exactly. By the way," John handed a taped manila envelope across to David. "Don't open this until we're alone at home." David took the envelope and placed it under the table in his lap. "It's a contribution from someone who tried to get me killed."

"Manny?"

"Right. It's probably drug money. I had to take it to leave the impression of another drug deal gone bad. The drug boys wouldn't have left that much money at the scene."

David lifted the envelope under the table to feel the weight. "There's a lot here."

"Actually I left some on the floor for effect. Anyway, you'll need it when you return to school, and Manny doesn't. Not now." John looked into David's eyes, measuring his recovery from Marcia's death. "I also kept a bit out for Jessica. She certainly needs it; if I can just figure how to give it to her."

"Yeah, she could probably use a car."

"Or a computer, or a cell phone, or a lot of other things I'd like her to have. I just have to determine how to give them to her without hurting her feelings."

David smiled at his dad. "I can think of a good way to do that. It's called a joint account."

John grinned. "Back to the plan."

David breathed deeply then continued. "Who's next?"

"Only Al-Falani. Then I think we're through."

"What about Sylvia?"

"I've been thinking about her. I may want to talk to her, but I've got to give that a bit more thought. I don't really know what we'd gain by that now. We know who made all the decisions. What could she add? Also, it could blow our cover. Thus far there's nothing to tie us to any of the killings."

"Good point."

"For now we just leave her out." John stood to leave and produced two tickets from his breast pocket. "If you don't have plans tonight, Manny bought us tickets to the Rockies game. I suspect we need a little excitement in our otherwise dull lives."

"Cool. That was nice of him."

"Yes it was. Let's enjoy tonight; tomorrow afternoon we develop the rest of our plan."

Chapter 30

Chicago, Illinois, April 25, 2018

Tony Valanetti stood impatiently in his ornate office; he was in a hurry, and this was a phone call he knew he would not enjoy. He also didn't like waiting; leaders of organized crime families generally did not wait for anyone. After the fourth ring, a familiar voice answered. "Hamad my friend, I'm afraid we have nothing to report on your friend Kinkaid. He seems to have disappeared. As I recall you said he was an average guy."

The voice on the other end of the line was less convincing than his answer. "Yes. That is my understanding."

"Well, we will keep surveillance for a few more days. I'll let you know if we get anything."

"Thanks, Tony."

Valanetti replaced the phone and rubbed his tired eyes. Glasses. He simply had to find time to have his eyes checked. He glanced back at the phone, then his very expensive watch. His "soldier" should have reported hours earlier. Tony didn't like to be uninformed. Control required knowledge, input from the field, and he had none. He had sent an experienced man, a dependable man who understood the rules. Frankie Joe had flown to the site as instructed, met his contact, picked up his weapon, and called in per plan. That was the last time Tony had heard from him. He glanced again at his watch. Six more hours and he would declare it a failed mission and send a team out to check. Who was this Jason Kinkaid? Is it possible that he could have killed Frankie Joe? No, he thought, that was highly unlikely if Kinkaid really were an average guy. Besides how could he have known that Frankie Joe was there? No, it had to be something else. But what? Tony rose and walked to the small wet-bar in his expensive mahogany office. He poured himself a drink and then crossed to the window. It was spring outside. New life. He wondered if he should have told Hamad that one of his key troops had failed to report. No, one had one's reputation to protect. He downed the drink in two large gulps and returned to the reports on his desk. He would force his disciplined mind to concentrate on the numbers that represented the health of his organization. *Damn*, he thought, *I'm little more than a fucking accountant.* That brought a small smile to his face as he picked up the report and prepared his mind for the task ahead. Corporate accountants could make mistakes or even lie. He could not; the penalty in his business was far too great. His accuracy would be unquestionable; it had to be. After all, it was all in the family, wasn't it? The last thought made him smile.

Tony looked at the stacks of paper on his desk. How the cops would love to see all of that. It could incriminate half of the "made" men in the state. But he knew the police would never gain access to his records. No judge in the state would ever issue a search warrant on his estate. The same law that protects the innocent also protects the guilty. There was never any evidence that could link him to a crime, no justification for closer investigation of his "business." His organization understood the rules. The "soldiers" were never to have any direct contact with him. They were not to call him or speak to him. Everything was handled by his lieutenants. He was never to be associated with any of the activities he controlled. The law is a beautiful thing he thought. One need only learn to use it well. He had.

Chapter 31

Madison, Wisconsin, May 3, 2018

It had been a difficult day. The small but cluttered office seemed to close in on Hamad as he placed his phone on top of the calendar on his desk. His role was to make sure that things ran well at CFT. He understood the skepticism with which the Saudis viewed Collingsworth, yet he also understood why they needed him. Collingsworth alone had dared to write the condemnations of the world order as a tenured professor at the University of Wisconsin. He alone had been interviewed on TV so many times by friendly advocates of every cause imaginable. The reporters found Collingsworth perfect for TV. He looked like a college professor, and he spoke with authority. His ideas were extreme, but his presentation was compelling. So, the Saudis had planned a little backup operation to ensure that everything was going well and that their money was well spent. That was the job for which he was responsible. Hamad stared at the stacks of reports on his shelf and wondered if there were others checking on him. Probably, he decided. And why not? Gavalas, alone, was secretly spending millions on this effort. That was a lot of money. Immediately the thought of so much money diverted his mind to his own situation. They had simply deposited a quarter million in an account for him in Switzerland and promised another million at the end of eighteen months— plus, he drew a salary in excess of $200,000 from *Citizens for a Free Tomorrow*. One and a quarter million, tax free, in a Swiss account, free from the prying eyes of a hungry government plus his salary; who knows, if all went well, he might well be kept on for another "tour." He had worked very hard to ensure the success of CFT; his problem was that he was a very intelligent man and recognized the stupidity of what he was doing. Immature students drove to their demonstrations in financed automobiles or flew in finely engineered planes and then protested big oil and the transportation industry. They had never worked a day in their lives, and they were the self-declared representatives of the masses who toiled in the sun. They consumed, but they had yet to produce even enough to sustain their own food intake. How absurd they were. Hamad smiled to himself. The wonders of youth. They had all the answers; they just misunderstood the questions. Their protests of the world banking system had reduced investments in parts of Africa by almost twenty percent. He wondered how much starvation that had caused. A movie star had protested labor conditions in a factory in China. It had closed, and now the people who had worked there were without any source of income. More starvation. People thinking with their emotions and not their heads; he had seen it so many times. Like communism, it all sounded so good until the cold light of reality shone in. International trade certainly hurt some but helped so many more. But it was so easy to concentrate on the few and not the many. It was so easy for the young to denounce poverty, but how many of them were out working to contribute production to those caught in the web of political, religious, social, and cultural causes of poverty? How many of the young people shouting in the streets had ever worked to alleviate physical suffering in the world, much less understand the real causes of the human pain they championed. How many had ever had the courage to demonstrate against a government, a religion, or a culture that contributed to the poverty of the people of a nation? No, it was far easier to blame the successful for the pain of those who had achieved less. Somehow they had always believed it to be a giant zero sum game. But Hamad knew that to be wrong. Intellectually he disagreed with his new bosses; he was far too practical, but outwardly he supported the cause like all the rest because of that same practicality. It was his bread ticket, his means of achieving a standard of living that had long eluded him. If people suffered as a result of CFT's successes, so be it. He just made sure he was not one of them. He was willing to adopt any view to ensure that. But working with intellectually inferior people infuriated him, and unfortunately he had no choice but to carry out that part of the charade. He was a director in CFT and had to be in daily contact with all of those seduced into doing the real work of the organization. The press, they were the most fun for him. His own IQ was quite large. He had been aware of that his entire life. He estimated the IQ of the reporters with whom he worked to be considerably less than his own. It had become a game for him, and that alone had broken the boredom of dealing with the inferior minds around him. He would ply them with food and booze then massage their egos. Eventually they were inventing the stories that he suggested. It had all been so easy since the incident in Chicago. It was unfortunate that it had been necessary, but it had worked so well. He had watched the organization, and his own stature, soar after that. It had been a masterful plan, and it had succeeded beyond his wildest dreams. Collingsworth had claimed all credit for the growth of CFT's influence, but Hamad knew it was not the articles, nor the TV interviews. He knew that it had been his brainchild to kill a demonstrator that had put CFT on the front page of every paper and the lead story of every newscast in the nation. The media longed for a breakout story regarding the demonstrations, and he had given it to them. He had done it; it was he who had found the daughter of a famous actor in their midst; it was he who had chosen her as their target, and one day he would declare that to the Saudis. But did it really matter? Only if it extended his "tour" for another million or so. Then it would matter.

Hamad looked at his watch; he was hungry. It was Friday night, and he felt like a steak and a couple of drinks. He had met a young woman from one of the demonstrations who was very attractive and totally devoted to CFT—and now, apparently, to him. Hamad could always find female company. It was easy to manipulate the enthusiasm of youth.   The phone rang again, but Hamad ignored it. He had talked to enough idealistic idiots today. Now it was time for dinner and a few drinks with his new found female friend. He rose slowly and walked to the elevator and his waiting car.   He was smiling. Idealism would never get in the way of his pragmatism. Only when one is a millionaire can one afford to worry about ideals, he thought.

Chapter 32

Seattle, Washington, May 24, 2018

The pensive detective sat upright in his chair as he scanned the morning papers. He reached for the coffee on his desk and took a long drink without taking his eyes from the page. "I'll be damned!"

"What's up Paul?"

"Looks like we've got another tie to the CTF murders." He reread the article more carefully as his assistant rose and walked around the desk to survey the article with him.

"That's three."

"No, it's more than that."

"What do you mean?"

"Read this." Paul reached over and retrieved a one-page fax from his inbox. "Two unsavory figures in Hawaii were murdered in what appears to be drug related killings. Cocaine found at the site was an identical match with cocaine found at all of the CFT killings. Now it really gets confusing." Paul looked up at the younger man. "Then just last week a body floated ashore near the town of Hana on Maui. Couple of fishermen found what was left of it. Turns out this guy had a hole in his shoulder, and that hole had a bullet from the same gun that killed the two men from the nightclub there. Tell me, how do a bunch of Hawaii's low life figure in CFT operations?"

"Any ID on the body that washed ashore?"

"That's the interesting part. Seems this John Doe was known in his prior life as Frankie Joe Carlotte."

"Frankie Joe Carlotte?" There was shock in the young detective's voice.

"The same."

"I'll be damned. So the Mob *was* involved."

"Appears that way."

"Somebody's going to be pissed when this news gets out!"

"You got it. There may be a war." There was a long pause before the older man spoke. "Anybody got anything on that gun yet?"

"No, but I'd hate to be found with it. You don't kill off Frankie Joe and just walk away smiling. Whoever did this better have lots of life insurance."

"You've got that right."

The young man looked at his friend for a long time before speaking. "You think there's a turf war going on among the drug kings?"

"It's hard to say, but someone is thinning the ranks."

"Were the two victims in Hawaii associated with CFT?"

"No. They were locals. One owned a nightclub there, and the other was his bouncer. Both appear to be involved in drugs."

"So what do we know?"

"Well, it seems they were all shot at close range with the same gun." Paul rubbed his eyes momentarily then continued. "Drugs were found at the sites, and those drugs just happen to match the coke found at each CFT murder. So the CFT killings and those in Hawaii have that in common. In Hawaii it appears that a large sum of money was taken as well. Robbery might have been a motivation, but I'm guessing the issue was drugs."

"What about evidence?"

"Whoever did this knew what he or they were doing. We haven't found a damn bit of evidence. No fingerprints that cannot be explained, no one who saw the perpetrators, nothing, not even a hair for DNA. No, these guys are pros."

"So the type of gun is all we've got—a 9mm."

"Right."

"Sounds like professional work."

"Exactly."

"Pros like Frankie Joe Carlotte."

"The Mafia is pissed about something."

"Most likely its drugs."

"Maybe we need to fly out to Hawaii and interview those guys." There was a big grin on the young face.

"Right. I'm sure the chief would approve." Paul, too, was smiling as he reached for the ringing phone that interrupted the levity of the moment. As he listened to the excited voice of a colleague in Wisconsin, the smile vanished from his face and his eyes narrowed in concentration.

Paul Hamilton replaced the phone in its cradle carefully. His eyes were focused somewhere beyond the cluttered gray desktop before him. Finally he looked at the younger detective across the desk. "Damn, this is all coming together. We were right."

"What's that Paul?" The younger man turned his attention from the attractive woman he was watching across the room and focused on his friend.

"You know we've always suspected the mob to be up to their eyebrows in the drug business, but we've never been able to get anything substantive on them. They're damn good at what they do. But if Frankie Joe Carlotte was involved in any way with the killings in Hawaii, we may have something to pursue."

"That would pretty much confirm the Mafia connection. Frankie Joe, Valanetti; this is making a lot of sense. The Feds have been watching Valanetti for years."

"Well, they may get their chance to do more than that if we could link the pieces. Then all we need is a judge with balls."

"Good luck with that. You'd need some pretty air tight evidence to get into Tony's estate."

Chapter 33

Chkalovsky Military Base, May 28, 2018

General Turgenov answered the phone that was ringing on his desk. As he did, he leaned to his right and looked into the lobby outside his office; the clerk was not there. *This army is falling apart*, he thought. *Now generals have to answer their own phones.* "Yes, General Turgenov here."

"General, your car is ready—as you requested."

Turgenov recovered from his shock quickly. He had not ordered a car, but his mind quickly recognized the code and the voice. "Yes, thank you. Please meet me at the main entrance to the headquarters building in twenty minutes."

"Yes general—twenty minutes."

Fifteen minutes later the decorated general stepped into the rear of the staff car and nodded to his driver, Major Rodion Mikhail Simkov. "Is the plan ready?"

"Yes, sir. Everything is in place. The officer in charge of nuclear records left yesterday on special assignment as you directed; I'll have complete control of the paperwork for all nuclear weapons." He paused momentarily as he pulled into the main road on the military base; he turned left toward the officer's club and continued. "I've arranged for the inventory tracker in Moscow to be "updated" as I explained. Everything is in order."

"Good."

"General, I have one question." There was concern in his voice.

"Yes?"

"I'm concerned about the men who will get this weapon and what they could do with it." Rodion knew he was broaching a dangerous subject.

"So am I." The general could hear the major's sigh of relief. "So am I. I don't trust these men at all. They are uncivilized barbarians. That is one of the reasons we will deliver the bomb in Chechnya. It is neutral territory. We will have a large Russian military presence nearby in case they try to double cross us." The general thought a moment. "I'm also considering a plan to stop them after we have our money, but it might be difficult."

"Then I have a suggestion. What about scrambling the enabling codes?"

"That is a very good idea."

"If they were given a certain code, which I have, dialing it into the bomb would cause an immediate explosion—but non-nuclear."

The general's face broke into a large grin. "We have a code that can do that?"

"Yes, Sir."

"Of course; how appropriate; and should we get a complaint, we simply accuse them of botching the code."

"Precisely."

"We get the money; they get a genuine bomb; and then they get blown away. I like your idea."

"It's true justice for the bastards."

"You know this code?" The general was surprised. He had no idea that such a code existed.

"Yes, sir. That's my job."

"Excellent. Do it."

"I feel better already."

"So do I, Major. So do I." They drove into the parking lot for the officer's club and parked in front of the entrance in the general's reserved spot. "I'm hungry. A good lunch and some vodka will be a fitting salute to our little joke."

243

The major climbed quickly from the car and opened the general's door.   It was important that they keep their professional roles intact. As they climbed the stairs to the door the general glanced back and spoke quietly. "You've done very well Major. Success will soon be ours."

"Thank you, Sir."   Both men were smiling as they entered the busy dining room.

*   *   *

Nina Simkova - "Minishna " sat quietly and stared out the dirty window at the new sprouts on the trees outside. New life, she thought, but not for me. A single tear trickled slowly down her left cheek, leaving a small trail of glistening moisture in the morning light. Her period had begun the prior evening. They had both tried so desperately. The teacup in her lap slid onto the large cushion on the window seat. She grabbed it without thought. Finally she rose and walked back to the small kitchen. She poured the cold tea into the sink and refilled her cup with hot steaming liquid. It was bitter as she tasted it, but that was how she liked it. Nina walked into the tiny bathroom and stood on tiptoes to see herself in the mirror. As she did, she pulled her worn sleeping gown over her head and stared at her body. The stomach was as it always had been, plump, but not extended joyously with a child. She studied her breasts. They were large; she smiled and considered that her husband would soon, perhaps, have to share them with a son or a daughter. Perhaps. She then looked at her face. It was no longer the face of a girl; it was that of a woman, one whose fertile years were numbered. She examined the tiny wrinkles around her eyes and on her forehead and forced herself to smile. That was how she would look as the baby would grow inside her; she would be smiling. And Rodya too. He would smile and be proud. She was so lucky to have such a fine man as her husband. And he was smart, too. Otherwise he would not have been chosen for this special assignment.

244

Nina pushed the thoughts from her mind and began selecting her clothes for the day. She would be late for work, but that was no concern. Tonight she was going to a fine restaurant in town, then later that evening, they would plan again the process of creating their child. She smiled, wishing her period were over already. But maybe, just maybe, Rodya may need a rest. She laughed softly and began brushing her long brown hair. Rodya never needed a rest, and neither did she.

* * *

Two weeks after the meeting of the General and his adjutant, a large canvass covered truck backed slowly to the loading dock of the camouflaged concrete building. Three soldiers climbed from the cab and waited for the large metal doors of the cold concrete building to swing open. A captain and three guards met the soldiers inside and surveyed the paperwork for the second time that day. It was routine with all of the required signatures. Once stamped it would be sent to the proper department for review, and then it would be entered into the base inventory computer system which would update the central inventory/tracking system in the Kremlin. Additionally, the hard copy would be filed and held at the base for future review. It was all very proper and efficient. Colonel Odintzov managed it well, and while he was away on special assignment, Major Simkov had everything under control and would continue the process.

The large wooden crate was carefully loaded on a pallet and then fork lifted into the truck. The sergeant in charge of the moving crew saluted the captain, and they pulled away. Twenty minutes later the truck exited the main gate of the base and turned east to the rail yards on the edge of town. It was escorted by two trucks with heavily armed guards. Three hours later the diesel pulled out of the military shipping area and headed south with supplies and troops for the growing conflict in Chechnya. The third from the last car of that train was occupied by one single crate, four heavily armed soldiers, Major Simkov, and Vasiliy Petrovich Kirzanov, the Russian arms dealer. Simkov inventoried the railcar quickly. There was food and water for the long trip, ammunition, hand grenades, two radios—plus his cell phone, and a box of tools. There were troops in each of the adjoining cars as well. He sent his sergeant to verify that they were equipped and ready. "Sergeant Orlov."

"Yes, Major."

"No alcohol. These men were hand-picked; I want them alert at all times. You stay with them and make sure that happens."

"Yes, Sir." With a salute he departed.

The train jerked suddenly as an old man waking from a deep sleep. It jerked again then slowly accelerated as it headed south. Simkov watched the familiar landscape disappear into the distance before he opened the toolbox and began to open the crate with the help of two of the soldiers. Fifteen minutes later the wooden crate was reduced to a stack of planks in the rear of the railcar. What was left was a black case, roughly five feet in length.

It had all been so easy. The reports were already shredded and burned, and by 1800 hours Moscow time, all computer records relating to NNP68FA0048 would be erased. It never existed. Major Rodion Mikhail Simkov knew, however, that challenges still existed, and he still had one important task to perform—ensuring that the fake enabling codes were passed with the bomb. Selling the terrorists a bomb was one thing; allowing them to explode it was another. He smiled; the non-nuclear explosion would still be large. When the Arab bastards dialed the codes to arm their weapon, they would all discover the truth of their religion in less than a mili-second. They would either stand before Allah, or they would simply be shredded like dried leaves in the wind. Either way, he would have his fortune and, with luck, a new son.

Chapter 34

Frankfurt, Germany, June 11, 2018

Walter reread the message on his desk for the second time. It was from a contact he had never met. Very simply it stated that two hundred fifty thousand US dollars had transferred from a flagged account to another controlled by a known arms dealer in Beirut, Kahlid Bahir. He looked at the account number carefully; the money trail had originated from the same account that had supplied a good portion of the initial startup money for CFT. Subsequently, one hundred fifty thousand had transferred to a suspected arms dealer in Moscow. Walter knew that the amount was chicken feed; perhaps someone wanted rifles or grenades. One hundred fifty thousand didn't buy much on the international arms market. The source, however, intrigued him most. Why would a wealthy Saudi with access to the Saudi military be involved in a small arms purchase? That didn't make sense. He could have a case of machine guns delivered to his house with a simple request. Could it be something else? A down payment perhaps? On what? A surface-to-air missile? He made a note to watch this one and placed the sheet in his "Current-Hot" file. Walter rubbed his eyes then stared out the window of his office. What had begun as a favor for a friend may well have uncovered a plot of great import. But why would a rich Saudi be involved with common arms dealers, and equally strange, why would he be financing an organization like CFT that was intent on reducing world trade? Where would he be without trade? Riding a camel? Obviously someone else was using the Prince's money—most likely one of his sons.

Walter rose and walked into the outer office for another cup of coffee, his third for the morning. The CIA agent sipped the bitter coffee and studied two sets of photos that had been delivered earlier that day. One set was from clandestine operations from his own people; the other was from Russian intelligence. Walter smiled, the photos could have been taken by the same man. Perhaps they were, sold in separate bundles to two different intelligence organizations. It would actually make sense. Who said the Russians didn't understand capitalism? There was one difference, however, the Russian photos had notes on the back—names. The pictures were taken late in the evening; it appeared to be raining. A tall Russian civilian was climbing into an Army staff car—with two stars flying from the small flags on the front fenders. The names on the rear caught his attention. Walter stared at the name a few moments then leaned forward and grasped the thick file on the corner of his desk. He sorted through it a few moments and found the report he wanted. Two hundred and fifty thousand transferred from Beirut to a Vasiliy Petrovich Kirzanov, suspected small time arms dealer. Below that, General Turgenov, regional commander, strategic nuclear forces. Walter sat upright in his chair and grabbed a highlighter. Was it possible that the small time operator was moving up the food chain? General Turgenov? He highlighted the appropriate sections, grabbed his pen and dashed a note on the top of the report, then copied it and placed it in a secure interoffice envelope. More eyes need to see this, he thought. This would bear watching.

The next morning Walter sat in his office rubbing his forehead vigorously with his fingertips. He had not slept well, and his head ached as if he had consumed far too much Jagermeister. Perhaps cold water would help. He was just rising when the phone rang. "Walter here." He listened for less than a minute. "Twenty-five million?" He listened further. Finally, "Thank you." Walter rose quickly and began pacing around his desk. He stopped momentarily, opened his top drawer and located a bottle of aspirin. He poured two in his hand, swallowed them without water then grabbed his phone and began punching in numbers to a secure phone of his intelligence counterpart in Moscow. The official stance of the Russian government was that no arms deals were taking place anywhere in the large country, but Walter's contacts were pragmatic men who worked diligently to insure no Soviet era bomb ever left the motherland. "This is Walter, the transfer has happened, and it's large."

"To our friend's account?" The English was perfect, but the voice had a distinct Russian accent.

"Yes, there in Moscow."

"Can I reach you on this number this afternoon?"

"I'll be standing by, but if you miss me, you can reach me on my mobile."

"I prefer the office; I'll try it first." The Russian intelligence officer replaced his phone and motioned for a subordinate to enter his office. "Call our contact at the bank. I believe a large deposit has just been received. I'd like to know who owns that account. I also want to know if any of it is transferred, and to whom."

"Yes sir."

"And tell them to keep it quiet, understand?"

"Yes sir."

Major Ruslan Mikailo Ondreevich, Russian Intelligence, walked out into the hallway and turned left for the coffee shop. It would be a long day; now he could only wait. The information he was pursuing was alarming, even if from a trusted colleague in America. There were some interests they shared in common, and the purchase of a nuclear weapon by terrorists was at the top of that list.

Chapter: 35

Madison, Wisconsin, June 12, 2018

Hamad Al-Falani sat in his cluttered office and watched the two detectives leaving his office. They had questioned him for over an hour about the possibility of drugs within his organization. Then they had discussed the deaths of Lonnie and Pierre. They had even shown him the pictures of the bloody bodies. Seldom in his life had Hamad been nervous, but today he could feel his nerves tightening within his body. He stared at the cold cup of coffee and finally rose and poured it into his waste can. Perhaps he had just consumed too much caffeine today. Perhaps. He was normally a man of clear thought and fast action, but today his mind was perplexed. He considered his situation for the tenth time this morning. Men he knew and worked with very closely were being killed. Lonnie and Pierre were both dead. The police felt they had been involved in drugs and perhaps even distribution. Hamad forced his mind with a disciplined will. Think! Reason! Would Pierre have been involved in drugs? That seemed unlikely to Hamad. He pulled a pad from his desk and reached for his pen. At the top he wrote Pierre's name. Suddenly his eyes narrowed. Slowly he wrote another name, Lonnie, above Pierre's. Maybe Lonnie didn't jump after all. What did the two have in common? Were they both involved in a drug ring? He considered that for a few moments. Lonnie? Possibly. Pierre? No. That just didn't seem possible; Pierre didn't use drugs. He was too smart for that. Hamad continued to look at the sheet, his ordered mind seeking

250

some kind of connection. Suddenly his eyes opened wide. As he focused on Lonnie, the connection became clear. Lonnie killed the girl in Chicago. Pierre hired Lonnie. Could that be it? Suddenly Hamad opened his bottom desk drawer and searched through the stack of paper there. He found what he was looking for on the bottom of the pile. It was Pierre's last email. He scanned it carefully for the third time. Strangely, Pierre had mistakenly sent it to himself. "Lonnie may well have leaked everything; they're really pissed; I'm worried. We need to talk." Perhaps it wasn't drugs like the police thought. Perhaps it was something else—the girl's death. But who? Who was pissed? Hamad wrote the word "police" on the pad and looked at it for several minutes. Finally he scratched it out. No, it wasn't the police. It wasn't their style; they wouldn't kill suspects. The rules wouldn't permit it, and they didn't have the balls to do it. Then who? Finally he reread the last sentence one more time. Who was "they"? Obviously Pierre knew "them." That eliminated a lot of alternatives. Slowly he scribbled CFT across the page and circled it. It had to be someone inside the organization. But how would they have known about the girl's murder? If they had, indeed, discovered the plot to kill the girl, they were the ones who had the most to lose if the word got out. And "they" might have been very upset at the decision to take such an action. Collingsworth? He was just dumb enough to think he could have captured the press without his brainchild. Could he be behind the killings? Perhaps he had hired it done. But no, Collingsworth could never order a killing; he was simply too weak for that decision.

Hamad tore the top sheet from his pad and began scribbling names on the next sheet. He wrote quickly, fighting the pen with anger and frustration. Who knew about the plan beside him? Lonnie, Pierre, Hamad, Sylvia, Anthony. Slowly he drew an X through the first two names. Besides himself there were two others remaining who knew about the girl's murder, two others who could implicate him in the killing. Though Sylvia never knew of the plot for sure, he guessed that she had figured it out after the events in Chicago. She had left the organization and had not returned since. Anthony Rice, the CNN TV photographer, had been escorted near the scene of the killing in order to get the news pictures they needed. He had not been aware of what was to transpire, but he may well have put the puzzle together. It was so convenient that he was there, ten yards from the dying girl. What dramatic film he had shot. It had appeared on most every TV in the free world that night. Could he have put it all together? Pierre had been rather obvious in keeping him in that location before the shooting, and Anthony was no dummy. Certainly he must know that the police were not involved. They were nowhere near the girl. Hamad drew two circles around the other two names: Sylvia and Anthony. They were the only keys that could link him to the murder. Hamad rose slowly and walked out into the office area. He poured another cup of coffee on his way to the receptionist's desk. As she talked on the phone he reached over the counter and picked up her addresses book. He smiled at her and motioned that he would return it soon. In his office he scanned the pages and quickly copied addresses and phone numbers beside the names he had just circled on his pad.

Hamad was a man of decision and action, and it was time for action. Tearing the pages from his pad, he folded them and stuffed them into his jacket pocket. Closing his office behind him, he dropped the address book on the desk in front of the young woman on the phone and walked out the door. He felt better; he had a plan to implement.

Chapter 36

Cairo, Egypt, June 21, 2018

The bright Egyptian sun sparkled from the large pool and warmed the sunbathers enjoying the afternoon. It was easy to distinguish the visitors with their pale skin from the dark complexion of the locals. But there were more of the pale visitors at the Mena House. This was a very expensive hotel. It was known to be an exceptional resort and drew travelers from around the world. Two young men made their way through the crowded pool area; they were obviously searching for someone. A waiter dressed in a well-tailored uniform approached the two, nodded, then led them to the far end of the patio. There, in the shadow of a large green umbrella sat Prince Fakhir. As the two approached, one of the young men stopped, scanned the terrace and then took a position south of the table, opposite the older man's guard. The two security men smiled at each other and nodded. They were cousins.

"My father." Hajid embraced his father then sat beside him so they might talk.

"Would you care for coffee?"

"Thank you, no. But an iced tea would be nice."

Fakhir raised his right hand slightly and a waiter approached immediately. Hajid was surprised; he had not seen him standing aside in the shadows of the patio. After they had ordered and the waiter left, the old man leaned forward and spoke quietly to his son. "Hajid, my son, I am very worried about Ammar. Are you aware of where he might be?"

"No, father. I have not seen him in several days. I thought he would be here with us in Cairo."

"As did I." The old man sat back and stroked his goatee thoughtfully, seeking the correct words to share with his youngest son. "I fear Ammar has become involved with friends who exercise poor judgment." Hajid looked at this father with surprise but said nothing. He simply leaned closer to his father. "There are those among us who take extreme positions and urge even more drastic actions. Their religious zeal overcomes rational thought." The old man leaned back and watched the waiter as he approached with coffee and iced tea. The waiter quickly placed them on the table and unwrapped a small plate of sliced lemons then left. Hajid watched his father carefully; when he failed to continue, Hajid spoke, haltingly.

"Father, Ammar has strong feelings to be sure, but he is far too intelligent to be led astray by impetuous men."

"Let us hope so." Fakhir was silent again. When Hajid failed to respond he continued. "I still worry, so I want you to do something for me. Find him, and tell him to come to me. I need to talk to him."

"Why are you so worried, father?"

The old man leaned closer to his son and spoke confidentially. "I have asked one of my senior men to check into concerns I have had. He reports alliances with men I disapprove of."

"Couldn't he find Ammar?"

"Yes, and he will help you locate him as well. But he cannot speak for me. You, however, are my son; surely Ammar will listen to his own brother."

"Then I will go to him as you ask."

The old man smiled and reached across the table to pat his son's hand. "I can always depend on you, Hajid. You have always given me great pride."

The young man smiled at his father and took a long sip of the bitter tea. He had forgotten to add the lemon and sugar.

Chapter 37

Evergreen, Colorado, July 3, 2018

John and David drank beer as they sorted through pages of information. They were in John's study, and paper was stacked around the stately desk in unkempt stacks. It was a beautiful room with large windows facing south and west. The views of the mountain ranges were breathtaking; still, the room had the feeling of emptiness. The entire house shared the mood. It was a house without heart; it was the dwelling place of one man; it was not a home, merely a structure. The mountains stretching off to the west were majestic, but they provided no warmth to the empty house.

John was enjoying the chatter of the younger man. It had been a long time since he had shared this room with anyone. Somehow it brought him comfort to work here with all the lights on and another soul working beside him. He half listened to David's mumblings, the rest of his attention divided equally between the information he was studying and the TV that was behind him.

David, seated on the floor, looked up from a tall stack of paper and grinned. "Damn, this Hamad is an ugly dude." He held up a photo for John's inspection.

John nodded with a smile and stopped as he was beginning to speak. He jerked his head around instantly to the TV. David's gaze followed his. The news announcer was discussing the death of Anthony Rice, a photographer for the news service that supplied his station with international news. As he eulogized the dead photographer and explained his sudden murder, famous footage he had filmed was featured. The last was a scene from Chicago showing a young man standing in shock holding the body of a beautiful young woman. It only lasted a moment on the screen, but it burned its image into the souls of both men. John turned suddenly and looked at the pale face of the young man staring blankly at the screen. The wave of sadness flowed over David like a wave crashing in from the sea. John watched his eyes grow dull, his shoulders slump. Finally David leaned back against the wall, staring at the floor. For a brief moment John's eyes dropped to the floor as well. Suddenly he jerked his head up and glanced back at the TV. The news anchor was introducing the weatherman when John switched the machine off. "David, did you look at that picture?"

"Yes." It was a small voice from far away.

John rose, excited. "Did you notice anything unusual about it?"

"No." David raised his eyes to the older man.

"David, think! When Marcia was shot what did you do?"

"I don't remember; I was numb."

"Think David. Did you lay her on the ground?"

"Sure."

"Did you do that immediately?"

"Yes."

"Are you sure?"

"Yes, I saw she was hurt, so I laid her down and began to shout for help."

"How long did you stand and hold her, David. This is important."

"Not long."

"Less than a minute."

"Probably less than thirty seconds. It just seemed natural to lay her down."

"Did you see that footage on the TV."

"Yes." It was the small voice again.

"David, he was there. Don't you see? He was right there. He was within fifteen or twenty feet of the shooting."

"Do you think he was part of the conspiracy?"

"Maybe he was directed to be there to get the film. Why else would he be in the back of the demonstration?" John began pacing the room as he thought. "He may very well have been a part of the plan, knowingly or otherwise."

"Yes. What would a news photographer be doing in the back of the demonstration? Most of them were in the front where the demonstrators were confronting the police. We were late; we were way the hell in back."

"He was just murdered. It's possible that his murder could be linked to Marcia's death." John was thinking out loud. "David, who else was there with you?"

"Just a bunch of CFT folks."

"You keep saying you were late for the demonstration. Tell me again; why was that?"

"Marcia got a note from one of the CFT secretaries that someone wanted to talk to her about being on TV. We went to the CFT office and were then told that we should go on to the demonstrations with a group from the office. She was to get in touch with their communications people later." David's head sank into his two hands as his mind slowly assembled the puzzle into his consciousness. "The bastards!"

"David, look at me." John waited until the young man's eyes met his own. "I think there is a good possibility that Anthony Rice was killed to prevent him from talking. I think the emails are working."

"Hamad?"

"Hamad. Who else."

"Why?"

"Look at the facts from Hamad's point of view, David. Lonnie and Pierre are both dead. What did they have in common? Drugs? He knew both of those men. Maybe not. "

"Marcia."

257

"Right. And my guess is that Hamad still doesn't know who is killing off his accomplices. If I were he, I would assume that it would have to be someone who knows what they did, someone with a motive. Now who could that be?

"The police? No, that wouldn't make sense." The young man frowned as his mind unfolded the mystery before him. Suddenly he looked up with shock and discovery. "Someone inside CFT? Who else would know they were involved."

"Right! We know that originally Collingsworth didn't know about their plan. Now what do you think his reaction would be if he later discovered what they had done?"

"He'd be pissed."

"I think he'd also be frightened out of his mind. If the word ever got out, his entire empire would crumble in ten seconds."

"So Hamad figures someone in the organization is getting rid of the evidence."

"Could be. So he's trying to cover his own tracks first." John stood and started pacing back and forth.

"So now there's no one left to implicate him in the murder." David thought for a moment. "Dad, do you think he might consider someone else—like us? Someone who loved Marcia?"

"No, I don't think so. There's little chance someone like us would know the truth about Marcia's death, and even less chance we'd kill his associates. No, I'm guessing his focus is in CFT. He's worried that Lonnie might have actually left a note. That is the only way the killing would be known. So if that is the case, it would be natural to suspect someone in CFT, not the police. This isn't their mode of operation."

"Right." John nodded thoughtfully. Suddenly his eyes widened. "Wait. There is one other person who might know what they did, Silvia. Remember, she was the secretary who did the research on Marcia. Pierre told us about her."

"You're right." David looked into John's eyes, searching. "What do we do about her?"

258

"Nothing. She had nothing to do with Marcia's death." John walked to the window and looked into the distance. Finally he continued. "My only concern is her safety. We have to be very careful. Thus far no one knows about our role in all this, and we run that risk if we contact her or if we alert the police she might be in danger. Let me think this over. I'll get her contact information. If I'm right, she may also be a target on Hamad's list."

"What you're saying is that we are the only protection she has right now."

"That's about it."

Chapter 38

Madison, Wisconsin, July 5, 2018

David nudged the man sleeping in the cramped seat next to him. "Dad, wake up, someone's approaching the house."

John woke with a start and reached for the infrared glasses. It was after midnight, but he could clearly see the outline of a man circling the small bungalow, obviously checking the small house. "Well, well. Seems our long hours of waiting are over."

"What's he doing?"

"Seems to be casing Sylvia's house. He just went around to the back of the house. Let's take this guy. I want to talk to him." John handed David the glasses.

"We could sneak up behind the hedge on the left side of the yard. I think we could get to within ten yards of him."

"He's certainly not expecting us. Let's give it a try." John pulled his pistol from beneath his seat and quickly screwed the silencer into place. He checked the ammo clip and slammed it back into place. "Just in case he's armed."

"I expect he will be."

"So do I." John slipped the weapon into his belt.

"Sure hope this isn't just some local burglar. If it is, he's about to get a real wake up call." David smiled as the two men climbed quietly from the dark rental car.

"Remember, Sylvia's bedroom is on the right rear of the house. We need to get him before he gets inside."

"Right."

Dressed in black, the two men walked quickly up the road, crossed to the tall hedge in the neighbor's yard and moved across the yard toward the house. John led with David following. Both men were moving quickly, but quietly behind the large hedge. John signaled David to hold his position and then crossed quickly to the side of the house. From there he walked to the corner, knelt down, and quickly peeked around the back of the yard. The intruder was nowhere in sight. John motioned David to follow and check the front of the house. John then looked around the corner again. Nothing. He saw a small porch halfway down the rear of the house. From there he could follow the intruder and ensure that he did not try to enter the bedroom where Sylvia lay asleep. John slipped around the corner and walked quickly to the porch. He crouched quietly behind it and quickly peeked toward the sleeping area of the house. A sound behind him startled John. A door opened slightly from the garage area behind him. The man was exiting, then he saw John's outline and dashed suddenly across the yard. John sprang to his feet and started after the fleeing figure. He heard David's voice call out. "Dad?" Then came the impact and sounds of two men scuffling. John rounded the corner in time to see David getting up off the ground cursing.

"David, you all right?"

"Watch out, he's got a gun."

John followed the man to the front of the house. As John crossed the driveway, a shot rang out. He ducked quickly behind a large Pinion pine and looked for the shooter. Behind him lights in the house flashed on. Off to the right side of the house he saw a figure dodging from shrub to shrub in the light of the bedroom windows. He recognized David sneaking behind the man who was hiding somewhere near the front gate. The assassin obviously did not know there were two after him. John rose, ran toward the front of the yard and dived into a mixture of flowers planted beside the driveway. Another shot rang out, followed closely by the sounds of two men struggling. John jumped to his feet and raced forward, his pistol ready in his hand. In seconds, he was helping David subdue the shooter. One crack from the butt of his pistol ended the struggle. John looked up as the lights in the house began to wink in the darkness. From the bedroom, Sylvia was obviously moving toward the kitchen. John was hastily tying the man's hands when he looked up to see one more light go on — the garage. He jumped to his feet and began to run toward the house when the garage door sprang open. As the ignition of the car echoed through the night, John stopped and watched helplessly as the entire garage exploded into a giant ball of flame. He watched momentarily then turned, ran back, and kicked the man on the ground. "Help me get him into the car. Put him in the trunk, quickly, we've got to get out of here."

A little over a block away John spotted a car parked beside the road. He clicked the key fob he had taken from the killer and the lights flashed on the car. "David, quick, get in that car and follow me." He tossed David the keys.

"What about him?"

"Not much he can do tied in the trunk. But stay behind me just in case. Use your cell phone if you see anything amiss. But I think he'll be out for a while yet."

The two cars drove for twenty minutes before stopping on a deserted road in a warehouse area. John opened the trunk of the killer's car. It was filled with explosives. "Look at this. We're definitely dealing with a pro."

"Wow, there's enough explosives in there to blow up half the city."

"Let's get him out. I want to talk to him." David unlocked the trunk of their rental car and pulled the man out onto the road. John jerked him up to a standing position and hit him in the face. The killer went down but was lifted again. "Okay, who sent you to kill that woman?"

"I don't know what you're talking about." John hit him again, in the stomach this time. The man groaned and fell again to the ground.

"Her name was Sylvia, and you just killed her for money. You son-of-a-bitch." John knelt beside the man. "Now, we may as well get one thing straight. You're going to talk, or I'm going to cut your tongue out. Do you understand?" The man groaned loudly but did not answer. "Now, I'll ask you again. Who sent you?" The man looked at him in silence without uttering a word. John smashed him in the face with the pistol. Blood gushed from his nose and the gash across his cheek. "One more chance. Who sent you?"

"Screw you."

"Okay, I've had enough. Bring him back to his car." The two men tied the killer even tighter, then locked him inside his own car. "Think he can move?"

"Not a chance."

"Good. Get in our car and turn it around. Wait for me half block down the street." David looked at this father for a moment then nodded and did as he was told.

John opened the trunk of the killer's car and pulled several blasting caps from among the items there. He held them before the bleeding man tied in the back seat. "Ever wonder what it feels like to be blown to pieces, like poor Sylvia tonight? Well you're going to find out, right here tonight."

"You can't do that. You've got to take me in."

John looked at the bomber, a slight smile on his face. "You idiot. Do you think I'm with the police?" John rolled up the windows of the car. "You wish I were a policeman. But I'm not."

"Who are you?"

"A friend of Sylvia's, one who failed her tonight."

"Hey, look, I'll tell you what you want to know." The man was breathing very hard and spitting blood intermittently.

"Who sent you?"

"I don't know. Really I don't. I just follow the orders on the phone."

"How do you get paid?"

"Money comes in an envelope. Shows up on my door."

"How much did you get paid for killing Sylvia?"

"Fifty."

"Fifty thousand for a life?" The man said nothing. "You have a cell phone?"

"Yeah, in my coat pocket." The killer was watching John carefully. He was obviously frightened.

John pulled the man's coat from the front seat and retrieved the phone. He looked at it for a moment then dialed Tony Valanetti's number. When a voice answered on the other end John just held the phone without speaking until the other voice hung up. Then he dialed the number he had gotten from Boone's wallet. Into it he whispered. "The job's done; send the money." David pulled the black rental car down the block and stood waiting.

John wiped the phone carefully then tossed it into the ditch beside the car. The bound man was shouting at him through the closed door. "I deserve my day in court. It's my right to have a trial."

John opened the door of the car and placed the pistol to the man's head. He ceased shouting immediately. John spoke very slowly, very deliberately into the man's face. "Scum like you disgust me. You're an insult to the idea of humanity." He shoved the killer onto his side and took his driver's license from his wallet. He studied it briefly. "Okay Fred, you'll get your trial. I'm the judge; you're guilty; I sentence you to death by explosion." He lit the fuse on the blasting caps, slammed the door of the car, tossed the blasting caps into the trunk, and sprinted down the road to the waiting car.

Chapter 39

Groznyy, Chechnya, July 11, 2018

Russian troops and supplies were abundant in Chechnya. In the last few years no one even stopped to notice the large brown trucks or even the angry looking tanks as they rumbled through the dusty towns. The stark reality of war had become commonplace.

Simkov had sent two of his men to reconnoiter the area. They needed a place that was relatively deserted, one that could be defended by a small contingent of troops, and most importantly, a place where one could easily see approaching danger while remaining relatively invisible to prying eyes. They had found the perfect site—a deserted hospital two kilometers from the town. There were small homes in the area, but most were rubble from Russian artillery. Few, if any, would be occupied.

The major returned with the men to check the location himself. He trusted his men, but he was their leader, and it was expected that he would confirm their choice. He also had other concerns. This was Chechnya. The local rebels had no compunction about killing Russians—even if they were delivering weapons to the rebels' friends. The major was a graduate of the finest military schools in Russia; he was also a practical man. General Turgenov had already introduced him to the local Russian commander, Colonel Pavel Matveevich Bazarov. Bazarov had been given clear instructions from the general; Major Simkov was on a special mission for the Army. It was top secret, and he was to be afforded that respect. Should the major request anything, it was to be given immediate priority. Like all good military men the world over, Turgenov and Simkov had devised a backup plan. Should the mission go awry, Simkov would simply call Bazarov and request backup in rescuing a "stolen bomb" they were tracking.

Simkov surveyed the deserted building. Most windows were broken and one entire wing was rubble. Fortunately, however, the operating room was intact and had no windows for prying eyes. The hallways could be cleared of litter and broken glass and would offer easy access for the bomb to be carted inside. There was also a loading dock to accommodate the truck and the unloading process. Best of all, Simkov noted that access to the building was across an empty field. No one could approach without being seen during the day. Night vision gear was available for the evening. He quickly analyzed his situation. He had one major problem. Ten troops and Vasiliy Petrovich would be stretched very thin to provide constant guard duty. He worried about the civilian, but Vasiliy had once been a soldier and had proper training. He would bear watching, but the arms dealer could stand guard duty too. He certainly had financial incentives to ensure the transfer went smoothly. Simkov found his sergeant. "We will need constant surveillance of all points of entry for two or possibly three days. We have ten soldiers and the civilian dealer. What are your suggestions?"

"The west wing was apparently destroyed by our artillery. It would be possible for one man or a small group to approach undetected from that direction. One man would therefore be required to stand guard in what remains of the western structure."

"I agree."

"One more man can survey all other directions from the top of the roof."

"I agree, but put two men there. That is a lot of terrain to monitor for one man. Plus," the major smiled, "it will help keep them awake if they have someone to talk to."

266

"Very good sir." Sergeant Orlov stopped and thought for a moment. "I'll put Filya with the civilian. He's our best man, and I'll also post a man in the eastern side of the structure to keep an eye on the buildings across the field. They would make an excellent hiding place for enemies."

"Good idea. That makes four guards posted and one to roam around. Ten men will require 12 hour shifts to cover guard duty." Simkov tested the wind with his nose and his eyes. "We'll store the bomb in the operating room. It offers the best protection and has no windows." The young sergeant nodded his confirmation. "I think we should move in before dark. I'd like someone on that roof as soon as we can get him there."

"Yes sir."

* * *

The first day at the hospital compound passed quickly. The soldiers backed the truck to the loading dock and moved the rebuilt wooden crate into the dusty operating room. Guard shifts were posted, and the entire team surveyed the compound. Then the major called his men together to brief them on their plan. They would be in place for an undisclosed time until contacted by the "agents" to make the exchange. Another truck would be driven to the hospital by the "agents." The crate would be loaded on that truck, then the troops would board their own truck and escort the second ten kilometers outside of town. At that point the deal was considered complete. From there the buyers were on their own. Guard shifts were to be standard. Each soldier would be diligent; if anyone became sleepy, he was to request replacement. The mission was too important to allow mistakes. Finally, two large boxes of food and a small stove were set up inside the room adjacent to the operating area. Twenty minutes later the smell of coffee permeated the evening air. *Now*, Simkov thought, *now we wait. I hope this doesn't take too long. I also wish I had three more troops.* He considered contacting Bazarov but decided not to invite questions from Bazarov's men. Only in an emergency would he call for their support.

The morning of the third day of waiting witnessed the promise of some respite to the heat and the boredom. A bicyclist stopped before what remained of the main gate of the hospital. The man carefully leaned his bike against a post, dusted his worn coat, and began to trudge up the small hill toward the wrecked building. He may or may not have been aware that a Russian rifle was aimed at the center of his chest. He walked forward with purpose, unafraid. When he was thirty meters from the front entrance, he stopped, reached into his right coat pocket and produced a red piece of cloth a little larger than a handkerchief. Holding it carefully in view, he resumed his trek to the front door. Major Simkov was there to meet him. The major was unarmed, but the sergeant beside him had an automatic weapon casually pointed at the ground. The man noted that the sergeant's finger was firmly on the trigger—just in case.

"Welcome to Chechnya, Major." Simkov grunted and nodded briefly as his blue eyes bore into the dark headed man with the well-trimmed beard. Simkov had watched him approach through his binoculars. He assumed the man to be between thirty-five and forty. He walked vigorously; he had never been wounded or injured severely. He also had few wrinkles around his eyes. Perhaps he was even younger. One of the soldiers stepped forward and motioned for the man to raise his arms to be frisked. It took only seconds and produced one large knife. The soldier walked five meters down the path and placed the knife there before returning.

Simkov watched the man carefully. "You can retrieve your knife after our meeting." The man smiled. "Come in and have some coffee."

The men drank their coffee in silence, Simkov watching his "visitor" carefully while the man glanced quickly around, obviously reconnoitering the premises and perhaps even searching for the bomb. Finally Simkov broke the silence. "When will the exchange be made?"

"You have the bomb?"

"Of course. That was our agreement."

"What about the enabling codes?"

Simkov regarded the man with new appreciation. Obviously they knew more than he had expected. "The codes are not here, but they are nearby. I will deliver both when the money is transferred. The major pulled a cell phone from his coat and held it up. "All I need is confirmation."

"May I see the bomb?"

Simkov nodded to the sergeant who rose and motioned for the man to follow. In three minutes they returned. Simkov could see the excitement on the man's face. "When will the exchange take place?"

"Thursday, July 26th."

"I had hoped it would be sooner." Concern was on Simkov's face and in his voice as well.

"We have transportation arrangements to make. It has been decided that a plane would be a safer way to move the bomb from this area. That takes time to arrange."

"Why don't we go ahead and made the transfer now. You can move it later."

"The bomb is far safer here with you while we wait for the plane. But if you wish, I can send a few more men to assist you."

"That will not be necessary; my men can secure this area for two more weeks." The Russian thought for a moment then added. "However, you could keep us informed of any threats you discover in the area."

"Don't worry Major, if we find any threats in the area, we will take care of them ourselves."

"Then we will see you again on the 26th."

"Yes, the 26th." The man thought for a moment. "You will escort us out of the town?"

"Yes. Three Russian regiments are in this area, but I have constant contact with them." He held the phone up. He wanted to ensure that no surprise Chechnyan attack would be considered. "We'll escort you out of town, beyond our troop positions, then you're on your own."

"Will we go north?" The man's dark eyes flashed in the shadows.

"I will decide the direction. I'll tell you as we leave town."

The man smiled. "Good plan. I will leave now, but I'll return early on the 26th. We'll be in a tan truck."

"We?"

"Of course. There will be three of us here. Only three. We will meet others after you escort us out of town."

"Stop just beyond the gate. One of my men will check the truck there. When he is through we'll motion you to approach."

"I understand." The man finished his coffee and stood to leave. "Till then."

Chapter 40

Beirut, Lebanon, July 11, 2018

Kahlid sat back in his comfortable chair and sipped the strong black coffee as he reflected on the fact that soon he would be sipping Cognac or Courvoisier. But today, however, he needed all of his wits. He was about to complete the largest arms deal of his career, twenty-five million US, and his share would be over five million. How easy, he thought. One simply needed rich terrorist friends and poor Russian generals to become extremely wealthy. He smiled in spite of the bitter brew. Vasiliy had come through. Kahlid had worried about his Russian contact. Hand grenades and AK-47s were one thing, but a nuclear bomb—that was a rare opportunity and a difficult arrangement to conclude. Yet, Vasiliy had come through; he had found the right contact. Even now the bomb was hidden somewhere in Chechnya, awaiting his agents. Kahlid considered his men; they were the best. They were carefully selected and thoroughly trained, men who could be trusted. They understood the importance of the mission, and unlike Kahlid, they were willing to die for the cause. He thought about that for a moment. What would lead a man to give his life for some cause? How could the zealots confuse reasonable men and lead them to such conclusions? It made no sense to him; perhaps they weren't so reasonable after all. Kahlid wondered what their target might be. Israel? London? The US? Perhaps even Moscow. Maybe they could smuggle it into Delhi and precipitate a war with Pakistan. Perhaps that might unite the various factions of Islam. Perhaps not. His cell phone lit up brightly and broke the silence of the moment. "Yes?"

"The exchange will be made on Thursday the 26th."

"Is everything ready?"

"As you ordered, but there has been a delay to secure a plane to fly the package out of the area. That will be far safer than dealing with local militias or the Russian Army. Both are unpredictable"

"I agree. Well done." He pressed the "end" button then began dialing a number memorized much earlier. "Ammar? It is ready. We leave for Paris on the 20th, then to our final destination three days later; be at the airport at eight o'clock on the 20th. You haven't changed your mind have you?" He smiled as he listened to the angry reply. "There were those who didn't think you would come. But I assured them that you would be there. It is important; after all, you did supply the money." Kahlid was still smiling as he placed the phone into his breast pocket. He pushed the coffee aside and rose, smiling as he walked to the powerful car waiting for his control, the car, like Ammar, controlled by his will. As he pulled out of the small street and into the busy traffic of mid-afternoon, a black Mercedes eased into traffic several cars behind him. Kahlid was smiling when he turned left into the better residential area of the tortured city. The men following him were not.

Chapter 41

Evergreen, Colorado, July 11, 2018

John stepped back in surprise as he opened the front door of his large home. The house was constructed of stone and stucco and had commanding views of several ranges of the Rocky Mountains. There in his doorway stood Walter, a long way from Europe. "Walter, what a surprise. Do come in."

"Are you alone?"

"Yes." Instinctively, John looked back over his shoulder. "What's up?"

"We need to talk."

"I've planned to have dinner with my son in thirty minutes. Should I cancel it?"

"I think that would be wise."

John ushered his friend into his study and picked up the phone. "David, something has come up. I need to cancel tonight." He listened to the phone a moment then answered. "I'll give you a call later." He sat in a large lounge chair opposite the one Walter had taken, but rose quickly. "Can I get you something to drink?"

"Do you have scotch?"

"Of course. I'll be right back." John returned in a few moments with two glasses in his hands. One was the color of scotch, the other the color of coke. "Now, what brings you here to Colorado?"

The agent sipped his drink and eyed his friend carefully. Finally he spoke. "Remember when you asked me to locate a

CFT staff member named Pierre and said you needed some time off?"

"Yes." John watched his guest without moving or even sipping his drink.

"When he turned up dead shortly thereafter, I became concerned. I wondered what was going on."

"Why didn't you just ask me?"

"I knew you'd tell me to mind my own business."

"I suppose you're right. I might have done that."

Walter placed his drink on the small table by his side and continued, leaning forward toward John. "Anyway, I decided to do some checking, just to make sure that my suspicions were correct. Seems they were." He stopped and took another drink of his scotch.

"Why did you feel the need to get involved?"

"I try to keep up with my friends. Anyway, I found out about the Bartlett girl's death, her relationship to your son, his disappearance from the university. It was easy to put the pieces together." Walter watched John's eyes carefully. "I suspected you were either onto something or making the biggest mistake in your life."

"And?"

"And I had one of my best analysts do a little checking around. Guess what he found?"

"I've no idea."

"Seems CFT was funded in large part from one account in a Swiss bank. That account was funded by an assortment of leftist organizations and from a bank in Saudi Arabia that just happened to belong to a very influential family there."

John was growing more uncomfortable and squinted at the CIA agent. "And?"

"Well, when we checked it seems that the money that backed old Collingsworth and the CFT is also linked to an account that I've been monitoring for several months. Whoever is doing this may also be involved in some kind of arms trafficking in Russia. Know anything about that?"

"No, arms sales was not my purpose."

"Well, when we tracked CFT's funding it turned up a lot more than we had expected. You have uncovered a den of vipers, my friend."

"Damn, that seems strange. CFT is a bunch intent on putting a thorn in the side of our government and especially our president, but they don't seem the types to buy weapons. Thus far they've hired out that kind of work."

Walter watched his friend's eyes narrow and his jaw clench. "John, I never officially asked you what kind of business you had with those guys. You said it was personal, and I can most likely guess what that entails. But I'm damn sure glad we checked. You know I trust you, but it would help me a great deal if I knew what you know."

John looked at the floor and spoke quietly. "You were right. It involved David's fiancée. They had her murdered in Chicago."

Walter also stared at the floor a long time before speaking. "I read the report of her death in the news. It was only after Pierre's death that I discovered her relationship to David. We were worried about you after that, but we had no idea they were responsible."

"They were. It was their way of getting TV coverage. Can you believe it, the bastards had her killed for five minutes of evening news."

"You're sure?"

"I'm sure."

Walter sat his drink on the floor and leaned toward his friend. "The bastards."

"David's also on their list." John watched his friend's eyes widen.

Walter picked his drink up again, leaned back into his chair and sighed. "I understand. If you are doing what I think; I would do the same." He said it without emotion. "Why didn't you ask for help?"

"It's personal. They stepped over a very important line."

275

"Do you need my help now?"

"No, but thanks." John relaxed a bit and sat back into his chair. "You've already helped a great deal."

"I need yours, however." As Walter spoke, John looked up quickly. There was a question on his face. Walter continued, "I need to know what that money was sent to Russia to buy."

"How much was involved."

"Not much. A hundred fifty thousand."

"That's a lot of money."

"That's peanuts in arms sales."

"Then why are you worried?"

"The guy behind this could get all the small arms you could ever want delivered to his front door by the Saudi army—no questions asked." Walter studied his friend's face. "Plus the account that the money came from had another thirty million—all newly deposited about three and a half months ago."

"Where did the one-fifty go?"

"To a small time gun runner in Moscow. He then took about one hundred thousand in cash, and that was spent somewhere."

"That's a lot of vodka."

"You bet."

"SAMs maybe?"

"Could be."

"Worse case?"

"Worse case? Down payment on a nuke." Walter paused, considering his words carefully. "I have some friends in Russian intelligence. They are cooperating and picked up something about a nuclear bomb in a conversation with someone in Lebanon."

John sat straight in his chair and eyed his friend. "That is ominous, indeed."

"John, you know CFT. I doubt they are involved in anything going on in Russia, but we need to be sure. I need your help on this."

"I have one more murderer to take care of."

"You'll have to wait. This issue takes precedence."

"How long do you think this might take?"

"Maybe a month; probably less."

"I need closure; can you give me a week?"

"No; we have to move now. We don't know their timetable, but it seems imminent."

John finished his drink. "Okay. I guess I can wait that long. But I will get the bastard—even if it takes me a lifetime."

"When all this is over, my friend, call me, and I'll help you."

"Thanks, but this is a job I can handle alone."

"I understand." Walter rose and started for the door. "I've got to run; I've a plane to catch." He looked straight into John's eyes. "Take care, and John, I meant what I said about helping. If you need me, just call." He stepped out the door but turned again to his friend. "How much longer are you going to be involved in this? How close to closure are you, really?"

"One more; maybe two; it's almost over." John looked into the eyes of his friend. "Walter, thanks for not trying to stop me."

"Stop you? Now that I know what's going on, I'd like to help." A small smile curved his tight lips. "But you really don't need it, do you?" John smiled back without speaking. "But I do need your complete concentration until we know what is going on in Russia. Think you could fly to DC for a few days? It would save us a lot of valuable time."

"I need to check in with my son, but I can fly out day after tomorrow."

"Great!" The two men shook hands and Walter slipped out the door and into the night. John walked back to the small bar in his den and made another drink. He had options to consider. First, however, he had to talk to David and advise him of the latest developments. It was important to get him to back off as soon as possible. It was also probable that the young man's reaction might well be much the same as his own. If necessary he would simply have to explain the reason; that should be enough. He had never told David about his "other" life. Perhaps it was time.

* * *

David watched the rental car pull from the curved drive and turn left down the mountain. He had never seen the man who stood on the stone porch and talked with his dad, but he recognized from their demeanor that they were friends. As the man turned to leave, John had put his hand on the man's shoulder as they walked to the car. David also realized that the conversation was serious; they had not smiled or laughed, even when the man was leaving. Both had stood silent in thought; both had stared into the evening, watching lights on distant mountains while listening to the other. Clearly the two friends were involved in a serious conversation, probably business.

David turned from the upstairs window and reflected on how little he knew about his own father. John was in some kind of business consulting, something to do with mergers. The large home, the cars, everything about John McClellan bespoke financial success. That had never impressed David; he had always taken it for granted. In the last few weeks, however, he had seen a side of his father that he had never recognized before. The businessman could damn well take care of things when necessary. David was both surprised and impressed. For the first time in his life he could envision his dad in combat, a young man just slightly older than David. He now also understood another chapter in his father's life. It must have been terrible what his father had endured as the woman he loved wasted away to the ravages of cancer. John must have felt so powerless, a difficult thing for a man like him. David walked across the spacious bedroom and looked into the large mirror on the wall. The room was dark, but the light from the hallway illuminated his face on the dark glass. Without thought he reached and touched his chin, then he looked into the eyes. Yes, he was his father's son. The McClellan genes were clearly evident. He stood taller and continued to gaze into the dark mirror. How long before he would surpass John in height. He was already close. Then a startling thought crossed his mind. Would he be the same man as his father; would he measure up to what he was finding his father to be? It had never been a consideration in his consciousness before. It was suddenly important that he do so; it was equally important that his father recognize it.

The front door closed and David heard John's footsteps across the tiled entryway. The young man walked quickly to the upstairs landing and proceeded down the stairs. As he turned into the study he saw his father standing before a large window, facing northwest. He was staring at the distant mountains in thought. "I heard a car leave."

John turned to his son and smiled. "Yes, it was an old friend. It was private business. I knew you'd understand my call. It was best that you not join us."

"Business?"

John thought a brief moment. "Yes, but nothing important. Are you ready for dinner?"

"You bet."

"How about barbecue? The sports bar down the road has great ribs."

"Sounds good to me."

*　*　*

As the waiter cleared the plates David turned to his dad. "I really miss school." He smiled. "Never thought I'd say that, but I do."

"I know. It won't be too much longer." John looked around, quickly checking the room. "Well, maybe a little longer than we planned, but soon."

"Could you be a little more specific, say a month or a year?" David was smiling.

279

"My friend who stopped by tonight needed a little help on a project. We'll finish our work with Hamad, but it may be delayed for a while, maybe a month or two." John folded his napkin and watched David's face for his reaction. He had decided not to confide in David regarding his work for the Agency. He had weighed the risks. David was young and might not value the Agency's work very highly. Divulging his status might also endanger his son. Both were risks he did not care to take. He was finally building a relationship with his son, and it was growing stronger each day. He would do nothing to risk that. John looked at the young man across the table. He was so young, but he also had such promise. David had handled himself well during their search for Marcia's killers, very well. John noted that David's reactions would have been his own at that age. David was also a quick learner. With a little training, he would be every bit as good an agent as John if he chose that life. All in good time; all in good time. And the same was true for his own revelation to his son. When this was over the two of them would take a trip, maybe to Australia, and they would talk, but for now the risks had to be managed carefully.

"Maybe I can do some research on Hamad in the meantime."

"Sure, that would be a good idea. Crank up your computer and see what you can find. In the meantime I promised my friend I'd fly up to Washington to help him with some planning. It may take a week. Are you okay here?"

"I'll be fine. I'll just do some research and maybe spend some time in the mountains."

"The condo's stocked with food; you know where the keys are."

"A little camping and fishing also sounds fun. Maybe I can locate some of my old buds."

John's face brightened. "That does sound fun. How about I join you as soon as I get back." John reached into his wallet and handed David some bills. "I suspect you may need this."

280

David placed his hand on his father's shoulder as the two men walked out into the brisk evening air. "No need for the money, but thanks, Dad. Remember, I still have Manny's contribution to my education." He smiled then added after a moment. "Thanks for everything, Dad." He didn't see the large smile on his father's face.

Chapter 42

Riyadh, Saudi Arabia, July 18, 2018

Hajid looked up as the black Mercedes pulled into the compound. Such a large car for such a small man. He knew his father's chief of security; he had always known his father's chief of security. Hamza was a middle-aged man when Hajid was still a small boy. Over the years Hamza had grown smaller, and wrinkles had covered his weathered face. Still, his mind was sharp and his will unbending. Though in his late sixties, he was a formidable man to cross. Even his name, Hamza, denoted a lion. Most importantly, his devotion to Fakhir and his family were unquestioned. Hajid released the rose from between his fingers and walked slowly from the garden to greet his guest.

"Welcome, old friend."

"Thank you, Excellency. How may I be of service?" The small man bowed slightly. He was dressed in a western suit, tailored exclusively in London.

"My father has spoken to you about my brother?"

"Yes, he has."

"Do you know Ammar's whereabouts?"

"We have tracked him to Beirut, he met with a friend there."

"A friend?"

"His friend, Kahlid."

"Oh yes, I recall him. He was Ammar's friend in school." Hajid studied the security man's face but found nothing there. "Is my father concerned about Ammar visiting an old friend?"

The weathered face remained blank for several moments. Hajid knew the shrewd mind was working tirelessly behind the expressionless eyes. "Your father is concerned about some of Kahlid's new friends."

"Women, drugs, or alcohol?" Hajid said it bluntly. He knew that would work best in the circumstances. He also wanted additional information. Just how much did this old man know?

There was another long pause before the director of security spoke. "Weapons."

"I see." Hajid rubbed his eyes to hide his face from his father's emissary. Finally he looked into the dark eyes before him. "Is my father aware?"

"Yes."

"I see." Hajid turned and looked into the late afternoon sky. "Are they bringing weapons into Beirut?"

"No."

"Saudi Arabia?" There was urgency in his voice.

"No."

Hajid turned back to the old man. "Then let's go to Beirut. I must speak with my older brother. When can we leave?"

"Some of my men leave tomorrow morning to prepare for a special assignment. We can leave after I give them their instructions." He watched Hajid carefully. "In the afternoon."

"Good, I shall meet you at the airport tomorrow at one o'clock. Please notify our pilot. Tell him when you wish to leave."

"Yes sir." The small man bowed and walked back to the car. The driver held the door as he climbed into the rear of the vehicle. Hajid watched as they pulled away, his young face dark with foreboding.

Chapter 43

Evergreen, Colorado, July 19, 2018

John climbed from the Explorer and wearily tugged his bags from the rear. It had been an exhausting trip. The work had been easy, the frustration with bureaucratic red tape immeasurable. Often during the endless series of meetings and preparations for more meetings he had seriously wondered how government managed to govern at all. John lugged the two bags and his computer case up the short stairs from the garage to the house, wishing David were there to open the door. It crossed his mind that David might not be home; young men have a way of escaping for more interesting things to do than wait for their fathers. He had noted that the house had been dark as he pulled up the drive. He hoped his son was out having fun, but he knew better. The pain of Marcia's loss was still too raw, too real. It would take months and perhaps years to heal those memories. Didn't he know? How long had it taken him?

John shoved the door with his foot and considered his son. They were making progress in their oft-strained relationship. In fact they were becoming friends. He was pleased that for the first time in many years he actually *liked* his son. Perhaps David felt the same. He had tried hard to please John recently; it was obvious he wanted his father's approval. Dumping his bags in the utility room, he walked into the kitchen and began sorting through a stack of mail. Then he saw the note on the refrigerator. He smiled; things didn't change much. He could remember David's first art, then later short notes on the refrigerator. A collection of refrigerator art would undoubtedly chronicle his son's growth into manhood. That had been, of course, Sybil's idea. Everyone would eventually find their notes there. Both of the men in her life visited that appliance often. John removed the magnet and focused on the note. As he read it his heart began to beat faster.

> Dad,
>
> I've found our man. He's in Atlanta for a few days to plan the next demonstration. There's a big liberal group meeting there next week. I'm leaving tonight to check things out (Tuesday – United 613). Couldn't pass up the opportunity. Hopefully I can locate him and get some helpful info. I'll be in the Embassy Suites by the airport. I'll give you a call Thursday morning.
>
> David.

John grabbed his phone and began scanning his messages. The last one was from David. "Hi Dad, your flight must be late. Anyway, I'm here in Atlanta. I'll check things out and give you an update in the morning. He's here."

John closed the iPhone and began rubbing his temples. "Shit! I should have told him. I should have told him before I left." He thought for several minutes then checked the Embassy Suites phone number. "Please connect me with your hotel in Atlanta, the one by the airport." He pressed the speaker button and stood staring out the window into the darkness. As he waited he walked into his study, picked up the phone on his desk, and began dialing the memorized number for United Airlines.

"Embassy Suites."

"Yes, may I speak to Mr. David McClellan please?"

"Standby."

John listened as the feedback simulated the ringing of a phone. After ten "rings" the operator interrupted. "I'm sorry,

285

Mr. McClellan is not in. Would you like to leave a message on his voicemail?"

"Yes please." John waited for the phone to cycle to the tone. "David, this is Dad. Stop all operations in Atlanta immediately; I repeat, stop all ops in Atlanta. I'll explain when I arrive tomorrow afternoon." He paused then added, "and call me on my cell to advise that you've received this call." He paused a moment wondering how to sign off. Somehow "I love you" just didn't seem appropriate, so he hung up without saying anything more. He pressed the desk phone to his ear. A voice was speaking.

"United 1-K desk; how may I help you?"

"This is John McClellan. I need a flight from Denver to Atlanta—tonight if possible."

Chapter 44

Atlanta, Georgia, July 19, 2018

David walked into the makeshift headquarters of CFT amid the crowd of students, union toughs, and environmentalists that filled the hotel lobby and hallways. They were an unkempt bunch. They were there to demonstrate, not look good, besides, if all worked as planned, many of them would be in jail before morning. They laughed, cursed, and sang in chorus with the blaring metallic music that echoed through the hallways. Inside various rooms throughout the hotel small groups of select demonstrators were being briefed on their task for the evening. One group was to set cars afire, another to break storefront windows and encourage the local looters. Another group was being briefed on what to say to the reporters—and which reporters were friendly to the cause. This last group was well groomed and clean cut—no metal in their ears, eyebrows, noses, or lips. They looked more like a group of young business professionals. They were being coached to seek out cameras. David walked through the building, scanning the crowd. He was looking for one man. If he were in town, Hamad would be in one of the executive suites; he would try there. If he could find him, John would be pleased. It would save them a lot of trouble and time later.

David stepped into the men's room on the lobby floor. He looked carefully at his face as he washed his hands. His goatee was growing in well. He had last seen these people as a redheaded union rep. Now his hair was dark, and he had a scraggly moustache and a neat goatee to disguise his face. He

287

felt a little nervous, but this was better than just sitting in his hotel room across the city. He was bored; at least this was something he could do to expedite their efforts. He would scout the area and try to locate Hamad. It had dawned on him that he did not know what Hamad looked like. John was working on that with his "friends." But maybe he would get lucky. As he stepped off of the elevator on the eleventh floor he was greeted by two men in suits. They were obviously security for someone important. The older of the two spoke first. "Can we help you?"

"No, just looking for some friends."

The older man appeared about fifty. He stepped closer to take a good look in the dim hallway. "You with the crowd downstairs?"

"Yeah. I'm here for the demonstration. One of the guys sent me up here to get briefed."

"I think they sent you to the wrong floor. What's your name?"

"James, James Morton."

"Well James, I'm Harold and I don't think you belong up here. Where you from?"

"California. I go to Berkley."

"I hear California is a beautiful state. You live there long?"

"All my life. I'm from San Francisco."

"That's a beautiful city." The older man reached into his pocket and withdrew his wallet and looked inside. "Say, would you happen to have change for a fiver?"

"I'll check." As David opened his wallet, the graying man noted the driver's license from Colorado. "No, afraid I don't."

"Tell you what, I know they have planned several briefings up here, but I'm not sure who will lead them." He looked at his cohort. "Gene, didn't they say the one in room 1104 would begin in about fifteen minutes?"

"I think so."

"Tell you what, since you are already here, why don't you go into 1104 and I'll check to see when the first briefing starts. It's going to be a busy night here." They led David into the room and left him alone while they ostensibly checked on the briefing. The older guard looked back at the door. "He may be a cop, but probably a reporter. Who knows, but we'll check him out. Mr. Al Falani is very nervous about strangers these days. He damn sure made that clear when he hired us. You watch the elevator while I ask this guy a few questions."

David sat by the door so when the two men walked in, he was closest to the door, and they were inside the room. Hamad studied the picture in the small notebook he held in his hands as he spoke to the young man before him. He was not sure who this might be. The picture of the two union reps who had escaped his friends was not very clear, but it was the only one that could be found among the footage that had been taken in Seattle. He assessed the size, tried to picture red hair, but it was too difficult. The picture was just too vague. Finally he spoke. "Hello, I'm William Morris, and I understand you're here for a briefing. And who might you be."

David looked right at the nametag on "William." It clearly said Hamad Al-Falani. He knew he was in trouble and made an instantaneous decision. He bolted for the door. As the two men watched him he grabbed the door and ran out slamming it shut behind him. He never saw the man behind the door or the pistol butt that crashed into the side of his head. He was out instantly.

Hamad studied the unconscious man for several minutes. "Get him out of here, and find out who he is."

"Shall we rough him up?"

"Just enough to find out who he is. Let me know when you do, then I'll decide what to do with him."

"How about the warehouse by the airport?"

"Good, but get him out the back. I don't want him seen in case he's a reporter or a security man. If he is, we'll have to decide how to handle that later." He watched as the younger bodyguard hoisted David's limp figure onto his shoulder. "Be careful getting him to the car. We don't want the cops on us now. Put a bottle in his coat pocket. Pretend he's drunk."

"Done."

"Use the back stairs. It's not so crowded." Hamad looked again at the picture in his notebook. "And check around for another unknown visitor about six feet tall with gray hair and a moustache that's dark."

The older guard fished through David's pockets. He took all of the money from his wallet and stuck it into his own pocket then pulled the hotel key card from his shirt pocket. "Well, well, what have we here? A hotel key from the Embassy Suites, not bad for a college student." He studied it for a few moments then called on his cell phone. "Bill, you and Bobby get up here."

Five minutes later two large young men with very broad shoulders swaggered into the hallway from the elevator. Harold studied the two. Bill, you help Jim with our drunk visitor." He smiled and nodded toward the unconscious figure on Jim's shoulder. "Bob, you and I will check his room."

* * *

It was after 6:00 pm and John was tired from the overnight flight, but his adrenalin kept him alert. It was the third time in thirty minutes that John had called David's room from the airport. The phone was still busy; that didn't make sense. Who would David be talking to this time of the evening? David knew that they had agreed not to make phone calls except to each other. Finally he called David's cell phone. A strange voice answered. "Yes? Who's calling?"

John's mind went into overdrive. He quickly answered. "Is this Pizza Hut? I want to order a Supreme pizza—with all the works." He paused a moment then added. "And a liter of coke. Can you deliver in half an hour?"

"Sorry, Buddy, you've got the wrong number."

"Thanks, sorry to disturb you." John looked at his cell phone; David had a preset number; there was little chance of a misdial. Something in his gut tightened. He quickly grabbed his bag from the conveyor belt and ordered a taxi. In the back seat of the cab he pulled the weapon from his bag, checked that it was loaded, and placed it, the silencer, and two clips of bullets into his coat pockets. "Embassy Suites please."

* * *

John stood outside the hotel door and listened to the noise of the two men talking in the back bedroom. He understood immediately what was going on. They were searching the room. He wondered if that meant they had his son; probably it did. A cold shaft of fear struck through his abdomen. John glanced down the hall; it was deserted. Quickly he reached for his pistol and attached the silencer. Lonnie may have been an idiot, but he did know good weapons. He checked the gun and then pushed the door open quickly. The front room was empty; the door to the back room was half shut. He moved silently to his left and stood next to the TV, hidden by the wall of the bathroom. Silently he waited and listened.

"What we looking for, anyway, Harold?"

"Anything. Names in a notebook, a weapon, addresses, even laundry marks. Anything that will help us determine who that bastard is. He damn sure ain't from California. Look at these clothes. Do these look like California to you?"

"Nope."

"Old Hamad is nervous as a wet hen about something. There might even be a bonus if we find the right things here."

"What if we do?"

"I'd not want to be in that young man's shoes if he's the one Hamad is after."

"Think they'll kill him?"

"If he's the one they're looking for they will."

291

"Let me know, I'll do it." Harold watched the young man swagger around the room and despised him.

"You'd piss in your pants if you ever killed a man."

"Oh yeah?"

"Shut up and keep looking."

"Not a damn thing. Guy must have been expecting this. Not even a prescription bottle."

"Check the front again. Try the kitchen; we didn't look there."

The younger security guard walked slowly into the front room. He was looking toward the small kitchen area and was totally surprised when John struck him in the face with a large glass ashtray. It stunned him; the second blow took him to his knees. John jumped over him and was standing in the rear room with his gun pointed at Harold before the man could speak. "Move. Into the kitchen. Now!" Bob was still on his knees, holding his bloody face when John and the older guard moved into the small room. "Okay, talk fast or you're a dead man. Where's my friend?"

"I don't know what you're talking about?"

"The one your friend here was saying he would kill." John raised the gun and pointed it at the older man's head. "I'm not a patient man. Where is he?"

For the first time in many years Harold was afraid. He recognized that there were just too many things that he did not understand. The job with the demonstrators was a good paying job; he couldn't turn down the money. But the man before him was too cold and the weapon in his hand had all the marks of a professional. He ventured a question. "Who are you?"

"Let's just say you don't want to ever get involved with my family. You idiots happen to have the son of a very, very pissed off Sicilian, if you get my drift. If he finds out you've mistreated him, he'll have your carcasses floating in the river by dawn. Capisch?"

Harold's face went white. "Shit man, we didn't know. We're just a couple of hired security guards. We didn't mean any harm."

"Where is he?" John pointed the gun at the young man who was still kneeling on the floor. "Now!"

"Wait. We don't want any part of this. He's being held in a warehouse by the airport. It's on the corner of Yosemite and Jackson Street."

John took the cell phone from his belt and keyed it. "Walter? Good, I need to take you up on that offer. I need some backup. Atlanta, warehouse at Yosemite and Jackson; they've got David. Make a call and get help quickly." He put the phone back on the clip and watched the two men before him.

The younger man started to speak very quickly. It was obvious he was frightened. "Look mister. We don't have nothing against you or the kid. We didn't know who he was. We just followed orders."

"Whose orders?"

"Mr. Al-Falani's."

"Hamad Al-Falani?"

"Right, that's him."

"Did you know why he needs protection?"

"No, sir."

"He's a dead man. He pissed off the don. That's not smart." He watched the blood flow from both of their pale faces. "Want to know how long you guys will survive if he wants you dead?"

Harold spoke slowly. "Look, we're not involved in whatever Al-Falani did. We're just security guards at the bank."

"Okay, I'm going to let you live. But I'd suggest you get the hell out of town as fast as you can tomorrow morning."

"Tomorrow morning?"

"Right. You are going to spend the night here, together. In case one of you decides to do something foolish—like calling the warehouse. If you do that, I'll have some of my friends make sure you never talk again. You understand?"

"Yes sir. We're not going to say anything to anyone, are we Harold?"

"Very carefully, take your driver's licenses out and toss them over. And don't move too fast." The two frightened men did as they were told. "Now, you." He motioned to Harold. "Tie the kid up—on his belly." John tore the phone from the wall and ripped the cord from the phone. "Use this—for starters. When that is finished, get the cord from the blinds and do it again." In twenty minutes the younger of the guards was hog-tied on the floor, and Harold was handcuffed to the door fixture in the bathroom. Finally he gagged them both. "Look. I'm going to call the hotel and have them come up and release you tomorrow morning. So, for now be really quiet and don't try to escape. If you do, we'll kill you. If I never hear from you again or see your pretty faces, you might just get out of this alive. Understand?" They both nodded. "And one last thing. You'd better be right about that warehouse address. If you aren't, there's no place you can hide from this kid's dad. You'll be dead in a week. The price on your heads will draw an army looking for you." He looked at Harold and checked his driver's license. "All right Harold. Yosemite and Jackson?" Harold nodded affirmatively. John walked to the door, looked outside quickly and then put the "do not disturb" sign on the door handle as he left.

* * *

John rented a car at the hotel and specifically asked for a dark Mustang. He was in a hurry so the ride to the warehouse was less than twenty minutes. Luckily most of the hotels used by the demonstrators were in close proximity to the hub of transportation. It was late, and the roads were not crowded with the normal Atlanta congestion. John located the warehouse and circled it twice. Few lights were on except the occasional floodlight to prevent unwanted visitors in the night. This was not a particularly safe part of town; theft in the College Park area was rampant. John pulled the car to a stop two blocks away from the building and walked quickly in the shadows to within half a block of the fenced building. In the distance he could hear the drone of jet engines as the commercial airliners waited their turn to depart from one of the busiest airports in the world. John watched carefully and walked slowly across the road and disappeared into the heavy growth beside the adjacent building. He was thankful that the local climate provided so much cover for his advance. He was also thankful that the local companies had not bothered to fight the encroaching shrubs and trees. He studied the fence and noticed that the gate was opened slightly. It was tempting, but it was also directly in front of the main windows of the large concrete structure. He turned south along the fence and soon found what he had been looking for—the west wall had no windows. The fence was tall but had no impediments like barbed wire atop the barrier. He crawled from the dense shrubbery and checked the fence for detection devices. There were none. The night security lights around the building were sufficient to check the ground behind the fence and then the walls of the old building. There were no cameras. In less than three minutes he was over the fence and sneaking to the back of the building to check it out. The back door comprised two large metal doors, padlocked. He was not concerned about the padlock. It was the sound of metal doors that bothered him most. He must gain entrance by stealth and surprise the men inside. He also knew he might have little time to wait. The thought of David inside at the mercy of Al-Falani's men caused a wave of rage to course through his body, but he fought to control that. He had to think logically. This was not the time to let anger cloud his mind. Above the rear door was a platform with stairs to the ground. They led to another single door for what he assumed to be offices. Quickly he checked the East side of the building. It had two loading docks and large metal doors that were controlled from within. The door on the second floor was tempting, but he wanted to see what was inside first. Opening a blind door could be dangerous. Quickly he walked back around the building and crawled into the shrubbery that led to the front door. There was one car parked in the otherwise deserted lot. That was good news; if Hamad's men were still around, chances of David being alive were better. The main floor appeared dark with the exception of one light in the rear of the building. That would be the storage warehouse, most likely where he would find David. John peeked quickly over the window frame and checked the first office. It was dark and deserted. So was the second. Lying flat on his stomach he eased his head around the wall to peer at the front door. It was closed; behind it was darkness with one light dimly shining in the distance. Suddenly he heard laughing from inside. He crawled to the door and carefully turned the handle. It opened. John peeked quickly through the top of the door that was a mixture of opaque glass and metal reinforcement. He could see nothing inside. Now he could hear voices shouting. They were the angry voices of violent men who were in control of their prey—his son. John made a quick decision. He slid his pistol from his belt, attached the silencer and rose beside the door. He waited until the men began shouting again, then he opened the door and slid inside. The hallway was over fifty feet long and dark. At the end were two doors that swung together in the center. They were green metal doors with the same opaque reinforced glass for the top half of the frame. Behind was the dim yellow light from the warehouse area. John walked quietly to the doors and slowly pushed one open a fraction of an inch. He could see David tied to a chair in the center of the room. His head was down; John could not ascertain if he were conscious or even if he were alive. One of the men grabbed David's hair and raised his face. One eye was already swollen shut; blood covered his face and the front of his shirt. John felt the weight of the pistol in his hand. It was time. As the man swung again at the tied victim, John slipped into the room and reached for the light switch. The man was just preparing to swing when the room was suddenly flooded with bright light. The two guards turned to see the pistol pointed at them, John crouching in a firing position. The man standing before David reached for his weapon, but the bullet from John's 9mm struck his right shoulder first. He screamed and fell to the floor. The other quickly stuck both arms into the air. "Don't shoot."

John stood steady in his shooting stance. "You, untie him." He nodded to David. "You okay, David?" As the tall blond young man moved behind David, John stepped quickly forward. "Don't do anything stupid. I could nail you from eighty yards."

The young man stuttered violently. "No, No, I, I just want, wanted to untie him."

On the floor the first assailant reached across his body with his left hand and retrieved his pistol. As he raised it, John fired one shot. It struck him in the middle of his face and splattered his head against the concrete floor. The second watched in shock and promptly vomited on the floor. "Untie him. Now!"

"Okay, okay. Just don't shoot."

When the ropes were untied, David fell forward onto his hands and knees. Very slowly he rose to his feet and began wiping the blood from his face. He turned to look at the frightened man standing behind him, then spun quickly with surprising strength and struck his tormentor in the face. The man fell to his knees, his hands on his face. David walked behind him and kicked him in the back as hard as he could. John spoke slowly to his son. "It's okay David. Let's get out of here." As he spoke, David stumbled to the chair where he had been tied and grabbed it. With all the strength left in his body he swung it, crashing the metal chair down on the kneeling adversary. The man went down and lay motionless, David falling beside him, exhausted. John crossed the room and lifted David. "Come on, we've got to get out of here." The two were slowly walking through the front door when the butt of a pistol slammed against John's head. Both he and David fell face forward into the grass beside the entrance to the building.

The three men surveyed the two men on the ground. Finally Hamad spoke. "I think this is the pair we've been looking for." He nodded inside the building. "Check inside." The shorter

297

man ran quickly through the doors and was back in less than a minute. "Jim's dead. Bill may be too. I'm not sure."

"Doesn't matter." He turned and started for a large black Lincoln parked just outside the gate. As he crawled inside he stuck his head from the door. "Shoot these two. Drag them inside and then torch the building." With that, he closed the door and the big car drove off into the night.

The fog in John's head was clearing slowly. He could hear incomprehensible voices, then slowly the words began to register. His eyes were still hazy, but sight was returning along with the sensation of intense pain on the right side of his head. He felt a body lying on his legs and looked to see David. One eye was opened as David fought for strength to rise. Then John saw the pistol pointed at his head; it was a Smith and Wesson .38. As he waited for the bullet, he felt the rage surging through his body. To lose to these men was almost more than he could bear. He opened his mouth to scream defiance at the shooter above him, but the words would not escape his throat. So this was how it would end. At least he had killed the others. That was some recompense. At least he had that much. He looked into the eyes of the young man with the pistol. The man was smiling, knowing he had won. Then suddenly, the smile vanished. In its place was a look of utter surprise. John blinked his eyes several times, slowly focusing on the face of his executioner. The young man's eyes were large as if in shock. Then the blood flowed down his cheek as he crumbled to the ground. Another silent round ripped through the left arm of the second man watching the execution. Another splattered in the concrete at his feet. Immediately the wounded man turned and ran toward their car which was also parked outside the warehouse gate. As he frantically climbed into the vehicle, another shot smashed the rear window. In seconds it accelerated away from the warehouse.

Slowly John pushed David from his body. He scrambled for his pistol. Finding it, he stood watching the fleeing enemy. He fired one shot but knew that his eyes were not yet clear. He heard the bullet ricochet off another warehouse wall down the street. He turned to see two men walking quickly toward him. "Walter called. I'm Wayne Simpson—based here in Atlanta. You guys alright?"

"They got away. They got away. Dammit!" John's hand dropped with the weapon beside his body. He stood there like a large defeated toy.

"Maybe not." Wayne reached into his pocket and extracted a small black box with a red button in the center. It was about the size of a cigarette pack and had a small coiled antenna extending from the top. John looked at the device for a moment then raised his head. He took it and nodded toward the car that had just disappeared over a small hill. The agent nodded affirmatively. John held the device into the air and pressed the button. The silence of the evening was rocked with an explosion that sent sheets of fire high into the air. The two men winced at the force of the bomb. As they watched the yellow flames climbing into the dark night, the sounds of metal parts falling to the ground echoed between the dark warehouses that lined the road.

"I'll be damned!" John smiled as large plumes of smoke climbed into the night sky. "But Hamad got away. Damn!"

"Right, just as planned."

"You wanted him to escape?" There was surprise in his voice.

"Right, but he won't get too far. There's a homing beacon attached under the fender of his limo, and if I'm right, he may just lead us to a bomb."

"Hamad was involved with the bomb?"

"Right. We intercepted a message he sent to the men we've been watching in Russia. He's working with the terrorist group that's buying the bomb."

As John turned from the burning car and knelt beside his son, the second agent walked to one of the bodies lying on the ground and tucked a small piece of paper into his jacket pocket. Then he reached into a small backpack lying nearby and extracted two large bags of white powder. He placed them beside the body after slicing one of them with his knife. John looked at him carefully. "Coke?"

"One is; this one is talcum powder."

"And the note?"

"Collingsworth's phone number and a notation about thirty thousand dollars due."

"That'll give the bastard something to sweat about for a while."

"Perhaps a long while." Wayne smiled at John who was helping David stand. "Especially after the authorities find a kilo of coke in his safe."

John spun around; there was a look of incredulity on his face. "Cocaine in his safe? What if he finds it first?"

"He won't. He doesn't know he has a safe behind the artwork on his wall, much less the combination."

"He doesn't?"

"No, it's new, an anonymous gift from Walter." He grinned, then walked over to help John get David on his feet. "Come on; we've got to get you guys out of here, but first we need to get rid of your pistol." John looked down at the pistol as if surprised to find it in his own hand. He handed it to the agent who studied the weapon carefully then wiped it and placed it in the dead man's hand and clasped his hand around the weapon and his finger on the trigger. "That's a nice silencer, professional work. But I happen to know two detectives have been looking for that gun. We've been helping them with the striations on the bullets. Let's help them find it. We may as well close that chapter, don't you think?" Suddenly he turned back to the body on the ground. "Oh, where is his original gun? We only want one with his prints." After a moment he located the .38 and placed it in his own pocket. "That should help those cops." He was smiling to himself.

John stood rubbing his head. The pain was still intense. "Look Wayne, I appreciate your help, but I'm not finished yet. I still have business with Hamad."

"No problem, we'll follow him wherever he's headed. Trust me. We will have another chance at our friend Hamad." He pulled a second detonator from his pocket that was carefully wrapped. Holding it with a handkerchief he tossed it aside in the street before the building.

"What are you doing?"

"Just leaving a little evidence with the correct fingerprints. Don't worry, they're not yours." He smiled at his friend. "Let's just say that I discovered who sent the shooter who tried to ruin your trip to Hawaii."

"You can do that? A fingerprint?"

"There's even a small hair caught on the antenna. Guess which barber shop we picked that up from." John was astonished. "Now, we've got to get out of here. Let's get your son to my vehicle; he looks in pretty bad shape." The three men carried David between them and helped him into a dark van parked just outside the fence. "Where are you parked?"

"Over there, a couple blocks up the street." John continued to unconsciously rub the side of his head.

"We'll drop you there, but I'll keep David with me. Do you know the Old Magnolia motel just north of West Paces Ferry off I-75? I think it's exit 33."

"I can find it."

"We're heading there. I'll have a "company" doctor on hand to check you both. David is going to need some stitches; you may too."

"Thanks, Wayne." John handed him the small black device from the first bomb. "That was nice."

"I thought that worked out very well myself. Now hop into the van and direct me to your car." He turned to the second agent. "Order a doctor ASAP." As he drove to John's car he dialed another number. "Walter, it's Wayne. We have them both; we'll talk more later."

John stepped out of the van and quickly climbed behind the wheel of the Mustang. He was exhausted, and his head was aching, but he knew he could drive. He had to.

* * *

The three men conferred quietly while David lay barely
conscious on the cheap motel bed. The doctor closed his bag
while watching the young man he had just checked. "He might
have internal bleeding, and I suspect a couple of ribs are cracked
or broken. We're going to need to get him to a hospital for a
few days."

Wayne snapped his cell phone closed and rejoined the
conversation. "How long do you think he'll need to be there?"

"Two days, maybe three if everything checks out okay."

"I'll get our nurse to stay with him." He grinned at John.
"She's a knockout; she's also a black belt in every hand-to-hand
combat known to man."

"I'll warn David. That's a dangerous combination." John
managed a small smile. "I'll be careful, too."

"No, you'll be with Walter. Our target just bought a one-
way ticket to Paris. Walter is already there."

"Paris?" John was surprised.

"Connecting to Groznyy, as in Chechnya."

"Of course. That makes sense. What a plan."

"If I were a Russian with a bomb, where would I want to
transfer control?"

"Chechnya!"

"Chechnya."

John looked at his son for several moments. "Let's go. I
want to finish this."

"You leave in two hours. Walter will meet you in Paris.
I'll have one of our guys take care of the Mustang, and I'll drop
you by your hotel room to pick up your things. I'll brief you on
what we know, and we can get anything else you need on the
way. Don't worry about your son; we'll take good care of him.
Oh yes, Walter also said to tell you not to disclose anything
about our trip. We won't even tell David. This is just too

302

important—we're talking about a nuclear bomb in the hands of maniacs."

"I understand. Let's get moving."

Chapter 45

Beirut, Lebanon, July 20, 2018

It was just after seven in the morning, and Ammar was sitting in the departure lounge for private aircraft at the Beirut International Airport when Hajid approached. He was followed closely by Hamza, the old security agent who had been a friend of his father for longer than he could remember. Ammar was surprised to see them; he had not told anyone of his plans to fly to Chechnya. Hajid walked over and sat on the white leather couch by his brother. Ammar sat up straight and looked at the two. "Hajid, what are you doing here?"

"I've been sent by father to fetch you back home. He needs to talk to you—now!"

"Now? Whatever does he need? Can it wait? I'm flying out today to Paris."

Hamza leaned forward and spoke very quietly. "Your flight plan is to Paris and then to Chechnya; perhaps the pilot made a mistake?"

"I'll have to confer with him. I'm going to Paris."

Hajid rose and stood with his hands on his hips. "You need to come with us. Father insists."

"I'm going to a party for a friend; it's his birthday."

The old man leaned in again and spoke with his typical quiet, but commanding, voice. "Kahlid's birthday was in February." He looked into Ammar's eyes and the look caused a chill to run down the young man's spine.

"But this is important."

"Your friends are not family, and your father requests your presence." Hamza's gaze penetrated Ammar's mind. "Our aircraft is waiting. Besides, your plane is not flying today. It needs maintenance."

"Why does it need maintenance right now?"

"Because I said it does." With that the old man took Ammar's bag and turned for the door to the parking ramp where the Prince's large jet stood waiting. Ammar looked around quickly; Kahlid was nowhere in sight. He stood staring at the floor for several moments, then followed Hajid to the family jet.

Chapter 46

Groznyy, Chechnya, July 26, 2018

There was a sense of excitement as the sun climbed over the horizon and shed light into the crumbling building. Atop the old hospital, two soldiers climbed onto the roof and replaced the two who were suddenly alert and voraciously hungry. The men inside were checking their weapons and loading the remaining food back into the large wooden boxes. There was expectancy in the air. In two days they would be back in Moscow, and they would be rich. Each would receive two hundred thousand US dollars, a fortune in Moscow.

Major Simkov walked slowly into the operating room and looked at the crate. There it sat, a weapon of death, in a room built to save lives. He unconsciously patted his breast pocket. He could feel the thick paper there—the other half of the bomb. But this half was the fraud; this half would ensure that the only casualties would be those men who practiced death and destruction. In this case, the destruction would be their own. Simkov smiled. What a laugh. If only he could watch as the cursed Arabs dialed in the code. How convenient that he would defraud the very evil that they fought even here in Chechnya. He smiled and walked out to check the guards and prepare contingency plans should anything go wrong.

Sergeant Orlov checked his men and noticed that young Nicolay was not eating his lunch. He seemed nervous, agitated. "Nicolay, you seem troubled."

"I have been thinking, Sergeant." Nicolay looked around as the major walked into the room with a cup of coffee in his hand. "I think we are making a great mistake." He then rose and looked directly at Simkov. "Sir, we can't do this. We can't give a nuclear bomb to these men. They're uncivilized. They're animals, terrorists."

Simkov turned toward the young man but stopped suddenly when he saw the pistol in Nicolay's hand. "Nicolay, we've discussed this already. We all committed to see this through."

"I know, but I've been thinking. These people could set this off in Moscow or Berlin or Rome, or Paris, or New York. Do we want that on our conscience?"

"Nicolay," Simkov stepped forward one step but stopped abruptly as the pistol was raised threateningly toward him. He thought quickly. Could he explain the enabling codes to the young soldier? He knew he could not. It would be entirely too risky. Only he and the general knew the details of the codes. He could not be sure whom he could trust with that information. No, he would simply have to talk this young man out of something he, himself, agreed with.

"No, hear me out, Major Simkov. These are the same animals we are fighting here in Chechnya. They would have no compunction to use this bomb on us. We cannot allow these men to have such a weapon." He looked down momentarily. "It's just wrong." In that brief moment, the sergeant stepped quickly behind the young soldier and thrust his knife into the young man's back. The shock of the blow caused a reactive jerk that fired a round from the pistol. It struck the major in his right shoulder and spun him around as he crumpled to the floor. The young soldier, his eyes wide in shock, turned to look at his sergeant. He stood there motionless, looking at his attacker then the bloody tip of the knife protruding from his shirt. Slowly he sank to the floor, his eyes wide in death.

Vasiliy and the two soldiers waiting for their shifts on guard duty stood, stunned, watching the events unfolding before them. The major lay groaning on the floor; Nicolay lay dead, bleeding onto the concrete floor, as Orlov rushed to the major's side. He quickly tore open the coat and shirt and examined the wound, speaking quickly as he pressed his handkerchief into the bloody hole. "It's not too bad, Major. You're injured, but you'll survive. We'll get you to the local regimental doctors as soon as this deal is finished." The sergeant looked up into the shocked faces of the men standing across the room. "Move, both of you. We must get Nicolay and the major into another room down the hall. If our visitors see a dead soldier and a wounded officer they'll depart as fast as the Russian Summer and this will all be for nothing. Now move. Get him out of here. You," he nodded toward Vasiliy, "help me with the major. When you two get back, clean up that blood. I want this place to look normal when that truck arrives. Move!"

Simkov and the dead soldier were moved down the north hallway to a windowless office there. A mattress was thrown onto the floor and the major was gently laid upon it. A blanket was placed over him to keep him warm, and another was brought to cover the dead soldier. The sergeant left and then returned with bandages that he tied carefully around Simkov's shoulder. "You're going to be fine, Major. I'll take care of transferring the bomb, then I'll get us all out of here." The major nodded; he was already feeling the shock settling into his body. Orlov pulled a cell phone from his pocket. "I'll check with the general. When he approves, we move. Right?" Simkov nodded as he grimaced. "Hang on Major, we should be out of here in about thirty minutes. We'll drive them South for ten clicks, then I'll be right back to pick you up. Think you can hold out for an hour?" Simkov nodded. "Good. Take care." Orlov rose and walked quickly down the hall.

The major painfully lay back onto the mattress. He felt weak and suddenly nauseous. He glanced over at the figure beneath the blanket across the room. Dark red blood flowed from under the blanket and oozed across the floor. He looked away rapidly, noting that his vision was slightly blurred. Perhaps he should have told Nicolay about the codes. Perhaps it would have been better. It was at that moment that he remembered the codes. They would need the enabling codes. Vainly he tried to sit or to roll over, but it was too difficult. Exhausted, he fell back, adrenaline coursing through his body. The fake codes; he had to get them to the sergeant. He lay there trying to gather enough strength to call out; then he heard footsteps. One of the soldiers raced into the room with a canteen. "Sergeant Orlov said you'd need water."

"Wait, the codes." Simkov reached his left hand into his coat and slowly pulled a thick, blood soaked package from his pocket. The bullet had ripped through the folded papers; the blood had done the rest. "Shit!" The major lay back and looked at the ceiling. "Shit!" He was struggling with the dilemma when the answer broke through his dazed mind. He called out to the young man who was hurrying out of the room. "The general can confirm the numbers."

"No problem; the sergeant brought another copy. He got them from the master files a week ago." As the words sank in, the young man walked quickly from the room, his footsteps fading as he ran down the hall. It took several minutes for what the young soldier had said to register in the major's mind. He suddenly realized that Orlov had the correct codes, not the fake ones. Panic raced through Simkov's mind as he realized the implications. The terrorists would have a "real" nuke, and he would have helped them get it. Instinctively his eyes moved back to the motionless figure across the room. Nicolay had been right; now the terrorists would get their bomb. He realized he had to stop it, but how? He might not be able to reason with Orlov. The sergeant had killed Nicolay; would he not do the same to a wounded officer? Could he convince him to call the general? Would that work? There was a lot of money at stake, and Orlov would want his share. Wait, through his fogged mind he recalled the escape plan—the local regiment commander! Simkov reached inside his coat pocket with great pain. Finally he was able to withdraw the cellular phone. He looked at it carefully, wondering how he would dial with his left hand. He managed to turn it on, and a small light flashed back at him. It worked. He dialed the phone slowly, considering the ramifications of his actions. The colonel would stop the transaction, but could Simkov escape being implicated? Perhaps, perhaps not. It didn't matter; he could not allow the bomb to depart with the terrorists—not with the correct codes. The voice on the other end was young. "Colonel Bazarov's office."

"Tell him Major Simkov is on the line and that General Turgenov requests his help."

Three minutes later the colonel's voice boomed over the phone. "Colonel Bazarov here. What do you need Major?"

Fifteen minutes later several armored personnel carriers and a tank pulled out of the Russian military complex east of the town and moved expeditiously towards the western outskirts. As they did, Military Intelligence in Moscow received a call from their counterpart in Chechnya. Another call was dispatched immediately to a very unlikely phone number. "Walter, my friend, it is Ruslan."

"It is good to hear your voice. How is the weather in Moscow?"

"Right now it is hot, but it is hotter still in Chechnya. You will recall your admonition last week in St. Petersburg? Well it is happening now as you predicted."

"You're right about Chechnya. I am in Groznyy."

"In Groznyy?" There was surprise in the Russian Agent's voice.

"I"ve been here two days. I'm following the man we discussed last week. He's somewhere here in the city."

"We have just received a call from a Russian officer who claims to be with the merchandise we discussed. He's been wounded." There was a short pause. "I think he's for real."

Walter's face turned suddenly pale. "Wait, did you say that it is happening? Now?"

"Do you know where he is?"

"Yes; we have troops on the way and will have the area surrounded in about an hour."

"Can you get there any sooner?" There was urgency in the voice.

"It will take an hour."

"What is your plan? Shall I get involved?" Walter knew the answer to that question before it was asked, but it seemed the politic thing to do on Russian soil.

"I'm leaving in twenty minutes."

"It's over 1500 kilometers to Groznyy."

"I have a Mig standing by; I'll meet you at the airport in two hours."

"Should I intervene here?"

"No, don't worry, the site will be isolated in an hour. I'll see you in two hours."

"Two hours, then." Walter placed the phone in its cradle and sat down heavily on the side of the bed. It was time to alert John who was resting in the next room. They had little sleep, but they had much to do before meeting Ruslan.

* * *

The two CIA agents walked across the hot pavement toward the Mig that had just parked on a taxiway opposite the civilian terminal. The shrill whine of the engines died slowly as the two approached with Russian guards trailing behind at a discreet distance. Ruslan walked quickly toward the pair, handing his helmet and gloves to the crew chief as he approached.

Walter smiled at his counterpart. "That was a quick flight."

The Russian smiled, looking back at the aircraft. "Yes, they are fast." John was studying the plane carefully. He was not so impressed. Somehow it didn't appear very substantial, but it certainly was fast.

"Are you ready to go? There's a helicopter waiting for us across the taxiway."

"Of course. But we must hurry. I received a message in-flight that a second truck has been spotted parked beside the Russian military vehicle. They are located outside the deserted hospital where the bomb is supposed to be hidden. We suspect the negotiations are going on inside. There has been no one in or out since we set up our perimeter a little over an hour ago. If we hurry, we can get there before the bomb is moved." The three men raced across the concrete ramp to the waiting Russian helicopter, a Mi-8. Walter recognized it by its NATO designation, "Hip." He had hoped the chopper would be one of the newer Mi-24's or "Hind" helicopters. He had long wanted to see one of them close up. The fuselage of the "Hip" was over sixty feet in length and almost nineteen feet in height. Inside was a squad of heavily armed soldiers. Twenty-three minutes later the large aircraft circled carefully and settled softly to the ground less than five kilometers from the abandoned hospital. The three intelligence agents stepped quickly into a waiting car and sped off into the afternoon heat. The car stopped three blocks from the hospital compound, and the men climbed out. A sergeant met them and escorted the team as they ran carefully down a street of wrecked buildings. Finally they entered the remains of what had once been a home. The walls were intact, but the roof had been destroyed and lay in pieces at their feet. Carefully the three men ducked into the last room in the skeleton of the home and peered carefully out the hole where a window had once allowed light into the small dwelling. "There, that's the building. It was once a hospital." The young officer pointed to the right. There are the two trucks. One is army; the other is probably for the terrorists."

"Where is Major Simkov?"

"We don't know. He's been shot and is somewhere inside. We assume he's dead. He hasn't been heard from in over an hour."

"What's the plan?"

"The colonel said for us to "standby" until he receives direction from General Turgenov."

"How long have you been here?"

"About forty-five minutes."

"Were both trucks there when you arrived?"

"Yes sir."

"And we don't know how many men are in there?"

"That is correct, sir."

The Russian intelligence officer leaned back against the crumbling wall and sighed, looking at the two Americans. "I guess we wait."

"I'm good at that."

"Comes with the job."

"It's the best part of the job, but I'd like a closer view if we can get it." Ruslan concurred and the three intelligence officers ducked from the destroyed house and walked fifty meters northwest to a spot overseeing the western wing of the hospital. It was, like the homes behind them, a mass of broken walls and crumbling structure. John looked from under two long pieces of roofing with his binoculars. "There he is."

"Who?"

"The guard. They'd have to have one on this side. Any on the roof can't get a clear view to the west. I figured someone would guard this approach." John passed the binoculars to Ruslan and took a long drink from the plastic bottle attached to his belt. "Can we take him?"

"If necessary, but it might be risky."

The CIA agent raised the glasses to his eyes again. "Damn, that guy is like a robot."

"What do you mean?"

"He hasn't moved once in over five minutes." John continued to watch the guard.

"Let me see." Ruslan put the binoculars to his eyes again. "You're right. Could it be a dummy?"

Walter took the glasses and checked the man as well. "Ruslan, throw a stone over to the left—into those ruins there."

The Russian officer selected a medium sized rock and lobbed it into the building across the litter-strewn street. "Nothing. You're right. That's either a dummy or he's asleep."

"Let's see if we can take him."

"Be careful; we don't want to spook these guys."

"No problem." Ruslan talked briefly with the junior officer who, in turn, rose and spoke to a sergeant. Ten minutes later a young soldier dashed across the open field north of the guard's location. Three other soldiers knelt nearby, the guard's chest clearly in the sights of their rifles. The intelligence officers watched in silence as the soldier raced toward the ruins of the west wing of the hospital. He entered the wreckage and disappeared. All of his comrades watched and waited. Time slowly ticked by. When he emerged from the crumbling structure, he was dragging a dead soldier. Immediately three men ran from their positions to the wreckage of the hospital. Walter and Ruslan arrived behind the young officer and several of his troops. The captain was leaning over the body. "His throat has been slit!"

"Your man did well."

"No, he didn't do it. The guard was dead when he arrived."

The two senior men looked at each other in confusion. "He was already dead?"

"For some time. Look at the dried blood on his shirt."

"You're right." Walter looked at Ruslan. "Damn!"

"What?"

"We may be too late. Maybe the Chechnyans knew about this and planned a double cross on your guys." Walter's face was one of shock. "If they got the bomb..."

"That's it!" The Russian intelligence officer put his radio to his lips and spoke quickly in Russian. As he finished the Americans looked up to see between fifty and a hundred Russian troops sprinting up the hill toward the hospital. More troops advanced from the west and the south. Two armored personnel carriers and a tank rumbled through the front gate and moved

314

behind the troops toward the hospital. "Let's go." Ruslan began running along the ruins of the west wing of the hospital toward the entrance. The CIA agents quickly joined in the sprint. They had only sixty meters to run, but the young troops arrived first and raced into the building. Several others raced to the trucks and surrounded them, weapons poised and ready. As the three agents caught up to the troops at the entrance of the building, a sergeant and two soldiers walked out of the front door and met them, their weapons hanging loosely by their sides. They were speaking excitedly in Russian. John understood no Russian, and Walter could only comprehend portions of the conversation, but he understood one key phrase—"all dead." The three men raced around the soldiers and dashed down the hall. Several soldiers stood at the entrance to the room on the right. Inside, bodies were scattered amid the wreckage in the room. Walter quickly checked the room. "Grenades." Ruslan nodded. John entered the adjoining room. It contained a large canvas sheet laying on the floor; under it was a large black case. He opened it carefully, studied it for a moment, then turned back to the first room. "It's here."

Ruslan quickly organized three teams of soldiers and sent them to search the premises for other insurgents. A fourth he sent to investigate the trucks. As he did, John and Walter began surveying the bodies. There were four army personnel and five men dressed in civilian clothes. Two of the civilians appeared to be Chechnyans; two were Arabs, and the other civilian appeared to be a Russian. Identification was difficult after the destruction of the grenades. The Arabs had also had their throats cut—it was either insurance or a message; it was hard to tell. Walter knelt beside the two and extracted their wallets. After a moment he looked at John and nodded. There was a small smile on his face. "This one appears to have been Hamad. I told you we'd find him, but it looks like someone else got to him first." Someone had beaten them to the punch. Someone had arrived first and had done their work for them. But who? Chechnyans? No, Chechynans would have taken the bomb. Whoever had orchestrated the attack must have known of the arrangement, and obviously they had disapproved. But who had known more than the Russian and US intelligence personnel?

An excited voice caught their attention. They turned to see two soldiers carrying the wounded major down the hallway. "We found Major Simkov. He's alive, but he's in very bad condition."

"Get him to a doctor quick. Take one of the APCs." Ruslan turned to the American. "Well, my friend, it seems we have averted another disaster."

Walter nodded. "Who do you think got here first?"

"I really don't know." Ruslan shook his head. "This is a mystery. Whoever it was; they obviously knew what they were doing. I salute them for that. They also knew the details of the transfer. Perhaps Major Simkov can help us when he recovers."

"Perhaps."

"I'll let you know if I discover anything."

"Thanks." The two Americans and the Russian agent walked out into the afternoon sun and headed down the hill toward the main gate, stopping momentarily to watch the soldiers load the bomb onto the Russian truck. They shook hands, and the Americans climbed into the rear of the Russian staff car. Ruslan waved, and Walter nodded as the car pulled off toward the city and the airport. Ruslan had been right. Another disaster had been averted. They had been lucky once more, but the question remained. Who had stopped the most dangerous contract in the world? Who had saved the world from an attack that could have changed history?

Chapter 47

Riyadh, Saudi Arabia, July 23, 2018

Ammar walked slowly into the room and took a seat opposite his father. The old man was drinking coffee and sat silently looking through the steam that curled around his nose. He was studying his son with piercing eyes, eyes that bore into Ammar's very soul. The younger man sat uncomfortably, squirming under the gaze of his father. Neither man spoke. Ammar was already unnerved; just this morning he had been advised of the mission's failure. Kahlid was dead as were the others he was to have met. Only his brother's interference had saved his life. Finally the old man placed the coffee on the tray beside his chair and closed his eyes momentarily. When they opened, he again pierced his son with his glare as he spoke. "You have disgraced this family. If you were not my son, you would be dead today." Ammar looked up at his father in shock then dropped his eyes to the floor. He said nothing; he only nodded. "You will remain in the family compound until I say otherwise. You will contact no one; you will talk to no one until I approve. Do you understand?" The younger man nodded. "Now go. You have brought great shame upon me and upon this family. I will excuse this only once. Now go from my sight."

"Yes father." The Prince picked up his coffee and nodded as his son walked slowly out the door. As he left, his father's old friend, Hamza entered the room without comment.

When Ammar was gone, the Prince spoke. "The bomb is secure?" The security chief nodded. "Well done, my old friend. You are the one man in this world I know I can trust."

Chapter 48

Seattle, Washington, July 24, 2018

"Billy Wong?"

"In person." There was a smile in the voice of the Hawaiian detective.

"Paul Hamilton here. Seems like we have your case solved."

"Really?" The voice was suddenly serious.

"Yeah. Seems we've found the gun that killed your local heroes."

"Where?"

"In the hand of a dead soldier for the CFT." He paused to let that sink in. "But I'm afraid we got there a bit late. Seems someone else was a bit distressed at the shooter and several of his friends and saved us the cost of a trial."

"Dead?"

"Yes. Six of them. Three were killed by a very elaborate bomb, one that took some real skill to produce."

"Any idea who did it?"

"I think we both know the answer to that. Seems the Mob was more than a little upset about losing Frankie Joe. At first glance it appears there might have been a turf war going on over drugs. You'd think the amateurs would know better than to tangle with the pros." He paused for a minute then continued. "We're going out for a little surprise chat with Mr. Valanetti tomorrow morning."

"You have anything?"

"We've found his phone number in several unusual places. Also seems that one of the deceased bombers had called him minutes before he was executed. It's not much, but it may be enough for a search warrant, and that's something we've wanted for years."

"Sounds great; good luck." The mirth had returned to the voice.

"We'll need it. Tony is a real pro; it's unlikely that he'll trip on his own shorts. I'll let you know if anything more comes up."

"I'll hold my breath."

"Don't think I'd do that, my friend. The Feds been after old Tony for a long time and haven't had a bit of luck. The FBI are checking a fingerprint they found on one of the detonators; it would have to be Tony's to get a conviction of that slippery eel."

"You're right. Fat chance. Talk to you later."

Chapter 49

Evergreen, Colorado, July 30, 2018

John walked into his house and nodded to the attractive agent sitting inside the living room. She smiled and nodded toward the stairs. "He's doing well. He's upstairs."

"Thanks." John placed his bags beside the door and turned immediately toward the stairs. He was tired, but he took them two at a time. As he opened David's door he was breathing heavily. He had been away long enough to feel the elevation change. "Dad?" David smiled at his father.

"You look terrible!"

"And I feel worse." David smiled though it pained him to do so.

"How are you doing? Can I get you anything?"

"How about a new head with a few less bruises."

"How about one that looks better?"

David smiled again, and again the pain returned to his jaw. "Damn, it hurts to laugh."

"Then let's be serious."

"Speaking of serious, you look pretty bad yourself. Where the hell have you been?"

"It's a long story, and I'll give you the details later. Basically our friend Hamad was in cahoots with a terrorist group that wanted to buy a Russian bomb, a nuclear bomb."

David sat silently looking at his father, a look of shock on his face. Finally he spoke. "So what happened?"

"The good guys got there in time, along with some Russian friends, and we took care of the situation." John thought a moment then continued. "Well, actually someone else took care of it for us, but we retrieved the bomb. That's what counts."

"Hamad?"

"Whoever beat us to the punch took care of him as well. It was not a pretty picture. Grenades."

"Wow! Any idea who did it?"

"No, but I found a small piece of one of the grenades. It looks like it might have been one of ours."

"Our guys?"

"Or an ally who has access to our weaponry." John smiled to himself.

"Have you seen Jessica yet?"

"We've been hard to reach this past week or so."

"She's been worried about you. I told her you know how to take care of yourself." David smiled even though it hurt his jaw. "She said she was aware of that. She told me about Hawaii."

"I'm glad you two are becoming friends."

"I'm glad you two found each other." David stopped and looked at John for several moments.

"Me, too."

"Are you going to marry her?"

"Yes." He said it firmly. There was no hesitation in his voice.

"Then get it done. She loves you too. We both know that. Don't wait. I never asked Marcia to marry me even though I wanted to. I regret that. Do you have any idea what I'd give for the opportunity to do that now?"

John looked into the young man's eyes and lowered his own. Finally he spoke. "Yes, I can understand that."

"Well, dammit, Jessica's down at the Cow café right now. As you always say, get a move on."

"Out of the mouth of babes." John was smiling.

"Damn straight, dude. Go for it."

John walked over to the bed and placed his hand on his son's arm. "You're right. Thanks for the nudge." The smile was growing on his face. "I'll do it. I'll do it now."

* * *

John stepped out of the shower and lathered his face. As his razor glided across his chin, he looked at the vision in the mirror. It was smiling. It grew until he laughed aloud.

John pulled into the parking lot and climbed from the Lexus. He was wearing tan slacks, a black silk shirt, and a dark brown sport coat. He looked like a man in control, but inside he felt the slight twinge of butterflies in his stomach. He took a deep breath and marched into the small café. It was 6:30 and the doors had just opened. There were two older men inside drinking coffee. He recognized both and nodded as he walked toward the kitchen. Before he could enter he was confronted by a tall fifteen-year-old with a hot pot of coffee. "Morning, Mr. McClellan. You looking for Jessica?"

"Yes."

"She's outside, I think."

"Thanks, Billy." John turned quickly and retraced his steps to the door. Before he stepped out, he saw her, sitting alone at the picnic table by the stream, staring at the creek below. The giant cottonwoods by the creek provided welcomed shade from the morning sun rising above. John turned abruptly and grabbed two empty mugs from a table by the door. He caught Billy's eye; the boy raced over and filled them both. "Thanks."

Jessica didn't see him as he approached. She was staring blankly at the dancing water crashing over the rocks in the swollen creek. He stood there looking at her back for several moments. Her hair was not brushed, and the sweater she wore was torn on the right elbow. John approached slowly and slid the coffee cup across the worn table. She turned her head slowly, then jerked around in recognition. There were tears on her cheeks. "Hi." She brushed her eyes quickly.

"Hi." John sat beside her and put his arm around her shoulder. Instinctively she put her head on his shoulder. "Are you okay?"

"I've been worried about you. I haven't heard from you in over a week, and George died four days ago. I needed you so much."

John looked at the woman beside him, uncertain of his own emotions. "George died?"

"Yes. I found him on the landing on the stairs." She began to weep softly. "I needed you so much then."

"I'm sorry, Jessica. That must have been difficult for you."

"I tried to lift him up, but I couldn't. I wasn't strong enough." John pulled her closer as she cried. "He was so good to me. He gave me a home when I had nowhere else to go." John's face was distorted in pain as he looked over her head to the cliffs of the hogback ridge in the distance. The sandstone cliffs sparkled in the sunlight, reminding him of their time by the ocean. "He was like a father to me; he would sneak up and put money in my tip jar; he thought I didn't know."

"How did he die, Jessica?"

"It was his heart. He just kept climbing those damn stairs. I told him he was too old for that." She blew her nose then wiped her eyes on her sleeve like a small girl. "I told him over and over that if he expected to make ninety he'd have to stay on the first floor. I told him not to climb those stairs."

"It's alright honey. He lived a long life, and he was loved. That's more than most can hope for." He pulled her closer as she wiped her eyes on her sleeve again. "I'm sorry I wasn't here. I should have been; it was my mistake." He lifted her face to his. "But I can promise you this, I love you, Jessica, and I'll never leave you again, never." Very gently he raised her face and kissed her.

"Promise?"

"I promise."

As they sat before the rushing creek, holding each other, they heard the echo of a cheering crowd. They simultaneously turned toward the café and saw the entire morning crew watching and cheering inside the large window that looked out onto the bright Colorado morning. John lifted his coat to block their view and kissed her again.

Chapter 50

Evergreen, Colorado, August 2, 2018

His head was not bowed, rather his eyes were lifted toward the farthest mountain range that stood dark blue against the bright morning sky. Overhead a gaggle of geese soared gracefully through the blue sky and turned abruptly in mid-flight toward the small lake to the east. It was a beautiful summer morning in Colorado; the smell of freshly mowed grass filled the air. Slowly his eyes shifted downward to the large granite headstone resting in the wet grass before him. One more time he read the name inscribed there: Sybil McClellan. The sadness enveloped him, along with the helplessness that one feels when facing the emptiness of death. Quickly John looked back up into the distance. There was something about the mountains that gave him strength. Perhaps it was their solid massiveness; perhaps it was their solitude. He stared at them a long time before he looked again at the grave. Finally he spoke.

"I miss you today. I miss you, and I still love you." John watched a single goose that flew close by and interrupted his conversation. "I know you would probably not approve of what I have done. For that I'm sorry. A better man might have done otherwise, but I guess I'm just not that strong. I can live with what I did; I could not have lived with less."

"Sybil, you'd be proud of David. He's become a fine young man. And I want you to know that I tried to keep him from getting mixed up in all of this. I really tried. I guess he has a stubborn streak, a lot like someone else we know." John

325

smiled faintly. "I'll keep an eye on him. We've finally become very close. I guess at least one good thing came from all this." John looked at the grave for several moments then continued; his voice was almost apologetic when he spoke. He did so very slowly. "Sybil, I've fallen in love again. You know I'll never get completely over you, and you know I'll always love you too, but I think it's time. She's very different, but she's a fine woman. She's brought joy back into my life and has given me a reason to live again. I hope you'll approve of her. She's like a rainbow on a cloudy day. I had almost forgotten how to laugh, to smile, to love. Jessica is a good woman, and she really does love me, although I can't imagine why." John kicked the earth at his feet absently then continued. "This has been a very difficult road to walk. I think it's time for me to give this tired soul a rest. It's time to find joy in life again. I'm going to give it another try, and I really hope you approve." In the distance he saw a car park behind his own. A young man climbed out and started toward him. "David needs to get on with his life, too. I'm going to try to facilitate that. He's young; he'll get over this in time. You raised a good one, honey. You did a great job."

David joined his father, and the two men stood in silence as the sun rose higher in the sky and warmed the earth at their feet. Finally they turned together and walked away as the green grass glistened in the morning sun.

Chapter 51

Chicago, Illinois, August 6, 2018

Shorty stepped off the old elevator and turned left into the offices of CFT. He stopped abruptly in the doorway; he hardly recognized the room. He stood there with two women and one young man, silently surveying what was basically an empty office. Since Collingsworth's arrest all CFT offices had been closed while FBI teams collected boxes of paperwork and computers. They had even taken the printers that had lined the wall opposite the windows. Shorty finally turned to his associates and nodded to the cardboard boxes they had brought. "Pack up everything that is left and put it in the van downstairs." He reached into his coat and pulled some envelopes from his pocket. Immediately the group assembled around him and held out their hands. "Remember to put your names, email addresses, and phone numbers on the clipboard in the van. I'll be in touch later." He smiled a thin smile to the crew. "We still have work to do, and we still have funding. I'll be in touch soon."

It only took the small team 15 minutes to complete their job. As they took the last box and started for the door the woman turned to Shorty and asked. "You coming?"

"No, go ahead. I'm meeting some of the demonstrator leads later."

"You talking about those foreign guys?" Shorty nodded, and she motioned toward the end of the short hallway. "I told them the meeting was in the big conference room down the hall." She looked at her watch briefly. "They should be here soon."

"Thanks." Shorty rose and started walking in that direction. Twenty minutes later the room was filled with various men dressed in jeans and dark shirts. Most had chains hanging from their belts and tattoos on their arms, shoulders, and necks. One had a clean shaven head; it was also covered with tattoos. There were few chairs left in the room, so they all stood in small groups speaking several different languages. Shorty stood near the door and watched the crowd carefully. He knew most all of them, but there were several he did not. Finally he checked his watch for the third time, squared his shoulders, and marched into the center of the crowded room. The group was surprisingly quiet, but as soon as he held up his hands, he was barraged by a series of questions before he could even speak. In frustration he raised his hands higher until the group became quiet. "Close the door." He motioned to one of the men standing against the wall. When it was closed he held his hands up once more until the room was quiet again. The room was old and dark, the lights clearly insufficient for the size room they were in. To accommodate that, every curtain had been removed so the bare windows could allow the maximum light. Without the activity of prior demonstrations, it was a depressing room for all. "Okay, here's where we are. Collingsworth was indicted and will face trial later this month or maybe next. That don't mean nothing to us. We go on as usual. From now on I am your contact." He smiled at the crew. "That means I pass out the money." With that he pulled a large stack of envelopes from the small handbag he was carrying and waved it at the men. "But first a few things I need to tell you, so pay attention. Number one. I need all of you to put your contact information on this clipboard I'll pass around. If you want to continue working with us, be sure to sign that, and write clear so I can read it. Number 2. As I said earlier, I am the new contact for all activities. I'll be passing along the directions—where we will be demonstrating, who our targets are, what our plans will be—and I'll also be passing out the money." He paused to let that sink in before continuing. "Our next target is the G-8 Meeting in Brussels. The top financial folks of the world will be there, and so will we. I need you there in two weeks. There are instructions for transportation and also for housing on sheets by the door. Check the table on the left. Any questions?"

After the professional anarchists had left, Shorty counted the remaining envelopes. There were six remaining. He tore them open, folded the cash together, and placed it into his left front pocket. When he exited the building he was smiling. He was now in charge, not just of some group of dumb students. Now he was in charge of a core group of hardened anarchists. It would be different, he knew. Perhaps it was even dangerous. But he also knew the bulge in his pocket was just the beginning of a long series of such rewards. Like his new crew, it was all about the money—and now he controlled the purse.

Chapter 52

Frankfurt, Germany, August 6, 2018

Walter studied the translation carefully. It was condensed from the Russian media and was fresh from the Moscow news service. He glanced over it quickly, then reread it carefully.

> **Officers from the Russian Army foiled an attempted theft of a Russian nuclear bomb. Troops under the command of General Ivan Sergeevich Turgenov tracked a team of renegade soldiers who attempted to steal a nuclear warhead for sale to international terrorists. All of the terrorists and traitors were killed in the raid. Major Rodion Mikhail Simkov, who led the investigation, was wounded in the brief battle, and one of his men was killed. Both will be awarded medals for valor and gallantry as heroes of the people by General Turgenov. Major Simkov is expected to recover fully and is to be promoted to the rank of Colonel for his bravery in action. The Russian president will meet with the general and the major as well as the parents of Private Nicolay Tribinski to give tribute to their service to Russia.**

Walter read on, finally looking up to rest his eyes. There were questions, to be sure. No one had accessed the money in the account. It was still in place—being watched, of course. Walter let his mind wander, as he liked to do. So many questions unanswered. Was it possible that a sergeant and a few soldiers could have pulled this off—or nearly so? Highly unlikely. Simkov did call in the troops, but what did he really know? Did the fake inventory forms really alert him? And why did he follow with only one soldier? The general had stated that there was never a real concern since the enabling codes were not compromised. That, at least, was comforting. Oh well, the world was safe for a short while longer. He imagined that the Russians were asking far more questions than he could even imagine. They had not realized yet that the terrorists were killed by American military grenades. That fact left a long list of candidates, but who would gain from such an act? That question narrowed the list considerably. Walter scratched his chin and smiled. He wondered if old Fakhir had removed the stains from his robe yet. Probably so, but maybe he should check. This incident would be filed, but not forgotten. Walter reached and switched on the TV beside his desk. He bypassed the national media and found the local news. The well-groomed face smiled into the camera then took a suddenly grave expression. "Police today arrested reputed underworld crime boss, Tony Valanetti, charging him in the murder of several alleged drug dealers who were operating from within the umbrella of Citizens for a Free Tomorrow. Dr. Lawrence Collingsworth, the founder and leader of CFT was also arrested and charged with conspiracy to distribute illegal drugs through his organization. The Democratic Minority leader advised the public to withhold judgement of CFT and lamented the failure of its leaders. 'Their actions should not reflect on the good works of the organization itself' she said in an interview on CNN." Walter smiled to himself as he sorted through his mail. *So, the spin starts, but the scum are brought to light; good riddance.* An expensive envelope from the stack on his desk caught his attention. It had his name in black ink neatly written across the front. He opened it and read the note. It was a wedding invitation. He smiled; summer would be a great time to visit Colorado.

Chapter 1

A sample from

2040 American Exodus

September 14, 2016
The Mediterranean Sea

As the nuclear submarine moved silently through the dark waters of the Mediterranean, the captain leaned against his desk and re-read the message he had received just five minutes before. Chaim's legs buckled as he struggled to comprehend it; he still could not believe the words. Slowly he sank into the worn chair beside the small desk. His heart said the message could not be correct, but his mind knew the codes checked out and therefore the message must be true. Once again he compared the security codes with the ones from his safe; they were consistent. He read the message again for the third time, carefully analyzing each word in case he had overlooked something.

At 1014 hours on September 14, 2016, an Iranian
nuclear bomb struck Tel Aviv; a second struck Haifa.
Execute: Special Order X-1003 immediately.

Beads of sweat gathered on his forehead and ran across the deeply furrowed face, joining the single tear that had escaped his right eye. He breathed deeply and steeled himself for the next vision that lurked in the recesses of his mind. Rebecca and little Daniel were gone; the wife and son who gave him purpose and joy were lost forever. His mind moved slowly toward the question he feared most. What was it like when the blast reached them? Did she call his name? Did she even realize what had happened? There were two nuclear bombs—probably dirty bombs set to explode several thousand feet above the ground to cause maximum nuclear fallout.

334

He knew what that would do to such a small country. There would be few survivors. How would he tell his men? How could he face them and still maintain control over his own emotions? But he was their captain; he was their leader. They needed him now.

Chaim wiped his face with a soiled handkerchief and stuck his head out of the small door to his room. "Call the entire crew together—everyone! Now!"

* * *

As the captain stared blankly into the darkness of his small room, the spirit of his wife moved behind him and silently watched the desolate man.

How could this happen, she thought? How could she be standing beside her husband in this dark vessel when only a moment earlier she had been rocking her child in her living room in Tel Aviv? And why does he look so sad as he leans over the small table with the map on it? The child in her arms was as light as a feather and looked so much like the tired man before her. Chaim was staring at the map, but he did not see it. His eyes were glazed, and tears blinded his vision. She called his name and reached to touch his shoulder, but neither of them heard her voice or felt her touch. She jerked her hand back and stared at it in disbelief. A long low moan came from his throat as he wiped his face and re-read the message he held with shaking hands. Chaim raised his eyes for a moment and stared off into space without seeing. He knew the message was real; it had all the proper codes. He also knew it would change his world forever.

Rebecca moved closer to him and spoke again—this time with fear in her voice. What did all of this mean? How, how could a person travel so quickly into such a desolate place? What was happening? Was it possible that the love between a man and a woman could draw them together like this?

Chaim grimaced in pain and anguish. She was gone, gone forever. And his Daniel; he was gone, too. How could he live with this knowledge? How could he live with this pain?

335

Rebecca watched his face. He was not aware of her presence. But why, she wondered? Could he not see her? She spoke again into the silence; then she screamed. He did not move; he did not hear; he only stood with his head down. A single tear rolled down his cheek and fell from his face. She reached instinctively and caught the tear before it splashed onto the map. She pulled it to her and looked into the prism of light sparkling back at her. It was then that she felt the pull that was drawing her away. It was a powerful sensation.

Something inside her cried out in defiance. She could not leave the man she loved in such pain—but the strange source that drew her was more powerful and so peaceful. She looked down at the sleeping child in her arms and smiled, then she looked back at her husband as she relaxed and submitted to the peace. She was smiling as she disappeared from the dark room and the sad man looking at the map. She raised her hand and looked briefly at the small droplet of water. The prism of light flashed a rainbow of colors into her eyes; she reached for him once more; and then she was gone.

* * *

The captain felt a sudden touch on his shoulder. When he turned, it was one of the sailors. As he moved, a prism of light flashed somewhere in the darkness of the room, and Chaim felt the anguish flowing from his body. There was a growing peace in his heart. Where had that come from? Was it his training? His discipline? Or was he simply accepting the reality that faced him the rest of his life—however long that might be.

"Captain, the men are assembled."

"I'll be right there." He brushed at the map to erase the tear that had escaped, but the tear was gone. He turned, confused for a moment, then stood as tall as he could and walked out to his crew. "Is everyone here?"

As the young sailors crowded together, a sense of shock hung in the heavy air of the submarine. Perhaps the rumors of the past ten minutes were true. But they couldn't be. The radio mate must have been wrong. Perhaps it was a military exercise. It had to be.

As the last members of the crew crowded into the cramped space, one of the junior officers spoke. "Captain, is it true?"

Chaim watched their eyes. He feared their reactions, but they had served together far too long to lie to them now. Inhaling deeply, he stood as tall as he could, and spoke very slowly, very deliberately. "At 1014 hours this morning, Tel Aviv was struck by a nuclear missile from Iran; another struck Haifa. They were most likely *dirty* bombs; we can assume that Israel was destroyed." The captain fought to maintain his own control and fixed his eyes on one young man before him. He watched the young eyes widen with shock; then the bottom lip began to quiver slightly as the sailor fought to control his emotions before his captain and his shipmates. Several others began to curse, while others cried openly. The captain slammed his fist on one of the small tables at his side. "Stop! Stop your weeping!" There was anger in his voice as he shouted at his crew. "There will be time for that later—after we finish our mission. Does everyone understand that?"

"Yes Sir." The entire crew mumbled in response.

"Now, put aside your thoughts of this day and concentrate fully on your jobs. We will not fail our nation; we will not fail the innocent blood of our people. Our enemies will know the price of their treachery!" He paused and watched the young men's faces. "We have spent years training for this day, a day we prayed would never come. Well, it is here. This is the measure of our will, the measure of our determination, the measure of Israel's response! We will not fail our brothers and our families; we will not fail Israel." He paused and then stood erect before his men. "We weep tomorrow—today we fight!" There was a shout from the back of the group. Others joined in, and the crew pulled itself to its full measure and screamed for revenge. "Now get to your battle stations. Let's show the cowards in Tehran that Israel still fights. As long as there is one lone Star of David worn by one lone Israeli, this fight continues. Today they may cheer in Damascus, in Riyadh, in Tehran, and Cairo, but their celebrations will be short!" As the men rushed to their stations, the captain turned to his second in command. "Dekel,

337

contact the American sub we are evading; tell them we have national tasking and will be ending the joint exercise."

"Yes captain. Do you think they might be a problem? Will they be aware of what we are doing?" There was neither joy nor fear in his voice, only a quiet resignation to a situation he did not desire or understand.

"It will take their government time to receive the notification and react. They will be in a state of shock for a while. Then they will start to assess the situation and make decisions. That should give us enough time to disappear. Turn to a heading of 240 degrees and tell the crew to run silent. After twenty minutes turn right to a heading of….no, turn *left* to a heading of 170 degrees. This time it is no exercise. We must evade the American sub."

"Why? They are our allies."

"We can't take a risk that the American President will support us. He has not been our friend in the past. The risk is simply too great; our mission is too important."

"Aye, Sir. 240 degrees then 170."

"And Dekel, monitor the American sub's position. If they follow us, let me know." He stood looking at the floor for a moment then added. "And start the launch checklist. Tell the men I want to beat our best time by five minutes. We've got to finish the checklist, stabilize, and launch before the Americans can find us. I don't know how much lead time we will have, so we must proceed carefully, but quickly." As Dekel departed Chaim turned and walked slowly into his small room and closed the door, something he seldom did. When he was alone, he hung his head and cried. How could there be a world without his family? After a few moments he raised his head, wiped his eyes, and washed his face in the small sink. He was focused on one thing; he had to slip away from the American sub and avenge his nation. He wasn't sure how long it would take the American government to assess the situation and make a decision, and he didn't want to commence launch operations with the American sub so close to his position. There was still a chance they might try to stop him. He wasn't sure how much time he had, but twenty minutes should be enough, he told himself.

* * *

338

Twenty-eight minutes after the Israeli sub had ended the exercise, Captain Donald Thompson in an American Los Angeles Class nuclear-powered, fast-attack submarine read the orders he had just received by coded satellite communication and shook his head in utter shock. He understood the words, but not the message. He read them again to ensure it said what he had read just moments before. For four days his crew had been shadowing the Israeli sub across the Mediterranean on a routine exercise. The Los Angeles Class attack subs had been around almost half a century, and less than forty remained in service. Though his boat was old, his crew was the best. They had silently located the sub, then they had shadowed it as it moved silently through the warm waters of the Mediterranean. This had started as a routine training exercise; now it had become much more than a simple test of skills. Thompson removed his ball cap and wiped the sweat from his forehead. It was decision time. The Israeli sub had disappeared immediately after breaking off the exercise. They had obviously received notification of the Iranian nuclear strike earlier than he. As usual, the U.S. government wheels turned slowly. Now he had to find his prey again, because he had just received orders to sink it. He understood the mission; but he also knew the Israeli sub was not his enemy. There had to be some mistake. He checked the code validation again. It was good.

Lieutenant Commander Francis Perez watched his captain with interest. "Captain, do we have confirmation of a nuclear strike on Israel?"

"Yes. It appears the Iranian leaders were as crazy as our intelligence suggested."

"How bad was it, sir?"

"The strike was against Tel Aviv and Haifa; I think it is realistic to assume that Israel is gone. I suspect that Gaza and Jordan were affected as well."

"Damn!" There was both anger and shock in the young man's voice. He looked at the official orders in the captain's hand. "What are we going to do, sir?"

339

Thompson looked at the orders a third time then back to Perez. "We've been ordered to sink the Israeli sub." His voice was low and controlled.

Perez's eyes widened in shock. "What? Sink the Israeli sub? There must be some mistake!"

"The codes check out. We have verifiable orders."

Like all men who wore the submariner's patch, Perez was a professional warrior. He had been trained all of his career to follow orders, but these were orders he found difficult to comprehend. They had to be wrong. "These orders can't be right." There was disgust and incredulity in the junior officer's voice; he paused before continuing. "Are we really going to do that?"

Twenty-seven years of Naval service had not prepared Thompson to answer that question. He was an Annapolis graduate with an outstanding career. Honor and integrity were burned into his very soul, and now he was being ordered to violate everything he believed in. He didn't understand the orders he had received, but he knew he would execute them to the best of his ability. Was this simply a decision to stop the carnage before it escalated even further? Was this a decision to save the oil rich region? Or was it a decision to buy time for negotiations? Someone with far more information had made that decision; his assignment was to follow orders, whether he liked them or not—whether he agreed with his Commander-in-Chief or not. He looked at the sonar scope; the Israeli sub had vanished, and now he knew why.

* * *

Dekel spoke quietly to his captain. "If the American politicians had courage, this would never have happened. Their lack of will allowed today to occur. When they were strong, we were safe. When they became weak and indecisive, we became a target."

Chaim looked at Dekel with deep lines on his face. "I probably know the captain of that sub. He probably wishes he could help us, but, like us, he is controlled by politicians. And the American President is not a friend of Israel."

"But the American military are our friends!"

340

"This is not a decision the military will make; the politicians will decide our fate. They deserted their own military just as surely as they deserted us. They took their weapons, their resources, their dignity—everything except their honor." The older man threw the papers in his hand onto the small desk at this side. "And as honorable professionals, they will follow the orders of lesser men who control them." Chaim rubbed his forehead vigorously. "But the very men who might order us destroyed will delay long enough in their arrogance to allow us to complete our mission anyway." Chaim looked away briefly and studied the sonar scope beside him. There was no indication of the American boat in his vicinity. "Our own American Jewish brothers helped elect the men who then abandoned us. I wonder what they are thinking today as they sit in their comfortable New York apartments and sip their morning coffee. Damn their arrogance! Damn their selfishness and their stupidity!" He stopped and visibly got control of himself. "We can discuss this tomorrow, if there is a tomorrow. Right now we have only one thing left to do, we launch our missiles, then we surrender to the Americans."

"Surrender?" There was shock in the younger officer's voice.

"Where would we go, Dekel? We have no home to return to."

*   *   *

Thompson and the American crew were scrambling. They knew the original direction of the Israeli sub had been southwest, but it could have turned in any direction after that. It had over half an hour head start and he needed to find it fast. He had turned southwest and was proceeding at full speed. The captain walked back and forth and talked to his crew. "Anything out there?" His voice was measured and low.

"Nothing, Sir."

"Turn right to a heading of 250 degrees. He turned right three times in a row. In fact, he always turns right. And keep listening. We found them before; we can find them again."

"I just got a sound."

341

"Where is it?"

"Is somewhere far behind us. Oh shit! They're flooding tubes." After a few seconds. "I can hear pressure equalization."

Perez looked at Thompson. "Does that mean what I think?"

"They are preparing to launch their missiles." Thompson's voice was no longer low. "Where are they?"

"I hear a hatch opening." Thompson walked quickly to the sailor's side. In slow cadence the sailor began counting. "One, two, three, four, five, six, seven, eight—eight missiles have launched. Wait! Nine, ten, eleven, twelve."

Another sailor called to the officers. "Sir, I have a message from the Israeli crew. They are surrendering. They will surface and surrender to us."

*　*　*

The Israeli sub was on the surface when an Iranian destroyer raced toward it from the northeast. It was traveling at a high rate of speed, leaving a large white wake through the clear blue waters. Commander Thompson was studying the Israeli sub when the destroyer suddenly showed up on the console next to him. He looked at both targets for only a second. He could see the smoke from the destroyer's guns as they fired toward the Israeli sub. "Prepare two torpedoes!" He looked at the sailor standing beside him, then at Perez. "Sink the destroyer!"

"Ready to fire."

"Fire one!" A few seconds later. "Fire Two!" The two torpedoes raced through the Mediterranean and caught the Iranian ship off guard. They had seen the first sub break the surface, but they had not seen the second that was following it. Both weapons hit the destroyer and enveloped it in a huge ball of fire. The captain watched the Iranian ship sinking into the sea; finally, he turned to his second-in-command who was smiling. "Good work men!"

"Good decision, Sir."

"I had no choice; we were under attack from an Iranian destroyer." The captain was grinning.

"That's right, Sir; we had no choice at all. Let the log show we were defending ourselves from an Iranian ship—that was firing in our direction."

"Mr. Perez, prepare to surface to take on our Israeli friends. Also, send an urgent message back to command headquarters to the effect that we captured the Israeli sub, but that we could not get to them before they launched their missiles."

*   *   *

On board the Israeli sub, Chaim watched the Iranian destroyer sinking into the sea. "I'll be damned, Dekel. In my haste I completely missed that destroyer, but the Americans sank it." Chaim walked back into his small room and retrieved a picture of his lost family. He looked at it for several moments then put it into his pocket. "Tell the men to come on deck. We may be close enough to see the result of our mission.   But unlike our barbaric enemy, we will not be celebrating the result. May God help us all."

At 1408 local time, September 14, 2016, the Israeli nuclear sub launched its entire arsenal of nuclear missiles. In the Middle East every major city from Tehran to Cairo was filled with people dancing in the streets, celebrating their great victory over Israel when the missiles rained down upon them. After centuries of warfare, the Middle East conflict was finally resolved in a ball of fire that reached into the gates of hell.

*   *   *

As the stunned Israeli sailors sat in the cramped American sub, they stared quietly at the floor, each lost in his own thoughts of the momentous and frightening events. Their world would never be the same, their lives changed forever. Above them the world was also changing very rapidly. The actions they had set in motion would leave much of the world in chaos. Entire cities were destroyed, countless people were killed, and a way of life had vanished. The horror of nuclear power was now evident to the terrified world and

343

would lead to cries to abandon such weapons. The fabric of humanity had been irreversibly torn, and the world would rise together to seek answers to prevent such catastrophes in the future. Fear would dominate international relations for years, and the United Nations would be called upon to rise above its mediocrity and act responsibly as a world organ for peace. Politicians the world over would find ways to use this disaster to enhance their own power and further their political goals. Citizens would demand their governments provide safety at all cost, and inept governments would find support from frightened citizens who would incrementally sell their precious freedoms for promises of safety and survival. And in that exchange, free people the world over would become little more than the children they insisted they were trying to protect. People would be pulled into a giant politically correct mold that regurgitated citizens of similar thoughts and values.

There would be some who would stand apart, independently defiant people of strong values and a passion for individual freedom. They would be ostracized and cast out by robotic citizens who would not accept their moral strength. Eventually they would be destroyed or incarcerated as enemies of the state, while very quietly a small, unseen group would mold the very thought processes of an entire generation mired in inertia. And in doing so, they would gain unquestionable power over the masses, while those they enslaved praised them for their beneficent wisdom.

Liberty would die a slow but inevitable death, and only a few patriots would stand at the graveside to mourn its passing.

Douglas Fain is a graduate of the Air Force Academy and holds graduate degrees from Georgetown University and the University of Southern California. He flew more than 200 combat missions over Southeast Asia and was awarded a Distinguished Flying Cross for Heroism, a Distinguished Flying Cross for Achievement, fourteen Air Medals, and an Air Force Commendation Medal. He is the president of CEBG, Inc., an international consulting company, and has worked in more than 30 different countries in that capacity. He has taught for four universities in both undergraduate and graduate programs as an affiliate faculty member and was a candidate for the U.S. Senate in 1992. Doug has served on several boards and is the author of *The Phantom's Song*, an award winning novel about the Vietnam Air War and *2040 American Exodus*, a warning about America's future.

www.ingramcontent.com/pod-product-compliance
Lightning Source LLC
Chambersburg PA
CBHW031428240626
47154CB00001B/253